SIZE STILL MATTERS

Short Stories Still Long
Enough To Satisfy

Published by
Dreamspinner Press
4760 Preston Road
Suite 244-149
Frisco, TX 75034
http://www.dreamspinnerpress.com/

Sight Unseen
Copyright 2007 by Shay Kincaid

Take My Picture
Copyright 2007 by Giselle Ellis

Start From the Beginning
Copyright 2007 by Chrissy Munder

Evan's Heaven
Copyright 2007 by Nicki Bennett
Portions of 'Cling Wrap' used with the kind permission of Ariel Tachna.

Cover Design by Mara McKennen

Storybook excerpt on pg. 219 from Goodnight Moon by Margaret Wise Brown and Clement Hurd

Storybook excerpt on pg. 284 from The Giving Tree by Shel Silverstein

ISBN: 978-0-9801018-2-9

Printed in the United States of America
First Edition
October, 2007

eBook edition available
eBook ISBN: 978-0-9801018-3-6

Table of Contents

INTRODUCTION

Hello.

It's great to have you back. "Size Matters" was wonderful, don't you agree? Hot and steamy and yummy and cuddly and *ohmigod do it again* – so here we are.

Doing it again.

Romantic homoerotica is no longer an oxymoron. It's an art form; it's a lyrical song. It's a soft, warm blanket that wraps you up at night; it's a wet kiss that revs you up inside. It's the smell of cologne and musk that intoxicates you; it's the sensation of slinky silk and satin sliding along your skin.

As I said in the introduction to "Size Matters," it's addictive. It's alluring. And once you've had some that really turns you on, you just want more and more and more. In a volume like this, you can find romance and teasing, and then work your way up to the sizzling, swamping, long, slow screw against the wall type of sex.

If you're new to the "Size Matters" concept, welcome! The works herein are, as billed, short stories long enough to satisfy. They're short enough for quick gratification and long enough to keep you toasty and titillated along the way.

Here's wishing you a steamy night,

Madeleine Urban
November, 2007

SIGHT UNSEEN

Shay Kincaid

CHAPTER ONE

THE phone rang three times before Devon Forrester decided to answer it. Sighing, he reached over to the end table and retrieved the receiver without bothering to take his eyes off the television screen.

"Yeah?" he answered, annoyed that the caller was interrupting his movie.

"May I please speak to Scott?" the caller asked.

"Sorry, but there's no one here by that name," Devon answered before disconnecting the call and laying the handset on the couch beside him.

Jackson Prescott picked up the piece of paper lying on his desk and dialed the number again.

"What?" was the answer that greeted him this time.

"Look, I know you said that Scott's not there, so could you please tell me when he left?" the caller asked.

"Again, there is no Scott here and has never been. Had a Steve once, but no Scott," Devon quipped as his mind recalled the young dark-haired man he had tutored a few weeks ago, both on and off the slopes.

"You sure? He gave me this number; told me this was where he was going to be if I needed to contact him," Jackson said as he became impatient all over again.

"I'm fairly sure I'd know if there was another person here with me," Devon quipped.

"Look, this is an emergency. I really need to speak to him."

Devon sighed. "And I really wish you'd believe me when I say that there's no one here by that name. Are you sure you have the right number?" he asked.

Jackson looked at the piece of paper again. "810-555-6754," he called off.

Devon laughed. "Then there's your problem. Would you like to know what number you called?" he asked.

The other man's brows furrowed. "I thought that *was* the number I dialed."

"Close. You called 801 instead of 810," he said with a smile.

"Oh shit," Jackson mumbled, somewhat embarrassed at the mix-up. "I'm sorry."

A light laugh teased Jackson's senses. "No problem, but in the future you should probably let someone else do the dialing for you," Devon suggested. "You might end up calling some place like Timbuktu and get stuck with someone who doesn't understand a word you're saying. God, your phone bill would be horrible."

The other man smiled. "You're probably right."

Devon watched the scene on the screen unfold. "Good luck."

"Thanks. And again, I'm sorry for interrupting your evening," Jackson offered.

"No problem," he said before disconnecting the call on his end.

As soon as Jackson had a clear line, he dialed the correct number and spent the next half-hour relaying bad news to his vacationing neighbor.

LATER that night, as Jackson sat on his back porch watching the falling snow, his thoughts drifted to the conversation with the stranger. There was something about the voice, something that had wrapped itself around him and wouldn't let go. It was soft, almost melodic, and definitely arousing. He had traveled the world over and never before had a voice, or accent, affected him as much as this one did.

He replayed the brief conversation several times and the artist in him constructed the other man's visage. An image of someone in their early twenties, younger than him anyway, with fair skin, light brown hair with blue eyes flashed in his mind's eye. He was of medium height, probably five-foot six or thereabouts, with a small frame. Jackson chuckled to himself when he realized he had just constructed what he considered a perfect little twink.

And don't forget the pouty lips that would look exquisite wrapped around your cock, his mind offered.

A small groan escaped from the man as he pictured his creation kneeling between his legs, administering what Jackson assumed would be the greatest blow job in the history of the world. It had been months since he had been with someone, and even then it was just a quick fuck, a way to release the pent-up tension that had been accumulating.

He had given up on relationships when he had come back from filming early to surprise his lover; only he was the one who had ended up being surprised. The signs had been there for months before - missed phone calls, working late, strange calls that Greg would take in another room 'so he wouldn't disturb Jackson' - but he had chosen to ignore them.

So maybe it really wasn't a surprise when Jackson walked into their bedroom to find Greg buried balls-deep in someone else's ass. Jackson was never one to lose his temper and blow up, except on the very rare occasion, which surprisingly this was not. He had calmly told Greg that when he was finished, he could pack his things and get the hell out of his house. And with that, he turned around and left two very confused men looking after him. He had locked himself in his studio with a bottle of Jack Daniels and did not re-emerge until late the next morning, sporting blood-shot eyes and a mouth that felt as dry as a desert. Jackson snorted at the irony of that little bit since he had just come back from filming *Dakota Plains*.

Once he had sobered up, he donated the bed to a homeless shelter and bought a new one to replace it. Out with the old, in with the new. It had taken him time to get over the loss, but eventually he moved on. Quick and discreet liaisons were his way of taking care of things now, and that suited him, and his partners, just fine. Jackson knew that they were with him because of who he was, and what he represented, but in the harsh light of day he wondered if there was anyone out there who would accept the man he was and not his public persona.

An idea struck, and before he could change his mind, he went back into the house.

DEVON had just stepped out of his shower when the phone rang again. Not caring that he was dripping water all over the carpet, he padded naked to his bed and picked up the extension.

"Hello?"

"I just wanted you to know that somehow I managed to dial the right number and talked to my friend," the voice said.

Devon laughed. "Oh, it's you," he teased. "Are you sure you meant to call me or is this another accident?"

Jackson propped his feet up on the coffee table, the fire in the grate warming his woolen-covered toes. "No, no accident this time. I purposely dialed 801."

"Well, good for you. Would you like a cookie for accomplishing your goal?" Devon asked as he stepped back into the bathroom and quickly dried himself off.

The other man laughed quietly. "How about your name instead?"

Not missing a beat, Devon quipped, "Well now, if I gave you my name, what would I go by?"

"Mouthy little bastard, aren't you?" Jackson mused.

Devon rubbed the towel briskly against his curls. "You make it too easy. So did you get your friend sorted out?"

"Yeah. Crises contained," the older man offered, surprised that he had been asked. Most people wouldn't give a shit one way or another. Feeling more relaxed about his current undertaking, he plowed on. "So, if you won't tell me your name, at least tell me where you are."

"In my bathroom," came the reply.

Jackson's arctic blue eyes rolled toward the heavens. "And where is that?" he prodded.

Devon grinned. *This is going to be fun,* he mused.

"Off my bedroom. You know, it's a small room that contains a sink, toilet and shower? People visit them when they need to answer nature's call, or their body odor starts to offend."

The older man groaned into the phone. "Walked right into that one, didn't I?"

"Smacked you square in the forehead," Devon said as he walked back into his bedroom and pulled a pair of cotton sleep pants from the drawer and slid into them.

Jackson sighed. "I'm not going to win, am I?"

"That remains to be seen," Devon said as he stretched out on his bed.

"Okay, you won't tell me your name or where you are, so what do you do for a living?" Jackson asked.

"Correction. I have told you where I am. Well, where I was."

"So you're not there now?"

"Nope."

"Where are you now?"

"Lying on my bed," Devon answered and Jackson nearly dropped the phone as the image he had created earlier flashed before him. The young man had been in his bathroom earlier and was now in his bedroom. Jackson could see him laid out, fresh from a shower, water droplets clinging to his skin. *Maybe this isn't such a good idea, after all,* he thought.

"Oh," was the only thing Jackson could manage.

BINGO! Devon had wondered where all of this was going, and now he knew. It wasn't that he was above a little phone sex every now and then; he just preferred the real thing.

He lowered his voice to what he would use when he wanted something, or someone. "Want to know what I'm wearing?" he asked as his fingers trailed over his chest, pausing briefly to gently tug on the sliver hoop adorning his left nipple. A shot of pleasure pooled low in his belly.

The older man took a deep breath. Fuck yes he wanted to know, but he wasn't ready to go in that direction just yet. Eventually, sure. But not yet.

Pulling himself back together, he went on. "No, I asked what you do for a living."

"And what if this *is* what I do for a living?" Devon teased. His hand skimmed his stomach and lightly stroked over his cloth-covered erection.

The tension inside of Jackson broke. "Well then, my guess is that you're flat broke because you're not going about it the right way."

"And what way would that be?"

"Asking for the money up front before you get down to business," Jackson said, completely horrified that he had just given that bit of personal information away.

Now it was Devon's turn to say, "Oh."

"Good try, though," Jackson offered. "So back to my question - what do you do for a living?" He heard a lengthy sigh before the answer.

"I'm a snowboarding instructor."

Jackson laughed. "Now, was that so hard?"

No, you fucker, but I am, Devon thought, but instead answered, "Nah. Your turn."

"Artist," Jackson conveyed. He had already decided that was the only piece of information he would divulge about his professions.

"Oh, now that was helpful. There's like a million things you can be under that title," Devon snorted.

"Yep," Jackson said with a grin.

"All right, you crazy artist, care to tell me where you call home?" he asked as he continued to tease himself. They might have moved on verbally, but his body hadn't caught up with that fact just yet.

"Where I'm at right now," the man said as he watched the orange flames dancing before him.

The brunette laughed. "I deserved that," he admitted.

"Damn straight, you did."

"Okay, let me rephrase. What state are you in? And don't give me any shit about confusion or depression or anything like that."

The word 'horny' came to mind, but the older man wasn't about to divulge that. "Montana."

"Lots of cowboys up that way. Do you ride?" Devon asked huskily.

Jackson's pulse raced at the seemingly innocent question. Either way, the answer was yes, and he said as much.

"Mmm, that's nice to know," Devon said with a smile.

Deciding that he'd better hang up before things took a turn for the worse, or better, depending on how one looked at it, Jackson offered, "Listen, I need to be going."

"No! Wait!" Devon said as he tried to calm himself down. He thought he had scared off his caller with his comment. "I'm sorry. I shouldn't have said that."

"It's okay. No offense taken," Jackson replied. "I just have to get up early in the morning."

"Oh, well, okay then. It's been real. Goodnight … neighbor," he said before disconnecting, knowing that he would be hearing from his inquisitive caller again. Exactly when remained to be seen, but he *would* call back. Of that he was sure. He quickly slid his sleep pants off and reached into the bedside table drawer for the bottle of lubricant he kept there, intending to finish what had been started earlier.

As Jackson lowered the handset to the couch, he wondered what the young man meant by that. Neighbor. Did that mean the young man lived in Montana? Could he know where Jackson was calling from and live close by? A thrill shot through his body at that thought. And then another thought crossed his mind, but he quickly discarded it. His number was unlisted and if the other man had Caller ID, his name and number would not show up. The only way to be found was if the man hit star-six-nine, the last call return feature. But even then, his information would not show up. He would only have his number.

Jackson thought that might not be so bad.

CHAPTER TWO

THE next morning, Devon walked into the Brighton Ski Resort office and checked the board for his assignments. He had a beginners group, ages eight to twelve, scheduled for 9:30, and then a private advanced lesson slated that afternoon for 1:15. He quickly checked the name on the private lesson form to see if he recognized it, but no such luck. He loved it when his previous students came back to pick up where they had left off. It might have been a month or two later, or even a year, but either way, it always put a smile on his face.

The morning class passed quickly, as it always did with a beginners group. After the standard safety speech, he showed everyone how to check their equipment, making sure that their bindings were tight and their boots laced properly, made sure they had both ski gloves. Once he was satisfied that everyone was ready, he gathered up his students and over to the starter slope they went. As with all beginners, they spent more time in the snow instead of gliding on top, but when everyone returned to the resort before noon, all agreed that they had a good time. He could hear the kids babbling excitedly to their parents about some of the things they had learned. A couple of them managed to traverse the entire beginner's slope without falling, and for someone just starting out, no matter how old you were, that was a great accomplishment.

After a quick lunch at the grill, he went back to the office to wait for his student. Casey Adams, age twenty-three, was an excellent snowboarder and Devon watched the way his body twisted and turned as he manipulated the board through the rough terrain they were covering. Devon followed the blur down the mountainside, his mind recording their entire run. At the end, when they slid safely to the rail, he pointed out a few places where Casey could improve, and back up the lift they went. They made three additional runs, and when they unhooked their bindings later that afternoon, both Devon and Casey felt they had a very productive afternoon.

As a repayment of sorts, Casey invited Devon to join him and some friends at Club Vortex, a members-only nightclub in the city. For a few moments, he had given the invitation some serious thought. Casey was a good looking guy and even if things didn't work out between them, since he had no idea what the other man's preferences were, there were always others at the club he could pick up, but Devon found himself politely declining the invitation as he had to work the next day.

It had nothing to do with a phone call that might - or might not - come later that night.

Nothing. At. All.

JACKSON spent the majority of the day outside as well. He managed to get a path cleared from the cabin to the barn and spent time with his equine friends, cleaning out stalls, replenishing food and water, and grooming each one. He briefly wondered if his new - friend? - enjoyed horseback riding. He was fairly certain he enjoyed the other sort of riding. Or being ridden. He would make a note to ask what his hobbies were the next time he called.

And call he would. He wanted to find out more about the person he spoke with last night, as much as he could. He was attracted to him, of that there was no doubt, and he wondered what opinion the other man held of him.

He probably thinks I'm some crazy person who dials random numbers when I get bored, he thought as he finished up his chores in the barn.

As he went back to the house, he gathered more firewood and stacked it by the back door, and then went inside. A stranger's face looked up at him from the sketchpad lying on the coffee table and he wondered, not for the first time, if he *had* lost his mind.

He had enjoyed their second phone call last night more than he probably should have, but it felt nice to just let go and be himself, minus a few pertinent details. The other man's cryptic parting words haunted him, and it was maddening to know that he was no closer to figuring out exactly what 'neighbor' meant now than he was when he finally drifted off to sleep last night.

It was one thing he hoped to rectify tonight.

"I was wondering how long you would wait," Devon said into the receiver that was currently lodged between his cheek and shoulder.

"You sound funny," Jackson offered. "What are you doing?"

Devon snorted. "Wouldn't you like to know?"

"Well, yeah, I asked, didn't I?" the older man threw back.

"Oh, there are *so* many ways I could answer that," the young man said with a grin. "But it's not late enough for some of them." Jackson's stomach clenched at the thought of what some of them could be. "Actually, I'm making a sandwich. And before you ask what kind, it's a ham and cheese sandwich. And I'm using wheat bread," he said as he spread Miracle Whip across the two pieces lying on the counter.

Jackson leaned back against the arm of the swing, his right foot nestled in the cushion while his left one rocked him back and forth. "What time is it there?" he asked.

"Dinner time," Devon quipped and called him on it. "I know what you're doing."

"So you're a mind reader. Then tell me, oh great seer, what am I thinking right now?" he taunted.

"You're trying to figure out exactly where I am."

"Besides the kitchen, of course," Jackson offered.

"Well, that goes without saying."

"Last night you said 'neighbor' before hanging up, which could mean one of several things. First, you know where I am…."

"Yep, cowboy country," Devon interrupted as he returned the jar to the refrigerator.

Jackson continued on as if the other man hadn't said anything. "So the term could mean one of three things. One, you're in the same city as I am, which is highly doubtful because I live in the middle of nowhere; two, you're in the same state as I am; or three, you live in one of the surrounding states. How am I doing?"

"Didn't ask," Devon said after taking a bite of his sandwich. "Sorry about that. So, how are you doing?"

"Smart ass," Jackson said with a smile.

"You've given this quite a bit of thought, haven't you?"

Jackson nodded, as if he could be seen. "Honestly, it's been driving me up the wall since we hung up last night."

"I really hope you didn't lose any sleep over it," Devon said before taking another bite.

Before Jackson could answer, an owl screeched somewhere in the distance and Devon heard it through the phone. "What in the hell was that?"

"Owl."

"Sounded like someone screaming, if you ask me," the young man offered.

"There's a parliament of Boreal owls that live in a stand of cedars about fifty yards from my cabin. They can be quite vocal when stirred up. And before you decide to interject your crazy thoughts, no, they do not have a Prime Minister, House of Commons, House of Lords, or anything of that nature."

Devon snickered quietly. "Well, of course they wouldn't. They live in America, not the United Kingdom."

Jackson dropped the receiver from his ear and shook his head. This one was definitely a handful. *No, don't go there,* he thought. His body began to shake as the laughter welled up inside of him until he could contain it no more.

Several hundred miles away, Devon sat at his dinner table and listened to the caller's voice as he laughed, and wished that he could see him. The laugh was full and strong, and he imagined someone who was solidly built, but not overly so like a lumberjack. Those guys were just.... Devon shivered at the thought. Gross.

When he finally recovered, Jackson picked up the phone again.

"Sorry about that," he said with a sigh. "I haven't laughed like that in I can't tell you how long."

"Well, glad to know you're getting your money's worth for this call," Devon said as he rinsed off his empty plate and left it in the sink.

"So now, where were we?" Jackson said as he settled back against the swing again.

"You were trying to figure out exactly where I am," Devon said as he moved into the living room and opened the vertical blinds, his sienna gaze taking in the lights of the city. "The weather report said we're in for several inches of new snow tonight."

"Not really helping," Jackson offered.

"I could turn this into something sexual and say that you're on top of me," Devon said with a grin.

Jackson's cock twitched at the thought. "You could, but don't you think we need to introduce ourselves first, before we jump to that point?"

"I guess. My name is Devon," the young man said as he settled himself on the couch. He hadn't bothered with any lights and the soft glow from his porch light filtered into the room.

Jackson knew if he gave his real name he was fairly certain the young man would recognize it and realize exactly whom he was talking to. Not for the first time did Jackson curse his fame. So he offered up the next best thing - the name he checked into hotels with.

"My name is David," he said as he slowly rocked the swing.

"Can I call you Davey?" Devon teased.

"Not if you expect me to answer."

Devon propped his left foot on the seat of the couch and rested his hand on his knee. "So we have David from Montana."

"And Devon from somewhere below me," Jackson supplied. "Care to be a bit more specific?"

The young man sighed. "Yeah, okay. I live in Utah."

"Yep, I'm on top of you," Jackson said with a smile.

"Not yet, you're not," Devon quipped.

Jackson laughed quietly. "You know, I didn't call you for phone sex, Devon."

"Maybe not, but it could be fun. You got me pretty worked up last night."

Jackson did *not* need to be reminded of the soft sounds that filtered through the phone during their conversation the night before. He took a few deep breaths and tried to get the conversation back on track. "As much as I'd love to, I'm not going there again. I...."

What should he say? That he'd been thinking of him all day? That his voice made him harder than stone?

"At the risk of sounding cheesy, I just want to get to know you," he settled on. "You seem like a very charming young man who has a wicked sense of humor. After spending all my free time around my horses, it's nice to have some human interaction, even if it's over the telephone."

"God, it's been forever since I rode a horse. How many do you have?" Devon excitedly asked.

Jackson breathed a sigh of relief that he had managed to get Devon's mind away from sex, at least for the time being. From that point on, they opened up a bit more and talked about their hobbies. Jackson was a bit dismayed to find that Devon seemed to love doing things that put his life in danger. Throwing himself out of a perfectly good airplane was not something Jackson would ever entertain doing, never mind dangling from a bridge with what amounted to a huge rubber band tied to his ankles. Snowboarding and surfing were Devon's passions, though, and Jackson was suddenly glad that he had not sold his condo in Santa Monica.

Devon learned that Jackson spent his free time riding, painting or sketching and was surprised to hear that the other man owned not one horse, but three, and figured he must be good at what he did. He wondered if the artist was good at *everything* he did.

From there, the conversation bounced from topic to topic and before they realized it, two hours had disappeared. Since the first time Jackson had heard the intoxicating voice, one question plagued the older man, but he was afraid that if he asked, Devon would hang up on him, and that was not something he wanted to risk. But in the end, he decided to take a chance, seeing as what he was doing was chancy, at best, anyway.

"I know this is going to sound weird, but what do you look like?" Jackson asked and then held his breath.

The question was unexpected and it caught Devon by surprise. "What do … what do I look like?"

He fell silent for a bit and Jackson thought that he had indeed scared the young man off.

"Why do you want to know?" he asked, his voice different now; softer than it had been before. Jackson recognized it from last night when Devon was teasing him. This was his bedroom voice and it would be the death of Jackson, he was sure of it.

"Just answer the question, Devon," Jackson said, exasperation tinting his voice.

Devon chuckled into the phone. "Can't blame a guy for trying. So you want to know what I look like. Well, obviously I'm a guy," he teased and heard the groan through the handset. "How specific do you want me to get?"

"Okay, let me go first then," Jackson offered.

"Hey! What if I don't want to know what you look like? What if I want to keep the image I have in my head?" he asked, knowing full-well that he wanted to know what the other man looked like, but was going to torture him just the same.

"Tough. If you don't want to hear, then don't listen," Jackson said before describing himself as best as he could. "I have what some would call sandy-blond hair and blue eyes, medium build, five-eleven and weigh about two-ten. I work out when I can, but the chores I do around here keep me fit."

"Not too bad," Devon said and then tried to describe himself. "Like you, I'm five-eleven, but I weigh somewhere around one-eighty, so I'm a bit on the thin side, but my job keeps me in shape, although I do work out at the resort a few times a week. I've got brown hair that has a mind of its own. Oh, and I have brown eyes."

Jackson closed his eyes and revised his picture of Devon in his mind. "Nice," he whispered. As soon as they hung up, he would make a new sketch of his friend from the description he had just been given.

Now it was Devon's turn to catch Jackson off-guard. "How old are you, David?" he asked. He knew the man was older than himself and that didn't matter. He was just curious.

Jackson closed his eyes and laid his head back on the swing. This would probably be it. "Older than you," he offered.

Devon was chewing on his thumbnail, something he did when he was nervous. "Yeah, but how much? I'm twenty-eight."

"Does it matter how old I am?" Jackson asked.

"No. I've had lovers who were older. I was just curious. You don't have to tell me if you don't want to."

"How old do you think I am?" Jackson asked.

"I'm taking a wild guess here but I'd say in your forties?" the brunette enquired.

"Ever had a lover that old before?"

"Um, no. I think the oldest one was in his late thirties. And I really shouldn't call them lovers, because it wasn't a relationship. Well, not a proper one. Just a few hook-ups, you know?"

"Been there and done that. Listen, it's getting late and I have to get up early - chores and all that," Jackson said as he slowly rose from the padded swing and stretched, his unused joints protesting.

"You don't have anyone there to help out?"

"Nope, just me and the horses."

"And don't forget the parliament," Devon teased.

"And the parliament," Jackson repeated.

"Get some sleep, David," he said, not really wanting to end their conversation.

"You too, Devon," Jackson said as he opened the door and slipped back into the warmth of the house.

"Wait! Before you hang up, you never answered my question," Devon chided.

Jackson smiled. "How about we save that for next time?"

A matching smile spread across Devon's face. "So will there be a next time?"

"I'd like for there to be, if that's okay with you," Jackson answered softly as he leaned back against the wall.

Devon nodded. "Yeah, I think I'd like that too."

Jackson's heart soared. "Until tomorrow."

"Tomorrow," Devon parroted before disconnecting the call. He closed his eyes and rested his head against the back of the couch. "Forrester, I really hope you know what in the hell you are doing." He shook his head and slowly stood. "Not a fucking clue, but whatever it is, it's … nice. Oh great, now I'm talking to myself … and answering! I must be crazy," he said as he made his way into the bedroom.

CHAPTER THREE

DEVON hurt.

And it wasn't just the ordinary, garden-variety hurt either. His muscles screamed in protest as he slowly removed his clothes, the tiniest of movements triggering another round of stabbing pain that left him gasping.

He finally managed to step into the steaming shower, but only after a litany of curses that could give a seasoned sailor a run for his money. Bracing his hands against the front wall, he bent his neck and let the hot water run down over his shoulders and back, hoping it would soothe at least part of the ache there. He'd deal with his legs later. Right now it was his back that needed attention.

Once the hot water had dulled the pain in his protesting muscles, he slowly left the confines of the shower and went in search of the muscle relaxers he had left over from his last bout of testosterone-driven insanity. Devon was nothing if not prepared. Experience taught him to always have an extra muscle relaxer, or two, on hand for just such emergencies. The effects might not last long, but at least they would alleviate some of the pain that was sure to return.

Not bothering with the hassle of getting dressed, he crawled onto his bed and waited for the medication to kick in. He had been floating in a haze of calmness for a little while when he heard his phone ringing.

"Yeah?" he managed to say when he pulled the receiver down onto the bed with him and laid it beside his face.

"Devon?" came the voice through the phone line.

"Mmm hmm." He really didn't have the strength for much more than that.

Jackson's brows furrowed and he looked at the clock. It was only seven in the evening. "Were you sleeping?"

Devon smiled. "Sleep? No. More like drifting," he mumbled.

Concern laced Jackson's voice as he spoke. "Are you okay?"

"Debatable."

"Care to tell me what's going on?" Jackson prodded.

"Fucking hurts," the young man whimpered.

"What does? Devon, what happened?"

"All fucking Chad's fault," he mumbled.

Jackson stamped down the fear that threatened to overwhelm him. The young man was making no sense, what so ever, and it was making Jackson a little worried. Fuck that, not just a little - more than that - a whole lot more than that, he thought.

"Devon, please tell me what's going on. What did Chad do?" The older man's imagination was running rampant and one thing stood out above all the rest. Jackson shivered. He did not want to think this Chad person had hurt his Devon that way. If he had, he was a dead man walking. He'd tear him from limb to limb, and then some.

Whoa, back the train up for a minute there, buster, he thought. Since when did he start thinking of Devon as his? *Try the minute you heard his voice and realized you felt something for him.*

Pushing his inner-voices aside, he concentrated on Devon.

"Devon," he said with a stern voice.

"Hmm?"

"Do I need to call 911?"

Devon snorted into the mattress. "No. 'M okay. Just a bit sore, is all."

Well, that was a little bit better, Jackson thought with relief. At least he was stringing more words together.

"Care to tell me why you sound like you're three-sheets to the wind?"

Devon smiled. "Muscle relaxers are excellent little pills, don't you think?"

"Not if they affect you like that, they're not," Jackson said honestly. "So, tell me what happened to cause you to sound this way."

The young man chuckled. "Just me being me, really," he started as he slowly rolled over so that he was lying on his back, groaning as he did so. Jackson closed his eyes against the pain he heard hiding just beneath the surface of the sound and wished he could help. "It was one of those extremely rare afternoons where a couple of us didn't have anything on the schedule, and we took advantage of our time off, so to speak. So there we were, Chad and I, tagging each other on one of the backcountry runs, which is out of bounds mind you, basically trying to outdo each other. We've ridden these slopes plenty of times before, so we know where each outcropping is, which ones we can do tricks from."

"Oh, Devon, no," Jackson whispered.

Knowing instantly what the older man thought, he rushed on. "No, nothing like that. No accidents, no broken bones. As soon as he hit the first drop-off, he started stringing together different aerials and it was amazing. So of course, me being the idiot daredevil I am, cannot allow him to have all the fun. I can't even begin to explain some of the things I did. Hell, I can't remember half of them now. All I know is that when I got to the bottom of the run, my body voiced its opinion about the afternoon's activities, loud and clear."

Jackson waited for his friend to continue, but nothing else was forthcoming. He breathed a small sigh of relief that it wasn't worse than a few sore muscles, and said as much.

"A few?" Devon protested. "Try damned near every one of them. I took a hot shower earlier and it helped ease the pain a bit, but the pill worked even better."

"Kids these days," Jackson said with a small smile.

"Yeah, well, at least I can still do that stuff, old man," he teased. "What can you do?"

"Whip your butt for being a smart ass."

Devon laughed, feeling somewhat better now. He didn't want to admit that hearing this particular voice on the other end of the line made him feel even better than the shower or the little magic pill. "You into kink, David?"

Jackson groaned. "I should just hang up and be done with you. It doesn't matter what I say - you're going to turn it into something sexual."

Devon's free hand settled lightly on his stomach, his thumb teasing the indention of his navel. "Yeah, well, sue me. I'm a young man with needs."

An idea was rapidly forming in Jackson's head. Before he could chicken out, he asked, "Where are you right now?"

"Lying buck-naked on my bed."

"Perfect," Jackson said with a smile.

"Finally gonna give me what I want?" Devon asked.

"Depends on what it is you want."

Devon's pulse quickened at the thought of what the other man might be thinking.

"I want you to lay face-down," Jackson said.

"Kinda hard to jerk-off that way," Devon teased.

"Just do as I say," he instructed and listened to the small sounds Devon emitted as he rolled onto his stomach.

Devon propped the phone on the side of his face. "Okay, I'm laid out and at your command."

Jackson groaned at the image that flashed across his mind. He lay back on his couch, the warmth of the fire relaxing him. "What's your favorite scented oil?" he asked.

"Fuck if I know. Never been asked. Does Astroglide have a scent?"

"Not that I'm aware of. So you're not into scented or flavored lube?"

"Nope. Dare I ask what are you up to?"

Jackson would have to remember that for future reference. "How about a nice imaginary massage from someone you barely know?" Jackson teased.

"As long as it's you, how could I refuse?"

A slow warmth suffused Jackson's body and he wondered if the young man realized what he had said. *Or maybe you're reading too much into things,* he thought, which was probably the more accurate of the two assumptions.

"Okay, now close your eyes," he quietly instructed.

"No problem there," Devon quipped as his eyes slowly shut.

"I'm pouring sandalwood scented massage oil in my hands. Now feel my hands as they slowly stroke your neck, my thumbs massaging the muscles at the base. I'm moving to your shoulders now, closing my hands over them and gently squeezing," Jackson said and through the phone line, heard a deep breath being inhaled.

Devon bit his lip as the words began to affect him. He slowly lost himself in the seductive voice, imagined that he could feel the work-roughened hands gliding over his body.

"I'm moving down your back now, slowly rubbing the soreness away. Does that feel good, Devon?"

Devon pressed his hardening cock into the mattress beneath him, trying to ease the tension that was building there. "Yesssss," he whispered.

"I'm moving down now, rubbing your thighs, relaxing all the muscles in your body with my hands."

The muscles in Devon's leg twitched in reaction to the soothing words.

Jackson took a deep breath and tried to calm his racing heart. He reached down to unbutton and unzip his jeans in an effort to ease the pressure off of his swollen member.

"My hands glide over your ass, slowly kneading each side."

Devon moaned as his hips slowly rocked against the surface below him. Jackson took in every nuance that spilled from Devon's lips, drank them in as if they were nectar from the Gods themselves.

"That sound, Devon," Jackson panted. "Jesus." He was silent for a moment, afraid of what might come out of his mouth if he tried to say anything else. His slid his hand into his boxers and slowly stroked himself.

Devon's moans became louder, his breathing ragged. The voice, the words … Devon reached into the nightstand drawer and quickly found what he was searching for. After rolling to his back, he closed his slicked hand around his cock. "Please don't stop."

Jackson heard the rustling through the phone line and knew what Devon was doing. "Devon, this is not…." Jackson started to say this was not where he had intended for this to go but was interrupted before he could finish.

"Too late," Devon said as he tugged on his nipple ring. "Just … oh fuck," he panted as want and need crashed through his body. Never before had he been so affected by someone. Devon didn't care if this wasn't what the other man wanted … he wanted it. "Fuck, I wish you were here, David," he said as began to stroke in earnest.

The name snapped Jackson back to reality but it was the whimpers and erratic breathing he heard that lured him back into the fantasy. He already knew he was going to hell - this just ensured him a first class ticket. His own fist closed around his member and he knew it wouldn't take but a few strokes and he'd be done for.

Might as well go out in a blaze of glory.

"So do I, baby. So do I," he said quietly, surprised at the ease in which the endearment rolled off of his tongue, as if it were said everyday.

The reply caught Devon by surprise. He'd been called 'baby' more times than he could remember, but coming from this man, it was somehow different. His cock pulsed in his hand, sending several pearlescent streams onto his chest as he realized that this was the first time he wished it was true.

Jackson's hand and shirt were covered with his own release, his heart beating frantically inside his chest. It was only when it had slowed to a somewhat normal pace that he finally dared to speak.

"Devon?"

"I'm here," he said quietly.

God, he felt like a first class asshole for what had just happened. "I'm sorry," Jackson offered. "That's not what I had in mind when I started it. I was just trying to help take your mind off of the pain."

Devon laughed. "It worked," he said as he reached over and retrieved a few tissues to clean himself off with. "Are you okay?"

Jackson chuckled. "I'll survive," he said as he tried to figure out what to use to clean up with. His shirt was a mess and he didn't have anything else close by. "Can you hang on a minute? I need to take care of the mess I made," he said as he pushed himself off of the couch.

"Take as long as you need," Devon said. "I'm not going anywhere," he said as he tossed the tissues into the trashcan beside the bed.

Jackson walked into the guest bathroom and set the phone on the sink before carefully pulling the soiled t-shirt over his head. With that done, he grabbed a washcloth and quickly wiped himself off.

"Done," he said when he retrieved the phone and tossed the shirt towards the mudroom.

"All better?" Devon asked as he slid beneath the covers.

"Yeah. So you're okay now?"

"Much better," the young man offered as he slowly stretched his back. "Back doesn't hurt as bad."

"That's good. What about work tomorrow?" Jackson asked as he settled on the couch again.

"Today was my last one. I work four on and four off," he offered.

"Good. You can take it easy tomorrow."

Devon rolled to his side, his eyes closing. He cradled the extra pillow against his chest. "Yeah, until about seven anyway, and then I go to my other job."

"Other job?"

"When I'm not working at the resort on the weekends, I'm a bartender at a nightclub here in town," he said quietly. "Not the most glamorous job, but it helps pay the bills."

Jackson heard the relaxing sigh and wondered how much longer his friend would be awake.

"I'm going to let you go now, okay?"

"I'll miss talking to you tomorrow night," Devon admitted as his mind slowly shut down.

"Me too."

"Gonna get some sleep now. Night."

"Goodnight, baby," Jackson whispered before disconnecting the call.

He lay on the couch and pulled the old battered quilt from its back, covering himself. It wasn't long before he succumbed to sleep's hold and dreamt of snow covered mountains and brown eyes.

CHAPTER FOUR

BEN Crawford stood, unobserved, in the doorway and watched his friend apply brown and golden hues to the canvas propped in the center of the room. He never claimed to understand Jackson's paintings, and this one was just as perplexing as all the others. No matter, though - it was beautiful. He lifted the cold bottle of beer to his lips and took another drink, wondering how long it would take the artist to realize he had company.

When he had stepped from his rental almost a half-hour earlier, the sounds of Jeff Healey filled the air. His knock on the door went unanswered and knowing the drill, he let himself inside the house. The unmistakable smell of Jackson's homegrown specialty assaulted his nostrils.

"So the artist is working," he said quietly as he closed the door behind him.

After dropping his bag at the foot of the stairs, he went back to the kitchen, pulled a beer from the refrigerator, and went in search of his friend.

Jackson had woke early that morning and after running through his chores quicker than he would have liked, immersed himself in a vision that came to him last night. Brown eyes, ringed and flecked with gold had teased him unmercifully in his dreams and now he was bringing that dream to life.

"If it were only that easy," he muttered to himself as he stood back and looked over his work thus far.

"I hear that talking to yourself is a definite sign of insanity."

The voice startled Jackson and he turned to find its origin. A broad smile lit the man's face as he saw who was lounging in the studio's doorway.

"Nah, it's only when you answer yourself that you've lost your mind," Jackson said as he moved towards his friend, enveloping him in a massive hug. "What in the hell are you doing here?" he asked, happiness flooding his voice.

Ben returned his embrace. "Was on my way to Los Angeles and thought you might like some company for a few days," he offered before the two men separated. He motioned to the canvas. "Another one of your mad creations in the making?"

Jackson turned back to the mess of colors and his heart softened. "Came to me in a dream last night."

Ben laughed. "You artists are a crazy bunch," he said with affection.

"Never claimed otherwise," he said as he threw his arm around Ben's shoulder and led him back into the living area. "So, how long can you stay?"

"I have a meeting scheduled for Monday afternoon. Think you can handle company until then?" Ben asked as he settled himself on the couch, stretching his legs out in front of him. Jackson claimed the other corner.

"My door is always open. You and the guys know that. Well, at least for the others a bit of notice is required, but you're always welcome, no matter what the time is," the older man said as he glanced at the clock on the mantel. Devon would be leaving for work in a couple of hours and Jackson wanted to call him before he left.

Ben noticed where Jackson's eyes had drifted. "Keeping time now?"

"Didn't realize it was this late. I've been in there all day," he admitted. "I need to go out and feed before it gets too dark. Care to join me?"

"Do I have a choice?" Ben asked as he stood and followed his friend to the door.

"Nope," Jackson said with a smile. "At least not with the late feeding. I won't make you get up for the early morning one."

"My body and I appreciate that ever so much," Ben teased as Jackson slid into his jacket.

DEVON was on his hands and knees looking under his bed for a missing black motorcycle boot. At least that's where he thought it might have been. He hadn't seen it in a few days so there was really no telling where it might be. He found one in the closet, but its mate had apparently taken off for parts unknown.

"Hot damn! Now that's what I'm talking about! Devon Forrester on hands and knees, ass ready and waiting," a voice said from Devon's living room.

"I'm looking for my fucking boot, you fuck-wit!" Devon yelled back at his friend.

"That may be, but I'll have to say that it looks like an invitation from where I'm standing," his friend commented.

"Shut up, Tyler, and help me find my other boot," he groused as he continued to move around the boxes that were stored under the bed.

"Fuck that," Tyler said as he eyed the leather-clad ass in front of him. "I'd rather watch you."

"Bastard," he muttered, and then, "There you are, you son of a bitch!" he yelled in triumph before dragging the wayward boot out from its hiding spot. He moved to sit on the end of the bed and slid his foot into the leather. As he was reaching down to do the buckles, his phone rang.

"Get that, will you?" he asked Tyler, who crawled across Devon's bed and reached for the receiver.

"Hello?"

Jackson paused and wondered if he'd dialed the right number. "Um, yeah. Could I speak to Devon?" he asked quietly.

He had left Ben in the living room watching Sports Center while he had snuck upstairs to make the call.

Tyler's eyes slid to his friend, who was in the process of pulling on his shirt.

"He's getting dressed. May I ask who's calling?"

Jackson's stomach plummeted. Devon was getting dressed and a strange man was answering his phone. For some reason, this made him very, very angry, but it would not do to let this person know that.

"Yeah, tell him it's ... David," he said in what he hoped sounded like a normal voice.

Tyler handed the phone to Devon. "Some guy named David," he said and watched the slight widening of his friend's eyes as the phone was taken from him.

Devon's pulse hummed at the name. He took the receiver and walked into the living room, leaving his friend on the bed.

"Hey," he said quietly as he moved to stand by the patio doors, his gaze taking in the colors of the evening.

"Didn't want to break with tradition, so I thought I'd call you before you left for work. Is that okay?" Jackson asked as he sat on the covered window seat in his bedroom.

Devon's features softened. "Yeah, that's fine."

"How's your back today? Been taking it easy?"

"It's fine. The *treatment* last night worked wonders," he teased. Heat spread throughout his body as he recalled their conversation.

Jackson leaned the side of his head against the window. "Glad I could help. You had me worried for a little while."

"Sorry about that," he offered.

"Kids will be kids, right?" the older man teased.

Devon leaned his shoulder against the doorframe. "I refuse to grow up, what can I say?"

"Dev, we need to be going," Tyler said from behind him.

Brown eyes drifted to his friend. "Give me a minute," he said with a small smile.

"Fine, but if we're late, it's your ass," the dark-haired man said as he went back into the bedroom.

"Sorry about that, but I do need to go," he said into the phone.

"That's fine. I just wanted to call and see how you were doing."

"Thanks. I … it means a lot to me that you called," he whispered as his heart thumped wildly in his chest.

"My pleasure, Devon. Be careful tonight."

"I will. I'll talk to you later? Well, not later because I'll be out … but, you know," he stammered.

Jackson smiled. "Yeah, I know. Oh, before we go, I wanted to let you know that I have a friend staying with me for a few days so we might not be able to talk as long as we have before. I hope that's not a problem."

"Depends on if your guest is a male or female," Devon teased.

"Male."

"Problem," slid from his lips before he could stop it.

"He's an old friend of mine," Jackson offered.

"Fuck buddy?" Devon asked.

"What color did you say your eyes are?"

"Brown."

"Sounds like they've got a green tint to them right now."

Devon shook his head, chestnut curls brushing his shoulders. "Nah, man, just giving you shit," he said, lied actually.

"Reaaally…."

"Yes, really. It's not like we … oh, never mind."

"You're adorable when you're flustered," the older man smiled.

"I am not flustered."

Jackson chuckled. "Go to work, Devon. I'll call you tomorrow."

Before the young man could reply, the call had been disconnected on the other end. As he slid into his leather jacket, he tried to squash the feeling that was growing in the pit of his stomach. He had no reason to be jealous. They weren't together, or anything like that. They talked on the phone and that was it.

Then why do you feel like smashing something if you are just 'friends'? a little voice inside asked.

"WHAT'S got your shorts in a knot?" Tyler asked when Devon slid into the passenger seat.

"Nothing," he said as he looked out the window. He did not want to discuss it - whatever it was.

"Could have fooled me. So who's this David guy? You been holding out on me?" his friend asked as he pulled into the evening traffic.

"Nobody. Just ... a friend," he offered.

"Just a friend. Well, care to tell me what this so-called friend said that pissed you off?"

"Drop it, Tyler."

"Okay, but if you want to talk, you know I'm there for you. Or, you know, if you and your so-called *friend* don't work things out, maybe you can put in a good word for me?" he teased, knowing how to get Devon to talk.

"Yeah, like I'd send him your way," he said and then turned to look at the driver. "I don't understand this, Tyler. I've talked to him for three days and it's like we ... I don't know ... like we are friends, but ... something else. It's crazy. He dialed my number by mistake a few days ago, looking for his friend, and I thought that was it."

"SO after I talked to Scott, I came out here for a little while and did some thinking. You know how I feel about people only being with me for who I am, what they think I can do for them, give them. So I got this crazy idea into my head. I went back and called Devon, let him know up front that I had called him on purpose, and we've talked every night since then," Jackson said as he and Ben sat on the swing and enjoyed the night.

"And he has no clue that you're you," Ben offered.

"No," Jackson said as he released a long breath. "I told him my name was David. Hell, you know that if I said my name was Jackson Prescott he would know right off the bat who it was."

"So now you're having second thoughts about it all."

"Try third and fourth thoughts. I'm in this up to my neck, Ben. It's exciting to speak to someone and let them know the real me, Jackson the person, not Jackson the actor. Just me. And it's been great."

Ben heard a 'but' coming.

"But now, I don't know. It's crazy. I feel something for him. Actually, I felt it the first time we talked. His voice, god, it's beautiful and does things to me that …." Jackson trailed off as lust slowly invaded his senses. He took a deep breath and tried to calm his racing heart.

"You want him, don't you?" Ben surmised.

"Yeah, I do," Jackson said with a sigh. "And I'm scared to death."

"YOU can't be serious, Devon. You've talked to him a handful of times and you think you feel something for him? You think … or you know?" Tyler asked as he maneuvered them through the traffic.

"I know, I'm a total spaz, but yeah, I feel something for him," Devon finally admitted.

"Horny," Tyler supplied.

"Well, that goes without saying," the brunette said with a laugh. "But it's, I don't know, different. More."

"So what got you all upset earlier? You seemed fine when I walked in."

Devon shook his head. "He told me that a friend was there for a few days and I sort of had a moment."

"Huh? What do you mean - had a moment?"

"I was jealous," the young man admitted. "And he called me on it."

"Reaaally?" Tyler asked, genuinely surprised by his friend's reaction.

"Oh shut up. I feel bad enough about it without you adding to it," Devon said as they pulled into the parking lot. "He said that they were just friends."

"Do you believe him?"

Devon shrugged. "Doesn't matter. It's not like we're together or anything."

"Obviously it does or else you wouldn't have reacted the way you did."

The brunette sighed. "No matter. It's over and done with."

"The two of you are, or just this incident?" Tyler asked as he opened his door, Devon doing the same.

"This incident. He said that he'd call me tomorrow," he said with a small smile.

Tyler was not about to point out the fact that his friend did not deny the first part of his question.

IN the darkness of his room later, Devon noticed the light on his answering machine blinking. He pushed the Play button and waited.

"Hey, it's me. It's 11:15 and I'm sitting in my studio thinking of you. I have a confession to make. You're not the only one who was jealous earlier. And don't try to deny it. I heard it in your voice even though you tried to play it off like it was nothing. So anyway, when you weren't the one who answered, I didn't like the things I was feeling. I know that I had no right to feel that way, but I can't help it. I'm not sure what this thing is that we're doing, but I'm enjoying it and I don't want to do anything to jeopardize it. My friend that's staying with me is just that - a friend. We've never been anything more and we never will be. I just wanted you to know that. I'll call you tomorrow. Goodnight, baby."

Devon smiled as he saved the message.

CHAPTER FIVE

"DEV, that guy has been giving you the 'Come Fuck Me' look all night long," Tyler said as he reached behind Devon to retrieve a bottle of Cuervo Gold from the shelf.

Devon looked up from where he was mixing his latest concoction and caught green eyes staring back at him. The stranger smiled and raised his drink to the bartender, saluting the beautiful young man. The brunette gave a small smile in return and looked away.

"Not interested," Devon told his friend.

Tyler nearly dropped the bottle he was holding. "Did I hear that correctly? Devon Forrester is not interested in what I would take to be a sure thing? Look at him! He's damn near perfect! Green eyes, light brown hair and a body that rivals yours," the dark-haired man offered as he looked Devon up and down. Tonight they were shirtless, both covered in a light sheen of sweat thanks to the place being packed; they were working non-stop. Tyler's gaze dropped to Devon's stomach and abs. "You, my friend, have the most amazing body. It's a shame you don't feel like sharing it."

Devon handed the drink to his customer and accepted the cash that was offered.

"Keep it," the patron said, and with a wink, disappeared into the crowd.

The brunette moved to the register and rang up the sale, added the difference to the almost-full tip jar and tossed the guy's phone number in the trash.

His friend's eyes widened. "Tell me you did not just toss someone's number away," Tyler said. "Have you lost your fucking mind?"

"No," he answered before taking the next customer's order.

"Then please explain what's going on," he said and then realization hit. "Does this have anything to do with that David guy?" Tyler saw the slight hesitation in Devon's movements and knew he had his answer.

Devon turned fully to his friend. "This is not up for discussion so I'd appreciate it if you dropped it."

Tyler acquiesced. "I will, for now. But later, you and I are going to sit down and have a talk."

"Fine," Devon sighed and went back to work.

IT was three in the morning when Devon and Tyler walked into the all-night diner they sometimes went to after work, when neither had a pressing engagement after closing time. Devon had turned down quite a few invitations for personal reasons, and Tyler had turned a few down as well because they needed to talk. A piece of ass was nice, but his friends came first.

Devon was sipping his coffee when the other man finally spoke.

"Now, care to tell me just what in the hell is going on with you?" he asked.

"I wish I knew," Devon answered honestly.

"Until this David guy showed up on the scene, you very rarely went home alone. What's changed?" Tyler asked as he cut his burger in half.

Devon set the cup down on its saucer and sat back in the booth. "I don't know. I mean, I still look, and all that. But it's like

I've lost my appetite or something. What's out there, what we see each weekend, there for the taking, is not what I want. I'm twenty-eight years old and tired of playing the game."

"What you want is an illusion, Devon. We don't get 'happily ever after'. You know this," his friend offered.

"Why not? Why can't we have it? I mean, it won't be the traditional 'happily ever after', with the white picket fence and the two-point-five kids, but who says we can't have our own version of it?" the brunette countered. "There are gay couples out there who have been together for twenty, thirty years."

"Yeah, and one of them probably has AIDS and will be dying here shortly," Tyler snorted.

"It's not funny, Tyler. So far, we've been lucky. But one of these days, our luck will run out. It might not be this year, or the next, but one of these days something will happen. And I don't want that."

"So, what, you want to find someone and become a 'kept man'? Is that it?" his friend asked.

Devon snorted. "I'll never be a 'kept man', as you put it. But yeah, I do want someone. I want to know that someone will be there when I get home, someone to cook dinner with, someone to argue about the laundry and grocery list with."

"Sounds to me like you need a wife," Tyler offered.

Devon mock-shivered. "Wrong equipment."

"So how does David fit into all this?" his friend prodded. "What is it about him that's made you turn guys down for three nights in a row?"

"I told you, I'm tired…."

"Of playing the game," Tyler finished. "I heard you."

Devon sat quietly for a few minutes, trying to put his thoughts in some kind of order. Finally, he looked up at his friend. "I think I'm going to ask him if we can meet."

"You what?!" Tyler exclaimed.

"I said…."

The dark-haired man waved his hand in front of his friend. "Hello! You can not be seriously considering this!"

Devon shrugged. "I am. I can't explain it. There's something between us, friendship, maybe something more. I want to know if the feelings I'm having are real or just a figment of my imagination because of the situation."

"So you're going to go traipsing off to Montana in hopes of finding, what? Your soul mate? Your other half? True love?" his friend asked.

The brunette knew he shouldn't get angry - this was his best friend he was talking to. If he couldn't handle what Tyler said, then why bother? But it stung when put to him that particular way. Just because Tyler didn't believe in it did not mean Devon had to follow suit.

"I don't know what's out there, but I need to find out," he admitted.

Tyler sat back in his seat and studied the man sitting across from him. Devon was serious about this, and when he made his mind up about something, he was like a bulldog - he would not let go until he saw it through. And for better or worse, as his best friend, Tyler would support him in this as well. He just hoped he wouldn't have to pick up the pieces of Devon's broken heart if things didn't work out.

"You know, Dev, you've done some crazy things in your life, but I have to tell you, this takes the cake," he said with a smile. "Just do me a favor."

"What?"

"Be careful. You don't know this guy from Adam, other than what he's told you on the phone. He could be lying about everything and you'd never know the difference, until it was too late," he offered.

Devon reached across the table and took Tyler's hand. "I'll be careful. I promise. I'll even do you one better. If this blows up in my face, you have the right to say 'I told you so'. Does that help?"

"Not really, but I'll be here if you need me."

"That's all I ask," Devon said with a smile.

DEVON was lying on his bed; the phone cradled between his cheek and shoulder, and listened as Jackson prattled on about his weekend. Ben had left earlier that day so the older man was free to spend as much time on the phone as he wanted and it appeared he was making up for lost time.

Devon's mind drifted back to the conversation with Tyler and he knew what he had to do.

"I want to meet you, David," he blurted out.

Jackson stopped mid-sentence, his train of thought derailed. Actually, the locomotive appeared to have been obliterated. It was as if an alien craft had swooped down from the sky and wiped it off the face of the planet. His heart thundered in his chest and he had to sit down. *He didn't really say what I think he just said, did he?* he thought to himself.

When no answer was given, Devon became worried. Maybe the other man didn't want to meet. Maybe he was satisfied with the way things were. Maybe he was married and this was just something he did for kicks.

"David?"

"Yeah," Jackson answered in a whisper.

"Oh, I thought you might have hung up or something. Look, if you don't want to, that's fine. I just thought that...."

"No," Jackson croaked and then cleared his voice. "No, you just caught me off-guard, that's all."

"So? What do you say?" Devon asked, his thumb finding its way between his lips; white teeth nibbling at the nail. "I mean, I'm … fuck, I don't know what I mean."

This brought a smile to Jackson's lips and he began to relax. "You mean to tell me that for once, you don't have a witty remark on the tip of your tongue? Devon, I'm so disappointed," he teased, trying to make light of the situation.

Devon forced a quick laugh. "Make fun of me, why don't ya?"

Now Jackson felt bad for teasing him. "No, I'm sorry, Devon. It's just that it was a bit unexpected. At least coming from you, anyway."

The young man sat up on the bed. "So you've been thinking about it, then?"

"Probably more than I should have," Jackson admitted as he ran a hand through his sandy-colored locks.

A sudden burst of energy assaulted Devon's system and he flew off the bed and began pacing his apartment. "So how do we do this? I've never done this before."

"Me neither. I don't know. We could meet somewhere, you know, halfway for both of us. Or you can come here, or I could fly down to ... where are you anyway?" Jackson asked.

"Salt Lake City. Where are you?"

"Livingston," Jackson offered. "Well, actually I live about ten miles west of Livingston, in the middle of nowhere."

"The middle of nowhere sounds great, if you ask me," Devon offered.

"It can be, but there's really not a lot things to do here. So we can either meet someplace or I could come to Salt Lake City," he suggested.

"Plenty of things to do here, that's for sure. Would ... would you want to stay with me or...." Devon started.

"I think I'll get a hotel room. That way if things don't work out, you won't feel pressured or anything," Jackson offered. *That way I'll have somewhere to hide and lick my wounds if you reject me.*

Devon leaned a hip against his kitchen counter. "Yeah, I think that'd be best."

"So when do you want to do this?"

Would yesterday be too soon? Devon thought with a smile. "Well, I'm starting my next run at the resort tomorrow, so anytime after those four days works for me. Or is that too soon?" he rushed. "Do you have anything going on next week?"

Jackson laughed at the nervousness Devon was exhibiting. It was comforting to know that he wasn't the only one who had been thinking about this. "No, but what about your bartending job at the nightclub?"

"I'll take the weekend off. I just need to give them as much notice as I can," he said.

"So how long do you want me to stay? A couple of days?"

Devon snorted. "My luck, you'll tire of me the first day and that'll be the end of that," he said with a laugh. "Really, it doesn't matter. I'm off for four days, so whatever you want to do is fine. Like I said, there's more than enough to do around here."

If things work out like I'm hoping, sightseeing will be the last thing on my list of things to do, Jackson thought with a smile.

"Any suggestions on where I should stay?" the older man asked.

Devon pulled a phonebook from one of the kitchen drawers and rattled off several hotels and their numbers. With that information secure, Jackson decided that he'd fly down the afternoon of Devon's last day of work and get settled in, and then Devon would pick him up for dinner later that evening. That would give them four full days together, and Jackson would make the flight back home on that fourth night.

If things don't come to a screeching halt before it gets started, Jackson thought.

"I only have one request," Jackson said after they had finally moved beyond the trip planning stage.

"What's that?"

"Promise me that no matter how surprised, or whatever you feel when you meet me, that you'll give me a chance," Jackson said quietly.

"As long as you do the same for me," Devon replied in kind.

Jackson breathed a sigh of relief. "Thank you."

"Now that we've got that out of the way, I guess we need to exchange last names, don't you think?" Devon teased.

"Miller," Jackson said.

"Forrester."

"Devon Forrester. Sounds posh," the blond man teased.

"David Miller," Devon said quietly. "Definitely sounds like an artist's name."

Jackson laughed quietly. *You have no idea.*

They talked a little while longer about things they might want to see and do, and it was only when Devon yawned that Jackson put a halt to their conversation.

"Get some sleep, Devon. Don't want you falling off a cliff before I get a chance to meet you," he said.

"Only if you promise not to fall off one of your horses and end up with a broken neck or something," he teased and then became serious. "I'm glad we're doing this. At first, I was afraid you might not want to meet me."

"I'm glad you asked. Much braver than I am, that's for sure," he said honestly. "Now get some sleep and I'll talk to you tomorrow night."

"Okay."

"Night, baby," Jackson said quietly.

"Night, David," Devon replied. He disconnected the call and looked at his shaking hands. In four days, he would finally meet the man whose voice had haunted his thoughts and dreams, and he was scared shitless.

Several hundred miles away, another man felt the same way.

CHAPTER SIX

JACKSON took one last look in the mirror and sighed, wondering again if he had completely lost his mind. He had only known Devon for two weeks, and now he was here to meet the young man. Only it wasn't Jackson Prescott the other man was expecting, but David Miller. This thought caused fear and uncertainty to flood the actor's system, his stomach roiling as if he were about to be physically ill. Closing his eyes against the nausea, he focused inward and within a few minutes, he had calmed himself - mostly.

He had dressed casually; black slacks with a loose burgundy button-up, in an effort not to appear too laid-back, but not over-dressed either. Devon mentioned dinner, but not where they would be dining. He had no idea what the dress code was, if there was one, so he settled for middle of the road. Grabbing his shoes and socks, he left the confines of the bedroom and made his way into the living area of the suite and settled himself on the couch to finish dressing.

And wait.

Devon stepped nervously from the elevator that had swept him up to the fifth floor of the Marriott Hotel quicker than he would have liked. The butterflies that had taken up residence in his stomach earlier were morphing into something larger, the frantic beating of their wings becoming heavier with each step he took down the hallway. By the time he had stopped in front of Room

332, inconveniently located at the opposite end of the long hallway, in his opinion, he was ready to take flight himself.

But if he did that, he would never know, and he would always wonder. Screwing up his courage, he lifted his shaking hand and knocked.

Inside, Jackson's eyes snapped to the door. This was it - the moment of truth. Slowly, he rose from the couch, not wanting to seem too eager to meet this young man who had brought to life something deeply buried, and moved towards the entrance. He fought the temptation to look through the peephole and reached for the knob instead.

What stood before Jackson was something he had never expected. The term 'beautiful' came to mind, but even that did not do this man justice. Jackson would never forget his first glimpse of heaven on earth. From the riot of wild chestnut curls to the large sienna eyes, his gaze moved to the sculpted cheekbones and a perfect pair of succulent lips. The young man was dressed casually in a gray button-up and black cargo pants that rode low on his hips, black boots, and a black leather jacket.

Devon had started opposite of Jackson, first taking in the long legs encased in black trousers, then moved up to the slim waist and torso wrapped in burgundy, and then finally higher, to the man's face.

And that was the moment his world fell apart.

Jackson knew the instant Devon recognized him and was at a complete loss of what to do next. He had rehearsed it all in his mind, time and time again: what he would say, how he would explain his deceit. But now, when it came time to follow through, he was lost. He saw the pain of betrayal in the young man's eyes and it cut him to the quick.

Before Devon could do or say anything, Jackson quietly asked, "Do you remember the promise you made? That no matter how surprised you are, or whatever you feel when you meet me, that you'll give me a chance?"

Devon did remember the promise. "Yes, but that's when I was expecting a real person," he threw at the older man.

Jackson sighed. He deserved that, and anything and everything the beautiful man standing before him would have to say. But not here.

"Devon, please, come in and let me explain," he said as he moved aside, his back pressed snugly against the wooden surface. His hand gripped the doorknob tightly.

The young man wanted to run; run far, far away and forget the last two weeks - two weeks of fun and quirky phone calls that had stemmed from a misdialed number.

A misdialed number by Jackson Prescott. Actor. Star. Not David Miller, the man he had felt a connection with more than anyone else - ever.

And it was all a lie.

Eyes the color of a clear sky on a summer's day pleaded with him. "Please? Just give me five minutes to explain things and if you're not satisfied, you're welcome to leave."

On their own volition, Devon's feet carried him inside the suite and it was only when the door had closed that he turned to face the other man.

"All I want to know is why. Why did you lie to me?" he asked quietly.

"Would you like to sit down?" Jackson asked, pointedly avoiding the question for now. "Maybe something to drink?"

Devon shook his head. "No," he stated and stood where he was. "I'm fine," he lied. He was not fine. Fine wasn't even a blip on his radar.

Jackson moved to the window that offered a picturesque view of the mountains beyond. They were what calmed him, what he was familiar with. Taking a deep breath, he turned back to Devon. "Would you have believed me if I had told you the truth up front, back at the beginning?"

"No."

"Which is precisely why I didn't. That first time I called, when I was looking for Scott, and I heard your voice, there was something ... I can't explain it ... but something was there and I

wanted … I don't know … more of it. So I called back. I still can't
believe that I had the nerve to dial your number again. But I did,
and I continued to dial it each day because I wanted to get to know
the young man who had entranced me. I know it sounds corny, but
you did. You do," he said as he paused to look at the rigid man
standing before him. "I was afraid that if I told you who I was, you
wouldn't talk to me. Or if you did, you would pretend to be
someone you're not."

"Ever heard of a pot and kettle?" Devon mumbled.

"Yeah, but tell me, if you had known who I was, would you
have continued to talk to me?"

"I don't know. Maybe," he offered with a shrug. "I guess
we'll never know."

Jackson moved to sit on the arm of the sofa. "There's a
reason I held my identity back. I'm tired of people using me for
their own selfish gain. They want the movie star, not me, the man
who lives on a ranch in Montana with nothing but his horses for
company. They don't want that. So I thought that if I showed you
who the real Jackson Prescott was … I don't know … I thought
that if we ever did meet, you'd already know me."

"Who is David Miller?" Devon asked, his voice tightened
by anger.

"Just a name I go by when I don't want to be found," he
answered. "Look, I know this is a lot to take in, but Devon, David
is me, as well. Everything that David told you, everything that
David felt, I felt those same things; me, Jackson," he said as he
placed a hand over his heart. "When you said you wanted to meet
me, I was shocked. I was excited. And I was afraid, because by
that point, it was too late to go back. I asked you to not make any
snap judgments for a reason. It was selfish, I know, but I had to. If
you'd give me a chance, you'll see that I'm the same person you
have been talking to for the past couple of weeks. Don't let the fact
that I'm an actor stand between us. That's just a job. It doesn't
define who I am."

Devon finally moved, his long legs taking him to the
opposite side of the room, away from the other man as he tried to

process everything. He could handle David. David was just a regular guy like himself. David made him laugh, took his shit and gave it right back. David was the one who had taken Devon's mind off of the pain he felt after the stunt he pulled with Chad. His brain almost shut down when he realized that he had gotten off with Jackson Prescott.

David Miller was safe. Jackson Prescott was in another category altogether. The man who had come to visit was someone else, someone Devon didn't know. But he had promised David, or Jackson, that he would give him a chance, and he would stick by that promise. After a few minutes, he turned back and looked at him.

"David ... Jackson ... fuck, I don't even know what to call you," he said as he looked at the floor, frustrated that he had been put in this situation. Never in a million years would he have expected this.

"Call me whatever you feel comfortable with," Jackson offered.

"Lying bastard comes to mind," Devon mumbled as he walked to the dining room table, his hands gripping the back of the chair tightly.

Jackson heard but said nothing. He would let Devon call him anything at this point, as long as they worked through this.

"Honestly, I have no idea what to do. I want to go to dinner with David. I want to laugh and cut up and have a good time with the man I've talked to for the past two weeks," he said. "I want to beat Jackson Prescott to a bloody pulp for lying to me."

Jackson chuckled to himself. At least he hadn't threatened to out-right kill him. Tense moments passed as silence descended in the plush hotel room while both men pondered what to do next. Jackson wanted to wrap his arms around the beautiful man and tell him that they could work through this. Devon was torn between wanting to walk out the door and never look back, and wanting to find out just how much of David was Jackson, or Jackson was David. Fuck, he was getting a headache trying to sort it all out.

Finally, he looked to where the man, Jackson, was still perched on the arm of the sofa. "I've half a mind to walk out and pretend this never happened, but I made a promise, and I don't go back on my word, regardless of how much I want to," he tossed at Jackson. "So we'll go to dinner, although it will have to be somewhere other than where I had planned. Heaven forbid the masses find out that Jackson Prescott is in town," he said snidely. He had promised to give this man a chance. Nobody said he had to be nice about it.

But how can you get to know him if you're a total shit to him? the tiny voice inside asked before promptly being told to shut the fuck up.

Jackson waited to see what the young man had planned for after dinner, but no additional information was imparted. "And after?" he asked.

Dark eyes pinned the other man. "Let's see about getting through dinner first, before we start making other plans."

The blond breathed a small sigh of relief. Score one for the good guys, or bad, depending on whose perception it was. Devon hadn't left when he found out the truth and they would be having dinner together. It was a start. He just hoped the young man lost the attitude and became the person Jackson had come to know, and care for. If not, well, he didn't want to think about that right now. He'd jump off that bridge if and when he came to it.

Right now, he had more groveling to do.

PERRY'S Italian Grille was a small, family-owned establishment located a few blocks from where Devon lived. Tables were covered with the traditional red-and-white checked tablecloths, a single candle gracing their center. Devon was greeted by name and after a polite request from the young man, he and his guest were shown to a place near the back, away from prying eyes.

"Our Devon here is a very nice young man, no?" Carmela, the owner's wife, asked as she handed menus to the two men.

Jackson looked up at the elderly woman and smiled. "Yes, he is. Most of the time," he teased.

Carmela looked at Devon and tutted. "What have you done now, Devon?"

Chocolate eyes cut to his companion and he had the sudden urge to kick him under the table. Manners won out and he turned to the hostess. "Nothing to concern yourself with, Carmela."

"I tell you now," she said to Jackson, "you need someone to straighten our Devon out, you come here. My Roberto will fix him."

Jackson smiled at the threat. "I'll keep that in mind if he doesn't get rid of his attitude."

"Devon," she said, punctuated by a few more tuts. "Why you have a bad attitude?"

"I've had a bad day," he said as he pinned Jackson with a stare.

"Well, Carmela know just the thing to cure your bad day. I'll send my Chessie over with something to make you smile again," she said before disappearing through the swinging café doors.

A few minutes later, Chessie arrived at the table bearing a plate of arancine and a loaf of bruschetta bread. What made Jackson smile, however, was the bottle of Secco Bertani Valpolicella and a pair of wine glasses. After their glasses were filled, the waitress slipped into the back.

"Now, what shall we drink to?" Jackson mused as he swirled the wine around in his glass.

"Hmm, let me think. Maybe someone telling the truth for once?" Devon snorted.

"If you'd tone down the attitude a bit, I could. Jesus, Devon, you act as if I committed a heinous crime or something," Jackson said quietly. "Yes, I lied to you about who I was but you're supposed to be giving me a chance to prove to you that I am the same person you talked to on the phone, the person you connected with, and I can't see how that's going to happen if you keep acting like that. What are you, twelve?" he taunted.

Before Devon could answer, Chessie was back to take their order.

"The usual," Devon said as he handed his menu to her.

"Should have known," she said with a smile and then turned to Jackson, who ordered the stuffed chicken marsala.

After she left the table, Jackson turned back to Devon. "What's your usual?"

"Chicken parmigiana," he offered as he placed a few arancine on his plate. "And for the record, you know how old I am," he said as he took a bite. "My question to you is just that. How old are you?"

"Devon, I'm sorry for that comment," he said with a small smile.

"Nothing I didn't deserve," he said with an indifferent shrug. He knew he was being a shit, but he honestly didn't know how else to act. Heartless bastard had worked for him before, but it was hard to be that person now. In less than two week's time, this man had waltzed into his life, made him realize things about himself, made him feel things for the older man, and then proceeded to yank the rug from beneath his feet.

And now Jackson Prescott was attempting to make things right. The least Devon could do was let him try.

"To answer your question, I'm forty-six," Jackson answered.

Devon took a good look at the man sitting across from him. He wouldn't have guessed him to be that old. "Do you really live in Montana?"

Jackson nodded. "For the most part. I like my privacy. I have a condo in Santa Monica where I stay when I'm working in Los Angeles, either with filming or if I have an art exhibition going on," he said before taking a drink of the ruby liquid. "When you said you liked to surf, I thought about us going there, spending some time at the beach together."

"That was only our second conversation."

"Third, if you count the one that started it all," Jackson said with a grin. "What ran through your mind when I called back the second time that night? And be honest."

Devon smiled a sly smile. "I thought you were crazy."

"You should do that more often," Jackson said before taking another sip of is wine.

"What? Tell you you're crazy?"

Jackson shook his head. "No. Smile. That's the first time I've seen it. Heard it through the phone plenty of times, but seeing it…." he trailed off, not trusting himself to finish the sentence.

Devon laughed self-consciously and set his glass on the table. "How about you start at the beginning. Tell me who the real Jackson Prescott is."

"You already know me, Devon."

"No, I know David Miller. Now I want to know Jackson. All of it, the good and the bad," he said quietly.

"From the beginning?"

Devon nodded. "From the beginning."

Jackson grinned. "Might take some time."

"You've got four days," he offered.

"And if I finish early?"

"Just tell your tale, Prescott. Then we'll talk about after," the young man said with a genuine smile.

It was an image that Jackson would never forget.

CHAPTER SEVEN

JACKSON talked. Devon listened. Devon laughed and asked questions. Jackson continued to talk. It was close to midnight and the man was still talking.

He should be. He has forty-six years worth of tales to tell, Devon thought to himself with a smile.

During their dinner, Devon slowly shed the attitude and by the end, realized that he was genuinely interested in this man ... Jackson. He was well educated, spoke several different languages, and considered himself an artist first, actor last. Painting was his passion. Acting was a job that helped pay the bills. He didn't play the games that other Hollywood types played. Jackson preferred his solitude.

Carmela had stopped by the table and squeezed the young man's shoulder. "Good to see you smile, Devon. Now Carmela no have to get Roberto after you," she had said before bustling off to visit with other patrons. Jackson laughed when he noticed the young man blushing.

They had left the restaurant and Devon had driven them to a nearby Starbucks where two cups of steaming coffee were procured, and then they were off again. The young man didn't want to go back to his apartment or to the hotel, for fear that it might give Jackson the idea that things were square between them. Although Jackson was making headway, Devon was not ready to forgive the man for his deceit just yet.

Devon pulled his Jeep Wrangler into a nearly deserted parking lot and parked next to a stand of snow-covered fir trees.

Before Jackson could ask where they were, the young man had already left the warmth of the vehicle in favor of the outside elements. It wasn't snowing, but it was damn cold. Jackson pulled his coat together and followed suit.

"Where are we?" he asked as they approached an outdoor skating-rink where several couples were gliding across the smooth surface, the blades on their skates leaving obscure designs on the ice.

"A little park I run in," Devon said as he made for the jogging path.

The light from the half-moon illuminated the path before them, the trail winding its way through the park, taking them away from civilization. The park was quiet, its occupants long-gone, taking the laughter of snow-covered children with them. An owl could be heard in the distance, its call answered soon after.

"Parliament?" Devon asked as they finally reached their destination.

"I don't think so. Sounds like someone's out on the town looking for company," Jackson teased as he took in their surroundings. They were standing on a stone bridge, the moonlight glistening on the snow-covered banks, reflecting off of the babbling brook below.

"I come here when I need to think," Devon offered as he braced his hands on the railing and looked out over the stream. "Sometimes I sit here for hours. The sound of the water rushing downstream is soothing," he said as he slowly closed his eyes and listened.

Jackson wished he had a camera with him. If he could capture one image of Devon, it would be right here, right now. The brunette's gorgeous face was upturned as if absorbing the moonlight, eyes closed, his features relaxed. He looked as if he had not a care in the world.

The artist thought about the two sketches hanging in his studio at home, the differences between his first impression of his new friend, and then the one drawn after Devon's description of himself.

Neither one came close to the real thing.

"What are you thinking about?" Jackson asked as he leaned his back against the railing, his eyes memorizing every detail of the moonlit face.

"David. And you," he answered quietly.

"Should I be worried?" Jackson asked as he gripped the stone beneath his hands.

Devon slowly opened his eyes and looked over at Jackson. "I understand why you did what you did. I don't like it, but I do understand. I've listened to everything you've said tonight, and it was quite a bit to take in, but I guess it's to be expected when you're as old as you are."

"Didn't your mother teach you to respect your elders?" Jackson muttered, although there was amusement in his voice. Devon making jokes was a good sign, as far as he was concerned.

"And didn't your mother teach you not to interrupt?" Devon tossed back. "So where was I?" he mused as he tried to gather his thoughts. "I've thought about everything you've told me, and I have a proposition for you."

"Hmm, a proposition," Jackson mused. "Does it have anything to do with sex?" He teased, earning himself a punch to his arm.

"Shut up. I'm the only one who gets to think about sex. Your privileges have been revoked for the duration of the trip. So here's what I was thinking. I know you're sorry for what you did, and I'm almost to the point where I can forgive you, because I do understand why you did it," he said.

"Is there a point to this?" the older man asked with a mock-sigh.

"I'm getting to it, but you keep interrupting me. My suggestion is this ... we start over. Right now. No more lying, no omitting the truth about anything. Everything has to be above-board or it won't work. I can see David in you, so I'm willing to put your lapse of judgment behind us and move on."

Jackson's heart took flight at the possibility that he might get what he came for after all. Devon hadn't sent him packing, and he would not have to hide in his hotel room and nurse his wounded pride over being rejected.

Before he could stop himself, Jackson quickly shed his glove, reached over and took Devon's hand in his, pulling the other man's leather glove off as well. The cold air wrapped itself around the young man's fingers, but it was quickly replaced with the warm breath spilling from Jackson's lips. Devon took a deep breath when lips caressed the back of his hand.

"It is my pleasure to make your acquaintance, Devon Forrester," Jackson said as he pressed Devon's palm against his cheek, his own hand covering the smaller one. He had taken the first step, and now it was Devon's turn.

The skin was cool beneath Devon's hand, but it was quickly warming from his touch. It felt so right to be here, with this man, and he was glad he had given him a chance. Whether his name was David Miller or Jackson Prescott, this was the man who had captured Devon's attention, made him yearn for something more.

He watched as Jackson slowly turned and pressed a kiss to his palm. "Is this okay?" the artist whispered, the warm breath teasing Devon's skin.

Devon nodded as he brought his other hand to Jackson's face, tracing a leather-covered finger from temple to chin as he moved closer to the man before him.

Jackson stood still, letting Devon do as he pleased.

The moment their lips touched, Jackson was lost. Devon was tentative at first, his lips barely moving against the other man's, and Jackson shuddered when he felt a warm tongue tickle the seam of his lips, requesting admittance. Willing lips parted, and the embers that had been smoldering since their first conversation slowly caught fire. Everything they felt for one another was poured into this first kiss as hands moved to cradle a face, caress a cheekbone, encircle a waist and pull the body closer. The kiss was broken only by the need for air, and then their lips met again and again.

Devon slowly pulled away and looked into the blue eyes. "It's a pleasure to meet you, Jackson Prescott," he said with a lazy smile.

Jackson wanted more of the tempting treat standing before him, but would not press his luck. Devon said that his thinking privileges had been revoked, and he would abide by the young man's rule.

For now.

"So where do we go from here?" Jackson asked as he pressed another kiss to Devon's fingers.

"Back to the Jeep. It's freezing out here," he said as he took his glove from Jackson and slid his hand into it. He smiled when Jackson linked their gloved fingers together and started back to the parking lot.

Jackson felt as if he were walking on air. "You know, if you wanted a kiss, all you had to do was ask," he teased, nudging his friend as they retraced their steps, earning a slight push back.

"Oh hush. I told you I come here to think."

"And I'm guessing that the fate of my visit was the topic of tonight's session," he hedged.

Devon nodded. "Yes, it was."

"Well then, I'm extremely grateful for your decision to extend my stay."

"Generous, aren't I?" the young man teased.

Jackson stopped and yanked Devon back to him, his arms snaking around the lithe body. "I don't know, are you?"

The brunette laughed. "Did you not hear what I said earlier about your privileges regarding the pondering of sex being revoked? Do you need a hearing-aid?"

"Brat," Jackson said before covering Devon's lips with his own, his tongue delving deep into the willing mouth, twining around its partner. His leather-covered fingers slid into the riot of chocolate curls, holding the instructor's head still while he did as he pleased, his tongue mapping the interior of Devon's mouth just as a cartographer would map a new world.

When he finally pulled back, Devon was dazed, his eyes closed, his breathing a series of white tufts of air floating between them.

"Nice to know that works," Jackson whispered against the moist lips before walking away.

Slowly the sienna orbs opened in time to catch the older man looking back over his shoulder. "You coming?" Jackson asked as he moved down the path.

"No, but it probably wouldn't take much," Devon mumbled to himself before following the other man.

"CARE to come up for a night cap?" Jackson asked when they pulled into the parking lot of his hotel.

Devon found a spot and quickly parked the vehicle. "I don't put out on the first date," he said with a grin. "Even if it's you. Especially since it's you," he added.

"I think I should be offended by that, but I'm not. Anyway, that's beside the point. I asked if you wanted to come up for a drink," Jackson repeated with a smile.

"Which translates into 'come up to my room so we can fuck'," the young man teased.

"Devon," Jackson said with exasperation.

"Jackson," the young man mimicked.

"What am I going to do with you?" he asked as his hand stroked the sable curls.

Devon leaned into the touch. "Nothing tonight. It's late and I'm tired. Some of us had to work today, remember? Actually, I'm surprised that a man your age managed to stay awake this long," he teased.

The fingers tightened in Devon's hair as Jackson brought his face within inches of the other. "You'd be surprised what a man my age can do. Of course, since you said you don't put out on the first date - and especially a first date with me - we'll just have to save it for some other time," he said quietly.

Sienna eyes met blue. "I thought I told you I was the only one allowed to think about sex."

"Baby, you can think about it all you like," he said as he brushed his lips gently against Devon's. "But me, I plan on taking a more pro-active stand on the issue."

A whimper escaped between Devon's lips as he pictured the two of them in a tangle of limbs, sprawled across his bed.

"But not tonight," Jackson whispered before nipping gently at Devon's lower lip. "Go home and get some sleep, Devon. I want you fully coherent when it happens."

It took monumental strength to pull away from the older man, but Devon managed. "I look forward to it. In the meantime, be ready to go at nine."

"What's on the agenda?" Jackson asked.

"Something you've never done before," the young man said with a calculating grin.

"From the look on your face, I'm thinking I should be afraid."

"You're in my hands, now, Prescott. Be very afraid," he teased before leaning over the armrest and giving Jackson one last kiss. "Sweet dreams," he said, moving back to his seat.

"Sweet dreams, Devon," the older man answered before leaving the vehicle.

Devon watched until Jackson was safely inside the hotel lobby, and then pulled away. His mind was a whirlwind of thoughts as he journeyed back home, but one stood out above all the rest - he was glad he did not walk away when he had the chance.

THE answering machine light was blinking when Devon walked into his bedroom.

"Hey, it's me. I just wanted to say thanks for giving me a chance and that I enjoyed this evening, once you dropped the attitude. It's been a long time since I could just let go and be myself with someone new. A very long time. And I promise, from here on out, no lies or half-truths. What you see is what you get. Of course, you may change your mind when you see me sans clothes, but I think I look pretty decent for an old fogie. You, however, will probably give me a heart attack. So I guess that's it for now. I'm looking forward to tomorrow, even if I have no clue what you're up to. See you in the morning. Night, baby."

A warm feeling spread throughout Devon's body as he saved this message with the other.

"Jackson Prescott," Devon whispered. "What have you done to me?"

CHAPTER EIGHT

"I come bearing gifts," Devon said when he stepped through the door of Jackson's hotel room, a navy blue duffle bag with the Brighton Ski Resort insignia in hand. "Well, it's not really a gift, more like a loan."

Before he could get too far, Jackson caught his hand and pulled the young man back to him, brushing his lips gently against Devon's. "Good morning," he said quietly.

"Morning," Devon whispered before moving away from the tempting man. There would be time enough for that later.

"So what's all this?" Jackson asked as he closed the door behind Devon and paused a few moments to take in the sight of his friend. He was dressed in black ski pants, a red turtle-neck that set off his olive skin, a matching jacket with a red stripe down the arms, and black hiking boots.

Devon shrugged out of his jacket and tossed it onto the couch beside the duffle bag he had just set down. The shirt he had worn last night was loose on him, so Jackson had no idea what his body looked like. Now, he could see the definition of his chest, and if he wasn't mistaken, a hoop in his left nipple. He wondered how sensitive he was there. Jackson knew that some men were more sensitive than others and wondered where Devon fit on the spectrum. He hoped he would find out.

The young man quickly opened the bag and laid the contents across the back of the couch. It was a pair of ski pants and jacket similar to Devon's.

"I take it we're skiing today?" Jackson asked as he moved to stand beside him.

"Did I say that?" he asked with a grin.

Jackson wasn't sure if he liked the mischievous look on Devon's face and then it hit him what Devon had planned.

"Oh no," he said with a shake of his head. "You're not getting me on a snowboard. I can barely stand on a pair of skis, much less deal with a snowboard," Jackson told his friend.

"Skiing is for wimps. Come on, Jackson; grow a set," he said as he picked up the clothes and handed them to the other man.

"I'm very comfortable with the set I have, thank you very much," he replied as he thrust the charcoal gray pants and jacket back at Devon.

Devon sighed. "Look, you've got a teacher standing right here in front of you. I won't let anything happen to you. We'll start out small and work our way up to the big stuff," he teased.

Jackson was not amused. Going home with a broken arm or leg was not something he had bargained for on this trip, unless it was from falling off the bed while fucking. Of course, if that happened, he'd have to make something up, but at least he'd have pleasant memories of the incident.

Devon dropped the clothes onto the couch and moved close to Jackson, his hands settling on the waistband of Jackson's jeans. "I promise I'll take care of you, Jackson. Just for a couple of hours? If you hate it, we'll do something else," he offered.

Large sienna eyes framed by impossibly long lashes looked back at Jackson and the man was lost. He'd do just about anything for the beautiful creature standing before him.

Two large hands framed Devon's face. "Okay, for a couple of hours," he acquiesced before brushing his lips against Devon's.

The allotted 'couple of hours' turned out to be most of the day. Jackson was relieved to find that Devon was an excellent teacher and that he was having such a great time learning.

"Okay, to turn, you use your toes and heels," Devon said as they stood at the base of the beginner's slope. "You're riding with your left foot forward, so when you want to go right, press the toes of your boots down. When you want to go left, shift your weight to your heels. But not too much or you'll wipe out. If you want to stop, turn your board perpendicular to your body and crouch down, and then sit."

Jackson had mimicked Devon's movements and when he thought he had a grasp on it, they moved to the top of the beginner's hill. As expected, Jackson hit the snow a few times, but once he had figured out just how much pressure to apply, he stayed upright for longer periods of time.

They decided to take a break for lunch and Devon led them to the resort's dining room. He covertly watched the people around them, wondering if any had noticed Jackson. He had seen several pairs of eyes drift their way, but nobody approached them, and for that, Devon was eternally grateful. He wanted Jackson's stay to be relaxing, especially after the rocky start they had.

After their meal, they had made a few more runs on the beginner's slope before Devon suggested they try something a bit more challenging. He decided Jackson was ready to move on, but the older man had his doubts. Be that as it may, they caught one of the lifts that whisked them up to one of the shorter runs.

"You'll be fine, Jackson," Devon said as they watched the people pass below their feet. To bolster the man's courage, he leaned over and placed a soft kiss to his lips. "I have faith in you."

"Glad somebody does," Jackson said as he gripped the board in his lap.

"If I didn't think you could do this, I wouldn't have suggested it," he said as he rested his hand on top of Jackson's, squeezing gently.

"You don't have plans for me jumping out of any airplanes, do you?" he asked as they approached their destination.

"Nah. This is about as dangerous as we get. I don't want you covered from head to toe in plaster. Kinda kills the mood," he teased.

The lift deposited the two men on the packed snow and Jackson grabbed the front of Devon's jacket, heedless of who might have been watching, not that anyone would have recognized them. When dressed in full gear, ski hats covered their hair and goggles covered their eyes and part of their face.

"If I survive this, you owe me," he said before covering Devon's lips with his own. Before things became too heated, Jackson ended it.

"Deal," Devon breathed as he led them to the edge of the hill. After checking their equipment, they secured their bindings and pushed off.

During the course of the ride, Devon never left Jackson's side, although he gave the man plenty of room to maneuver. For the first minute or two, he was doing great. And then someone cut in front of him, causing Jackson to overcompensate his turn and he ended up face-first in the snow.

Devon glided over to where his friend was spitting out a mouth full of snow, and then crouched down beside him.

"You okay?" he asked and earned a glare in return. "Oh, come on. It wasn't that bad of a spill. You're not hurt are you?"

"No," Jackson groused as he managed to get up to his knees. "If I see the little shit that did that, he's toast. Help me up, will you?"

Devon reached for Jackson's arm and before he realized what had happened, he was in the snow as well. Jackson pushed him onto his back and hovered above him.

"I think you'll owe me anyway," he whispered before dipping his head and claiming the enticing lips below his.

Jackson's body pressed him further into the snow and Devon grabbed the artist's face, holding him close as they kissed. And then reality set in.

"As much as I hate to do this, we need to get up before the ski patrol comes over," Devon said when they finally came up for air. "I don't want them ragging on me when I come back to work in a few days," he said as he pushed up to his elbows, his lips swollen from the intense kiss.

It took a few minutes to get straightened out, and then they were on their way down the slope again, this time with no mishaps.

Devon kept a close eye on Jackson's progress, giving him tips, watching as the other man implemented the suggestions.

"Good job," Devon said as they slid to a stop at the base. "Ready for another run?" he teased and earned a face full of snow for his effort. "Guess not," he said as he unhooked his bindings and stepped from his board.

Jackson leaned over and did the same, except he was slower to get up again.

"I think my snowboarding days are over," he said as he placed his hands on his lower back and stretched. "Yeah, definitely over."

"And here I was hoping you'd be the next big thing to hit the circuit," the young man said as he retrieved Jackson's board from the snow and handed it to his companion.

"Thanks, but I think I'll stick to raising horses," Jackson said with a small smile.

Devon reached over pulled the goggles from Jackson's face, brushing the hair away from his eyes. "Are you okay or are you humoring me?" he asked, genuinely concerned about the other man.

"Would you be disappointed if I asked you to take us back to the hotel? I think I'm in need of a hot Jacuzzi bath," Jackson said as he captured Devon's hand in his.

"Well, that all depends," he said with a grin.

"On what?" the blond asked.

"How big is the tub?"

Jackson's smile was the only answer Devon needed.

DEVON turned on the faucet of the garden tub and watched as the water slowly filled the fiberglass oval, his thoughts drifting. He hated the fact that Jackson was hurt, hated that he was the one who'd caused it. He should have listened to the older man, but he had wanted to share this part of his life with him.

"Why the long face?" Jackson asked as his fingers threaded through chestnut curls.

"I'm an idiot," he said as he turned from where he was perched on the side of the tub and looked up at the man standing before him. "I'm sorry about...." he started, only to have two fingers placed against his lips.

"I've already told you I'm okay. It's just a muscle spasm, that's all," Jackson said as he knelt beside the tub, balancing on the balls of his feet. He ignored the twinge of pain in his lower back. "I get them from time to time. Seems to be part of the whole getting old thing," he said with a grin.

"You're not funny," Devon said as he tried not to smile.

"No, I'm crazy, remember?" Jackson asked as he slowly closed the distance between them and pressed a light kiss to Devon's lips. "Now, how about we make use of this monstrosity?"

"Sounds good to me," Devon whispered as Jackson slowly stood and stepped away to undress. Devon's hands stopped him.

"I want to do that," he said as he stood as well. His own hands went to the hem of Jackson's long-sleeved shirt and slowly lifted it up and off of the artist, tossing it somewhere behind him. His eyes took in the partially dressed man before him. Jackson's abs, chest and arms were defined from hours spent in the barn, mucking out stalls, stowing bales of hay. Tentatively, Devon reached out and ran his hands from Jackson's shoulders down his arms, and then back up his torso, his fingers sliding through the reddish-blond hair on his chest.

Jackson's hands went to Devon's shirt and it was quickly removed and tossed aside as well. Smooth, bronze skin covered the lithe frame, but the large dusky disk sporting a silver loop caught his attention. His index finger ghosted over the pierced nipple, and he watched Devon's reaction.

The beautiful eyes closed and a deep breath was inhaled. The nub hardened.

"Sensitive. I wondered about that earlier today," Jackson said as his fingers moved on, tracing the planes of Devon's chest and lower, stopping only when they encountered the waistband of the black ski pants. His fingers teased the trail of soft hair below the young man's navel.

"It's very sensitive," Devon said as he unbuttoned Jackson's pants and then remembered the running water. "Hang on. Wouldn't want to flood the place," he said as he moved back to the Jacuzzi to shut off the faucet and turn on the jets. When he turned back, he found Jackson pushing his pants down, his hardness springing forward.

Devon's eyes widened as he got his first good look at the older man. His mouth had gone dry and his thoughts seemed to have taken a vacation.

"Didn't your mother tell you it's not polite to stare?" Jackson teased as he stepped out of his pants, leaving them in a pool of charcoal on the white marble floor. A few moments later, he slowly lowered himself into the steamy, churning water. "Damn, that feels good. You planning on standing there all afternoon or are you going to join me?"

Within a few seconds, Devon was as naked as the day he was born and then it was Jackson's turn to stare. He wished he had something handy to sketch the beautiful body with.

"What were you just saying about staring? Scoot up so I can get in," Devon said.

Jackson did as he asked and Devon settled himself behind him. He sighed when he felt strong hands on his shoulders, felt long fingers slowly massaging the tight muscles.

"Damn, that feels good," Jackson said as he relaxed under Devon's ministrations.

After a few minutes, Devon leaned forward and pressed a kiss between the artist's shoulder blades. "I am sorry about this."

Jackson leaned back against Devon's chest and captured the young man's hands in his own. "I'll be fine," he said before pressing a kiss to their twined fingers.

"How about we ditch the tub and I'll give you a real massage," Devon whispered against Jackson's neck. "I think I owe you one."

A few minutes later, they were in the bedroom with Jackson lying face-down on the enormous bed, Devon perched on the tops of the older man's thighs as he poured a small amount of Astroglide into his palm.

"Never used this stuff for a massage before. Well, except for the internal kind," Devon said with a snicker as he placed his hands on Jackson's back and began to slowly knead the muscles again.

"I can't believe that you've never taken the time to enjoy everything that goes along with a sexual relationship," Jackson said, his voice muffled by the pillow he was hugging to his chest.

"*Relationship* would be the key word of that sentence," Devon offered as his hands slid smoothly over Jackson's back. "I told you before that I've never had a proper relationship. At most, it was just few fucks, nothing more."

A soft moan slid between Jackson's lips. "You're good at that," he said as nimble fingers relaxed his body.

The sound went straight to Devon's already hard cock. His hands slid to Jackson's lower back, his thumbs rubbing circles at the base of his spine. Jackson shifted on the bed.

"You okay?" the young man asked.

Jackson chuckled. "Yes and no," he answered as he moved again.

Devon trailed a teasing finger lower. "Anything I can help you with?"

"I'd say that's a fair assumption," Jackson said as he reached over to the nightstand and opened the drawer. He tossed a condom over his shoulder. "Make yourself useful," he said before relaxing into the mattress again.

The brunette picked up the foil packet lying on the bed. "Roll over," Devon said as he rose to his knees so that the other man could move. He loved to put a condom on his partner, teasing while he did so.

"I'm not moving," came the muffled reply.

Devon stared at the broad back for a moment and then realization hit him like a ton of bricks. If Jackson had looked over his shoulder, he would have seen the young man's impression of a fish out of water, his mouth opening and closing several times.

"You want...." Devon started, genuinely surprised that Jackson would allow this.

"Yes, I want," Jackson said as he rolled onto his side and looked at the young man. "I want very much."

"But, I...." he stammered.

Jackson sighed. "Let me take a guess. You thought that since I am who I am, I'd top, right?" he asked and earned a nod from Devon. "Oh, I plan to, many, many times before I head back home in a few days. But today, right now, I'm not in any shape to do that. So, if you're not interested...." he said with a grin.

Devon leaned over the man and captured his lips in a searing kiss.

"Oh, I'm interested, all right," he breathed after he pulled away. He found the bottle of Astroglide again and quickly slicked his fingers before he rolled them to their left side, pushing Jackson's right knee forward, his own following.

Deft fingers found their target and before long, Devon had Jackson gasping as he teased the puckered opening, and slid one and then two fingers into the artist.

"When was the last time you bottomed?" Devon asked as he slowly prepared his soon-to-be lover.

"Couldn't tell ya. It's been awhile," Jackson said as he concentrated on relaxing his body. Devon's fingers were long and had no problem finding the bundle of nerves that reduced the older man to what amounted to putty. But when the third finger was introduced, Jackson's body tensed.

"I'm sorry," Devon whispered against Jackson's cheek. "Just a bit more, okay?" he asked as he slowly stretched Jackson's entrance.

Jackson sighed when he heard the packet being ripped open and the reassuring click of the bottle of lube being opened.

Devon draped his body across Jackson's back, his cock nestled between the firm globes. "Look at me, Jackson," he said and waited until blue eyes locked with his. "If this gets to be too much, tell me and I'll stop. I don't want to cause any additional pain," he said and smiled when Jackson's lips brushed against his.

"I promise," Jackson said as he held Devon's gaze.

There was a brief moment of pain as Devon breached the outer ring of muscle, but it was worth it to finally have what Jackson wanted, and that was to be connected to this young man.

"Okay?" Devon whispered as he held himself in check, not wanting to hurt the man who had come to mean so much to him in such a short period of time. While he wasn't sure he could voice exactly how he felt about him, he could show him.

Jackson nodded and then closed his eyes, relaxing his body even more.

Devon's left arm slid under Jackson and curled around his chest while his right hand rested on the artist's hip as he started to move in slow, lazy strokes, each one taking him deeper into the tight passage. Long minutes passed and the only sounds that could be heard were soft sighs, gasps of pleasure, and whispered words of encouragement.

Jackson's paint-stained fingers dug into Devon's thigh as the thick cock brushed the sensitive spot deep inside of him. "Yessssss," Jackson hissed as he arched his back, ensuring that Devon hit the same spot over and over.

Devon pressed his face between Jackson's shoulder blades. His hand left Jackson's hip and slid to his stomach, caressing the muscles that contracted and released as Jackson moved in counterpoint to his thrusts.

Devon kissed Jackson's shoulder. "Still okay?" he asked and earned a nod in return.

Their bodies broke out in a light sheen of sweat as he slowly increased the tempo of their joining. A few minutes later, Devon felt Jackson's fingers link with his and then their joined hands were moving down, entwined fingers raking through the nest of reddish-gold curls.

"Yes ... please baby ... need you...." Jackson babbled as their hands stroked his weeping flesh.

As soon as the words were out of Jackson's mouth, Devon's hips moved faster, bringing them both closer to the edge. His body felt as if he were on fire and he knew that his own release wasn't far off.

"Oh fuck … gonna … nnnngggghhhh," Jackson shouted into the bedroom as his orgasm hit him like a runaway freight train. Wave after wave of ecstasy rolled through his body as his cock pulsed in their joined hands, his release jetting across the spread.

"Jaxxxx," Devon moaned as his lover's body contracted around his cock and pulled his own orgasm from him. The brunette lay unmoving, panting heavily against the sweat-covered back, his cock still pulsing inside his lover.

It was several minutes before either could speak. When Devon finally regained a portion of his senses, he slowly withdrew from Jackson and dropped the used condom beside the bed.

Jackson rolled onto his back and gathered Devon in his arms. "That was so much more than I ever imagined," he whispered against the sweat-soaked curls.

"I have to admit it was pretty amazing," Devon said with a smile. "How's your back?"

"It's fine. We made a mess on the bed," the older man commented, his voice sounding tired.

Devon chuckled. "You mean you made a mess on the bed."

"Hmmm, your fault, though," he said as his fingers linked with Devon's.

"This is true," he said as he snuggled closer to Jackson.

Jackson's arms tightened around Devon's body. "Cold?"

"Yeah, a bit," he admitted.

"I'd offer to cover us up but seeing as how the blanket's a mess...." he trailed off.

Devon nodded, understanding. "How about we go back to my place? Right now my blanket is come-free."

Jackson turned his head so that he was looking into Devon's beautiful eyes. "And how long do you think that will last?"

The young man lifted his shoulder as an answer. "Don't know, but at least I have others to replace it with. Plus, my place has food."

"Ever heard of room service?" Jackson teased as his fingers threaded their way through the chocolate-colored curls.

"Yeah, but I'd rather go back to my place and do it myself. Get your stuff packed," Devon said as he slid from the bed. "You're staying with me until you go back home."

"Oh, really?" Jackson asked as he propped himself up on his elbows, missing the warmth Devon's body offered.

Devon nodded. "Makes more sense than me driving all the way over here to pick you up so we can go out," he said as he walked into the bathroom to retrieve his discarded clothes.

"And who says we're going out? Once we get there, I might tie you to the bed," Jackson shouted.

"Don't tease me, Jackson," came the reply through the open doorway.

"Who said I was teasing?" the older man mumbled as he slid from the bed and pulled on the jeans that he had been wearing earlier that morning.

CHAPTER NINE

"SO where are we off to today?" Jackson asked as Devon navigated through the morning traffic heading East on I-80. "You're being awfully secretive about all this."

Devon looked into his rear-view and side mirrors before signaling and changing lanes. "I've told you all you need to know."

"Oh yeah, right. 'Jackson, grab your coat and camera. We're going somewhere,' really helps," the older man said before taking a sip of his Starbucks coffee. He wondered if Devon even owned a coffee maker. He didn't recall seeing one in his kitchen.

"Where's your sense of adventure?" the young man asked with a grin.

"Oh god," Jackson moaned. "We're not going to do something crazy like bungee jumping, are we? Because if that's what you've got planned, you can turn this Jeep around and take me back."

The brunette shook his head. "No, nothing that extreme. I promise you'll enjoy it. Now stop asking questions and enjoy the ride."

Jackson settled back in the seat and looked out the window. This was going to be a long day.

AT ten forty-five, the two men boarded the last vintage coach of the Heber Valley Historic Railroad and found a seat near the back, away from the crowd. Instead of sitting side-by-side,

Devon opted to sit across from Jackson, their seats facing each other, wanting to see the expressions on the man's features on their journey.

The instructor had taken this trip a few times, and during each trip had wondered if he would ever find someone to share it with. This was like his special place in the park - he wanted to share as much of himself as he could with Jackson. He had never taken anyone else to the bridge, just as he had never invited anyone on one of these excursions. Devon hoped that one day he could tell Jackson these things.

The artist caught the wistful look on Devon's face and quickly raised his camera.

"What were you just thinking?" he asked after snapping the picture.

"That I'm glad you're here," was all Devon offered.

Jackson set the Nikon on the seat beside him and leaned forward, bracing his elbows on his knees, hands in front of him. His fingers caressed Devon's denim-covered knee.

"I can't think of anywhere else I'd rather be," he admitted. "Except maybe back at your place," he added with a smile.

Sienna orbs caught the mischief playing in the azure ones across from him. "And exactly what would we be doing if we were there?" he asked as he mimicked Jackson's seated position. His breath caught in his throat as Jackson leaned forward and whispered, in explicit detail, what they would be doing. Devon was suddenly glad he had chosen to wear a pair of baggy cargo-style jeans.

"Later," he managed to croak before leaning back in his seat, propping his booted right foot on the edge of Jackson's seat, inconspicuously adjusting himself as he did so.

"Definitely," Jackson promised and then they felt the train lurch as it began its journey to Provo Canyon.

It was a three-hour round-trip to Vivian Park and back, but with the extra hour they would be spending at the park for sightseeing, the total time stretched to four hours. During their journey, they crossed the farmland of the Heber Valley and followed the snow-covered banks of Deer Creek. The railway descended into a glacier-carved canyon and then slowly wound its way along the ice-cold waters of the Provo River.

They had remained inside the heated coach for a good portion of the trip, and then the artist in Jackson had taken over. He and Devon had moved to the observation deck at the back of the train where he took several shots of the snow-capped mountains, frozen waterfalls, the undisturbed landscape, and Devon.

Several of the more hardy tourists had joined them for a little while, capturing their own memories, and Devon felt a small thrill run through his system as he watched Jackson discussing photography with an older gentleman. Of course, he had no clue what they were talking about - apertures, F-stops, masks - these things were beyond him, but his lover definitely knew what they were.

Lover. Was that what they were? Devon wondered. Yes, he had feelings for Jackson, more than he ever had for someone before, but didn't the term lover imply that they were together, as in a couple, as in a relationship? Devon had had his fair share of one-night stands, a few fuck-buddies, but never someone he truly cared for; never someone he wanted to share his time, his life, with.

Until now.

He heard Jackson's camera click again and turned to find the man's eyes on him.

"I really wish I knew what went on inside that head of yours," he said as he moved close to Devon, his hand brushing a stray curl away from the beautiful face.

After a quick glance around, Devon realized they were alone, the gentleman Jackson had been talking to opting for the warmth the inside of the coach offered. Devon pulled his hands from his coat pockets and slid them under Jackson's jacket, his fingers hooking around the belt loops of the artist's jeans, pulling him closer.

"Is this okay?" he asked as their bodies touched from thigh to chest.

"More than," Jackson answered as he pressed Devon's body against the outer wall of the coach. "So, are you going to tell me or should I guess?" he asked quietly.

"Maybe some day I'll tell you," he offered.

Jackson nodded. "I'll hold you to that," he said before dipping his head and capturing Devon's cool lips with his own. The kiss was unhurried, and Devon found himself melting under the man's assault, allowing Jackson to do as he pleased. He felt an identical hardness pressing against his own and wished they could take this further. Knowing that was next to impossible, he slowed the kiss.

"Thank you," Jackson said when he pulled away. "I've never had anyone do something like this before."

"You mean you've never made out on a train before?" Devon quipped.

Jackson tweaked the young man's nose. "That's not what I'm talking about. I mean this trip. Where we are," he said as he looked at the scenery that passed them by. "It's beautiful, Devon. It's like we've stepped back in time and we're just discovering it."

"I was hoping you'd like it," Devon said as he turned to the railing, Jackson wrapping his arms around the young man's waist. "When we were talking about what to do when you came to visit, I thought about this. I figured it would appeal to the artist in you," Devon said as he snuggled back into the warmth of Jackson's shearling coat, laying his head back on the strong shoulder.

"You appeal to the artist in me," the older man whispered.

"Folks, we should be arriving at Vivian Park in a few minutes," a voice on the speaker informed them. "We'll be there for an hour, which should give you plenty of time for a quick lunch, if you so choose, and maybe a little sightseeing as well. We'll sound the whistle about ten minutes before we're set to leave so you can finish up and make it back to the depot. Please be sure to have your ticket handy so you can re-board the train at no charge. Enjoy your afternoon."

"Well, I guess it's back to the general population," Jackson said as he pressed a kiss to Devon's temple and led the young man back inside.

AFTER a quick lunch of homemade chicken-salad sandwiches purchased at the depot, the two men struck off on their own. Jackson had been mulling over an idea and he hoped he could bring it to fruition. He just had to find the perfect spot.

They had been wandering for a bit, Jackson snapping pictures here and there, of a snow-covered picnic table, snowdrifts at the base of trees, anything that captured the artist's eye.

"Stay right there," he told Devon and then disappeared into a stand of trees that were on the outskirts of the property.

"What are you doing?" he asked as he watched Jackson walking back and forth, looking for god only knew what.

"You'll see," came the muffled answer.

"I see the crazy person is back," he teased.

A few moments later Jackson reappeared, took Devon by the hand and led him into the trees. Now it was his turn to pull Devon to him, his hands sliding around the slim waist to settle at the small of Devon's back, pressing the lithe body against his own that was leaning back against the trunk of a tree. "Now, what were you saying earlier about the crazy person?" he asked before nipping at the plump bottom lip just inches from his own.

Devon moaned. "You're driving me insane, you know that?"

"Think they'll let us share a padded cell at the asylum?" the crazy artist asked as his right hand came up to cradle Devon's face, the left sliding into the riot of velvet curls. Before Devon could answer, Jackson's mouth was on his, robbing him not only of speech, but of breath as well.

The kiss flared red-hot, threatening to burn anything in its wake, including the both of them. It was a battle of dominance as their tongues dueled, thrusting and retreating, pulsing against each other. And then, as if by mutual agreement, the tempo slowed, both taking and receiving in a more equal measure. Jackson moaned into the quiet of the forest as Devon teased his bottom lip, catching it between his teeth and tugging gently, and then it was Devon's turn as Jackson's lips surrounded his tongue and sucked gently.

"Where's a fucking bed when you need it?" Devon panted as his forehead rested against Jackson's.

The train whistle sounded in the distance, alerting the passengers that they had ten minutes to get back.

"Fuck!" Devon yelled into the snow-covered trees.

Jackson kissed Devon's forehead. "We need to head back or we'll be left," he said as he pushed them away from the tree, Devon taking a few steps backwards.

"Now we have an hour and a half ride back to Heber, and almost an hour back to the apartment," he lamented. "I'm going to go fucking nuts!"

Jackson chuckled. "No you won't," he said as he reached up and retrieved his camera from a limb next to them while he slid the infrared remote control back into his pocket.

Devon's brows furrowed. "What the hell?" he asked as he watched what Jackson was doing. And then it dawned on him. "You ... you took pictures of us?" he shouted.

Jackson smiled and nodded as he checked to see how many exposures he had left on this roll of film.

Devon was torn between wanting to hit the arrogant son of a bitch for doing that and being even more turned on because of it. He settled on punching the crazy artist in the arm.

"When we get back to the train, I expect you to tell me exactly how you managed to do that. And ... I want a set of those prints," he said with a grin before leaving their impromptu hideaway, leaving Jackson to follow.

"I was wondering what in the hell you were up to, disappearing into the forest like that," Devon said once they were back in the warmth of the coach, a cup of hot coffee in hand. "So tell me, my crazy artist, have you taken any other pictures of us?"

"No," Jackson said with a shake of his head. "I was going to surprise you with these. And before you ask, I develop all my own stuff so there's no chance that someone will get hold of them."

"Is this something you do on a regular basis? Taking photographs of your partners?"

Jackson's shoulder lifted a fraction. "I have other pictures, yes, but not like this, and not like you're thinking."

"Why not?"

"Haven't wanted to," Jackson admitted.

"Then why with me?" Devon asked before taking a careful sip of his java.

"Because I'm crazy?" he teased. "I don't know, Devon. It was just something that hit me while we were wandering around. If it hadn't worked out, it would have been okay, too."

Devon thought it over for a bit and then nodded. "You, Jackson Prescott," he whispered, "have to be the craziest person I've ever met."

"Do the words 'pot' and 'kettle' ring any bells?" Jackson asked with a smile. "So am I forgiven?" he asked.

The young man shook his head. "Not quite. But if you'll meet me in the restroom in a few minutes, I think something can be arranged," he said before leaving his seat and heading to the back of the coach where the restroom was located.

Jackson watched his lover walk the length of the car and disappear through a small door to the left. He sat motionless for a moment, knowing he should not do this, but Devon had a point - he owed him. Jackson and his crazy idea had put his young friend in a certain mind-set and now he had to pay.

He just hoped a trip to jail wasn't included in the fee.

Devon jumped when the small door opened and Jackson stepped in. The sight that greeted the artist was one he would never forget. Devon was leaning against the small counter, his jeans around his ankles, two fingers buried inside himself. Jackson quickly closed and locked the door.

"Jesus, Devon!" Jackson whispered in the small compartment.

"Here," Devon said as he passed a condom over his shoulder with his free hand. "Hurry up! You fucking owe me, Prescott. You're the one who got me wound up. You're the one who's going to take care of the problem."

"How about a blow job, instead?" he hopefully asked.

"Your cock, my ass ... now," Devon ordered as he continued to open himself up.

In a matter of moments, Jackson's pants were around his ankles as well and he was rolling the condom over his shaft. "I can't fucking believe I'm doing this. Lube?" he asked and Devon handed a small packet to him. He squirted the contents into his hand and quickly covered the latex.

Devon removed his fingers and bent over the small counter. "Fucking do it!" he whispered loudly and before he knew it, Jackson's cock was buried to the hilt. "Fuck, yeah," he said as his internal muscles clenched around Jackson's length.

The kiss beneath the snow-covered tree served as foreplay, and the thrill of getting caught fed the desire both felt flooding their systems.

Jackson's hips moved quickly and a few minutes later, Devon's whispered, "I'm close," caused the man to speed his thrusts as Devon stroked himself. "Oh fuck, Jax...." was all the young man said before the small sink was dotted with his release. Jackson slammed into the receptive body one last time as he reached his completion.

He would have liked to stay there, buried deep inside his lover, but common sense won out and he slowly disengaged and tossed the condom into the toilet. Devon handed him a few paper towels to clean up with and then he was dressed and out of there.

He had been back in his seat for a few minutes when Devon joined him, a satisfied look on his face. Jackson glanced around the coach and breathed a sigh of relief that nobody was paying attention to them.

It was only when he relaxed back into his seat did that change.

"Lucky bastard," was muttered from the person sitting in the seat behind him, and when Jackson finally found the courage to look at the reflection in the window, he found the gentleman he had spoken to earlier smiling back at him.

Sky-blue eyes slid to the young man sitting across from him and he had to agree. He *was* a lucky bastard to have the attentions of this lovely creature, at least for the next couple of days.

After that, it was anyone's guess.

SANTANA played softly in the background, filling the apartment with songs that were a mix of Latin jazz and Afro-Cuban rhythms, as Devon prepared dinner that evening. His CD collection was an odd one, Jackson had told him. The young man listened to anything from Audioslave to Led Zeppelin, and although he tended to listen to mainly rock/alternative rock, there were a few rap and blues CD's thrown in the fray. He was stirring the boiling pasta when a pair of warm lips brushed his neck.

"Something smells good," Jackson said quietly and then slid his arms around Devon's waist, peering over the young man's shoulder as he eyed the pots on the stove.

"That would be dinner," the brunette said with a laugh. "Enjoy your nap?"

Jackson placed a kiss behind Devon's ear. "I'm thinking it might be something else," he said as he buried his nose in the riot of curls and inhaled. "Are you on the menu, by any chance?" he teased.

"Possibly," came the breathy reply as Jackson's right hand slid lower.

"Missed you when I woke up," the artist admitted. And he did. He had enjoyed the feel of Devon's warm body pressed intimately against his when they awoke that morning and realized it was something he wanted to have happen every chance they got, naps included.

"I thought I'd get dinner started," Devon said as he relaxed in Jackson's embrace. "One can't live on sex alone, can one?"

The warm lips nipped at the sensitive skin. "Probably not, but it'd be nice."

The doorbell rang and Devon had half a mind to ignore it and let Jackson continue.

"Expecting someone?" Jackson asked as he teased the trail of hair beneath Devon's navel.

Devon shook his head. "No, but I'd better see who it is, just the same," he said as he turned the heat almost all the way down on both the spaghetti and homemade sauce and reluctantly moved out of Jackson's arms.

After a quick peek through the peephole, he debated whether or not he should answer the door. Tyler was nothing if not persistent, and Devon suspected that if he didn't answer, his cell phone would be ringing shortly thereafter. Sighing, he opened the door.

"So?" his friend asked as he breezed into the apartment. "How goes it with the mystery man?"

"And hello to you too, Tyler," Devon said as he closed the door and then leaned back against it, his mind going in ten directions at once. Was he ready to reveal his visitor? Was Jackson ready to meet his best friend? What would Tyler do when he realized exactly who the mystery man was?

"Yes, hello, Devon. Well?" the dark-headed man asked when he turned around to face his friend. "How are things going? *Are* they still going or did you send him packing? Spill, man!" he demanded, and then caught a whiff of something cooking. "You're cooking? You never cook," he said, and then a smile spread across his face. "Oh shit, is he here?"

Devon pushed away from the door and joined his friend in the living room. "Yes, he's here and yes, I'm cooking dinner. Well, I was before you dropped by. And contrary to what you believe, I do cook from time to time."

"So, can I meet him?" Tyler asked excitedly.

"Umm, well," Devon said as he fidgeted, uncertain about what to do next, but the decision was taken out of his hands when Jackson walked into the living room after disappearing into the bedroom first to retrieve a t-shirt.

Jackson approached the two men and held out his hand to Tyler. "Hi, I'm...." Jackson started, only to be cut off with a gasp from their visitor.

"Jackson Prescott," Tyler whispered. "Son of a bitch. You've been talking to Jackson Prescott? Jesus H. Christ, Dev! Only you could get this lucky," he said once he had recovered and then quickly shook Jackson's proffered hand. "I'm Tyler Pierce," he said, awe tinting his voice. "It's very nice to meet you."

Devon stifled the laughter he felt welling up inside of him. To see his normally unflappable friend completely star-struck was something he would always carry with him. He remembered sitting in the theater watching Jackson's latest movie, *No Man's Land*, listening to Tyler's comments about the various cowboys on the big screen. Some Devon agreed with, others he didn't. The character of Rafe Morgan was one they both agreed on. He was definitely fuckable. It was something about all that dirt and sweat - sexy as hell.

Dark eyes turned to Devon. "This is … fuck, this is unreal. You've been talking to Rafe Morgan this whole time?"

"No, I've been talking to Jackson," Devon clarified.

"I thought you said his name was David," Tyler mused as his eyes slid back to Jackson, who had moved in behind Devon, and noticed the older man's hand resting possessively on Devon's waist.

"It's a long story," Devon sighed. "One that I'll tell you some other time. So, what brings you to my neck of the woods?"

"Just checking to see if you were okay," Tyler said as he moved to the sofa and took a seat. "I hadn't heard from you and thought I'd stop by on the way to the club."

Devon leaned back a bit, reveling in the feel of Jackson's chest pressed against his back. "Couldn't be better."

Tyler looked at Devon and noticed something different about his friend. Devon always had a smile handy for those around him, but for the most part, it was forced. The one on his face now was genuine, just as it was the night they had talked, when Devon told him about how his mystery man made him feel, made him want something different.

If he wasn't mistaken, he had a sneaking suspicion that his friend was falling for ... God, he still couldn't believe it ... Jackson Prescott, of all people. He just hoped that the older man wasn't toying with Devon; that this wasn't just something to pass the time until something better came along. Tyler admonished himself. You couldn't get any better than Devon Forrester.

"I think I'll let you two talk while I go check on dinner," Jackson said before he pressed a quick kiss to Devon's temple.

Tyler watched the show of affection and the resulting blush that stained Devon's cheeks. Yep, his friend was definitely smitten.

"No, it's fine," Tyler said as he stood. "I didn't mean to interrupt you guys. I just wanted to see if Devon was okay. And now that I have, I'll be heading out. It was a pleasure to meet you, Mr. Prescott," he said with a grin. "Dev, take care and I'll talk to you in a few days?"

Devon nodded. "I'll call you," he said as he walked Tyler to the door and Jackson disappeared into the kitchen.

"So, tell me," Tyler said quietly as they stood in the doorway. "Is he good?"

"I'm not one to fuck and tell," Devon said with a smirk and quickly closed the door before his friend could ask any more questions.

Jackson was sitting on the counter next to the stove when Devon walked back into the kitchen to check on their dinner. He caught the young man as he walked by and settled him between his legs.

"Well?" he asked as he tucked an errant curl back behind Devon's ear.

"Well what?"

"Am I good?" the artist asked as his index finger traced indiscernible patterns over Devon's face.

Devon's eyes widened. "You heard him?"

Jackson nodded. "Yep. And I also heard your answer, both vague and telling all at the same time, if he knows what to look for. But now I want to know the real answer," he said as his finger teased the plump lips.

Devon's tongue snaked out and teased the pad before gently nipping at the digit. "How about we have dinner first, and then I'll tell you?"

"How about we skip dinner and you tell me?" Jackson taunted as his free hand slid to Devon's chest and tugged gently on the silver hoop, which sent shocks of erotic pleasure through the young man's body.

"Fuck," Devon breathed before Jackson's lips crashed against his own.

Jackson reached over to the stove and quickly turned the knobs to the off position before dragging Devon back to the bedroom. It would be hours before they finally ate dinner.

CHAPTER TEN

EVERYTHING Devon had chosen for their outings during Jackson's stay had been geared towards the artist, this one doubly so. For their last night together, he had decided on an early dinner at The Aerie, a beautiful restaurant perched on the uppermost floor of the Cliff Lodge at Snowbird Resort, that offered spectacular views of the mountains through unencumbered floor-to-ceiling windows that lined the dining and bar areas. Following that, they would take the aerial tram up to the lookout at Hidden Peak.

They had arrived at the restaurant early, their reservations not scheduled for another hour, but Devon knew his artist would want to spend time outside, absorbing his surroundings like a sponge, capturing his discoveries on film. When the cold became too much, they found a quiet table in the bar area, ordered two beers, and waited until their pager went off telling them their table was ready.

In the dining room, numerous candle-lit tables covered with white linen, accented with bone china and crystal glasses, filled the open area, and a smile lit Jackson's face as the hostess seated them at an intimate table set for two near one of the windows.

"If I didn't know better, I'd say that this was a set-up for seduction," Jackson said quietly once the hostess had left them.

"In certain instances, I guess it could be," Devon offered as he looked over his leather-bound menu, taking in the different food selections the restaurant had to offer.

Jackson's eyes scanned his own menu for a moment and then looked at the beautiful man seated across from him. "Certain instances?" he queried and earned a nod from Devon. "How so?"

"This has been labeled the most romantic restaurant in Utah. You do the math."

"Why sir, you are trying to seduce me," Jackson whispered and watched the corner of Devon's inviting mouth quirk.

"Hate to break this to you, but I don't need some elaborate scheme to get into your pants," he said with a grin.

"Oh really? And what ploy would you use?"

Devon set his own menu aside and leaned forward, his long fingers brushing over Jackson's. "If memory serves me correctly, I'd say a day on the slopes would do the trick. Nothing romantic about that, as far as I can tell."

Jackson's pulse increased at the mention of their first time together and wondered what Devon would say when he told him the real reason things had progressed the way they did. Unfortunately, that was not a discussion he wanted to have here and now, but later, in private.

"This is true," he admitted as he linked their fingers together.

A few moments later, an impeccably dressed waiter arrived to take their orders and then disappeared just as quickly. After dining on Barbecue Glazed Filet of Beef served with Potato Risotto, the men settled back in their seats with cups of coffee, enjoying the easy conversation that flowed between them. Each nugget of information imparted was filed away, added to the chest of gems they had collected thus far. After a minor disagreement over the check, Jackson winning this time, they retrieved their coats and stepped into the elevator that would take them to ground level.

It was early evening now, the sun beginning its descent behind the white-capped mountain range, giving off just enough light so that the passengers on the aerial tram could watch the glistening snow-covered landscape pass beneath their feet as they were transported up the mountainside.

Devon and Jackson had nabbed a vacant corner of the car when they boarded, out of the way of others, yet still able to take in the sights. Devon linked his arm with Jackson's and let his head fall to the other man's shoulder.

"What will you be doing this time tomorrow night?" Devon asked quietly, and Jackson noted the sadness in his voice.

Jackson placed a kiss to his forehead. "I'm not sure. I could be in the barn, checking on the horses or I could be in my studio, working on a new painting. Or, I might be stretched out in front of the fire, listening to your voice on the other end of the line."

Devon nodded, not trusting his voice at that particular moment. He still wasn't sure what the other man wanted beyond tomorrow, but Jackson's answer quelled a few of his fears that things would not end when the artist went back home.

"I vote for the last one," Devon said with a smile and then snuggled closer to Jackson.

"Well then, I'll see what I can do," the blond offered as the tram approached its destination.

The lookout at Hidden Peak provided a breathtaking view of the Rocky Mountains at their finest. At eleven thousand feet, the air was crisp and clear, and in the night sky, stars glittered like diamonds tossed into the heavens, something that could not be seen while in the city proper. Devon pointed out different areas in the distance, like the Alta resort that was up canyon from Snowbird, then east to Sundance. The lights of the resort below twinkled like lights on a Christmas tree, reminding Jackson that the holidays weren't far off.

His eyes sought out his lover and he wondered if he would be alone this year, or spending it with someone special.

AFTER they arrived back at Devon's apartment, Jackson quickly undressed himself before turning his attention to his young lover. As this was their last night together, he wanted it to be something both would always remember. He slowly and reverently undressed the beautiful man, pressing kisses to each area of newly exposed skin, nipping and teasing places that he knew would drive

Devon crazy with want. With gentle touches, he took Devon to the edge only to pull him back, much to the young man's disappointment.

Now Devon was lying across his bed, his breathing labored once again, as warm lips skated across the toned chest. Jackson reveled in the sounds that spilled from the young man when he tugged gently on the silver hoop, laving the distended nub after. Each breathy sigh, each erotic moan was recorded in the artist's mind so they could be played over and over later. The lips moved lower, Jackson's tongue darting out to lap at the sheen of sweat that covered Devon's body, then dipping into the depression of his navel.

"Jax, please," the young man whispered as his body was played like a finely tuned instrument that only his lover had the score for.

Warmth suffused Jackson's body as the abbreviated version of his name tumbled from his lover's lips. "Wait, baby," Jackson said softly, his fingers reaching up to twine with Devon's. "I promise it will be worth it."

The brunette groaned his frustration. "If it's not, old man, your ass is sleeping on the couch."

"What about the rest of me?"

"That too!" Devon fairly shouted.

"Hmm," Jackson hummed against the overly sensitized skin, before sucking gently on a hipbone. "Guess I'd better make this good then."

"Damn right, you'd better," was the answer that floated down to Jackson's current position. He was lying on his stomach now, his aching cock pressed into the mattress below, but he would not give in to his desire just yet. He was going to drive his lover completely out of his mind first.

Those same lips, teeth and tongue played over the inside of a muscled thigh, and then moved to lavish the same treatment to its twin. Next, teasing licks were applied to the backs of knees before sucking gently on an ankle.

Devon's fingers tightened around Jackson's as he struggled to remain still. His body was perilously close to sensory overload, but he would try to hold out, to wait until Jackson slid into his body, claiming him once again. He nearly sobbed with relief when the artist released his aching fingers and moved them to his shins, gently pressing them back against his body, opening him to his lover's gaze.

"So beautiful," Jackson whispered before his tongue traced a path starting at Devon's cleft, passing over the puckered entrance and up his perineum before teasing the pouch that was drawn up against his body. "And all mine."

"Yours, Jax," the young man panted, his sweat-soaked curls sticking to his forehead and neck. "All yours." He wanted to touch himself, wrap his hand around his cock and finish this insane teasing his lover was administering, but knew if he did, he would disappoint his lover and probably miss out on something special. Jackson said it would be worth it; he just hoped he was still coherent enough to enjoy it.

Jackson's tongue circled Devon's entrance and he knew his lover was on the edge again, could hear it in his breathing, could feel it in the slight tremors that were snaking their way through his body.

"Think you can hang on for a bit more?" Jackson asked as he rose above the supine man, his hand retrieving the bottle of lube on the nightstand.

Devon shook his head. "Probably not, but … just hurry," he mumbled.

The artist leaned down and pressed a kiss to Devon's lips. "I will," he breathed before slicking his fingers and lowering them to the man's entrance.

Devon's eyes closed and he fought to retain control of his body as Jackson's fingers massaged the tight ring of muscle before slipping inside. His cock was leaking copious amounts of viscous fluid onto his stomach and he wanted nothing more than to give in to the pleasure that had been assaulting his senses for what seemed like forever. He felt the thick fingers stretching him, knowing it had to be done, but when they brushed over bundle of nerves deep inside him, he could not help his reaction.

"FUCK!" he screamed into the silence of the night. "Jax … I can't … now … pleeeease…." he begged as his head thrashed left and right on the pillow, his fingers clutching the sheets, knuckles white under the strain.

Jackson took pity on him and quickly took the straining shaft into his mouth. When his tongue flickered over the knot of nerves at the head, Devon's release hit the back of his throat in three short bursts.

Devon's world went dark after that and it was several minutes before he came back to himself. When he did, Jackson was lying on his side next to him, his head propped on his hand, a very satisfied smile hovering over the man's lips.

"Don't look so smug, you fucker," the instructor said as he snuggled into the man's warmth. "I'd like to see how long you last under an assault like that."

"Feel free to test me any time you like," Jackson offered before leaning down and brushing a kiss to Devon's cheek.

"Hmm, afraid I can't do it right now. Maybe tomorrow," he said sleepily.

"Oh no you don't," Jackson said as he rolled Devon onto his back and pressed his cock against the young man's thigh. "You're not about to leave me like this."

"You've got a hand," Devon teased and earned a raised eyebrow in return. He chuckled lightly. "Well then, get on with it," he said with a grin. "Just don't expect much from me. You nearly killed me."

The artist reached over and snatched a condom from the bedside table, quickly rolled it on and moved between Devon's lax legs. After coating himself with lube, he pulled the unresisting body onto his thighs.

"We'll see about that," Jackson said as he nuzzled the blunt head against the relaxed portal and then gently pressed inwards, Devon's body accepting him immediately. He started moving in slow, measured strokes and smiled when he felt the passage flutter around his shaft. "I think your body has other plans, baby," he said as he slid deep on the next thrust, causing the young man to moan.

"Traitor," Devon managed to ground out as his cock stirred in the nest of curls.

Jackson kept to the slow tempo he had set and then Devon was moving with him, the long legs wrapping around his waist and pulling him deeper into the unrelenting heat. His hands left Devon's hips and linked their fingers together, settling their hands on either side of his lover's head, their bodies pressed together tightly.

Amidst the gasps of pleasure, words spilled from Jackson's lips, words he wished he were strong enough to say in his native tongue, instead of hiding behind foreign languages. He hoped that one day he would be able to tell Devon how he felt, what he wanted. Until that time, he would continue to show him, would let his body convey his emotions.

Devon felt the fire ignite low in his stomach. "Touch me," he said and earned a shake of Jackson's head as his answer. "Please." Another shake of blond hair.

"I want you to come like this. Just from me being inside you," the older man requested and pressed his body harder against his partner's.

"I've never ... I'm not sure I can," Devon answered honestly.

Supple lips caressed Devon's. "Yes you can, baby. Just let yourself go and feel it. Feel me moving deep inside of you, giving you all that I am," he said as he continued to make love to the man who had captured his heart. "Concentrate on that, on what you're feeling inside. Everything else will just fall into place," he said before he dropped his head to Devon's shoulder.

Devon's focus turned inward and he thought about everything he had felt for this man since their first conversation. He had never felt anything like this before. It was new, and exciting, and also scary as hell. He didn't want his artist to catch a plane the next day, taking him back home to Montana. Devon wanted Jackson to stay there, with him; wanted to wake up in his arms each morning, wanted to share breakfast, lunch and dinner with him; wanted to share every facet of his life with the other man, good and bad.

When he finally admitted to himself that he had fallen in love with the crazy man who had dialed his number by mistake, everything did fall into place, and his body responded to the revelation. Clutching Jackson's fingers tightly, he let the wave of his orgasm roll over him, through him, sweeping him away.

Jackson felt the sudden change in the body below him and a moment later, their stomachs were covered in Devon's release. It was only then that the older man gave in to the passion he had been holding at bay.

"So good, baby," Jackson whispered against Devon's neck as his cock pulsed deep inside his lover. He lay there for a minute or two before he pulled himself together and rolled to the side. "Be right back," he said as he slid from the bed and disappeared into the bathroom where he discarded the condom, grabbed a washcloth and quickly wet it with warm water. When he returned to the bedroom, he smiled. Devon had not moved a muscle. After a quick cleanup, he tossed the washcloth towards the bathroom and pulled Devon to him, then grabbed the covers from the foot of the bed.

Silence reigned supreme as the two sated men drifted in their thoughts, both wanting to acknowledge that what had just happened between them went beyond desire, yet both afraid that their feelings would not be returned.

Finally, before he drifted off, Devon pressed a kiss to Jackson's neck. "Goodnight, Jax," he whispered and settled himself against the warm body, his hand resting on Jackson's chest, above his heart.

Jackson twined their fingers together and lifted them to his lips. "Sweet dreams," he whispered before closing his eyes and succumbing to sleep's hold.

CHAPTER ELEVEN

THE first rays of the morning sun filtered through the curtains, bathing the two sleeping forms in golden hues. Strands of dark hair mingled with light, just as pale limbs intertwined with tanned, the contrast beautiful in its simplicity. Fingers of light teased a bronzed back as an outstretched arm lay across a lightly-furred chest that rose and fell with a hypnotic rhythm.

Slowly emerging from the last vestiges of sleep, Jackson smiled as he felt the warmth of the body lying beside him, the weight of his lover's hand resting on his bicep, the way Devon's left leg was thrown over his own. He lay there for a long while doing nothing more than listening to the sound of the other man's breathing and watching the day assert itself, chasing the traces of night from the room. It was only when nature called that he reluctantly left his private haven. Not wanting to disturb his sleeping lover, he slowly slid from the bed, padding quietly across the room to the adjoining bathroom.

A few minutes later, he returned to find the gorgeous body lying across the bed. Devon had rolled onto his back, his right arm resting against his toned stomach while his left arm was thrown across Jackson's side of the bed, the navy blue sheet pushed haphazardly below the trim waist as if he had been fighting with it.

The artist drank in the sight of Devon on display before him, taking in as much as he could, burning the image into his mind, into his soul. Starting at the sleep-tousled mane of chocolate curls, his eyes caressed the chiseled face, noticing the long lashes resting against dark skin, lips relaxed and parted ever so slightly, the strong jaw, the long column of neck.

Twin dusky discs sat atop lightly muscled pectorals, and Jackson fought the urge to reach out and caress the silver hoop and watch the pierced flesh pebble and tighten. Cerulean eyes followed the fine line of soft hair that ran from navel to abdomen and further down. Jackson's cock stirred as his eyes lingered on the outline of raised flesh that was hidden from his gaze by the bedclothes. He wanted to pull the sheet back and taste his lover, but first there was something he had to do.

He made a quick trip into the living room and retrieved his camera before slipping silently back into the bedroom. After adjusting the settings, he took several photographs from various places in the room, and then crouched beside the bed, inwardly cursing his weary bones as they threatened to give away his game. Devon's face was turned towards him and Jackson snapped a few close-ups of his features - mouth, one closed eye, then both, and then one of the beautiful face. Right before depressing the shutter button, Devon's lids fluttered open and Jackson captured the bleary sienna orbs on film.

The hand that had been lying quiescent on Devon's stomach clumsily reached out and pushed the camera away.

"Too early. Come back to bed," he mumbled before rolling away from the artist, taking the sheet with him and effectively presenting Jackson with more body parts to capture: the lean back, tapered waist, the swell of a toned buttock. When the artist was satisfied with his collection, he abandoned his camera and joined his lover once again.

Devon wrapped himself around Jackson. "Much better," he said before gently pressing a sleepy kiss to the strong shoulder and then drifting back to sleep. Jackson followed not long after.

The next time the artist woke it was to the feeling of warm lips surrounding his cock. Sleep-blurred eyes looked down his body and met mischievous sienna ones looking back at him. A quick wink from his young lover had Jackson groaning, his head falling back onto the indented pillow.

"As much as my body is obviously enjoying that," the gravelly voice started, "it also needs to relieve itself."

"Tough," Devon said after he pulled his mouth from the hard flesh and then licked a wet stripe up the sensitive vein underneath. "This is payback for the hell you put me through last night."

Jackson snorted. "What? Sucking me off when I need to piss? While I agree it's torture in itself, I'm also inclined to say you might get more than you bargained for if you keep it up."

Devon thought for a second and released his prize. "Go," he said as he motioned to the bathroom. "But when you get back, your ass is mine," he informed the man and watched as his artist crawled out of bed. When he had disappeared, Devon stretched out on the bed and planned his attack.

When Jackson returned to the bedroom, he stopped in his tracks. After a quick search of the room, he realized that his camera was too far away to capture this particular image on film. Devon was teasing himself, his long fingers trailing up and down the thick shaft, gently squeezing the head between his thumb and index finger, and collecting the clear fluid there before moving down once again.

"Better be careful or you won't be able to punish me," Jackson said as he crawled back onto the bed, laying himself over the young man, sliding his erection next to Devon's.

A smirk played at the corner of Devon's tempting mouth. "That's what you think," he whispered as he twined his fingers into the blond hair and pulled Jackson's face to his. Before their lips touched, he whispered, "I've already come once this morning so I have no doubt I'll be able to hold out," and then his lips devoured Jackson's.

JACKSON sat propped against the headboard with Devon's head resting on his stomach, the two men enjoying what was left of their time together. Work-roughened fingers threaded their way through the dark curls, Jackson memorizing the texture on every pass. Devon's digits were teasing the coarse hair on the older man's shin when a loud rumble erupted in his ear, causing him to snicker.

"Guess that means it's time to get up," he said as he rolled to his side and looked up at Jackson.

"Considering the fact that it's nearly noon, I'd say that we both probably need to eat something," Jackson surmised as his fingers moved to Devon's face, tracing an invisible line from forehead to chin.

Reluctantly, the young man sat up and moved to the side of the bed. "Feed me, suck me, fuck me," he teased. "Needy bastard, aren't you?"

"No more than you." Jackson leaned over and as Devon stood, left a red handprint on the left butt-cheek.

"Ouch, you sadistic bastard," he grumbled as he rubbed the offended flesh and moved to his dresser to grab a pair of boxers and t-shirt.

"Oh, stop your whining. You weren't the one who was just folded damn-near in half and drilled into the mattress," Jackson tossed back as he retrieved his tried-and-true paint-stained jeans.

A dark eyebrow arched. "Are you complaining?" he asked as he stepped into the shorts and then donned a t-shirt.

The artist moved to where Devon was standing at his dresser and brushed his lips against the young man's. "Never," he said before leaving the bedroom and heading for the kitchen.

They worked well together in the small space, Jackson at the stove, scrambling a dozen or so eggs and adding heaven-only-knows-what to the mix, while Devon popped several slices of bread into the toaster, buttering them when they were done. The oven timer dinged and the artist retrieved the bacon, careful not to tilt the cookie sheet and drip grease all over everything.

When Devon asked why he cooked bacon that way, he laughed. "Less mess. No grease splatters all over the kitchen." His young lover nodded and moved to set the table.

It was all done with an ease that surprised them both, and a warm feeling of rightness settled over them.

Devon was munching on a slice of bacon, lost in thought, and then his eyes slid to Jackson. "Last night, you said something in another language. What was it?"

Jackson opted for swallowing the mouth full of orange juice rather than spraying it all over his inquisitive lover. Of course, he had to swallow around the lump that had suddenly formed in his throat, but he managed, just barely. He wasn't ready to have this talk, wanted to wait until right before he left, chicken that he was, but it seemed Devon's question was rearranging his timetable.

"Actually, it was a mixture of Spanish and French," he admitted. "And before you ask what was said, let's finish breakfast and then we'll talk."

Devon's stomach dropped. Jackson wanted to talk, and when people said that, it wasn't a good thing. Maybe Jackson *was* just playing with him, and none of this meant anything to the man sitting next to him. Devon was just someone to fill the time, an exciting adventure he had taken and now it was time to go back to the real world, a world that didn't include a young snowboarding instructor-slash-bartender.

Jackson saw the war of emotions flicker across Devon's face and he reached out, turning the sad eyes towards his.

"Baby, it's nothing bad," he said as he caressed the soft cheek. "I promise."

The young man nodded and forced himself to finish the rest of his breakfast.

After the table had been cleared, dishes rinsed and loaded into the dishwasher, Jackson took Devon by the hand and led him into the living room where he sat the young man on the couch, while he opted for the coffee table.

He ran a nervous hand through his sandy-blond hair, trying to piece together his thoughts, trying to decide how to tell Devon that he had become his world in just a short period of time.

He took a deep breath and leapt.

"What I said last night, in the other languages, were things I was afraid to say in the light of day: thoughts, feelings, wishes, desires," he said quietly. "And they were about you, about us."

Devon shifted on the couch. "Us?"

Jackson nodded. "Yeah, us," he said as he reached out for Devon's hands. "I want there to be an 'us' after I leave. I want you to know that this isn't just another series of casual fucks for me. Since the first time I talked to you, I felt something for you, something I thought I'd never feel again after...." he trailed off, not wanting to get into the whole Greg thing right now. "Anyway, last night, when I said those things, I meant them with everything I am. I want us to be together, whenever we can; however we can manage. I want to know that I'm yours, and that you're mine, in every sense of the word."

The words wrapped around Devon like a blanket, and he realized that his earlier fears were unfounded.

"I care for you, Devon, a great deal. And I have a feeling that you might feel the same way towards me, or am I reading you wrong?" he asked and earned a shake of russet curls. "So that brings me to my next point. Before you make a decision on whether or not you want this as well, there are some things you need to know."

Devon nodded and Jackson continued.

"There are things in my public life that you might not want to deal with. The pressure of being with a celebrity, and I really hate that word because that's not who I am, as far as I'm concerned. Unfortunately the masses see it differently," he said with a grimace. "But the pressure takes its toll on most couples. I'm not doing anything other than living at the ranch and painting right now, but my manager has a few scripts he wants me to look at, which I may or may not accept. But if I do, then that means time away for filming, and it could be anywhere in the world."

Devon wasn't so sure he liked that part of the deal, and briefly wondered exactly how much time they would manage if he chose to pursue a relationship with his artist. It would have been difficult, to say the least, if Jackson were just a regular Joe. But he wasn't, and Devon wondered if that was a good thing or bad.

"And then there are the vultures, the press. They are relentless. They'll do damn near anything to get a picture or a story, and when they can't, they'll make things up."

"So have they made things up about you?" Devon asked, his curiosity piqued.

Jackson nodded. "Everyone, at some point, has shit made up about them. My life has been under a microscope for a very long time, so the crap they print doesn't bother me. I know the truth, and that's enough for me. I think the biggest bug up their ass is that I don't play the Hollywood game like others do. I'm not going to say that it'll be easy for us, if you decide you want to be with me. It'll be hard as hell," he said as he brought Devon's hands to his lips. "But I think we'd be crazy not to try it. There's something between us, something I want to explore, to discover with you. But you have to want it too. And if not, then that's okay. I completely understand that you might not want to be in the spotlight. Because there will be times, premieres, openings, art shows, things like that, where I'll want you by my side. Actually, I want you with me all the time but real life isn't as obliging. You're here in Salt Lake City and I'm either in Livingston or Los Angeles or somewhere else while filming. I'm not going to ask you to make a decision now. I just wanted to lay it all out for you so you'd know what you would be getting yourself into if you choose to give us a chance."

Devon listened to everything that was being said, and it scared the hell out of him. That this man, Jackson Prescott, could have feelings for him was something he had only wished for. To hear the admission from the man sitting in front of him twisted his insides, but in a good way.

"Now, do you have any questions? Concerns? Thoughts? I'll try to answer them as honestly as I can," Jackson offered.

The brunette sat quietly for a few moments as everything sank in, or at least attempted to, and then he nodded to himself.

"Everything we've done over the past four days, it's what you do in a relationship, isn't it? Spending time together, eating, laughing, cutting up. You've been showing me how it could be, haven't you?" he asked.

"In a manner of speaking, yes. You've never had a relationship, so you had no clue what being in one entails. It's great, it's scary, it's tough. If I didn't think you were worth it, I wouldn't have behaved that way. Oh, and just so you know, I don't bottom for just anyone," he said with a grin. "There was a reason our first time was the way it was."

The sienna eyes widened. "What do you mean?"

"I may be old, but I'm not a cripple. I might have played up my aching back a tad more than I should have. But I did it for a reason. I wanted to prove to you that I wasn't here on some whim, that I trusted you; that I have feelings for you," he stated.

Devon could understand that, and even applauded the man for his underhanded scheme to influence the way things happened that day, and then another thought came to him. "You made love to me last night, didn't you? It wasn't just sex, was it?"

Jackson nodded. "Yes, I made love to you. It's just another facet of being in a relationship. Of course, sex is great and all, but when there are feelings involved, it's so much more," he said as he reached out and cupped Devon's face, his thumb tracing along the instructor's lower lip.

Devon's eyes closed as he leaned into the touch. "Show me again," Devon whispered. "Show me how it could be." He had never before felt such a strong need to be connected to someone, but looking back on the past few days, he realized it had been there, lurking beneath the surface if he had chosen to look for it.

When Jackson finally joined with him, he felt as if he were home, as if this was what he was made for. Everything that had happened before, everyone he had been with, none of that mattered now. Devon responded to every touch, every word with abandon, showing the man that he was not alone in his feelings. He gave his artist everything he was, heart and soul. He might not be able to say the words, but he showed him as best as he could. When he reached his completion, it was with Jackson's name on his lips, in his heart.

As Jackson held his love in his arms after, he knew that getting on a plane in a few hours would be the hardest thing he had ever done in his life. He had made love to Devon as if it were their last time, which it very well could be. He would be crushed if the young man did not choose them, but he would not pressure him in any way. Devon had to make the decision himself. And whatever he chose, Jackson would accept.

"I know I said that I would talk to you tonight, but I'm not so sure that'd be such a good idea now," Jackson said as he pressed a kiss to Devon's forehead while people bustled around them in the Salt Lake City airport. "You have some thinking to do, and I don't want to do or say anything that might sway your decision one way or another."

Devon wrapped his arms around the older man and held him. "I understand, Jax. I don't like it, but I understand."

"I left my numbers on the refrigerator before we left. When you make your decision, call me. Whether it's yes or no, call me. Okay?" he requested and earned a nod from the now quiet young man. "As much as I hate to say this, I want you to do whatever it takes for you to decide if you want this or not. Do you understand?"

Another nod. Devon understood the message loud and clear. He just didn't think he would ever be able to be with anyone else other than Jackson now, now that he knew what it felt like to be cherished, wanted, and loved. Jackson might not have said the words, but he knew, just as he had a feeling Jackson knew how he felt as well.

Jackson pulled back a little and looked at Devon. "No matter what happens, I'll always cherish these past few weeks. And if you don't choose us, I hope you find someone who will make you happy, because you deserve that, and more."

Devon leaned forward and captured Jackson's lips in a loving kiss and then he was standing alone, watching his lover walk away from him, watched until he disappeared from sight. He did not remember the drive back to his apartment, his thoughts filled with the man who had waltzed into his life, turned it upside down, loved him, and left him to decide the fate of their relationship.

His fingers caressed the scrap of paper he found secured to his refrigerator by a magnet with the picture of a beach on it. He had never seen Jackson's handwriting before and he laughed when he realized the man could have been a doctor; it was that bad. He turned the paper over and found a note.

Destiny is not a matter of chance; it is a matter of choice; It is not a thing to be waited for; it is a thing to be achieved.

No matter what you choose, I'll always treasure our time together.

Jax

Devon brushed away a lone tear that slid down his cheek and realized that whatever decision he made, it would impact the rest of his life.

He just hoped he made the right one.

CHAPTER TWELVE

"SO let me get this straight," Tyler said as he handed a beer to Devon, and then settled himself on the couch since his guest had opted to take the oversized chair. "He wants you, you want him, but he wants you to be sure so he basically told you to go out and screw around to make sure you know what you want."

"Fucked, isn't it?" Devon queried as he twisted the top off of the bottle.

Tyler nodded. "Definitely. I mean, if I were him, that offer would have never been on the table."

"I know, but I understand why he did it. I've never been in a relationship before and what he showed me while he was here was how a relationship worked. Well, the basics anyway. We went out, had a good time, had some amazing sex, and fell asleep together. But I think the best part of it all was waking up next to him, knowing that he was going to be there, that I wouldn't be waking up alone."

"And yet he wants you to fuck around so you'll know that's what you really want," the dark-headed man surmised and earned a nod from his friend. "Fuck that. If I were in your shoes, I'd have already called him and gave him his answer. It's what you want, Devon, you said so yourself."

"Yeah, in a roundabout way, it is. Although there's the whole long-distance issue we'd have to work through, not to mention the fact that our privacy will be practically non-existent if I choose to pursue this. Even with me here, you know the press would get wind of it and the next thing I know, they'll be camped out at the base of the mountain, waiting to get pictures, or worse, on the mountain while I'm trying to give a lesson. Wes would have a fit if that ever happened," Devon said before taking a drink. "I don't even want to think about them lurking about the club while I'm working."

A comfortable silence settled between them for a few moments, and then Tyler spoke again. "I still can't believe it," he said with a grin. "You nabbed Jackson Prescott! Do you know how many men, and women, would love to be in your shoes right now?"

Devon chuckled. "Yes, I'm looking at one of them," he teased. "But as strange as it sounds, I don't see him like that. It's hard to explain. Yeah, I was furious when I realized that I'd been duped, but he proved to me that the man I had spoken to on the phone was Jackson, as well as David. During his stay, every now and then, it would seem a bit surreal, that the man I had developed feelings for was the man you and I had made some pretty interesting remarks about, but he's a person first, an artist second, and an actor last."

"And he never tried to sneak in under the radar, to do some recon before he showed up?" Tyler asked.

"No. It was bad enough that he was lying to me. He didn't want the fact that he had spied on me hanging over his head as well."

"And you never checked the number he was calling from," his friend stated.

A quick shake of Devon's head. "No. It was easy to sit back and let him take the lead with things. Actually, it was kind of nice, being pursued for something other than sex, for once."

"So what now?"

Devon leaned his head back in the chair and closed his eyes. "Now, I have to figure out how to push my feelings for him aside and see if he's what I truly want."

"By fucking around," Tyler stated.

The instructor nodded. "I don't want to, Tyler. I don't want to mess up what Jackson and I have. But I have to know."

Tyler slumped down on the sofa and hooked his booted feet on the side of coffee table. "That's messed up, Dev. But if that's what you gotta do, then do it."

A cold tremor ran though Devon's body at the thought of being with someone else. He knew what he had to do. He just hoped he could go through with it.

IT was snowing again as Jackson carefully pulled his white Chevy Silverado 4x4 into a vacant parking space in front of Cassie's Photography Studio. Everyone who had half a brain was tucked away somewhere, nice and safe, warm and dry. Jackson wasn't one of them. He had something to do and nothing but a full-on blizzard would deter him from the task at hand. Reaching over the armrest, he grabbed his camera bag and quickly left the warmth of the vehicle.

The bell over the door jingled, alerting the proprietor of the shop of his arrival.

"You know, I really didn't expect to see you today," Cassie said as she rounded the counter and gave her friend a hug. "How was the drive in? Not too bad, was it?"

"Nah, it was fine. Nothing I haven't driven in before," Jackson offered as he returned his friend's hug.

Cassie Shepherd had owned the studio for as long as Jackson could remember, and the two had struck up an immediate friendship back in the early days, when Jackson had first moved to the small community.

The petite woman with brown shoulder-length hair and hazel eyes stepped away from Jackson. "So what have you been up to lately? Haven't seen you around for a few weeks," she said as she stepped behind the counter again. "I was a bit surprised when you called yesterday."

Jackson set his bag on top and pulled out several rolls of film. "Been painting mostly. Took a few rolls of film while I was in Salt Lake City for a few days," he said as he zipped the bag closed, hoping he wasn't grinning like an idiot. The thought of Devon always put a smile on his face.

And made his dick hurt.

The images of their last time together, of Devon laid out before him, accepting him into the young eager body, responding to the artist's touch, the cries of pleasure that spilled over kiss-swollen lips, had caused Jackson to become painfully hard more times than he cared to admit. Now was definitely not the best time to be thinking of that. He'd have enough trouble when he got into the dark room to develop and print his pictures.

"So which room is ready?" Jackson asked, and a few moments later, disappeared down a long hallway and into one of the studio's three dark rooms.

Cassie's was a true full-service photography studio. Not only did they do sittings and the like, thanks to modern technology, they also developed film and printed photos for the residents of the community.

And then there were people like Jackson, the eccentric artists and die-hard photographers who insisted they would take care of things themselves. Cassie had no problem with that as there was always someone needing one of the dark rooms to create the many works of art that hung on the walls of galleries, restaurants and homes in Livingston. Unfortunately, the prints that Jackson would leave with later in the day would never be seen by anyone other than the artist and his muse.

Carefully extracting the roll of film from its canister, Jackson methodically went through the first series of steps that would bring his photographs to fruition. Developing solutions, stop baths, fixers, and fixer removers were all part of the time-consuming process. Once the roll had been sent through the solutions, he hung the strips of film to dry, and left the room in search of food.

"I'm going over to the diner for lunch," he said as he pulled on his coat, secure in the knowledge that his things would not be disturbed. Everyone knew that when Jackson Prescott was in the dark room, he was working, and nobody bothered him. "Want me to get you something?"

Cassie looked up from the photos she was retrieving from the automated machine. "Nah. I'll go over a bit later, but thanks."

Jackson nodded. "No problem. See you in a few," the artist said before pulling his battered cowboy hat down and braving the elements once again.

As he consumed his bowl of homemade stew, Jackson wondered what Devon was doing at that moment. Was he teaching a class, on a break, or was he eating lunch as well? Had he thought about them as much as Jackson had since returning home? Was he close to making a decision about them?

Jackson sighed, knowing that he was just chasing his tail in a never-ending circle. He had come so very close to calling Devon just to hear his voice, but stayed true to his word that he would not contact the young man.

The majority of his being screamed with need for his lover, to have the younger man by his side, to know that Devon had chosen them; while a much smaller, but very stubborn, part knew he had to wait, had to let his lover decide for himself if this was what he wanted.

He didn't like the thought of someone touching what he had come to think of as his, but he knew deep down it was a necessary evil for Devon to realize that what he had shared with the older man was so much more than anything anyone else could ever offer. Jackson had showed him one last time how it could be between them, and as they reached the pinnacle of pleasure together, he had to fight to hold the words back that begged to be said.

But it wasn't the right time, so he'd said nothing. He tossed a few bills onto the table, slid from the booth to collect his coat and hat, and hoped that one day soon he would have the chance to tell Devon his true feelings.

He spent the afternoon enlarging and printing his treasures, using different methods to lighten or darken the images, and his heart ached with longing for the face that slowly appeared on the coated paper, time and time again, as the solution brought the photos to life. His azure gaze lovingly caressed each sheet that was pulled from the final tray and hung on a line behind him. Memory after memory assaulted his senses as he relived their time together and wondered if he would survive the wait.

OVER the next couple of weeks, Devon agonized over what he had to do, and after several more arguments with Tyler, none of them pleasant, decided to just get it over and done with. A fuck was a fuck. He used to do it all the time. He could do it again. Then he would have his answer, one way or the other.

Screwing up his resolve, he joined Tyler and a few friends for dinner one evening after work, followed by a night of drinking and dancing at one of the clubs in town. Devon only had one thing on his mind. Well, two, if he included Jackson. He knew he should not be thinking of the man at that moment, but then again, his artist was never far from his thoughts, no matter what he was doing.

From his position at the bar, Devon watched the sea of bodies moving to the trance mix that poured from the speakers, trying to find someone that appealed to him. He knew what he used to like, but his taste had been drastically altered by a blue-eyed devil in the guise of one Jackson Prescott. He shook the thought from his mind and scanned the area once again.

The opportunity finally presented itself a few minutes later. The young instructor was at the bar, waiting for his drink, when someone slid into the space next to him. Devon looked up to the stranger's face and he saw that the man was older, had reddish-blond hair and blue eyes that reminded him of Jackson's. Of Jackson, period.

Maybe I can do this, Devon thought.

"I'm Rick," the man said, his voice low and thick.

"Devon," he answered and then he was being kissed, the stranger's lips caressing his own, and he was a bit dismayed at his body's response. But, he was young, and it had been several weeks since anyone had touched him, not counting himself, so it was only natural he would react this way.

"You live nearby?" Rick asked when he pulled away and Devon shook his head.

"Just here visiting a friend," he lied. He was not about to bring someone else into the bed he had shared with Jackson.

"I'm here on business. Guess we'll go back to my hotel room then. That is, if you're up for it," he said as his hand slid up Devon's thigh and cupped the growing bulge he found.

"Lead the way," Devon said in what he hoped sounded like an excited voice. After a quick side-trip to let Tyler know where he would be, he left the security of the building, climbed into his Jeep and followed Rick's rental car to the hotel.

Once inside the room, Devon watched as the older man unbuttoned his shirt, mentally comparing him to Jackson. He had a nice build that spoke of time spent in a gym, whereas Jackson's body was toned from hard work. Rick's hands were delicate, he had noticed at the club, and not rough like his artist's.

Stop it, Devon, he chided to himself. *Just get on with it.*

Those same hands were now lifting his shirt and tossing it aside.

"My God, you are beautiful," Rick said as he ran a hand over Devon's torso. "May I?" he asked as the long digits paused over his nipple ring. Devon nodded and he could not stop the involuntary groan that rumbled within his chest as Rick gently tugged on the hoop. His mind might not want this, but his body definitely had other ideas. He leaned back against the wall and gave in to the need that rushed through his system.

A warm tongue teased the furled nub for a moment before making its way down his torso.

Rick squatted down in front of Devon and quickly unbuttoned and unzipped the young man's jeans. "Now, let's see what you've got for me," he said as his prize was revealed. "Mmm, perfect, just as I suspected."

Devon closed his eyes and let his head fall back against the wall with a thud as his cock was enveloped in wet heat. There were no teasing licks, no knowing touches, just the no-nonsense business of an impersonal blowjob.

He tried to think back to the time before Jackson, before it didn't matter, tried to remember how to just let his body go and enjoy it, but he couldn't. Jackson had claimed Devon's heart as well as his body, and nobody would ever come close to making him feel the way he did when Jackson loved him, worshipped him.

After a few minutes, his hands went to Rick's shoulders and gently pushed the man away. "Rick, I'm sorry," he said as he looked down into the lust-filled eyes. "I can't do this. It's … I need to go," he said before stepping away from the older man and quickly pulling up his jeans. He grabbed his shirt and before Rick could say another word, Devon had disappeared through the door.

The shaking young man ran down the hallway and ducked into the stairwell, hoping that Rick wouldn't come looking for him. There he collapsed against the railing; his heart thundering furiously in his chest, and reality hit him like a ton of bricks.

No one other than his artist would ever touch him again.

CHAPTER THIRTEEN

JACKSON was bone-weary and half-frozen when he rode back into the warmth of the barn late one afternoon. He and his neighbor, Scott, had spent the day riding their fence lines, looking them over, testing their strength, making repairs where necessary. It was something they had been doing for some time now, enjoying each other's company as well as nature at its best.

He groaned when he slid from the saddle and he felt the slight catch in his back, that tiny twinge that let him know he wasn't as young as he used to be. A smile formed on his wind-chapped lips as he remembered the last time he had felt that twinge. Too bad his snowboard instructor wasn't here to give him another massage.

Devon.

He was never far from the artist's thoughts, that was certain. Jackson unbuckled the cinch, removed the saddle and bit, and stored them away in the tack room. After that, he tossed the blanket over the stall railing and brushed Midnight down. Long, sure strokes with the medium-bristled brush covered the equine's body, Jackson's thoughts wandering with the repetitive action.

Why hadn't he called? It had been almost six weeks since he had heard his lover's voice, looked into the beautiful coffee-colored eyes as they kissed one last time before he boarded the plane. Maybe Devon had decided that a relationship wasn't in the cards for them; maybe he had decided he didn't want that kind of life. The thought pierced Jackson's heart and he lowered his forehead to rest against the black-as-coal withers. He knew he had told Devon to take his time, but how long would Jackson have to wait before closing this chapter in his life?

Images of his time spent with the young man skittered through his mind and he fought the wave of sadness that threatened to drown him. He had to trust his lover with this, had to hope that the love he had shown the young man would be enough.

Midnight turned his head and nudged Jackson's shoulder, whickering softly, the air expelled from the horse's muzzle stirring the artist's shoulder-length locks.

Tear-filled eyes looked up at his friend and he smiled softly. "Yeah, I know, buddy. It's a mess, isn't it?" he asked and switched brushes, a soft-bristled one this time, and gently brushed the horse's head. With that done, he reverently pressed a kiss to the blaze of white on Midnight's forehead, and then moved to the opposite side to continue his brushing, while Honey and Firefly looked on from their neighboring stalls.

His cell phone vibrated in his shirt pocket and he fought to contain the bodily flinch that usually accompanied the call, not wanting to spook Midnight. Being trampled in a horse's stall was not the way he wanted to bid farewell to this world. Extracting the device from its resting place, he smiled when he saw the caller's name.

"I've tried you at the house for over an hour. Where the hell are you?" The baritone voice wrapped itself around Jackson like a friendly hug, something he surely needed right about now.

"In the barn, brushing Midnight down. Scott and I rode fence lines today," Jackson said as he continued to brush the dark hide in front of him.

"Well, I'm glad you remembered your cell," Ben said with a chuckle. "I can't count how many times you've ridden off without it."

Jackson smiled. "And I wouldn't ask you to. You probably couldn't count that high."

"Bastard," Ben said affectionately. "So, does a certain snowboard instructor have anything to do with you remembering it now?"

"Could be," Jackson replied evasively.

"So, have you heard from him?"

The artist let out a long sigh.

"I take it you haven't," Ben surmised.

Jackson dropped the brush into the bucket of supplies and moved to sit on a bale of hay outside Midnight's stall. "No, and I'm starting to wonder if he's going to call at all. It's been weeks, Ben. I'm just afraid that he decided to forget the whole thing," he said as he leaned back against the railing.

"Why don't you just call him?" Ben asked. "I know you said you wouldn't, but if you're this down about the fact he hasn't called, just bite the bullet and do it."

The artist shook his head, as if his friend were sitting next to him. "No, I can't do that. I told him to take as much time as he needed. I just didn't expect it to be this long. Oh God, Ben. What if he...." he started, only to be cut off by a stern voice.

"Listen to me, Jax. You did everything you could in the small amount of time you had, short of telling him your true feelings, that is. If he can't see that, then you're better off without him."

Jackson pinched the bridge of his nose. "I know. You're right. I just wish he would call."

"I know, Jax. I know," Ben said in a soothing tone. "You'll keep me posted? I mean, I'll be out in a couple of weeks, but if you hear from him before then, you'll call, right?"

"Yeah, I'll call. You don't know how glad I am you're going to spend a few days here before heading back home for the holidays," Jackson said as Sasha, his half-wild barn cat, jumped onto the bale of hay with him. She gently butted his hand and he obligingly stroked her soft black and white fur.

"I'm not one to break with traditions," Ben said, thinking back on the numerous holidays the two men had spent together, and they spent the next twenty minutes or so catching up.

"I'm glad you called," Jackson admitted after wiping tears of laughter from his eyes. "I really needed this."

"Chin up, Jax. Sometimes no news is good news."

Jackson nodded. "Sometimes. I sure as hell hope this is one of them."

"Well, no matter what, you still have me, even though I refuse to cuddle with you when you get in those strange moods of yours," Ben teased. "See you in a couple of weeks, then."

"See you in a couple of weeks," Jackson said before disconnecting the call.

Sasha had curled up beside Jackson's leg and he slid his fingers through her fur, wondering if he would ever get to run them through Devon's sable curls again.

CHAPTER FOURTEEN

TWO weeks later, Jackson's house was full of friends, laughter and songs. The cast members of *No Man's Land* had been reunited and the Christmas party was in full swing. Jackson felt truly blessed with his extended family, but wished with all his heart that he could look out into the fray and find a certain pair of sienna eyes looking back at him. Several people had adjourned to the kitchen table for a few hands of poker, while the others mingled, catching up on what everyone was doing.

A little while later, Jackson was returning from the restroom on the way back to the poker game when the phone rang. Jeff, being the closest person to it, answered.

"Hello?"

"Could I please speak to Jackson?" the caller asked.

"Sure. Who's calling?"

A smile. "Devon."

The young man handed the receiver to Jackson as he passed. "Some guy named Devon is on the phone for you," he said and then disappeared into the kitchen in search of more beer.

Jackson's stomach fell to his feet.

The normally calm and collected actor had finally found something that would shatter his calm. His stomach ached, his heart thundered in his chest, and his body had broken out in a cold sweat. His palm was damp as he held the receiver, looking at the piece of plastic as if it were a foreign object.

Devon was on the other end of the line, and it scared Jackson more than anything ever had. By the end of the conversation, he would have Devon's decision regarding their relationship, and hoped with all his heart that he had chosen in favor of it. A burst of laughter from the kitchen snapped him back to the here and now, and he lifted the receiver to his ear.

"Devon?" he asked and then felt like an idiot. *Of course it's Devon. Jeff just told you that.*

"Hey," the beautiful voice said. "Sorry about calling so late."

"No, it's no problem. Let me get somewhere where it's quiet," he said in what he hoped was a calm voice. He didn't want Devon to know how shaken he was from the phone call.

Devon chuckled. "Yeah, I hear noise in the background. I take it you're not alone."

Jackson left the living room and slid into his studio, closing the door behind him, effectively shutting out the noise from the party. "Okay, that's better," he said and leaned against the door, trying to calm himself. "And to answer your question, no, I have a house full of people right now. Christmas get-together with my extended family."

"Oh," came the small voice through the airwaves. "I'll let you go, then."

"No!" Jackson rushed and the young man smiled. "It's okay, really. I'm glad you called," he said. *You have no idea how glad,* he thought. "So, how have you been?"

"Tired right now, actually," he admitted. "But I've been working quite a bit lately. Christmas vacations and all that, which translates into extra instructors needed to keep up with the demand for lessons."

Jackson chuckled. "Good for business."

"Very good for business," Devon agreed. "How have you been? Keeping busy around the ranch?"

"Never a dull moment around here, that's for sure. Went out riding the fence lines a couple of weeks ago, making repairs and such. Done a bit of painting for an exhibition I have planned for February," he said and wondered why it was so hard to talk to Devon now.

"That's good," the instructor offered and then was silent for a moment. "This is a bit strange, isn't it?"

Jackson nodded. "Yeah. I didn't expect it to be like this when you called."

"What did you expect?" the young man asked as he snuggled further into the cushions.

A chuckle met Devon's ear. "Not exactly sure. I guess I thought it'd be like it was before."

"But it's not," Devon surmised and Jackson agreed.

"No, it's not. Would I be out of line if I said I've missed you?" the older man said as he moved away from the door and opened one of the storage cabinets that held his supplies. His eyes lingered on a photograph of Devon he had hung on the inside.

Devon breathed a sigh of relief. "I've missed you too," he said quietly and then it was Jackson's turn to let out the breath he had been holding. "So, there're actually two reasons for my phone call. One, I guess you want my answer, but before we get to that, I wanted to see if you received my gift yet."

Reddish-blond brows furrowed. "Gift? No, I haven't seen anything from you."

"Strange," Devon offered. "You should have received it today."

"Sorry, I haven't had any deliveries in the past couple of days," Jackson said, now upset that he hadn't received Devon's gift.

"Damn it," the young man groused. "Will you do me a favor and go check by your front door? I told them I specifically wanted it delivered today."

Jackson complied and left his quiet studio.

"Everything okay?" Ben asked as Jackson made his way through the living room towards the front door.

Jackson gave Ben a small smile. "Be right back," he said before he disappeared outside. "Okay, I'm on the front porch," he said into the phone as he looked around the doorway. "No package."

"Fuck," Devon swore.

"How big is the box?" Jackson asked, wondering if he might have overlooked it.

Devon snorted. "It's not something you're likely to miss. Is there any other place they could have put it? Maybe the back porch?"

"It's possible. They've left things there before," Jackson said as he followed the wrap-around porch towards the back. When he rounded the last corner, he stopped dead in his tracks.

Devon.

Was here.

On his porch.

Sitting in his swing.

Jackson watched as the young man closed his cell phone and slowly rose from the swing. He sincerely hoped this visit meant the end of his torture. His azure gaze drank in the sight of his lover; the long legs encased in black jeans, the lithe torso covered by a forest green shirt, which, in turn, was covered by the black leather jacket. He smiled as Devon approached him, his strides confident.

"Dare I hope that Santa came early?" he asked when the young man finally stood in front of him.

Devon's smile could light the entire west coast. He raised his hand and cupped Jackson's cheek. "Is this what you wished for?"

"Yes," Jackson whispered as he leaned into the touch.

As Devon leaned in to capture Jackson's lips, the back door opened.

Ben's head appeared through the doorway and he looked around. His eyes widened when he spotted the two men who were only a few inches apart.

"Oh, sorry," he said with a sheepish grin. "Just wondered where you got off to, is all."

Jackson turned his head toward the voice and Devon fought the urge to bring it back around so they could get on with things. Instead, he let his head fall back against the post and looked at the intruder as well.

"No problem," Jackson said with a smile.

"Says you," Devon grumbled, which caused his lover to laugh.

The artist pressed a kiss to Devon's forehead. "Impatient brat," he said affectionately and then turned back to Ben. "Give me a few minutes and then we'll be in."

"Right," he answered and disappeared back inside.

Before the door closed, Devon had grabbed Jackson's shirt and pulled the man back to him. "Now, where were we?" he asked before closing the distance between them. This time, their lips met with a hunger that begged to be sated. Jackson's hands framed the beautiful face and held the young man still as he plundered the warmth of Devon's mouth. The instructor's hands slid around the trim waist and pulled Jackson even closer, their bodies pressed together from knees to lips.

Jackson slowly pulled back, his teeth nipping at Devon's plump bottom lip. "I've missed you," he admitted.

Devon gave him a small smile. "I'm sorry I took this long. I...." he started but Jackson's fingers placed against his lips silenced him.

"How long can you stay?" he asked.

"You have me for fourteen days," he said. "That is, if it's okay. I know I didn't call ahead or anything, so I don't know if you've got other plans or what. But if you do, I can go back," he rambled and Jackson silenced him with a kiss.

"Then we have plenty of time to talk about everything. And while I want nothing more than to take you upstairs and make love to you, I need to see to my guests," he admitted. Jackson linked their fingers together and led Devon inside.

It was bound to happen sooner or later, his meeting Jackson's friends. He just hadn't planned on it being this soon, and certainly not before they had a chance to talk about everything. Oh well, it was out of their hands now. Devon felt like a bug under a microscope and realized that this was probably how they, as actors, felt all of the time. Jackson had introduced Devon to everyone, and the young man knew he was being sized up, could imagine everyone going through their mental checklist as they spoke, wondering if he was only out to make a name for himself, or if he truly cared for Jackson. Jackson never wandered far from him, his presence calming, and his touches familiar. Whether it was his artist's hand at the small of his back, or resting on his hip, or their fingers entwined as they moved through the house, it made Devon feel wanted, included.

Jackson had brought in an extra chair from the studio so Devon could join the card game, at Jackson's side, no less, and once he had a beer or two in him, he relaxed and began to enjoy himself. He listened as everyone recounted their filming days together, as well as other, more personal, tidbits of information that Jackson's 'extended family' chose to reveal. Devon learned a great deal about his lover through this avenue, and was now beginning to see 'the actor' part of Jackson's persona.

Devon laughed when Ben told him about the things that Jackson had done to 'become' Sheriff Rafe Morgan: the way he wore the black oilskin duster and battered cowboy hat as long as he could, repairing the costume himself when need be, and even wandering off into the woods 'to better understand the character'. He had almost fallen out of his chair when they told him about Jackson sleeping in the barn with his horse 'so they could bond'. Jackson just shrugged and upped the bet.

Sometime around midnight, everyone who was staying in town bid their farewells and made the long trek back, promising they would meet up around noon at Cecil's Bar and Grill, leaving Ben and the newly reunited couple at the cabin.

While they were outside saying their goodbyes, Jackson spotted Devon's Jeep.

"You drove?" he asked with a smile on his face. "No wonder you said you were tired earlier. And here I thought it was from working."

"Actually, it is. The drive just added to it," he said before bounding down the steps to retrieve his bag from the backseat.

"Why didn't you fly?" Jackson asked as he took the bag from Devon and led them back to the porch.

"Thought I'd drive the first time and see the sights."

The first time, his young lover had said. Jackson definitely liked the sound of that.

"So how did you find me? Besides in your Jeep," he said before the young man could form a flippant reply.

"Actually it was Tyler who helped me. He has a friend at the phone company who can find all sorts of personal information, for the right price," he said with a grin.

"So Tyler...." Jackson trailed off and Devon picked up.

"Gave him head in exchange for your 'personal and confidential' information," he supplied. "Not that he minded, of course."

"I guess in this case I won't press charges against Ma Bell for the invasion of privacy," Jackson conceded. "It brought you to me," he said as he opened the door.

Devon snorted. "Yeah, but only after I realized that I had passed your road … twice. You weren't kidding when you said you lived in the middle of nowhere."

Ben was cleaning up when the two men returned to the house.

"I'll be back down in a bit," Jackson said as he led Devon to the stairs. "Gonna get Devon settled in."

"Take your time," Ben said with a friendly smile.

The young man was impressed with Jackson's cabin. He had expected something small, quaint, but the reality of it was much different. The first floor was an open layout; the only breaks in the flow were Jackson's studio, the guest bathroom, and the mudroom off the kitchen. The stairs led to the second floor, where a guest bedroom and bath were immediately to the left, while the master bedroom and bath was across the landing, on the opposite side of the house.

Jackson led him into the master bedroom and tossed Devon's bag onto the window seat. He watched as his lover walked around the room, looking at the different photographs on the dresser, chest of drawers, and nightstands. He saw the smile on Devon's face when he came across several of his own pictures in the mix. He had dreamed of this moment, of finally having Devon here, in his home, in this very room, and wanted nothing more than to reacquaint himself with his lover's body, but knew if things got started, he wouldn't make it back downstairs to help with the clean-up.

"Listen, if you want to shower, or whatever, it's through there," Jackson said as he pointed to the open doorway on the opposite side of the room. "And since you're going to be here for awhile, you can unpack your things and store them in the chest of drawers, if you want. Just shove my stuff over. Dirty clothes, just toss in the corner of the bathroom. I do laundry when I can't find something clean to wear," he said with a grin.

"I can identify with that," Devon said as he walked over to where Jackson was. Long fingers fanned out over Jackson's chest and slid upwards until they linked behind his neck. Devon leaned in and placed a gentle kiss to Jackson's throat.

The older man took a deep breath and moved his hands to Devon's arms. "Baby, don't. Not yet. Let me go help clean up and when I get back up here, you can do whatever you like," he said as he stepped way from the temptation that was Devon Forrester.

A mischievous glint appeared in Devon's sienna orbs. "That's giving me quite a bit of latitude, Jax. You realize that, right?"

Jackson nodded and quickly kissed Devon's nose. "I wouldn't have it any other way," he said before disappearing through the open doorway.

The wheels in Devon's sex-deprived brain started to churn.

CHAPTER FIFTEEN

"SURPRISED to see you back down here," Ben said as he pulled a now-clean bowl from the sudsy water and gave it a quick rinse before adding it to the rest of the washed dishes.

"I'm not leaving you alone to clean up everything," Jackson said as he motioned to the mess that was his living room and kitchen. "We've got two weeks together, so there's no...." he said and was interrupted by Ben.

"You haven't seen him in almost two months. I know this because I was the one you called during that time, so I'd imagine you'd rather be up there with him than down here cleaning. I know I sure as hell wouldn't be down here," Ben said as he dipped another plate into the water. "Go. I'll take care of everything."

The artist knew when to admit defeat and nodded. "You're a good friend, Ben," he said with a smile that Ben hadn't seen on his friend in quite awhile.

His bedroom door was closed and when he turned the knob, the sound of the shower met his ears. Desire coursed through his veins and he quickly undressed, not wanting to spend another moment away from his lover.

When Jackson stepped into the steam-filled room, Devon's form could barely be seen through the glass walls. It was only when the artist opened the shower door that he finally gazed clearly on the lithe body he was eager to reacquaint himself with.

Devon's head was tilted back, his long fingers threading their way through the drenched locks, washing away traces of shampoo. He moaned when he felt Jackson's hands slide around his waist, felt his artist's lips at his throat, felt the hard column of flesh against his hip.

Jackson feasted on his lover's freshly washed skin, reveled in the fact that they were together again. He bestowed loving nips and kisses everywhere he could reach. He smiled against the hollow of Devon's throat when the young man's fingers slid into his own sandy locks, holding him in place or serving as an anchor for Devon, he wasn't sure. Either way worked for him. His hands slid down the silken skin of his lover's back, stopping when they covered firm buttocks.

The brunette arched his back when Jackson squeezed, pressing his own hardness against Jackson's abdomen.

"Thought you were going to help clean," Devon said as he leaned back against the tiled wall, letting Jackson do as he pleased. He'd get his turn later.

"Was told I had a night off," Jackson murmured against Devon's shoulder.

Devon tilted his face down and to the right, nudging Jackson's a bit, and then their lips met. The water from the shower drenched both men, splashing between them, dripping into their mouths when they pulled apart slightly, their tongues playing in the open space between them.

Jackson gasped when Devon's fist closed around him, the young man's thumb teasing the skin below the flared head. Ever the gentleman, Jackson reciprocated and then it was Devon's turn to be surprised.

"Fuck," Devon mumbled as Jackson slid his body closer and wrapped his fingers around both of them. The young man followed suit and together they began to stroke. The slip-slide feel of their flesh pressed together was electric, and the sound of the shower drowned out the gasps and moans of pleasure that filled the room.

"Come for me, baby," Jackson said as he increased their pace. "I want to watch you."

Devon flexed his hips, repeatedly thrusting his cock into their joined hands. When he felt Jackson's tongue on his nipple, lips tugging on his silver hoop, he threw his head back and let himself go.

Azure lust-filled orbs watched as Devon gave in to his passion, watched the toned stomach contract as the cock in Jackson's hand swelled and then his lover was coming, his essence covering their stomachs, their joined hands. The erotic display caused Jackson to fall into his own orgasm, his release mixing with Devon's on their bodies.

"You don't know how badly I needed that," Devon said as his forehead rested on Jackson's shoulder.

A chuckle rumbled from Jackson's chest. "You're not the only one. Now we can take our time," he said as he wrapped his arms around the sated body and held Devon close. "You don't know how happy you've made me."

"Give me a bit and I'm sure you'll be even happier," the young man quipped as he held Jackson close.

"I'm not talking about that. I mean, having you here. I was getting worried you weren't going to call," he admitted.

Devon pressed a kiss to Jackson's lips. "I know we need to talk about things, but right now, I just want to enjoy being back together. We've got quite a bit of time to make up for," he said with a smile.

And make up for lost time they did.

A few minutes after their shower, Jackson found himself pinned to the bedroom door by his very insistent lover. The sound of his head hitting the wooden surface was audible downstairs, causing Ben to smile. It sounded like the real reunion was just getting started.

Devon laughed at the startled look on his artist's face.

"You said I could do anything I want," he said with an impish grin that, for some reason, made Jackson nervous. "And right now, that's where I want you," he informed the older man before claiming his lips. Now it was Devon's turn to dominate the kiss as he pressed himself harder against the body pinned to the door. He tugged at Jackson's bottom lip, and then he moved on, his lips trailing over the strong jaw to spend a few moments at the spot right beneath Jackson's ear that caused the older man to dig his fingers into Devon's hips.

"Like that, do you?" he whispered before he captured the fleshy lobe between his teeth, and earned a small moan as his answer. "Thought so," he said before moving on. Devon took his time rediscovering his lover's body, reveling in the sounds that he pulled from the other man. Long fingers caressed the artist's thighs, both inside and out, while his mouth paid homage to Jackson's upper body. He earned a deep moan when his tongue teased the tight nubs and then moved lower to dip into the enticing navel.

Jackson's hands moved to Devon's shoulders when the young man knelt in front of him.

"No. Palms against the door, and don't you dare move them," Devon ordered as relocated his lover's hands. "No matter what I do, they better stay there."

Stormy eyes looked down at Devon. "You are an evil little fucker, you know that?"

"You brought this on yourself, Jax," the young man reminded him.

"Yeah, but when I said you could do anything you wanted, I was thinking more along the lines of making love in the bed, not being tortured against the bedroom door."

"We'll use the bed a bit later," Devon promised as he ran his fingers through the coarse hair on Jackson's legs, slowly stroking the strong thighs, his thumbs gently brushing the pouch hanging beneath the semi-erect shaft with each pass. He saw Jackson's fingers clench against the wooden door and wondered how long the man would obey his rule.

Leaning forward, Devon inhaled his lover's musky scent, burying his nose in the nest of curls at the base of his artist's cock.

"Mmm, I've missed that smell," he admitted and took another deep breath. He felt Jackson's cock twitch against his cheek and he laughed quietly. "That's better. I was wondering if you were done for the night," he teased as he rubbed his nose back and forth against the coarse hair.

"Not by a long shot," Jackson said through clenched teeth.

"Good," Devon said as he ran a finger down the vein of the shaft, from head to base, teasing the sac beneath. He took his lover in hand and slowly stroked a few times before releasing him.

Jackson's eyes closed and his head hit the door again when he felt Devon's tongue on him, licking a path now from base to tip, where it swirled around the head and then disappeared for a second, before the motion was repeated time and time again.

This time it was a frustrated fist that hit the door. "Baby, please don't tease me," Jackson begged.

Devon placed a kiss to the head of Jackson's cock and then stood. Strong arms captured the young man and walked him a few steps backwards. When the backs of Devon's knees came into contact with the mattress, he fell back onto the bed with Jackson following.

"Now we can use the bed," the young man said with a grin as he reached up and threaded his fingers through Jackson's towel-dried hair. "Make love to me," he said before he brushed a kiss against Jackson's lips.

The artist smiled as he reached over to the nightstand and opened the drawer. "You know, I should pay you back for that little stunt, but I think I'll save it for later," he said as he retrieved a condom and the lube, and placed them on the bed beside Devon.

"Can I ask you a question?" Devon asked as he picked up the condom.

"Sure."

Sienna eyes searched his lover's face. "When was the last time you were tested?"

"August," Jackson answered as he brushed a few damp strands of hair behind Devon's ear. "Why?"

"I don't want to use these," the young man said as he waved the foil packet around. "I've always been careful and never not used them, but now, with you, I don't want to. I want to feel you, just you, and not you covered by a thin piece of latex," he admitted.

Jackson's heart soared. Devon was that serious about them.

"When was your last test?" the older man asked.

"After I finally 'saw the light', as Tyler called it, I went and had the tests run again, even though they were less than six months old. I just wanted to be sure," he said with a small smile.

"I know I have no right to ask, but did you...." he trailed off, not wanting to finish his question.

"You have every right to ask. But the answer is no, I didn't sleep with anyone after you left. I went home with a guy, an older guy who resembled you in a way, and he went down on me, but I couldn't go through with it. I knew then that nobody but you would ever touch me again," he informed his lover. "Nobody, Jax. I only want you. I made him stop and then I ran like hell."

Jackson captured Devon's lips in a loving kiss. When he pulled away, he took the condom from between Devon's fingers. "No more, baby," he said as he tossed it back towards the nightstand. "From now on, it's just you and me."

"You and me," the instructor repeated with a relieved sigh. "Now, will you please make love to me?"

Jackson reached for the lube. "It will be my pleasure," he said before moving to his knees so he could prepare his lover.

Devon pulled his legs up and braced his feet on the covers and then Jackson was there, his finger teasing and then pressing inwards. Devon let out a soft moan. "No, I think it'll be both our pleasure," he said as he closed his eyes and gave himself over to the sensations that were spiraling through his body. After a few minutes of exquisite torture, Devon had had enough.

"You do that too much longer and I'll be finished before you even begin," the young man said as he concentrated on not coming.

Jackson slowly slid his fingers from the tight passage, teasing the bundle of nerves one last time. "You're young. It wouldn't take long for you to be raring to go again." He quickly coated his shaft, and then nudged the slippery opening.

Devon wrapped his long legs around Jackson's waist. "Stop teasing me and get on with it."

"Damn, you are such a bossy bottom," Jackson said as he slowly breached the outer ring of muscle, causing his lover to gasp.

"Oh fuck," he moaned. "Go slow, Jax. Want to feel you."

The older man did as requested and slowly entered his lover. With no barrier between them, Jackson felt everything - the incredible heat, each minute tremor that wracked his lover's passage, the soft walls that hugged his member lovingly.

Devon felt the thick shaft stretching him, filling him. It was indescribable, and he rejoiced in the feeling of finally having this connection with Jackson. Once his artist was snugly ensconced within his body, he brushed the long reddish-blond locks away from Jackson's face.

"Hey," he said with a soft smile.

"Hey," Jackson parroted and kissed Devon's palm. "You ready for this?" he asked as he flexed his hips, pushing himself just a tad bit deeper into the man beneath him.

Devon nodded. "Always."

"How you do you want it?"

"Long, deep and slow," he said. "There's only one 'first time', and I want it to last."

Jackson brushed a kiss to Devon's lips. "Whatever you want, baby," he said and then began to move.

They took their time and constantly fought the urge to speed things along, knowing that the payoff would be better than anything they had ever shared before. Devon's shaft leaked steadily between them, coating their stomachs, but he never made a move to touch himself, nor did Jackson. Sweat dotted the older man's brow, pooled between his shoulder blades, but he held himself in check.

The room was filled with soft sighs, gasps of pleasure, murmured words of encouragement. Devon came close to losing it when Jackson spoke to him in Spanish, but a hand over his artist's mouth put a stop to it.

"You keep that up and that'll be the end of it," he informed his lover.

"For you maybe," the artist taunted.

"Jackson, please don't," he said, his large sienna eyes pleading. "Not yet."

"Later then," he offered as he continued with the slow pace he had set for them.

Moments later, Devon felt liquid heat spreading through his body, signaling his oncoming release.

"Oh, God, I'm close," he said quietly as he locked his legs tighter around Jackson's waist.

"Just let go, baby. Let it wash over you," the artist said as he finally gave up the tentative hold he had on his own desire. "I'll be right here."

The intensity of Devon's orgasm surprised him. It wasn't like the others, the quick, erratic pulsing. This one was smooth as it rolled through his body, as if it were filling all of the empty places inside him, filling him with sunlight and clear blue skies, but most of all, filling him with hope for the future. It left him thoroughly exhausted, but yet, wanting more.

The clenching of Devon's passage pulled Jackson into his own orgasm, his seed spooling out into his lover, bathing the pulsing sheath with his essence.

Devon gasped when he felt Jackson coming inside of him, felt the thick cock twitching with his release. He pulled Jackson's lips to his, conveying everything he was feeling at that moment. "So much better," he whispered as he brushed the sweat-soaked hair away from Jackson's face.

"You've got that right," Jackson agreed before he slowly pulled away from his lover. At Devon's whimper, he pressed a quick kiss to the plump lips. "I'll be right back. Just gonna get a rag so we can clean up a bit," he said before disappearing into the bathroom.

Devon closed his eyes for a few moments, and then his lover was back, tenderly wiping his stomach, and then moving between his legs to clean there as well. A quick intake of air had Jackson worried.

"What's wrong?" he asked as he stilled his movements.

"Just a bit tender," Devon admitted.

Jackson lightened his touch and continued to clean his lover. "Why didn't you tell me?"

Sienna eyes met blue. "What, and have you stop? Not a chance in hell of that happening. I'll be okay."

Jackson tossed the washcloth back into the bathroom and they crawled beneath the covers, Jackson gathering Devon in his arms. "I never want to hurt you, so if it's uncomfortable, please tell me. We'll figure something out."

Devon nodded as he settled himself against Jackson's body, his hand resting above Jackson's heart. "What was it you said earlier, when I made you stop talking?"

"Tu eres mi mundo, Devon, eres mi todo," Jackson repeated.

"What does that mean?"

Jackson smiled. "You are my world, Devon, my everything."

If it were possible, Devon fell a little bit more in love with his crazy artist. He rose up and left a lingering kiss on Jackson's lips. "And you are mine," he said with a smile.

Long fingers brushed the sweat-soaked hair away from Devon's face. "Can I ask you something?"

"Sure," Devon said with a nod.

"What took you so long to call?"

The young man linked their fingers together and let them rest on Jackson's chest. "It was a combination of things, I suppose. First off, it was several weeks before I could even entertain the idea of being with someone else. You would not believe the arguments Tyler and I had over that. He told me to just call you and be done with it, but there was always this little voice in the back of my mind telling me not to call you, not yet, that I had to find out for myself. The night I finally did it, or at least tried to, I wanted to call and tell you, but I needed to take care of a few things before I did."

"Like your tests?" Jackson pondered and earned a nod from the other man.

"Yeah. And then I had to practically beg my boss to let me take time off, but I had it coming. I knew there was a reason I was saving my vacation days," he said with a grin. "In order to appease him, I ended up working on most of my days off."

"What about the club? Did they give you shit for taking off during the holidays?" the artist asked.

"No. There were plenty of people wanting the extra hours, so that wasn't a problem. The holidays are quite busy for the bar industry," he quipped.

"You don't say?" Jackson teased.

"Fucker. So I finally got my schedules coordinated and made the drive. And here I am. Think you can handle me for two weeks?"

Jackson leaned up and captured Devon's plump lips. "Probably not, but I'm always up for a challenge."

"Need to make a run to the pharmacy and get your Viagra filled?" the brunette teased.

"Brat," Jackson said as he pushed his lover back onto the bed once more and proceeded to show him that he didn't need any help in that department. The temptation that was Devon Forrester was more potent than any pill.

Much later, as Devon's sated body relaxed into his lover's embrace, there was no doubt in his mind that he had made the right choice.

DEVON woke to the feel of cool air against his back, but it was quickly replaced with the warmth of the comforter. Thinking that his lover was making a quick trip to the restroom, he burrowed deeper into the covers and started to drift back to sleep. The sound of the closet door opening had him peering through one sleepy eye a moment later. Jackson was pulling on a blue and white-checkered flannel shirt.

"Where are you going?" Devon whispered into the quiet room, causing his lover to turn back towards the bed as he slid one arm into the shirt.

"Sorry, did I wake you?" he asked the man who was peeking over the edge of the blanket, his sable curls wild on his head.

"Cold air woke me when you disappeared," he said with a grin. "Why are you getting dressed?"

"Have to go feed the horses and turn them out," the artist answered as he leaned down and grabbed his boots, closed the closet, and then moved to sit on the edge of the bed.

"Oh," Devon said as he sat up, bracing himself on his elbows. "Want some help?"

"Nah. I can get it," he said as he pulled the brown Ropers onto his sock-clad feet. "You stay here and keep the bed warm," the artist instructed as he leaned over and quickly kissed the young man. "I'll be back."

Devon nodded and lay back down. He turned to his side and wrapped an arm around Jackson's pillow, pulled it against his chest and inhaled his lover's scent before he drifted off once more.

Jackson closed the door behind him and quietly made his way down the stairs. On a normal morning, he would start a pot of coffee before he went out to feed, so it would be ready when he came back in. Today, however, he decided to forego that indulgence in favor of getting his chores done as quickly as possible and getting back upstairs to his lover.

As he opened the back door, he heard footsteps on the stairs and was surprised to see Ben coming down, fully dressed. His friend motioned to the door and Jackson nodded before he stepped through and waited for Ben to join him.

"Didn't expect to see you up this early," Jackson said as he looked out towards the barn. "No new snow. Good, won't have to shovel our way out there this morning. Maybe the water trough isn't frozen."

Ben buttoned his coat and pulled on his gloves. "Actually, I wasn't expecting to see you up, so I thought I'd take care of things," he offered.

Jackson patted Ben on the back. "You're a good friend, Ben," he said with a smile before they stepped off of the porch and made their way to the barn. They worked in companionable silence, adding feed to the bins in each stall and topping off the hay in the racks above the feed. With that done, they settled on a bench, waiting for their charges to eat so they could turn them out into the paddock.

"Devon seems like a good guy," Ben said as he leaned back against Honey's stall. "A bit young, but other than that, he seems to genuinely care about you."

The artist smiled and turned towards his friend. "I still can't believe he came all the way out here."

Ben jammed his hands into his pockets. "Well, he did. So I'm guessing you guys are going to try to make a go of it?"

Jackson nodded. "Seems that way."

"It's going to be a hard road, but if anyone deserves to be happy, it's definitely you. After the Greg fiasco, I wasn't sure you'd ever settle down again," he admitted.

"I didn't want to, until Devon. And yeah, it's going to be hard, with him in Salt Lake City and me here and just about everywhere else, but we'll find a way to make it work," Jackson declared.

"I don't doubt that for a minute," his friend said with a grin.

Midnight whickered in his stall and then poked his head over the gate.

"Guess they're ready to start the day," Jackson said as he rose from the bench and unlocked his stall. The Morgan nudged his owner's chest in greeting. Jackson scratched behind Midnight's ears and with a few soft words and a pat on his hindquarters, sent him down the center of the barn where Ben had opened the gate into the paddock. Firefly and Honey followed shortly after. When all three were outside, Jackson checked the water trough and after chipping a few pieces of ice from the sides, grabbed the water hose and filled it. Ben closed the gate and they made their way back to the house.

"You up for the day?" Jackson asked.

"Nah. I'm going to try to get a few more hours in," he offered and then smiled. "I'd be willing to bet this is the first time you're going back to bed, isn't it?"

Jackson chuckled. "Do you blame me?"

Ben threw an arm around Jackson's shoulder. "Just do me a favor and try to keep it down this time."

The artist nodded. "We'll try," he offered with a grin.

It wasn't Jackson's fault that Devon squealed like a girl when he pressed his cold skin against his lover's warm body. Nor was it his fault the young man decided to thoroughly berate him for said infraction. After a quick wrestling match, Jackson managed to wrap his arms around his struggling lover and suggest that if he didn't like him cold, he needed to find a way to warm him up.

Ben pulled the spare pillow over his head to block out the racket that was coming from the master bedroom and prayed for another visit from the sandman.

CHAPTER SIXTEEN

ARRIVING back at the cabin after spending the majority of the afternoon at Cecil's Bar and Grill with everyone, Ben disappeared inside while Jackson took Devon's hand and led him out to the barn.

"I want you to show you something," he said as he pulled the side door open and allowed the young man to enter first. They made their way down the walkway between two rows of stalls, and Devon easily identified the three where Jackson's horses stayed while indoors. Instead of a cramped, single stall, Jackson had combined two small stalls into one larger one, allowing more room for each of them.

A piercing whistle brought his three charges to the gate of the paddock and Devon's eyes widened at the sight of the beautiful creatures. He followed Jackson's lead and climbed to the upper railing and sat next to his lover.

Midnight was the first to greet them, followed closely by Honey and Firefly. "This is Midnight," he said as he patted the coal black horse's neck. "The tan mare is Honey and the chestnut roan is Firefly."

"They're beautiful," Devon said with awe. "May I?" he asked as he slowly raised his hand.

Firefly leaned over and sniffed the newcomer. The two-leg smelled like his owner, so the roan nudged the hand, causing Devon to laugh. Long fingers threaded their way through the dark mane before Devon's hand moved back to the face. "He's beautiful," he said quietly.

Not to be outdone, Honey immediately jockeyed for position, causing Devon to nearly topple over backwards. "Jealous?" he asked with a grin as he gave the mare his attention.

"Ben is leaving tomorrow, so after that, we'll go riding. I want you to see the place," Jackson said as he continued to stroke the black hide.

"How much land do you have?" the instructor asked as he eyed his immediate surroundings.

"Couple hundred acres, but the majority of it is forest. The house, barn, and pasture sit on about ten of it," he offered.

Devon let out a low whistle. "Nice little get-away you have here."

"No, this is home," Jackson said with a smile. "I spend more time here than I do in Los Angeles, and that suits me just fine."

"Who takes care of the horses when you're away filming?"

Jackson laughed. "The man I was trying to reach the night I dialed your number by mistake. Scott Morgan, my neighbor to the east," he said as he motioned to the far side of the clearing. "We've been friends since he moved in about twelve or so years ago. We look after each other's places if one of us is going to be gone."

The horses shifted positions, each of them vying for more attention, causing both men to laugh.

"Just like kids," Devon said as he divided his affection between Midnight and Honey. "Always wanting more."

A brisk gust of wind wrapped itself around them, causing Devon to shiver.

"How about we head inside?" Jackson suggested as he climbed down from the top railing. Devon nodded and followed suit, but instead of making their way to the house, the artist led them back inside the barn and into an empty stall where several bales of hay were waiting to be untied and distributed to the horses.

"Never made love in a barn before," Devon said with a grin as he watched Jackson grab a blanket and toss it over a hay bale.

"I'm sure you will a time or two before you have to head back to Salt Lake City," Jackson said as he settled himself on it, pulling Devon into the vee of his open legs, the young man's back pressed snuggly to Jackson's chest. "But right now we need to talk." Jackson slid his arm around Devon's waist and settled his hand against the warm skin of the young man's stomach.

"About us and how we're going to make this work," Devon added as he relaxed into Jackson's embrace.

The artist pushed the riot of curls aside and pressed a kiss to his lover's neck. "Yeah. You know it's not going to be easy, and it's going to take work on both our parts. I'll fly down to see you as often as I can, and you can come up here if I'm not off filming or promoting. I have an exhibition scheduled for February in Venice Beach and I want you there with me, if you can manage it," Jackson said as he absentmindedly traced circles around Devon's navel.

"A trip to California sounds nice," the instructor admitted.

"I have a couple of scripts on my desk in the studio that I'm giving some thought to, and if I say yes, I'll be gone for a few months after that," Jackson informed him.

"And I'll be stuck in Salt Lake City," Devon grumbled.

"Not necessarily. You could take a leave of absence and come with me," Jackson said hopefully.

"Right," Devon snorted. "I'll just sit in the hotel room all day while you go out and do your thing. Tyler would give me shit for months about it, saying that I *had* become a 'kept man'."

"Would that be so bad?" Jackson asked, only slightly joking. "At least we'd be together. And we'd get to travel, see different parts of the world."

Devon bristled at the words, threw Jackson's hand aside and quickly stood, his body tense with anger. "Would that be so bad?" he parroted as he turned back to his startled lover. "That is so easy for you to say because you would be the one out there doing things. My life is not like that, Jackson. I can't just say, 'Hey, I think I'll ditch my responsibilities and play house for a few months'. I'm not like that. If you thought I would just blindly follow you wherever you went, then I'm sorry, but you've made a huge mistake. I have a life of my own!" he shouted into the silence of the barn.

Jackson closed his eyes and let his head fall back against the barn wall. This was not how the conversation was supposed to go. They were supposed to calmly discuss their future and how they would manage it. Instead, Devon looked ready to do battle for Jackson suggesting what he had. Taking a deep breath, he looked to where Devon was standing in the center of the walkway.

"I know this is all new to you, but it's not just you any longer. A relationship is comprised of two people, Devon," he said as he slowly stood and walked to the gate of the stall. "It's me and you, now. And what affects you, also affects me, and vice-versa. It's a balancing act, an equal give and take. I never said that you had to come with me. I would never presume to tell you what to do. I was just making a suggestion that would allow us more time to be together."

Devon stood quietly, listening to Jackson's words, wishing now he could take back what he'd said. Jackson was right - they had a relationship, and to make it work, both parties had to be flexible. But why did it sound like Devon would be the one giving and Jackson taking?

"Listen, it's not something that has to be decided right this very minute. I don't even know if I'm going to take the parts yet," he said as he approached the wary young man. "I'm just letting you know that no matter where I am, I want you by my side."

The instructor turned and looked at Jackson, his brown eyes hard. "But that's just it. You want *me* by *your* side. What about what I want? Call me selfish, but from where I'm standing, it seems that I'd be the one giving up more."

Jackson sighed. "Devon, that's not what I meant," he said as he ran a frustrated hand through his hair. "I want us to be together as much as we can manage, and it doesn't matter to me where we are, whether it's here, at your place, or somewhere else."

The young man sat dejectedly on the bale of hay Jackson and Ben had shared earlier that morning, thinking over everything that had been said. "I'm sorry," he said quietly as he picked at a few loose pieces of the dried grass. "I didn't mean to be like that. I've never done this before, so I'm bound to make mistakes."

Jackson knelt beside his lover, his hands resting lightly on Devon's knees. "Devon, look at me," he said and waited until sienna eyes met his own. "I know it's going to be hard, but we'll manage it. We'll take it one day at a time. Besides, there's always the phone," he added with a grin.

"Isn't that what got us in this mess to begin with?" Devon asked with a small smile. He still wasn't sure how they were going to manage, but if Jackson said they could do it, he would trust his lover.

The artist raised his hand to Devon's face and cupped his cheek. "Believe it or not, I'm kinda thrilled about the 'mess', as you call it, that we're in. We managed to survive almost two months apart, although I thought Ben was going to rip me a new one each time I called him, which was quite often," he admitted. "And we just survived our first argument. Well, second if you count your initial reaction when we finally met. But neither one of us stormed out, or said this wasn't going to work, which you could have easily done, because it's a new concept for you. I'll let you in on a little secret. If you have to work at it to make it work, it's worth it," he said as his thumb stroked the full lower lip. "And I think we're worth it."

Devon sat quietly for a few moments, his eyes noting the sincerity shining in his lover's pale blue orbs. He slowly raised his hands and slid his fingers into Jackson's already-ruffled hair. "I think we are, too," he whispered before brushing his lips against his lover's.

The sound of the barn door opening stopped things before they became too heated.

"Sorry to interrupt," Ben said with a grin.

"No you're not," Jackson said as he rose from his kneeling position, a matching smirk on his face as well.

"Anyone ever tell you that you have the world's worst timing?" Devon grumbled as he eyed the other man from where he was still sitting.

"What's up?" Jackson asked.

"Weather service just issued another warning; said we'll be getting somewhere between eight and ten inches of new snow tonight. Thought you might like some help getting things ready out here," Ben said as he approached the two men.

Jackson glanced at his watch. "Yeah, it's almost time for them to come in anyway," he said before walking to the large doors that led into the paddock. His shrill whistle carried across the snow-covered pasture, and a few minutes later, all three horses bounded into sight.

Devon stood to the side and watched as they filed into the barn, going immediately to their stalls to wait for dinner. The young man watched everything his lover did with Midnight, and followed suit, feeding Firefly while Ben worked in Honey's stall. Once all three horses were tucked safely away for the evening, Jackson closed the barn doors and the men made their way back to the cabin.

CHAPTER SEVENTEEN

THE new-fallen snow crunched under the horses' shod hooves as they bore their passengers around Jackson's ranch. The day had dawned bright and clear, and after waking for the second time that morning, something that was quickly becoming a habit, Jackson had suggested they take this opportunity to see his place, since Mother Nature could change her mind on a whim.

They rode along in companionable silence, Midnight walking slowly beside Firefly, the stallion only leading by a head's length. Devon took in the sights around him: the evergreens that stood like quiet guardians, protecting all that was within the boundaries of Jackson's domain, the seemingly endless snow-covered meadow that led to a stand of bare aspens and the dark forest beyond. His knee occasionally brushed against Jackson's as the horses waded through the knee-deep drifts.

"Where are we going again?" he asked, suddenly tired of the quiet.

"To my special place," the artist replied, not looking at his lover, whom he could tell was pouting.

"Is it close by?"

"Yeah." Jackson smiled.

Devon grumbled, "You could at least indulge me with more than just barely worded answers."

Jackson turned to the side, reached out his hand and flicked the delectable lip that protruded far from his lover's mouth. "You better put that up before it gets frostbite."

"Make me."

Never being one to back down from a challenge, Jackson grasped the back of Devon's head and crushed their lips together. Midnight faltered only for a second at the change of his charge's position, and then continued on, Firefly plodding alongside.

Desire surged through Devon's body as their tongues slid sinuously against each other, mimicking actions that had just taken place a few hours before. He silently cursed the man for this asinine idea. He would much rather be back at the cabin, enjoying another round of mind-blowing sex, than out in the cold. He shifted in his saddle, trying to alleviate some of the tension that had gathered in his lower region.

Jackson slowly pulled away and licked his lips. "You taste like a Pina Colada," he said as his breath lingered between the two men.

"Yeah? Never been told that before. How about we go back to the cabin so you can suck on my straw?" Devon suggested with a grin before he lightly touched his heels to Firefly's flanks and left a gaping Jackson behind.

He rode for several seconds when he realized that he still had no idea where they were headed, and reined in Firefly. Turning in his saddle, he looked back at Jackson. "Come on, Cowboy. Since you're the only one who knows where we're going, I would suggest you get up here and lead. If not, I'm going back to the house."

Jackson nudged Midnight and quickly caught up with his snarky lover. "Cowboy?" he asked with an amused smile.

"If the hat fits," Devon retorted as he reached up and tugged on the brim of Jackson's battered cowboy hat.

"Well then, I guess it's only fair that I get to call you my snow bunny," the artist tossed back and with a flick of the reins, took off through the woods. Now it was Devon's turn to gape like a fish.

When he finally recovered, he shouted, "Jackson Prescott! You are so going to get it when I catch up to you!" and then took off after the older man, trying to stay on the same path that

Midnight had left. Devon was unfamiliar with the terrain and did not want to risk Firefly becoming injured from a blind ride through the forest. Devon laid himself over Firefly's neck and gave the horse his head. He was surprised to find that he did not have to do much as far as directing Firefly. It seemed that the roan knew this was a game, and as such, followed his instincts, racing after his equine brother.

The wind was cold against the instructor's cheeks as he rode, causing his skin to prickle. The brown Carhartt knit cap he was wearing protected his head and ears, but he was fairly certain it would take some time before he felt his nose again.

Jackson led his lover on a merry chase, dodging back and forth between trees, snow and dirt flying up from the horses' hooves, marking their passage, as they neared their destination with each step.

Devon's eyes widened at the sight that greeted him when he and Firefly burst through the last stand of trees. He quickly reined in his steed and sat in awe of the natural beauty that he had found. The lake that lay before him was enormous; its surface slick as glass, reflecting images of the surrounding trees and mountains in the distance, and it took his breath away.

"Beautiful, isn't it?" came the voice somewhere off to his left. He turned to find Jackson standing beside Midnight, reins held loosely in his gloved hand.

Devon had been robbed of speech, and could only nod.

Jackson hobbled his horse and walked over to Firefly, taking the reins from Devon. "You plan on sitting there all day?" he teased and then stepped back so the young man could dismount. Once his lover's feet had safely touched the ground, Jackson led Firefly over to where Midnight was standing, and then joined his stunned instructor once again. "You have your bridge in the park and I have my mountain lake," he said as he slid his arms around Devon's waist from behind.

It was like stepping into another world, Jackson's special place was. Devon had never seen anything like it. The sheer magnitude of the area was enough to humble him, but this - what he was seeing now - was so much more. His heart swelled from the simple fact that Jackson was sharing this with him, just as he had shared his special place with his artist. As he stood in his lover's embrace, he thanked his lucky stars that this man had dialed his number by mistake.

"It's so much more than beautiful," Devon whispered into the silence that had settled around them once again. "If there is such a thing."

Jackson knew there was, because at the moment, it was standing in the circle of his arms, reacting the same way Jackson had when he first found this spot. When he was looking at different places to buy, the realtor had mentioned a lake, but he was thinking along the lines of something small, a watering hole for the horses. When he stumbled upon this piece of Heaven on earth, he knew he had found his home.

"Come on," Jackson said as he loosened his arms and took Devon's hand in his. "There's more."

Devon wasn't sure if he could handle 'more'. This was almost too much, as it was. They walked side by side, their gloved hands clasped together as best as they could with the extra bulk, skirting the water's edge. Jackson pointed out several sets of tracks that ran between the lake and the forest as they went; raccoon, deer, and surprise was evident on Devon's face when Jackson showed him a set of tracks that belonged to a mountain lion.

"He hasn't bothered the horses in quite awhile, so I'm guessing that he took the hint he wasn't welcome when I peppered his ass with buck-shot one evening," the older man conveyed.

"How big was he?"

"Big. Probably weighed somewhere between one-twenty, one-thirty. I hated that I had to do what I did, but it was either that, or say goodbye to one of my prized possessions, and that was not an option," Jackson explained. "I've seen his tracks in different places, claw marks on the trees, so I know he wasn't fatally wounded. Probably pissed off as hell, but he's not dead."

Devon's sienna gaze drifted to the tree line.

"Don't worry, the horses will let us know if he gets near," he offered and watched as his lover looked over their shoulder at their so-called alarm.

Both horses were huddled together, apparently sharing their warmth and Devon wondered if they were paying attention. He really hoped he wasn't about to become some hungry mountain lion's meal.

Jackson leaned forward and quickly kissed Devon's cold nose before pulling his lover's cap down over his eyes. "Now no peeking. I want this to be a surprise," he said and earned a huff from the young man.

"Oh come on," he groused as he tried to pull the hat back up so he could see. "What's so special that I can't see just yet?"

Jackson slapped Devon's hand away and pulled the hat back down over his eyes. "Stop acting like a baby and trust me," he said as he took his lover's hand and slowly led him a few more feet. "Okay, now there's a small step up, and then you'll be back on solid ground again."

The instructor took a tentative step with his left booted foot, and when it connected with whatever it was he had found, he stepped up with the other. Jackson was by his side, a strong arm wrapped around his shoulder, leading him to where ever it was they were going. He had a brief moment of panic when Jackson let go of him, but then his lover was standing behind him, both arms wrapped possessively around his waist.

"Okay, now you can look," his crazy artist whispered.

Devon slowly pulled the tan hat from his head, his chestnut curls in wild disarray, and gasped. They were standing on a pier that jutted out from the bank, placing them about thirty yards out over the clear water.

"This is my special place," Jackson said and Devon smiled at the pride in his lover's voice. "I can sit here for hours on end, just enjoying the solitude. Sometimes I bring my camera, snap a few pictures here and there, or sit here and sketch."

"It's amazing," the young man said with a smile as he looked over the edge. "You can see the bottom."

Jackson moved to stand beside him. "Yeah. I've got large-mouth bass, crappie, perch, and catfish in there; although I'm sure they're hiding in the deeper water in the center, where it's not so cold. When it warms up, we'll have to do some fishing."

Warmth suffused Devon's body at Jackson's mention of him being here again. It still gave him a small thrill to know that they were together, and that they would take every opportunity they could in order to spend time together.

"Deal," Devon said with a smile as he looked out over the water, memorizing every little thing. "I can't get over how peaceful it is here. No wonder you decided to buy this place."

A quick tug on Devon's hand brought his attention back to the man beside him. "Come here," the artist said as he led them to the extra wide, weather-beaten Adirondack chair that was on the finger pier. Jackson sat first and pulled Devon down onto his lap.

Devon quickly made himself comfortable by sliding his arm behind Jackson's neck and resting it on the man's shoulders, his legs wedged firmly between the artist's own, their temples touching.

"When I got back from my trip out to see you," Jackson said softly, "I can't tell you how many times I found myself here, thinking about you, about us, about our future. Every time I became restless because I hadn't heard from you, I would saddle up one of the horses and ride out here. Actually, there were a few times I rode bareback, not bothering with the extra time it took to dress one of them. I needed to get out here quick, or I would go mad," he admitted.

"I'm sorry it took so long," Devon offered.

"You're here now and that's all that matters," Jackson said as he turned to capture the enticing lips with his own.

When they finally separated, Devon looked out over the lake. "I wish I could stay here forever," he said wistfully. "There are several beautiful lakes in the valleys outside of Salt Lake City, but they are nothing compared to this."

Jackson wanted to tell the young man in his arms that he never had to leave, if he didn't want to; that he wouldn't mind one bit if he didn't so they could live out the rest of their days together. But he held his tongue, not wanting to jump too far ahead. There was still so much out there, in the real world, they had yet to tackle.

He had briefly entertained the idea of flying the two of them to New York to ring in the New Year, maybe get a suite at one of the hotels and watch the ball drop from their balcony, and then make love the rest of the night. But the idea of all those people, in one place at the same time, made Jackson's skin crawl. No, better ease his lover's way into the limelight and start small, like his exhibition in February. After that, it was anybody's guess.

A movement in Jackson's peripheral vision caught his attention. "Look to the right, about fifty yards or so down the bank," he whispered.

Devon's eyes widened when he spotted what Jackson was referring to. A large bull elk had slipped from the safety of the forest for a moment to take a quick drink.

"Oh my god," the young man whispered. "Jackson, he's huge! What else do you have living on your land?"

"Turkey, deer. I haven't seen a bear yet. Not sure if that's a good thing or not," he said with a teasing glint in his eye.

"I'd say it's a damn good thing if you haven't seen one. They're worse than mountain lions."

Jackson chuckled. "During the spring and summer evenings, we'll be able to sit here and watch the heard of deer come down to drink. Last summer I counted fifty-seven of them."

Devon leaned up and looked at his lover. "You're serious. Fifty-seven deer? How in the world did you count fifty-seven deer?"

"One, two, three," Jackson counted, which earned him a smack to the side of his head.

"You're not funny," the young instructor imparted.

Jackson reached up and rubbed the spot that Devon had just cuffed. "You left yourself wide open for that."

"I'd rather be wide open for something else," Devon whispered against the shell of Jackson's ear, the tip of his tongue teasing the sensitive skin as he pressed himself harder into his lover's lap.

"Stop that or I'll rip your clothes clean off of you right here," Jackson said as he ducked his head in an attempt to dodge the persistent tongue.

Devon's lips captured the fleshy lobe and he sucked gently for a few seconds. He nearly fell out of Jackson's lap when two very demanding hands lay siege to his jacket. When it was unbuttoned, they started on his shirt.

"Jackson, don't!" Devon shouted into the quite afternoon as he fought the searching hands and scrambled to get away. He managed to escape Jackson's clutches long enough to stand and move a few steps away. "Are you crazy? It's freezing out here!"

The smile playing on Jackson's lips worried Devon. "I'm going to give you until the count of three, my little snow bunny, and if you're still within reach, you're fair game. What the hell, you're fair game no matter what. One," he said as he slowly stood from the chair and watched his lover's eyes widen. "Two," he taunted and Devon had taken off, running like the hounds of hell were nipping at his heels. His booted feet took him to the end of the pier in a matter of seconds, and then he stopped, which was where he made his mistake. "Three!" Jackson shouted and took off after him.

Devon was surprised to find the man as fast as he was, considering his age. But then again, Jackson was in excellent shape, so maybe it shouldn't have been that much of a surprise. He looked over his shoulder as he raced towards the horses and found his lover gaining on him. As he ran, he wondered if their hasty arrival would cause the horses to bolt, leaving them without a way back. He made a snap-decision and slowed just a bit, and a few seconds later found himself hurtling towards the ground, encircled by a pair of strong arms.

Jackson quickly turned them so he would absorb the impact of the fall, and they both landed with a thud on the cold ground, the air knocked from their bodies. The men lay there, Devon looking up at the cloudless sky, Jackson looking at the back of Devon's head. It took a few seconds, but their bodies remembered that they needed to breathe, and then Jackson tightened his hold on Devon.

"Look what I caught," he said with a smile as he wrapped his legs around Devon's. "My own little snow bunny."

Devon mock-struggled. "Keep calling me that, Cowboy, and you and I are going to have problems," Devon warned.

Jackson stuck his index finger in his mouth and tugged the glove from his hand. "Seems to me you're the one who's going to have a problem," Jackson said as his hand slid down the writhing body, not stopping until he found what he was looking for. Deft fingers made quick work of the five buttons of Devon's Levis, and stroked his lover's arousal through two additional layers of clothing.

"Damn long johns," he grumbled as he felt for warm skin. Once that had been found, he plunged his hand beneath the elastic waistbands until his fingers encountered the silken flesh they were searching for.

Devon canted his hips, pressing his growing shaft into the circle of his lover's hand. "Dammit, Jackson. It's freezing out here and you're ... ohhhh fuck, that feels good," he said as his lover stroked him quickly.

"Come for me, baby, and I'll let you go," Jackson said into the mass of curls that were covering his face. "We're in the middle of nowhere; I've got my hand in your pants, stroking you just the way I know you like it," he said as his hand continued its pace. "I know how you like me to squeeze right beneath the head, and then twist," he said and did just that, earning a long moan from the man who was lying atop him. "That's right. Give me what I want, baby. I want to hear you scream my name. There's nobody here to hear you, just the two of us."

"Ohhh, God ... so fucking good," he panted as he was pushed to the edge by his lover's masterful strokes. He felt Jackson's own hardness pressing against the cleft of his ass, and wanted nothing more than to take the other man deep inside his body. Later, he promised himself; when they were back at home.

Home.

The word wrapped itself around Devon and he screamed his release to the heavens. "JAXXXX … oh … yeahhhhhh … AAAHHHHHHHH!"

Jackson's hand was covered with Devon's release a few seconds later. He held the panting young man through the aftershocks, crooning soothing words to him. When he felt Devon's breathing even out again, he finally let him go.

The sated young man sat up and looked at the mess on his shirt. "Look at the mess you made," he said with a grin.

"Not my fault you're young and can't hold out," Jackson said as he wiped his hand on Devon's shirt.

"Evil bastard!" he exclaimed. When Jackson pulled his hand away, there was a perfect imprint of all five fingers. Sienna orbs met icy blue. "You're doing the laundry, I hope you know," he said as he got to his knees and righted himself.

Jackson braced himself on his elbows. "Nope. When we get home, I'm doing *you*," he informed his lover. "The laundry can wait. I can't."

WHEN they returned to the barn, Devon cared for Firefly as if he were his own, removing all of the gear and stowing it in its proper places, and then gave him a thorough brushing.

As Jackson watched this, an idea took hold in his mind and he planned to make a phone call to a friend of his as soon as he could slip away.

CHAPTER EIGHTEEN

CHRISTMAS morning found Devon and Jackson sitting quietly in front of the fire, steaming cups of coffee in hand. Devon had opted for the corner of the couch and Jackson had no problem with propping himself back against the warm body, smiling as a lightly muscled arm wrapped around his chest.

"This is nice," Devon said as he watched the flames licking their way over the logs in the grate.

"Know what would be even nicer?" Jackson said as he kissed the bicep that was a few inches away.

"We go back upstairs and you make love to me again."

"Later," Jackson promised as he slid from his lover's embrace. "Right now I want you to open your gift," he said as he set his coffee mug on the side table and disappeared into the study.

Devon's eyes widened when Jackson returned carrying a large, and from the way he was holding it, heavy box. After setting it on the coffee table, Jackson rejoined him on the couch.

"Merry Christmas," he said with a grin.

Sienna eyes darted between the gift and his lover. "You're joking, right?" he asked and watched as Jackson shook his head.

"Nope. It's all yours." He propped his feet up on the end of the low table and waited.

"Hang on. I want you to open yours as well," Devon said and jumped from the couch to rummage through the various gifts beneath the tree to find the one he had hidden the day before. He found the flat box he was searching for and handed it to the older man. "Here, you open yours first. Age before beauty," he quipped as he took his seat again.

Jackson hadn't realized Devon had brought anything and guessed he must have hidden it when he was outside at some point. The box was heavy, maybe a couple of pounds, and he wondered what it was. He methodically unwrapped the gift, taking care not to tear the paper. He liked to savor every moment, but even more so now because it was from the man who held his heart.

Devon sat next to him, his thumb firmly wedged between two rows of gleaming white teeth, his nerves on edge as he watched the gift being unwrapped.

The artist's eyes widened as his paint-stained fingers caressed the oiled beechwood box, noting the leather handle and brass fittings. He lifted the lid and to find a multitude of drawing and sketching materials housed within: pastel pencils, charcoal pencils, graphite, drawing leads, charcoal, erasers, and a sketch pad.

"I wasn't sure what sure what medium you used when painting, so decided to play it safe and get you something for sketching," Devon said quietly.

Jackson felt the curious prickling at the back of his throat, and fought to hold the threatening tears at bay. "It's beautiful," he whispered, not trusting his voice at that moment. "No one has ever given me such a thoughtful gift. Thank you," he said as he leaned over and brushed his lips against Devon's. "I love it." *And I love you* was on the tip of his tongue as well, but he held the words back for fear that the young man wasn't ready to hear them just yet.

Devon visibly sighed with relief. "I'm glad you like it, because for a minute there I was worried," he admitted.

"I'm sorry. It just touched me in a way that no other gift ever has," he admitted as he sat back and looked over the contents. Even when he and Greg were together, he always received the standard cologne or shirt, nothing as thoughtful as this. "How did you know what to get?"

"Went to an art store and asked," the instructor said with a shrug. "The lady there said that this set was a nice combination of everything someone needed for sketching, so I bought it."

"She was right. I just hope you don't get tired of sitting for me now because I plan on putting this to good use in the near future," he informed the beautiful man. "Okay, now it's your turn." He pointed to the gift on the table. "Knock yourself out."

Devon was not as meticulous as Jackson was and in a matter of seconds, the area around them was littered with scraps of wrapping paper, which caused Jackson to laugh.

"Just like a kid," he teased which earned him a peek at the delicious tongue that drove him crazy.

Devon turned back to the box and his eyes widened when he lifted the lid. A beautiful blanket woven in an intricate southwestern design in shades of brown was folded neatly on top. His breath caught in his throat when he lifted the blanket.

"Jackson," he whispered as he stared at the gift. "I … oh my God!"

The artist rose from his place on the couch and hoisted the saddle from the box. "Merry Christmas, baby," he said as he leaned over and kissed Devon once again before moving the box and setting the gift on the coffee table.

Devon was speechless. The gift was so unexpected, so overwhelming that all he could do was stare at it.

"It's not gonna do any tricks, so you can blink," Jackson teased when he saw his lover's reaction.

The young man quickly did so and slowly reached out to touch it, making sure it was real. "It's beautiful," he said as he trailed his fingers over the hand-tooled leather.

"It's similar to the one you used when we went riding a few days ago," Jackson offered. "It's called an endurance saddle, and the biggest difference between that and a regular western saddle is that this one is smaller, lighter, essentially easier on the horse. The stirrups hang underneath the rider instead of forward, like other saddles, which makes it more comfortable when you travel over long distances. And it doesn't put as much of a strain on the horse's shoulders because of their positioning."

Jackson's words were lost as Devon reverently caressed the supple leather, cool and slick beneath his fingers. Silver lacing trimmed the light tan seat and pommel, and then his gaze landed on the leather tie strap holder and he smiled.

"A snowboarder?" he queried and earned a grin from Jackson. "Crazy artist," he said affectionately as he fingered the small piece of leather. "Jackson, this is ... I have no words to explain how I feel right now."

"Welcome to my world," the older man said as he ran his fingers over the wooden box sitting beside him. "However, that's not all." Jackson reached back into the box and pulled out an envelope, handing it to Devon.

"The saddle is more than enough, Jackson," Devon said as he opened the envelope. Tears gathered in his eyes as he read its contents. He looked up at his lover. "I ... I can't...." he whispered as the emotions running though him at the moment threatened to steal his voice. Sienna eyes went back to the papers he was holding. Transfer of Ownership papers. Jackson was giving Firefly to him.

"Yes, you can," Jackson said as he slid his fingers into Devon's curls, cupping the skull gently. "I've watched you with him and I'd say you two are a perfect match."

Devon was speechless. Finding Jackson had been a gift in itself, but to have his lover turn around and do something like this was more than he had ever imagined possible. He looked up from the paper into the sky blue eyes and smiled. "Thank you," he whispered and then he was being gathered into strong arms, an embrace he never wanted to end.

"That's more like it," Jackson said as he held the man who held his heart. "How about we get dressed and go for a ride?"

"Can we go to the lake?" Devon asked, hopefully.

"We can go anywhere you'd like."

Reluctantly Devon pulled away. "Then we're off to the lake," he said before leaning forward and brushing his lips against

Jackson's. "And when we get back, I'll thank you properly because if I do it now, we'll never leave the bedroom."

"Promise?" Jackson queried as Devon moved away from him and stood.

"Cross my heart," Devon said before heading up the stairs and disappearing into the bedroom with Jackson following.

LATER that evening, Devon sat quietly by the fire, his eyes closed, arms wrapped around his drawn-up knees, feet planted firmly on the worn, braided rug, listening to the sounds around him. The combination of the fire crackling, the cold, winter wind lashing at the windows, and the soft scratching sound of a pencil moving across paper had lulled him into a trance-like state.

In his mind's eye, he pictured the two of them living together in this beautiful place that he suspected was the closest thing to Heaven on earth, not counting being wrapped in his lover's embrace. He wanted a life with this man, his crazy cowboy-artist who had entered his life like a fresh spring rain, washing away the traces of winter that had surrounded his heart.

Devon knew he was in love with the man, and the thought of leaving caused his heart to ache. He never wanted to leave, never wanted to be separated from his other half, because that was precisely what Jackson was - the other half he had been missing, whether he realized it or not.

A warm finger brushing over his cheek startled him momentarily, and he opened his eyes to find his lover kneeling beside him, concern etched in his features.

"Baby, what's wrong?" Jackson asked quietly as he lovingly stroked the soft skin, brushing away a stray tear that had fallen, unbeknownst to Devon.

The young man blinked several times and realized that he had been so lost in his thoughts he didn't know that he was crying.

"Nothing," Devon said as he reached up and wiped at his eyes with the back of his hand. "I was just sitting here and things kind of hit me all at once," he admitted and when he saw the alarm on Jackson's face, he rushed on. "No, Jax, it's nothing bad, well, in a way it is because I'll have to leave eventually, but I was thinking about us, and how we came to be together and everything that we've gone through to get to where we are today. You didn't give up on me when you could have, and for that I'll always be thankful," he said as he leaned into Jackson's touch.

Jackson's knees protested the strain of squatting down so he slowly lowered himself onto the rug beside Devon, sitting so that they were facing each other.

"You don't have to thank me for that. I told you to take all the time you needed to be sure you wanted a life with me," he offered as he reached up and brushed several curls away from the beautiful face.

"I know, it's just that, now, looking back, I knew in my heart I wanted to be with you, and I'm so sorry for putting you through the hell I did," he said with a voice that was almost a whisper.

Strong arms wrapped around Devon, pulling the young man closer. "That's in the past, Devon. You're here with me now."

"And I wish I could stay here forever and never go back," Devon admitted.

"I wish that as well. I would love to see your beautiful smile before I close my eyes each night and when I open them again the next morning," the older man whispered against the dark hair.

A slow warmth suffused Devon's body from his lover's words, and his stomach felt as if the butterflies he had before their initial meeting two months ago, were back. He pulled away from Jackson for a moment and studied the blue-gray eyes of his lover, his heart thundering in his chest.

There, in the quiet evening, he finally gave voice to his true feelings.

"I love you," he said with a tremulous smile.

Jackson's fingers slid into the riot of chestnut curls and gazed at his lover. "You don't know how happy you just made me," he said with a small smile before leaning forward and capturing the alluring lips with a kiss that reinforced the bond that had grown between them. It was slow, passionate, and thorough, leaving no doubt in either man's mind how the other truly felt. When they finally separated, Jackson returned Devon's sentiment.

"I love you, too. For now and always," he vowed.

LATER that night, as snowflakes danced outside their window, swirling and dipping, finally landing with their partners, Devon slid into the velvet heat of his lover and he knew he had truly found his haven, the other part of his soul. Tears were shed as they moved together, tears of happiness and joy, and when they reached their completion sometime later, their hearts were filled with the love they felt for one another.

It was a moment in time they would never forget.

EPILOGUE

IT was a difficult road they traveled, but one that both men agreed was worth it, in spite of the curves that life threw them.

Devon was by Jackson's side for the Venice Beach exhibition and had survived the media circus that surrounded the event relatively unscathed. There had been a few uncomfortable moments early on, but Jackson had stepped in and handled the press with ease, answering their questions with a genuine smile. Yes, he and Devon were in a committed relationship and yes, they understood how difficult it would be when his job put hundreds, if not thousands of miles between them. It was like he had said to Devon once before, "If you have to work at it to make it work, it's worth it."

Several months later, Jackson was by Devon's side when a friend of his was attacked one night outside of a club in Salt Lake City. A hate crime, the police had said. It was a gay bashing, plain and simple, as far as the gay community was concerned and the incident left Devon shaking for hours on end.

That night, wrapped in Jackson's embrace, Devon made a decision.

"I don't want to be here any more," he whispered into the darkness. "I want us to be together, Jackson. I want to fall asleep every night in your arms, to wake up each morning knowing that you'll be there. I want to go to the lake each evening and watch the sun set. I want to make love beneath the stars."

It was the one thing Jackson had always hoped for but had never asked. He knew it had to be Devon's decision, just as he had left the fate of their relationship in Devon's hands, all those months ago.

"What about your jobs? Your friends?" Jackson asked.

"My friends will be harder to leave than my jobs. Well, the job at the resort, anyway. The other I was thinking about quitting anyway. It's not the type of atmosphere I want to be a part of. And Tyler can come for a visit every now and then, and vice-versa. Bozeman is a half-hour away from Livingston, and they have a couple of ski lodges that might need a ski or snowboarding instructor next season."

"So what will you do until then?"

"Guess I'll just have to swallow my pride and become a 'kept man'," he said with a smile.

Jackson pressed a kiss to Devon's temple. "I think that can be arranged. When do you want to leave?"

"Is tomorrow too soon?"

"No, babe. Tomorrow sounds perfect."

Shay Kincaid calls herself a dreamer; her husband and two children call her crazy, although they are smiling when they do so.

Born and raised in Southeast Texas, a young Shay would do anything and everything she could to avoid reading, until her senior year in high school where her English teacher introduced her to *The Mists of Avalon*. It was then she learned that there was a huge difference between reading because she had to, and reading because she wanted to.

Romance novels and action-adventure stories were her genres of choice until 2001 when she discovered 'fan fiction' dedicated to one of her favorite actors at the time. After dabbling in that arena for a year or so, as both an avid reader and writer, she was introduced to what she now calls 'home', also known as romantic erotic fiction.

Shay hasn't looked back since.

http://www.shaykincaid.com/

TAKE MY PICTURE

Giselle Ellis

5 YEARS AGO....

AARON was waiting in a hallway outside an apartment in Manhattan's Upper Eastside. He had no idea how he'd gotten there, but there he was. He was waiting to be ushered inside with a string of other guys to see who would be chosen to be some photographer's next model for his new series. Aaron had no idea who the guy was, some weird last name, but that didn't stop him from waiting in line. He needed to eat just as much as the next guy.

Since moving from London to New York three months ago, he had basically taken any job he could find that would supplement his income and allow him some time to go on auditions and to sculpt or to throw an occasional pot on the wheel at the community school near his dreary flat, or apartment. Whatever.

This gig should be easy. In the door to stand around in odd poses and then out again. Two hundred dollars was two hundred dollars. He imagined he'd have to put up with a temperamental arsehole photographer, some diva who was probably extremely famous judging from the swank hallway he was standing in at the moment. Fuck, he'd rather live in this hallway than in his own apartment. There was lovely soft carpet on the floor and it was blessedly cool, a far cry from his sixth floor walk-up with nothing but a rotating fan to move the putrid, humid air from his solitary window through his solitary room.

This place was fucking posh; if the hallways were this nice, he could only imagine what the inside of the bloody apartment looked like.

"You can come in now," a soft voice came from the now

open door.

As Aaron followed the line of guys ahead of him and walked through the doorway, he looked at the person belonging to the soft voice. She was nearly as tall as him with dark hair and pale skin. She was quite lovely and he noticed several of the others taking a quick peek as they walked by her.

"Thanks for coming. My name is Alyson and if I can get you anything to drink or eat while you wait, just give me a holler. Jake should be ready to see you soon."

Aaron looked around and noticed no one was taking her up on her offer. Fuck, he hadn't eaten all morning. He'd have loved to have a go at whatever food the bird was offering, but since no one moved, he didn't want to act a ponce and be the only one asking for something. He frowned as he looked around some more, willing anyone to speak up and ask for something. Shit, they'd probably get champagne and caviar, or some smelly arse cheese at least, by the looks of this place. Though food was fucking food, now wasn't it?

Dammit.

Aaron was shifting from foot to foot as he crossed his arms and began to put a pout on when the other door leading into the room they were in opened and some kid walked through the door. Must be the diva's son from the looks of him, he thought, couldn't be much more than twenty-one, twenty-two.

"Jake, these are…." began Alyson before she was abruptly cut off by the kid's, "Yeah, okay."

He started walking quickly past the row of guys just standing there with their thumbs up their bums until he came to Aaron.

"That one. I want that one," he said abruptly before turning and walking quickly back through the door through which he had entered.

Okay then.

"Well," said Alyson as she cleared her throat, "I guess that takes care of that. Thank you for coming, gentlemen."

Aaron watched as she efficiently herded the lot of them to

the door while deftly ignoring their complaints and protests of time wasted, and from those to the right of Aaron, of not even being looked at.

Once they were all gone and only Aaron was left, she turned back to him and said, "If you'll follow me, please?"

"Hold on a tic. What's up with all this? I mean, some kid wanders in and points at me in like ten seconds and I'm supposed to go into the lair blindly? Jesus, you two could be fucking serial killers for all I know."

Alyson laughed, "I'm so sorry. I'm just used to him, I guess, his abruptness doesn't even faze me any more. You'll get used to it."

"I don't think I'll be staying around long enough to get used to anything, much less some weirdo."

Alyson just smiled, "We'll see."

"No, I don't think we will," said Aaron, turning to leave, "thanks for the ... well, whatever the fuck this was. It's been ... unusual."

"Wait," she said as she reached out to grab Aaron's wrist. "He really does just want to take your picture. Nothing odd, unless you consider his style odd ... which it isn't," she hastened to inform him, "he just knows what he wants. He doesn't waste time. Give it a chance. Where else are you going to get a couple hundred dollars on such short notice?"

"Without dropping my trousers?" asked Aaron with a raised eyebrow. "Nowhere."

Alyson laughed again and gave his wrist a gentle tug. "Come on, if nothing else you can brag to all your friends in a few months that you're part of Jake's newest exhibition. You'll be the talk of Manhattan."

"Yeah," began Aaron with a scowl, "what parts of me will he be exhibiting? Because I like all of my parts, you know ... I wouldn't want to be parted with any of my parts. Truly."

"He's not a serial killer," insisted Alyson with a grin.

"All serial killers say they're not serial killers. Do you

think he's going to wear a badge that says, *Hello, My Name is Psychotic Serial Killer of Young and Very Poor Men*? That's bad serial killer form, you know."

"Okay, fine," sighed Alyson, "let's put it this way, if you don't get your cute little ass in there in about another thirty seconds, he's going to chew my equally cute little ass out for not bringing you in to him. How's that?"

"What the fuck? Does he think he's the sultan or whatnot? Like I'm to be brought forth? Tell him to piss off."

"Come on," pleaded Alyson, "think of my cute little ass. Take one for the ass."

"Now if you said, '*take one up the ass*,' I'd be a bit more willing."

Alyson threw her head back and laughed, "Oh, he's going to love you."

"Yeah, love to *kill* me," muttered Aaron, following her through the door that Jake had disappeared through.

Aaron's mouth dropped open when he entered the "room;" it was more like a huge open loft ... no walls, huge floor to ceiling windows, shiny hardwood floors ... perfect for a studio. He had no idea how Jake had acquired such a huge space in Manhattan.

As if reading his mind, Alyson leaned over and whispered, "He bought the place next door and tore down the walls."

"Perfect," replied Aaron, "and did he happen to find a treasure chest hidden in one of the walls as well?"

"What do you mean?"

"I mean, how the holy hell does he afford this place? He looks like he's twelve."

"He's twenty-two, and he happens to be quite successful."

"At twenty-fucking-two?"

"He was born with talent?" Alyson said questioningly.

"He's a lucky wanker who blew the right people?" suggested Aaron.

Alyson tried to scowl but grinned instead, "A child

prodigy?"

"A deal with the devil?"

"Naturally gifted?"

"An indulgent sugar daddy?"

"How about '*c) All of the above*'?" asked a third voice from behind the partition at the far corner of the studio.

"Does your sugar daddy mind when you interrupt conversations like that?" asked Aaron.

"Does yours like it when you talk shit about people in their own home?" asked Jake as he came out from behind the partition.

"Kind of, yeah, he likes my filthy dirty mouth."

"Oh, so he's one of those?" asked Jake, raising an eyebrow.

"One of who?"

"One of the kinky old bastards that ask you to talk dirty to them, call them *Daddy*, give you spankings…."

"Nothing wrong with the occasional spanking … or daddy issues."

"I doubt your friendly neighborhood psychiatrist would agree with you."

"My friendly neighborhood psychiatrist was my friendly neighborhood spanking daddy-issues sugar daddy."

"Figures."

Alyson was staring at them as they went back and forth like a tennis match.

"Yep, it does," said Aaron happily as he began to wander around the room touching and picking things up.

"Don't touch my stuff."

"Sharing issues?" asked Aaron absently, picking up yet another thing.

"No, breaking issues."

"So you better make sure not to drop anything then."

Jake frowned.

Alyson grinned.

"Where do you want me, Ansel? Naked? On all fours? Ready to get spanked?"

"Do you ever stop being annoying and irritating?" asked Jake. "You're like a herpes outbreak."

"Know a lot about that, do you?" asked Aaron, pushing buttons on the camera he was holding.

"Would you stop!?" Jake practically yelled as he charged over to Aaron and grabbed the camera from his hands.

"Sharing issues," he mouthed in Alyson's direction, who put her hand up to her mouth to hide her smile when Jake turned an angry face on her.

"You know, you can stop laughing at him any time, Aly."

"What?" asked Alyson as she shrugged. "*You* picked him."

"In an obvious fit of insanity."

"Obviously," she agreed with a knowing look.

Jake pulled a face at her.

"Come on, Mozart, what do you want me to do?"

"Mozart?" Jake and Alyson asked at the same time.

"Child prodigy...?" supplied Aaron helpfully.

"Your brain works in mysterious ways, doesn't it?" asked Jake.

"You'll never be able to fathom the deep recesses of my mind."

"Do I really want to? I have a feeling the fathoms of your recesses would make me cry."

"My recesses have been known to make grown men cry," said Aaron agreeably, picking up a different camera.

"God, you really are annoying."

"Yeah, lucky for you, huh?"

"Are you high? Because if you're high, I don't want any part of you."

"See!" Aaron hollered at Alyson who jumped at the sudden outburst, "He *does* want my parts! What did I tell you? Serial killer!"

"Look at his pupils," Jake directed at Alyson, "and tell me if they're dilated or not."

"You two are idiots," said Alyson as she started to walk away.

"You're leaving me alone with him!" Aaron and Jake demanded at the same time.

"You picked him," she directed at Jake, "and you followed me in here," she said to Aaron, "enjoy each other."

"Dammit, Alyson," shouted Jake, "I told you that you could quit, but he hasn't even agreed yet so don't you dare walk out of here just yet."

"What is she quitting and what am I agreeing to?" asked Aaron.

"Alyson wants to quit being my assistant to get married and have babies or some shit like that. Honestly, marriage," Jake all but shuddered, "and you're going to agree to take her place so she can go breed."

"Gee, thanks, Jacob, I love it when you compare me to a dog."

"Well, if I'm comparing you to a dog and you're breeding, then obviously you're a pedigree, right? A perfectly perfect specimen."

"Yes, a perfectly perfect specimen. Of. A. Dog."

"Don't go all girly on me now, Aly."

"I wouldn't dream of it, you asshole."

"There's my girl back."

"You're making a real solid case on your behalf, acting like your lovely and charming self in front of the newbie. He already thinks you're a serial killer."

"Yes, well, I've found people can put up with a lot of shit, including serial killer behavior, if they're paid enough."

"Um, excuse me," interrupted Aaron, "I'm not fucking working for you so I think this little conversation is over. Thanks for the brief moment of mildly disturbing entertainment, but I'm out of here."

"Wait," said Jake as he stood between Aaron and the door, "you wouldn't be here if you weren't short on cash. Desperate, maybe?"

"I happen to *like* posing for pictures in the homes of strange men. This is a typical Tuesday for me, I'll have you know."

"Whatever. I'm sure I can pay you a hell of a lot more than whatever it is you're making now doing whatever the hell it is you're doing, which with all the talk of sugar daddies and spankings is probably prostitution or S&M work."

"So," said Aaron, "I'm to believe you want a person who you think is a master of pain, or Julia Roberts, to be your assistant after looking at him for about a half second in a line of wanks in your living room?"

"Yes."

Aaron shrugged, "Okay, then. I'm in."

Alyson mimicked a blessing as she moved her hand in the shape of a cross in front of Aaron and said, "God be with you, my son."

"I'm not that bad," said Jake, pushing Alyson's hand out of Aaron's face.

"He really is," said Alyson as she walked over to a desk and pulled open the top right drawer. "I'll give you my holy water. Just splash some on him and chant *'the power of Christ compels you'* and he should either stop or start smoking - either way, he stops."

"Does he spit pea soup, too?" Aaron asked eagerly, "Because that would be fucking awesome. And gross. But more awesome."

Alyson rolled her eyes, "You two are perfect for each other. He's an emotionally retarded asshole," she said, tipping her head toward Jake, "and you're clearly insane and find emotionally retarded assholes amusing. This should work out smashingly."

"I thought he was the devil," said Aaron, scrunching up his face in confusion. "Emotionally retarded assholes general don't start smoking after being doused with holy water … they usually start smoking after fucking some random guy, then kicking him out of bed before the condom comes off."

"He has a point," said Jake as he gestured in Aaron's general direction.

"Yeah, I'm leaving now," said Alyson. "I'll be back to show Aaron the ropes. Or not. Maybe I'll just run far, far away."

"You couldn't leave me if you tried, Aly," said Jake confidently.

"Oh, that's right, I forgot. I'm madly in love with you. Leaving you and your 3 a.m. phone calls and demands for Ho-Ho's only from the market on the corner of 78th is a pain I'm not sure I can bear."

"He only likes Ho-Ho's from a particular market?" asked Aaron.

"Yes, along with a weird obsession with having me wait at the fucking crack of dawn every first Thursday of the month to get him that month's issue of *Field and Stream,* even though I suspect he's never been out of Manhattan, much less near a field or a stream."

"Yes, well, when our plane crashes in the woods and I save your ass from a bear and catch trout for you to eat instead of the dead pilot, you'll be appreciative of my *Field and Stream* obsession."

"Whatever, Jacob," said Alyson before turning to Aaron. "I'm running out for lunch, you want something?"

"Some trout sounds really good."

"What did I say … crazy!" exclaimed Alyson as she walked out the door.

"She'll be back," said Jake, wandering over to his cameras.

"I should hope so," replied Aaron. "I want my fish."

"She's not going to get you fish, you know. She'll more than likely get you the chicken salad sandwich I always get on Tuesdays from the deli down on the corner."

"You eat the same thing every Tuesday?"

"And Wednesday and Thursday and Friday … do you see a pattern?"

"I think you and your Ho-Ho's need to branch out more."

"And eat trout?"

"Maybe even bear."

"Yeah, uh-uh … I'm thinking no on the bear."

"You gotta live dangerously, Mozart, there are only so few days each year bear is in season, you know."

"When exactly is bear season?"

"How the hell should I know? You're the one who reads *Field and Stream,* for christsake."

"This conversation is going nowhere fast."

"It's not my fault you're a conversation killer."

"Is that in any way, shape or form like a serial killer?"

Aaron grinned, "A little, only with slightly less body parts in your freezer."

"That's good, because then there would be no room for the bear."

"Exactly."

PRESENT DAY....

"AARON!"

"What?"

"I'm out of film."

"Sucks to be you."

"Get me some more!"

"Hold on, I'm busy."

"Flip, I didn't get you that potter's wheel so you could fuck around on it when I need you," whined Jake.

"Flip? I thought his name was Aaron," said the guy waiting very patiently for Aaron to get up from his wheel and bring Jake more film.

"It is Aaron, I just call him Flip," answered Jake.

"Why?"

"Because he always flips me off when he should be kneeling before me waiting to do my bidding," replied Jake at the same time Aaron answered, "Because I flip his pompous ass off when he's being obnoxious and whiny."

"Oh, okay then...." the guy trailed off in confusion.

"Aaron, come on," said Jake, "could you at least *pretend* that you work for me and that I have actual control over your actions in said work environment?"

"I *could* do that, but it would throw our whole relationship off balance ... you giving orders, me actually listening ... just doesn't work, Jacob."

"One day you'll actually want to humor me."

"I'll be looking forward to it, babe."

Jake scowled as he walked over to a nearby table to change out the film in his camera. "I'm going to take your wheel away from you one day, young man."

"No, you won't," came Alyson's voice from the open door. "That wheel's here to stay, along with the dink attached to it."

"Love you too, Alyson," sang out Aaron, then, "Milo! My man! Come on over here and get dirty with Uncle Flip."

Alyson's son, Milo, raced by her legs yelling, "Unc Fip! I wan sum mud!"

"Aaron, don't you dare get him dirty. That's the first time he's worn that outfit," Alyson hollered as she walked in the room.

"He's a little boy. He's supposed to get dirty."

"Yes, well, not when he's on the way to meet Grandma who's the person who got him the outfit."

"Aw, Grammy Schmammy ... we're men and we do manly things and get full of manly dirt, don't we, Milo?" asked Aaron, wiping off his hands and grabbing Milo up to set him on his lap.

"Yes, you're very manly," said Jake, "what with all the pretty pots you're making over there. You're the manliest of the manly."

Aaron whispered something in Milo's ear who then yelled, "Unc Dake, you stink like farts!" before bursting into laughter.

Alyson tried not to laugh as she admonished, "Milo! That's not nice. You shouldn't tell people you stink and you should *never* listen to what your Uncle Flip tells you."

"Always say no to Uncle Flip," grinned Jake.

"Just like you do, huh?" Alyson muttered under her breath.

"I say no to him," Jake answered back in a whisper.

"So that's why you're over here putting film in your camera and he's over there getting my son into trouble at his *very* expensive potter's wheel, then?"

Jake tried to scowl at Alyson but his cheeks burst into flame, completely ruining the effect. Alyson just smiled and leaned over to kiss him on the temple, "You two will be so cute when you finally figure it out."

"Figure what out?" Jake asked in a huff.

"I have *no* idea!" Alyson said happily.

CHAPTER ONE

EVER since Aaron walked into Jake's apartment on a Tuesday in July, his world had been turned upside down and inside out. Aaron breezed in and took over.

Everything.

His space.

His things.

His peace of mind.

His life.

The next day, when the first thing Jake did upon walking into his studio was trip over Aaron's sneakers because Aaron liked to "*let my feet air and my toes roam free during the day*", he knew he was in for it. Gradually, day by day, more of Aaron snuck into Jake's life, from changing the CDs in his stereo, to a discarded t-shirt that mystified Jake since Aaron would have had to walk home topless without it, to a fridge full of weird British food concoctions and a cupboard full of tea.

Jake had no idea how it happened, but in a span of a few weeks, Aaron became his best friend as well as the person he most wanted to impress and please, which was an odd concept for him since he had never given a fucker's fuck before about what anyone thought or felt. But here was an obnoxious little Muppet who was *always* in the way, *always* loud, *always* opinionated and *always* annoying and yet Jake cared what he thought.

A lot.

It was fucking irritating and more than a little troubling. Troubling simply because if he were to choose a person whose opinion he'd value, it certainly wouldn't be a person who sang '*I'm too Sexy*' at the top of his lungs whenever Jake tried to photograph him … or ate bananas with a knife and fork after making Jake peel them for him because they "*taste yummy but feel icky and naughty*" … or laughed at the commercials for M&Ms.

So before Jake knew it he had a stereo filled with CDs that weren't his, a closet missing half his shirts because Aaron decided they looked better on him, and a potter's wheel and kiln in the corner of his studio that got the most light, because the thought of Aaron traipsing across his fucking dump of a neighborhood in the middle of the night to work on his pots because Jake kept him too busy during the day sent a stab of fear and worry through his gut so intense that only the purchase of said wheel and kiln could alleviate it. Alyson had been the first to see it, even before Aaron, and all she had done was stare at it, then at Jake, and back and forth until Jake had finally asked, 'What?' in exasperation.

"How much did all of that cost?"

"Does it really matter? It's not *your* money, now is it?"

"No, but I was just wondering why you'd spend this amount of money on someone who's an employee. Allegedly," she added with a smirk.

"Do you know where he lives? And he's skipping around like a Pollyanna in the middle of the night to go make ashtrays and kitty statues, or whatever the fuck he makes. He's going to get mugged … or killed, for christsake!"

Alyson just smiled.

Jake fumed.

At least he fumed until Aaron showed up and saw the wheel and kiln and started yelling and jumping around like an idiot.

Then Jake just smiled.

He smiled even more, although he *tried* his damnedest to scowl at Aaron's stupidity, when he insisted on calling the wheel

Wilbur and the kiln Charlotte.

"For the love of god, why must you give them names?"

"Why wouldn't I give them names?"

"Because they're a wheel and a kiln, not a trout and a bear."

"Why would I have a trout and a bear? Honestly, Jacob, you're ridiculous," answered Aaron happily as he fiddled with the settings on the kiln … no, correct that, on *Charlotte*.

"Why wouldn't you have a trout and a bear … you have a wheel named Wilbur and a kiln named Charlotte."

"Exactly."

"What does that even *mean*?" asked Jake in frustration.

"Exactly is a word, first of all," stated Aaron as Alyson grinned and Jake rolled his eyes. "It means precisely, often used to emphasize a point."

"I find it's a word often used to emphasize your psychosis."

Aaron shrugged and smiled.

Alyson stepped in and asked, "So I take it you like them, then?"

At her question, Jake suddenly uncrossed the arms he had crossed while trying to decipher the intricacies of Aaron-speak to push his hands into his back pockets and ask, with an uncharacteristic insecurity, "Do you? Like them, I mean … Wilbur and Charlotte?"

Aaron stopped toying with the kiln and looked at Jake and answered, with an uncharacteristic seriousness, "I love them. They're the best gifts I've ever gotten. Ever."

"Yeah?" Jake asked again as he pulled his right hand out of his back pocket and ran it through his hair.

"Yeah," said Aaron walking over to Jake and hugging him tight. At first, Jake stood there rigidly, his left hand still in his back pocket and his right tangled up in his hair, until he realized Aaron wasn't letting go any time soon. He gave up and awkwardly wrapped his arms around Aaron briefly as he patted his back, then let go.

Aaron had teased him about hugging like a dude. "Awwww, we were having a moment here and then you do the awkward guy-hug, you totally ruined the lovefest. Now, what could have been a Barbara Streisand '*misty water-colored memory*' is just an unremarkable dude moment."

Aaron had laughed and gone stumbling after Alyson to get some "*love from the willing*," leaving Jake standing with his arms hanging at his sides.

Although Aaron had declared it an "*unremarkable dude moment*", Jake remembered it down to the minute. Even now, nearly five years later, if anyone asked him when he had first touched Aaron, he could say with certainty, "10:37, Monday morning, August 22, 2001."

Exactly.

SIX months later, Aaron came to work over three hours late. Jake had prided himself that he only called Aaron's place six times and Alyson three times during those three hours. When the door opened, he was ready to chew Aaron a new one, but was instead tackled to the ground by a giant pile of mud and stink.

"Isn't he adorable?" asked Aaron.

"He fucking smells," whined Jake, trying to push an overly large, overly shaggy, overly slobbery dog off his chest.

"That's because I found him eating out of the dumpster in the alley next to my apartment," Aaron said cheerily, like it was a *good* thing.

"Get him off me!"

"Come here, Harold … come on, boy … come on, Harry!" Aaron hollered as he patted his thighs and whistled.

The dog licked Jake's face one last time before bounding over to Aaron at the sound of his voice.

"That's a goooood boy! That's a good Harold! Aren't you the best boy there is?!?!" Aaron cooed, letting the dog slobber all over him as he scratched him behind the ears.

"Harold? You named him Harold? What is it with you and

naming shit?"

"Yes, Harold ... Harry for short, and why *shouldn't* I name a dog?"

"We're not getting into this again...."

"It's not like he's a trout or a bear ... he's a *dog*, Jacob, dogs have names ... it's the law of the universe, give thy dog a name and it shall be good, or something like that."

"Okay, fine, whatever ... but he's not your dog ... and he probably already has a name."

"What am I supposed to do? Ask him what it is? Has a dog ever talked to you, Moz? In actual people-talk? In English? Because if one has, you need to up your meds."

Jake huffed, crossed his arms and glared ... which was all summarily ignored by Aaron so he said instead, "I'm just saying don't get too attached to him. He probably has an owner and you'll have to give him back and then you'll be sad and mopey, which is annoying and irritating for me."

"Yes, and you're *never* annoyed or irritated so those will be two new emotions for me to experience. I can hardly wait!"

Jake frowned and turned to walk away while mumbling, "I just don't want you to be sad."

Even though it was said under his breath, Aaron heard him and sprang up from the crouch he'd been in while playing with Harold to run over and hug Jake from behind. "Thanks ... ya big girl," he whispered and was gone.

Back to play with Harold.

Harry for short.

Jake stood still for a second before rubbing his neck and shaking himself out of his stillness. He walked over to his desk where he said in a louder, firmer voice, "Well, if that smelly-ass thing is going to spend another minute in here, you better wash it."

"He's not an it! He's a Harold!" said Aaron indignantly.

"Well, go wash Harold then ... Harold fucking reeks."

"Come on, Harry," whistled Aaron, walking toward Jake's bathroom.

"What the fuck do you think you're doing?"

"Washing him, you jackass, you know … that thing you told me to do about five seconds ago."

"Not in my bathroom!"

"Where, then? In the portable tub I carry around with me in my pocket in case of stinky Harry emergencies?"

"No. But not in my tub!" Jake whined some more.

"You're so cute when you think I'm going to listen to you," said Aaron as he pushed Harold through the bathroom door.

"I don't want fucking dumpster dog hair in my tub!"

"It's only your studio bathroom, it's not like you actually bathe in this one and besides, I'll clean the tub when I'm done … it's this magical concept that works wonders for keeping things shiny and bright."

"Bite me," Jake muttered from his desk.

"I'll have to be paid more for that!" yelled Aaron from inside the bathroom.

"Dammit! Are you fucking Spiderman with the hearing everything I say shit?" growled Jake.

"Ew! No! Spiderman's outfit … SO not cute!"

"Name one superhero that *does* have a cute outfit."

"Wonder Woman!"

Jake grinned and shook his head.

"Are you grinning out there?" hollered Aaron, "'Cos I can hear you grinning, too, I'll have you know."

"Wow! Kind of like how I can hear you pout," answered Jake.

There was a brief moment of silence before Aaron responded, "Did you hear that, too, cunt?"

"Yep, you're flipping me off again, aren't you?"

Jake chuckled when he heard a quiet "*dammit!*" come from the bathroom.

Later that day, when Harold was blessedly clean and non-smelly, Jake took his picture so Aaron could make 'Found' posters.

Jake insisted on printing his number on the posters so if anyone actually called about the damn dog, he could deal with them instead of Aaron … the man who had just found a piece of blue ribbon and tied it in a bow around Harold's neck … yep, right decision … definitely *his* number on the posters.

Every day for a week, Aaron showed up with a hopeful look on his face when he asked, "Anybody call?" And every day Jake was happy to report, "Nope, not a soul."

He never told Aaron that the owner had called on the third day and hung up five minutes later, with his next month's rent paid in full in exchange for Harold.

Jake considered it a fair exchange when he saw the look on Aaron's face on the day he bought a dog bed to put in the corner of the studio for Harold and said, "I think you can stop worrying now, I'm pretty sure the damn dog is yours."

Definitely a fair exchange.

AROUND the third month was when the first of the boyfriends showed up.

Boyfriend Number One: Michael.

Michael was beautiful and tall and funny and brilliant.

Michael was a doctor.

Michael would come over on his breaks or shift changes to see Aaron because he "missed his boy."

Michael worshipped the ground Aaron walked on.

Michael was perfect in every possible way.

Jake hated him.

The only redeeming quality he possessed, or the only one Jake was willing to concede him, was the fact that he obviously adored Aaron, but then he ruined that by making Aaron adore him in return.

Jake hated him.

He hated him until Aaron dumped him because he said he was "too perfect" and that the combination of Michael's perfectness and his own imperfect strangeness would cause some sort of tear in the time-space continuum and would end the world.

After that, Jake liked Michael.

Very much.

He wasn't such a bad guy really, quite nice actually.

Then came ... Boyfriend Number Two: Nate.

Nate was a surfer dude who had somehow ended up in New York. Jake asked him how he wound up there, but suspected he was sufficiently stoned that his answer of "Man ... I have NO fucking idea" was the best he could muster.

Jake was duly unimpressed.

He was even more unimpressed when Aaron started showing up late for work on a daily basis reeking of pot and sex with eyes at half mast.

He told Aaron that Nate was toxic and Aaron got predictably pissed at him.

It was not a pleasant month.

Every day Aaron came to work and hardly spoke more than two words to him made him sicker and sicker. When he didn't show up at all for three days, Jake stopped all pretense of carrying on with his life to sit by his phone day and night, willing Aaron to call and say he was sorry or that he was coming back to work.

Or just to say something at all.

On the fourth day without him, exhausted from sleepless nights and too much worrying, Jake fell asleep on the couch in his studio with the phone clenched in his hand. He only awoke when he felt a warm body pressed next to his and the weight of a curly brown head on his shoulder.

"You were right about him, Moz, he's bad news. I'm sorry," the head sighed.

Jake nodded to indicate he had heard him before his eyes slid shut again, content now and able to sleep the whole night through.

Neither one mentioned Nate again and he was soon forgotten, but Jake *always* remembered that Aaron came back.

Boyfriend Number Three: Chris

Chris was as American as apple pie.

And as boring.

Chris ran a bookstore and was as predictably dull as one would imagine a bookseller to be.

Jake imagined Aaron needed a dose of boredom to alleviate the chaos left behind in the wake of Nate. He knew poor Chris wouldn't last very long.

Which still didn't make Jake like him, not one little bit.

The Era of Chris was short-lived and completely unremarkable.

Boyfriend Number Four: Mikos

Mikos was Greek.

And looked like a god.

Paired with Aaron, they were a sight to behold. If Jake hadn't disliked the asshole so much, he would have insisted they pose together.

That, of course, did not happen.

Mikos had millions, which he never hesitated to spend on whatever Aaron wanted.

Or thought he wanted.

Or might think he'd want in the future.

Aaron said Mikos's father was one of those Greek tycoons who made money just by being Greek.

Jake told him Mikos was probably a drug dealer.

Aaron laughed and asked for a month off so Mikos could sail him around the world.

Jake said no, then asked who the fuck did he think he was, a pirate?

Aaron laughed again, then asked for two weeks off instead.

Jake didn't have an excuse for two weeks so he had to let him go.

Jake forgot how long fourteen days could be.

Mikos lasted a long time.

But suddenly, he was gone.

No explanation from Aaron as to what happened or where he went.

Jake didn't care enough to ask, he just knew he was gone.

After Mikos came Jamie, then Connor, then Riley, then Lawrence ... who Jake called Larry in an effort to annoy and irritate to which Aaron replied, "*Awww, Larry ... that's cute!*" Jake stopped calling him Larry.

There were also Ben, John and Paul.

Jake asked if Ringo was far behind.

Aaron assured him if there was a Ringo out there to be had, he'd find him just to please Jake. He said for him he'd fuck a Ringo.

Jake told him to eat shit which, as it always did, only made Aaron laugh.

So, there they were, a string of boyfriends Aaron left behind. A string consisting of periods of time, anywhere from a month to seven or eight, that Jake growled and grumbled through. Periods of time with which he measured his life. The Month of Riley, the Stage of Connor, the Phase of Paul. All strangely upsetting to his equilibrium, all throwing him slightly off-balance until they ended and it was just him and Aaron again.

Until another period began.

Then it was back to the confusion. And the annoyance. And the displeasure that always simmered beneath the surface.

Jake complained to Alyson about each and every one. Sometimes he pouted and complained. Sometimes, such as in the period of Nate, he raged and roared. Alyson sat and listened to Jake's endless list of character flaws and defects that he assigned to each of them. The countless, and baseless, reasons they should hit the road and never ... ever ... come near Aaron again. Every time, Alyson would ask him why he had any say whatsoever in who Aaron dated.

She asked him why it mattered to him.

Why it bothered him so much.

Why he cared.

That always shut him up because he *didn't* have any say in who Aaron dated.

And he didn't know why it mattered to him.

And he refused to think about why it bothered him.

Or why he cared.

CHAPTER TWO

EVEN though Jake appeared calmer and saner than Aaron, in actuality he was just as insane as he was, and Aaron knew it. Right from the beginning. Right from the moment Jake looked at him for all of two seconds and said, "That one. I want that one."

Aaron had gone into the whole situation with a surprisingly light heart. He had no idea why a weirdo photographer who never even bothered to interview him, much less ask him if he knew anything at all about photography or how to be an assistant, would trust him enough to ask him into his home. He simply had a good feeling about it and went with it, like he did everything else in his life. Usually his penchant for never thinking things through and trusting his gut landed him in a shiteload of trouble but this thing with Jake, this job, this friendship, so far had not led him astray. It was one of the few things in Aaron's life that he had managed not to fuck up by being random and careless.

Because he found, with Jake, that he could be random and arbitrary, but never careless.

Never careless.

He found Jake to be rather fragile beneath his gruff and highly irritating exterior. He was brilliant and amazing at what he did, he was strong and bold in his studio, in his world, but take him out of that world and he was uncertain, almost shy. Aaron could never understand how someone could be so in control of their world, their own little environment, but be so out of control in the bigger world.

Jake very rarely left his apartment, and when he did, he never ventured far. Sometimes Aaron would be able to cajole him into a walk in the park with Harold, sometimes even a lunch or dinner out. It was like Jake was afraid he'd get lost and never be able to find his way back. Whenever they were out walking anywhere, he was constantly looking at the landmarks surrounding them, taking them in like his own version of breadcrumbs that would show him the way back. Aaron would always grin at him, hook his arm through Jake's and say, "*No worries, Moz, I know the way home.*" But still Jake would usually only leave if he knew his destination or had a purpose for leaving.

Or if Aaron was with him.

Otherwise he was content to stay in his studio. Aaron could never figure out how someone could be so content just to stay in one place, to have such a small world. He had always craved being somewhere else because somewhere else had to be better than the somewhere he was at the moment. He wanted to see every place in the world and devour everything in those places. Swallow them whole. He realized his own restlessness and was completely aware of it, he just didn't know where it came from exactly or why it had come into being at all. He always figured that his restlessness would collide and crash into Jake's contentedness with tragic results. Instead, as Jake's studio and apartment became more of a home than any place he'd called that word previously, he became less and less restless. He didn't quite know why that was either, he just knew that for some reason curling up into a ball in one of Jake's window seats and falling asleep with his face pressed against the window as rain fell down in streaks along it was often more appealing to him than the idea of flying to far off places that were wild and beautiful and more than a little bit like a dream.

He also found out that all Alyson had told him about Jake was true.

Jake *did* make odd requests, but Aaron sometimes suspected he only did it to test him, to see if he could trust him, to see if he cared enough to actually do what he was asked. He suspected that Jake was so scared of people not caring that he invented crazy and unusual requests or missions simply to reassure himself that there was at least one person in this great big lonely city that cared whether he had Ho-Ho's from the right corner market or had dish soap that didn't smell too "dish soapy."

Jake *did* try to run everything in his life, but again, Aaron suspected it was because Jake found everything outside of his world so massive and unrestrained that he needed some sort of way to manage the things, the people inside his universe.

Jake *did* get in a strop over the littlest things, but all Aaron ever needed to do was look at him and say *"stop it"* and he would. Simple as that. Alyson stared at him in amazement the first time he did it and later told him that it took her almost a year to figure out to just tell him to stop.

Aaron figured it out in three days.

Jake *did* in fact call him in the middle of the night. Sometimes at three, sometimes at four, sometimes at midnight. Aaron was never sure when, there was no set schedule in that regard, but he was always sure he would. He'd maybe do it once every week or two or sometimes every night for a week straight. Whenever Aaron would pick up the phone and grunt, since he was fairly incapable of speaking when woken from a deep sleep – much to Jake's amusement since he insisted that Aaron was incapable of *not* speaking during his waking hours – Jake would seem confused, as if he wasn't quite sure why he had called in the first place. The first few times it happened, Aaron thought he might be drunk or high, and had teased him mercilessly about it, but after getting to know Jake better, he knew he wasn't drunk and would never be high so it was something else altogether. As time went on, and the calls coincided with Jake's foul moods, his odd request moods, Aaron came to realize he only really needed to do one thing. Whenever the phone rang and he grunted his version of hello and Jake would say hello in a small quiet voice, Aaron would simply say, "I'm still here."

And Jake would say, "Okay."

And Aaron would ask, "Can you sleep now?"

And Jake would reply, "Yes, now I can."

And then the phone would click and Aaron would fall back to sleep again. Sometimes he wasn't even sure the next morning if Jake had really called or if it had been a dream, sometimes the only indication was the phone still clenched in his hand that he had been too tired to place back on its receiver after Jake clicked off. Instead of being irritated with those late night calls, Aaron came to expect them, and although they would wake him from sleep, they never caused him restless nights. In fact, he sometimes wondered if maybe he didn't need the reassurance as much as Jake did, that Jake calling to make sure he was still there actually made him be there. He sometimes worried that if Jake stopped calling to make sure he was somewhere out there, then maybe he would cease to be there entirely.

Maybe he'd just disappear.

Without a trace.

Gone in the night like he had never been there at all.

So he welcomed the calls and made sure to tell Jake he was still there, because by doing so, he reassured himself he was still there as well.

THEIR working relationship was another thing that was alternately wonderful and strange.

At all of Aaron's other jobs, of which there had been many, he was expected to keep his mouth shut, or at least not call his boss a raging twat. He was expected to be on time. Be prudent and wise. Be dependable and reliable.

Be boring and dull.

Jake never minded when he was called a twat because he'd turn right around and call Aaron a fucker. He never minded that Aaron came in at nine-ish ... or maybe ten-ish ... or perhaps noon-ish. He didn't mind that Aaron would sometimes be walking across the studio and stop dead in his tracks because he completely forgot what he was doing or why he was even walking anywhere at all.

Jake knew things about him, too, things no one else ... especially a boss ... had ever bothered to know about him before.

Jake knew he could talk non-stop but could also sit silently and listen for as long as he was needed. Everyone else always assumed he never listened to anything that anyone other than himself had to say.

Jake knew he was deathly afraid of elevators, and if it was one of those days he didn't feel like climbing up the endless number of stairs to Jake's apartment, he knew all he had to do was buzz him and he'd come down in the elevator to ride up with him.

Jake knew he made up stories for every piece he sculpted, every pot he spun, and would ask him to tell them to him as he sat cross-legged on the floor and cleaned his cameras.

Jake knew about his weird relationship with bananas and he would only need to call out his name from the kitchen and Jake would put down whatever it was he was working on to come in and peel a banana for him.

Jake knew he had loved Harold from the start and had somehow gotten him for him. Aaron knew who he had belonged to, he had seen him yelling at him on the sidewalk outside his building, so when the opportunity presented itself, Aaron went ahead and *accidentally* lost the collar that was around Harold's neck before bringing him over to Jake's. He worried every day for a week until one day when a dog bed appeared and Jake told him the damn dog was his. Aaron didn't know how Jake had managed to procure Harold for him, he only knew that he did.

There were some things, however, that Jake did *not* know about Aaron.

Jake didn't know that sometimes, as he was pretending to work at his wheel, he was actually watching Jake work. He'd sit at his wheel for amazingly long bouts of time for one not used to sitting still for any length of time at all to watch Jake take pictures. Picture after picture as his clay spun round and round on his wheel, his pots wearing thin and collapsing in on themselves, as he forgot to mold them and coax them into the form they were meant to possess because he was too busy watching the way Jake moved with a camera.

Jake didn't know that the reason Mikos disappeared was

because he had insulted Jake and given Aaron an ultimatum. He told Aaron that Jake was a worthless, talentless hack who tried to control him by being bitchy and whiny. He said Aaron would have to quit his job, toss Jake to the curb. It was either Jake or him.

Mikos was out the door before he even had a chance to realize where he had gone so deathly wrong.

Jake didn't know Aaron wondered endlessly about where all the pictures he took of him went. At least once a month Jake would ask him to sit for him, but Aaron never saw the resulting pictures, nor did anyone else. He always wondered if maybe he just didn't know how to sit properly for Jake, if perhaps the pictures he took were so awful that he didn't want to show them to Aaron for fear of hurting his feelings. He was sure there was something wrong with them, why else would no one but Jake ever see them? Why else would he try again and again, session after session, if it weren't in an effort to get Aaron to finally do it right?

Jake didn't know that Aaron hated everyone of Jake's *"boyfriends"* as well, if boyfriend is what you could call a one-night stand. He hated the look Jake got in his eyes when he decided on a particular model. He was never quite sure when the fancy would strike, but he knew the look and hated it. Jake would go for long periods of time disregarding every single model that came in to sit for him, but then one would come in and he'd get a gleam in his eye and he'd decide to make that particular ass his *Fuck Du Jour*. The only thing that kept Aaron from punching each of the *Fucks* in the face was that they stayed around for one night only, and usually not the entire night either.

AARON used his key to open up Jake's front door and came crashing in, dropping bags all over the entry and leaving his shoes in two different spots as he kicked them off.

"Jacob! Jaaaaaaaay-cooooooob! Jacob!"

"Bedroom," came the faint reply.

"Get your lazy arse out of bed, you twat, I'm here on time for a change even though I'm still tired and sleepy and would much rather be in bed, so be duly impressed and bask in my promptness, for godsake!"

Aaron wandered down the hallway leading to Jake's bedroom and popped his head in, "Up you go, wakey-wakey Jakey-bakey ... and you're not alone ... oops," mumbled Aaron when he walked in on Jake pushing his current *Fuck Du Jour* out of bed with his foot.

"No, wait!" called Jake as Aaron turned to leave. Both Aaron and the *Fuck* stopped and turned. "Not you, you still need to go," Jake said to the *Fuck*, "I'm talking to him," he added as he pointed at Aaron.

"Jesus Christ, Moz, I don't want to see your bits and pieces this early in the morning," grumbled Aaron.

"I've got boxers on, you idiot."

"Still, ew," Aaron said, tipping his head in the *Fuck's* direction.

"He's leaving," Jake reassured Aaron before turning to the *Fuck* and saying succinctly, "Leave."

The *Fuck* finished zipping up his pants and reached down to grab his socks as he walked out mumbling under his breath. When he walked past Aaron, identical brown eyes stared each other down frostily before Aaron smiled brightly and said cheerfully, "Bye-bye! Don't let the door hit you on the arse on the way out!"

Jake grinned when Aaron waited until the *Fuck* was out the door and no longer in sight to make a face at him, pulling up his hands like claws and hissing at him.

"Down, Fifi."

"Man, you have *got* to stop doing that!" Aaron said as he walked over to Jake's bed.

"Doing what?"

"Letting the *Fucks* stay until I get here. I don't wanna see the *Fucks*. The *Fucks* are evil."

"The *Fucks* are fun."

"So say you."

Suddenly Jake leaned forward and grabbed Aaron around

the waist and dragged him into bed with him.

"Sonofabitch!" screeched Aaron, laughing and kicking at Jake.

"Aw, come on, Flip, gimme some love," grinned Jake, trying to hold down a flailing Aaron.

Aaron started to yell and curse even louder when Jake turned him toward the other side of the bed. "Don't you dare throw me on the other side of this bed, you tosser!"

"Why not? Huh? Huh?" asked Jake as he pulled at Aaron's waist and tried to flop him over to the other side.

"Why not?!?! I'll tell you why not, you assfuck," Aaron hollered, digging his heels into the bed to try to stop Jake's momentum, "I don't want to land in *Fuck* spooge!"

Jake was laughing so hard he lost his grip on Aaron, who took advantage of the situation to roll off of him and stay on his side of the bed. Jake remained lying on his back, laughing until his sides ached and he could barely breathe. Once he managed to calm down, he flopped onto his side and wrapped his right arm around a pouting Aaron, who was still lying beside him on a precariously small piece of mattress. Jake scooted back and pulled Aaron with him.

"You're gonna fall off, Flip."

"Yes, well, the floor is less likely to be contaminated."

"Ah, there's where you're wrong. My floor is quite the slut, you have no idea where it's been."

"Jaaaaake!" whined Aaron.

"What?"

"Quit being so fucking gross, I don't want to hear shit like that."

"You don't want to hear about my slutty floor?"

"No," Aaron answered in a near pout as he turned to face Jake and ineffectively pushed at his chest with his hand, "and I don't want to hear about your slutty *Fucks* either."

Jake saw the look on Aaron's face and stopped teasing instantly. "No, I don't either," he whispered into Aaron's hair, pulling him closer.

Aaron pressed his face into the curve where Jake's neck met his shoulder and closed his eyes. Jake followed suit when he felt Aaron's breath brush across his skin. They lay there in silence for a while before Aaron suddenly inhaled deeply and let out a near sigh.

"What?" asked Jake quietly.

"I don't like it when you don't smell like you," was the equally quiet reply.

Jake's hands clenched into fists briefly before they curved back around Aaron, lying flat against his back and winding tightly in his curls, "It won't happen again, Flip. I promise."

"Okay," muttered Aaron.

Jake shivered when he felt Aaron's eyelashes brush against his skin as he closed his eyes again. "Go to sleep," he whispered. "It's too early in the morning, I think."

Aaron didn't respond other than to snuffle slightly as he settled down into sleep and his fingers curled against Jake's chest.

CHAPTER THREE

FOR all they knew of each other and all they didn't know, there were still a few truths that existed between them that both took for granted because they just were. There was never an explanation, never a mention of them. They were the things that happened nearly every day between them that never faltered or changed.

Almost daily, Aaron would get so lost in his work, in his wheel or sculpture or kiln, that he wouldn't notice Jake stopping his own work to click his camera in his direction.

Almost daily, Jake would take a break during which he'd lie on his back near Aaron's feet, letting the whirl of his wheel hum him to sleep.

Almost daily, Aaron would move his left foot ever so slightly so it would rest against Jake's shoulder as he slept a half hour away and Aaron let the clay spin and form in his hands.

Almost daily, Jake would ask Aaron a random and completely unnecessary question simply to hear him speak.

They had their schedule and their routine, which was so ingrained in them that they never even noticed they had one until Alyson would make fun of them or point out what they were doing. Jake would curse her out and Aaron would laugh and try to break up the moment by turning to Milo to swing him about by his hands, his childish giggles obliterating the moment when things got too close to truth.

"I know you hate them, but do you ever stop to look at what the *Fucks* all look like?" asked Alyson as she and Aaron went on a shopping trip to fill Jake's nearly empty fridge. They had left Milo behind to hopefully drive Jake insane.

"Why would I bother looking at them? They're always gone before I have a chance."

"Except the ones who aren't, the ones that make you pick up the phone and bitch me out like I'm supposed to do something about it."

"You should be able to, you know."

"Should be able to do what?"

"Talk some sense into him."

"Sense and Jake do not go hand in hand. Besides, what makes you think I'd have any influence over him?"

"Because you've known him longer. You know how he is."

"So do you. And that is bullshit about me knowing him better just because I've been cursed with knowing him the longest. You knew more about him in a month than I did the entire three years I worked for him."

"But you're Alyson."

"Meaning?"

"He'd listen to *you*."

"That's the dumbest thing I've ever heard."

"Hello! Look who you're talking to," said Aaron emphatically as he waved his hands in front of her face, "it's me, Aaron, the dumbest things say-er!"

"Say-er isn't a word."

"See! Dumb! I just proved my point!"

"So what am I supposed to do? Go, '*Hey Jake, would you mind not fucking the boys so Aaron isn't thrown into a tizzy*'? Because I'm sure that would work and make everything all right."

"But you could talk to him and explain how these one night stands aren't doing him any good and they never will. He's never going to find what he's looking for if he keeps up with the *Fucks*. They don't know him, they don't care about him, all they know is that people in this city know his name and his pictures are in magazines and galleries. They're fucking groupies … literally, fucking groupies. They're just going to drag him down. He's already lonely enough. He needs someone who will be there in the middle of the night and someone who will make him get out of his little self-imposed prison. He needs someone to look after him."

"Like you do."

"Exactly, he needs…."

"You."

"Yes … no! … I mean, yes he does, but not like that. We're just friends and he needs me as a friend. A friend. What he needs is someone to take care of him as more than a friend. He needs someone that will love him because he's amazing and strange and beautiful, because he's … Jake, not because they like the sound of their name said after his. He doesn't need hangers-on, he needs something true, something real."

Alyson stared at Aaron's reddening face as he stuttered out his ramblings, and when he was finished said, "You are infuriating, Aaron."

"Why? What did I do?"

"Everything, you do everything and you are everything to him and both of you know it but neither one will see it. You're both so fucking stupid and infuriating that I want to stab the two of you in the head sometimes. You're absolutely fucking perfect for each other because you're the only person I know that could possibly tolerate him for more than a fifteen minute interval of time, and he's the only one that understands everything that comes out of your mouth, he's the only one that understands and speaks fluent Aaron, yet neither one of you will see it!"

Aaron looked completely flabbergasted. "We're not like that! Jake doesn't think of me as anything more than a friend. I mean, why would he have all his *Fucks* if he wanted to be with me?"

"He has his *Fucks* to try to make you jealous, you stupid

shit. To counteract all your ridiculous boyfriends that you parade around in front of him - you're lucky you don't see *more* of his *Fucks* than you do."

"You're seeing things, Aly, or you're seeing what you want to see."

"Fine, you know what I see? I see a man who has one night stands so randomly as to be laughable until you see what they look like. Have you not noticed what they *all* look like?"

"I'm not checking them out, they're not my type."

"Well, I should hope not or you'd be completely narcissistic!"

"The fuck?"

"They all look. Like. You. Every single one of those assholes that you despise so much looks exactly like you. They're carbon copies of one another ... tall, lean, dark curly hair, brown eyes, big smile. They're all you. Why do you think they're so random? Why do you think you can never figure out when he's going to fuck one? Because he doesn't either, not until he sees what they look like. He's trying to get as close to you as he can and the reason none of them stay around longer than a night is because that's all it takes him to realize they're a poor substitute for you. But, he keeps trying to find an acceptable substitute because the real thing is too fucking dense to figure it out."

Aaron looked at Alyson with what could only be fear in his eyes. He shook his head violently, "No. No way. If he really felt that way about me ... if he ... if he loved me, I wouldn't ... wouldn't know what to do. Everything would be thrown out of whack. I wouldn't know him any more ... I mean, I wouldn't know what was going on in his head and I've *always* known that. I don't want to not know what he's thinking. I'd lose him," he said in a panic.

Alyson reached out to grab a hold of one of his wrists as he paced back and forth in front of her. "You'll lose him eventually if you don't figure this out and I'm telling the same thing to him. You'll lose each other and then where will you be? Don't use that as a cop-out, Aaron, because you know damn well if you ever lost him, he'd find his way back to you, but if you both lose your way, then you're just lost."

Aaron pulled his wrist out of Alyson's grip and started walking down the sidewalk again. "I've got to go get Jake's food, it's a long list and will take bloody forever. You don't want him locking Milo in a closet before we get back, do you?"

Alyson started following him, reaching out with her hands as if to strangle him before shouting, "Aaahhh!" and running her hands through her hair instead.

ONCE Jake realized Aaron knew exactly what to say to him when he called in the middle of the night, he came to depend on it and when he wasn't there to say the things that needed to be said, when he wasn't *there*, Jake would get out of bed and go in search of him. He'd throw a jacket over his pajama pants and slip his feet into his shoes and walk toward Aaron until he spotted a cab that would take him there faster.

Aaron had given him a set of keys to his place which Jake kept on his keychain next to his own house keys. Once the taxi dropped him off in front of Aaron's building, he'd look up to the sixth floor and the windows on the right to see if there were any lights on. If there were, he'd sit on the curb and press the button for Aaron on his cell phone and wait until he answered. If he answered, he'd turn right around and start walking back to his place in search of a cab that would bring him back home. If he didn't answer, Jake would let himself in with his key, kick off his shoes, drop his jacket in a pile on the floor, and crawl under the covers of Aaron's bed.

Even if Aaron wasn't there to tell him so, Jake would know he had been there and it would only be a matter of time before he was back there again.

So he'd wait.

Until Aaron was back again.

THE door slammed open as Aaron was pushed through it

by the most recent of the phases, the boyfriends, Matt. He stumbled backwards until his back slammed against the wall as Matt barreled into him. It was all tangled limbs and heated kisses from Matt, and Aaron was trying to focus, trying to bring himself to participate wholeheartedly, when the voice that was the source of all his distraction called sleepily from the corner of the room.

"Flip?"

Aaron instantly pulled his lips away from Matt, who sighed and dropped his forehead against the wall near Aaron's shoulder. "Yeah, it's me. I'm home," he called back.

"You weren't before."

"I am now."

Aaron pushed Matt off of him and wiped his mouth before asking him, "Can we do this tomorrow?"

"This is fucked up, you know that, don't you?" Matt asked.

"I'm sorry, but I wasn't home when he called, he likes me to be home when he calls."

"It sounds like he likes to keep you on a short leash."

"He needs me."

"*I* need you."

"Tomorrow, I promise."

Matt sighed again and rubbed his eyes, "You know what, babe? You're going to have to decide what this really is between us sooner or later. I know he's your boss and your best friend, but I'm your boyfriend, Aaron. Me. Not him. I understand that he's an important part of your life, but you're going to have to realize sometime that he's not always supposed to be first, there are other people in your orbit."

Aaron smiled up at Matt and in an effort to try and lighten the situation asked, "So I have an orbit, huh? Is this your subtle way of telling me I'm from outer space?"

Matt cracked a slight grin as he leaned in to kiss Aaron on the cheek. "No, it's my not so subtle way of telling you you're the fucking sun," he whispered before pulling away and walking through the doorway.

"Tomorrow. Promise."

"Tomorrow," Matt agreed as he quietly shut the door behind him.

Aaron pushed away from the wall and ran his hands through his hair. He was so stupid. Why was he tossing Matt out when what he should really be doing is putting Jake in a cab to take him back home? Matt was right, he was his boyfriend for christsake, *he* should still be here.

"Flip?"

"Coming," Aaron sighed as he toed off his shoes and started shedding clothes on his way over to his bed. He grabbed a t-shirt and pajama bottoms to sleep in before slipping into bed behind Jake, who reached back and pulled Aaron's arm around his waist. Aaron muttered *"lift"* and Jake lifted his head so Aaron could snake his other arm under it and the pillow, bending his elbow so he could bring his hand up and rest it against Jake's chest. Their breathing soon synchronized and Aaron thought Jake had fallen asleep, so was slightly startled when his whispered question pierced through the quiet darkness.

"Why have you been so far away the last couple of weeks?"

"I've been right here."

"Your body has, but your mind is a million miles away, which it usually is because you're crazy and all that," Jake grinned faintly when Aaron pulled his hair, "but this is different."

"I guess I've just been thinking."

"Dangerous undertaking, Flip."

Another hair tug.

"Alyson said some things to me that day we went grocery shopping for you and I haven't been able to get them out of my mind."

"What did she say to you? You know I could hire her again just so I could fire her if that would make you feel better."

"Awww," sighed Aaron, "you'd do that for *me*?"

Jake just laughed, "I'd like to say it would be just for you, but I think I'd enjoy it, too."

"You're so mean to poor Aly."

"Ah, she still loves me."

Aaron grew quiet. "That she does, Moz, she's always looking out for you."

"Just like you," Jake added in a whisper, wrapping his hand around Aaron's which was resting at his waist.

"Just like me."

It was quiet for a few minutes as Jake concentrated on the feel of Aaron's breath against his neck and Aaron concentrated on Jake's smell as he pressed his face against the back of his neck.

"Why are you so far away?"

"I don't know, Moz, I'd tell you if I could explain it myself."

"Well, come back soon, will you?"

Aaron squeezed his arms extra tight around Jake. "I'll try."

THEIR nighttime assignations didn't merely go one way. There were nights Aaron travelled the many blocks uptown to Jake's apartment to let himself in with his own set of keys so he could sit at his wheel, the light coming through the window his only illumination.

He never knew when the mood would strike him, but it would come over him in a powerful wave when it did, and the only rest he'd get would be after he found his way back to Jake's. He'd sit down at his wheel, trying to be as quiet as he could, as the mild humming from the turning of the wheel was the only sound to cut into the night. But no matter how quiet he tried to be, Jake always wandered into the studio to find him. He'd never say a word to Aaron, not even a brief "hi", he would just walk over to the window closest to Aaron, but not the one providing him his only light, and sit down on the ledge, pull his knees up to his chest and simply watch him.

Watch as his hands moved over the malleable clay, smoothing it, forming it, guiding it into what it was meant to be.

He would watch until his eyes drifted shut and he'd fall into that world of half-sleep, oblivious yet aware, asleep but not. He swore he could still hear the humming of the wheel and the movement of Aaron's hands over the clay even though he knew the last part was impossible. He swore he wasn't asleep but inevitably he would wake up the next morning tucked in on the couch in his empty studio, Aaron gone. The only evidence of him even being there was the light flashing on the kiln as it worked away to harden his clay into something stronger than what it started out as. Aaron would come back later in the morning and go about his business until he could pull his creation from the kiln and begin glazing it, usually in the most brilliant and beautiful shades of blue Jake had ever seen.

Every other pot or bowl Aaron made would leave the studio soon after it was properly glazed and fired, but not the nighttime ones. Those stayed on the shelf Jake had decided to build on a whim one day. It ran around the entire studio at just the right height so Aaron could reach up and place his pots and bowls on it.

One right after the other.

Blue as the sky.

Blue as the sea.

Blue as twilight.

Blue as Jake's eyes.

Those were the ones that never left the studio.

Never would leave the studio.

Not as long as Jake had any say.

And not as long as Aaron continued stealing over in the night to make them.

AS Alyson let herself into Jake's apartment, all she could hear was the thump, thump, thump of the bass on a stereo turned up far too loud. She wandered through the living room to the door of the studio, the music getting clearer, more distinct, as the pounding of the bass rattled the pictures on the wall near the studio door. She opened the door and was assaulted with a blaring wave of Rolling Stones washing over her and nearly blowing her eardrums out.

Jake was busy photographing a man and woman in a most interesting position. Alyson cocked her head to the side and shrugged. Both of the models were fully clothed and not in a sexual position per se, but the way they were positioned made it somehow more erotic than if they had been posed in a blatantly sexual way. She had never pretended to know exactly what Jake's photographs meant, or what he was trying to do, she only knew that she liked them and that was enough for her and Jake both.

Aaron was curved over a spinning pot, his long fingers bringing up its lip. He was almost writhing as he moved with the pot, his back bent, the painfully thin cotton fabric of the t-shirt he wore showing every movement of his back muscles. His foot tapped a steady beat with the music, causing his entire leg to shake and jerk. He had what looked to be an even older and more worn t-shirt somehow tied around his head to keep his hair out of his face. She could almost feel the wave of energy coming off of him as he moved with the wheel and thought if Jake wanted to photograph blatant sex, all he had to do was turn to his right and snap a few of Aaron.

Neither one was paying the slightest bit of attention to the other but Alyson was certain she could see a strand of nearly invisible light connecting them. She stared at them and thought if she had one of those giant novelty scissors they used to cut red ribbons at the openings of new businesses, she could walk over and sever that connection with one snap of her shears and they would both crash to the floor like puppets shorn of their strings. Both would falter and fall without that rope of support holding them up. But instead of finding scissors to cut them apart, she chose to walk over to the stereo and shut off the Stones.

The second the music stopped and silence exploded through the studio like a bomb, both men stopped what they were doing to look around in flushed confusion. Jake stumbled as he changed positions and nearly dropped his camera. Aaron jerked so violently that his hands closed up and smashed the pot through his fingers. Twin sets of startled and somewhat glazed eyes turned toward her, one brown, one blue.

"The fuck, Aly?" Jake finally asked as he blinked a few times.

"Yes, dear?"

"You scared the shit out of me, and I think you broke Flip's pot."

"Well, he'll make another one. Besides, I think I just spared you both from inevitable deafness in your very near future."

"We always have it that loud when we work," Aaron supplied helpfully from his corner.

"And I always smoke after meals, doesn't mean it's good for me, now does it?"

"No, but it's pretty fucking great, isn't it?" grinned Aaron.

Jake laughed under his breath as he rearranged his models.

"So," Aaron continued, "what brings you to the humble abode? A dying urge to annoy?"

"The urge is always there, but this time, that's not my sole purpose, although what I have to ask may annoy you anyway which is surely just an extra bonus."

"I'm sure it'll annoy that one," said Aaron, jerking his elbow in Jake's direction as he tried to salvage his pot somehow, "but I'm too mellow to be ... hey Moz, move her arm down, otherwise she's a little teapot except tall and svelte and not short and stout but you get me ... annoyed by you."

Jake adjusted the woman's arm, muttering a "thanks" over his shoulder. Alyson just laughed and said, "What part of that conversation was directed at me exactly?"

"Ah," said Aaron absently as he fiddled with the clay, "most of the beginning words and all those fun ones at the end."

"Yeah, okay."

"He said I'll be annoyed by whatever you have to say but he won't because he's mellow, much like a pothead," Jake supplied helpfully as he started to snap pictures again, stopping abruptly to raise his hand and say without turning around toward Aaron, "and don't even say what you were going to say, Flip."

"I wasn't going to say anything!" Aaron whined.

"You were going to say like a fucking Beavis, *'you said pothead,'* and then do that laugh that you *think* sounds like Butthead but what really sounds like you're in the throes of a stroke."

"I was not, you tosspot!" Aaron yelled at the back of Jake's head before turning to Alyson and mouthing, "Yeah, I was," and grinning like an idiot.

"As much as I would love to continue this mentally stimulating conversation, I need to know if you two can watch Milo tonight. I know it's last minute but our regular baby-sitter had something unexpected come up and I'm fairly desperate."

"Well, yeah, you would be to ask us," said Jake.

"Why do we both have to watch him? I was thinking about how later I was going to think about having plans tonight."

Alyson sighed, "What in the hell does that mean?"

"It means he doesn't have plans yet, but he's seriously considering coming up with something later on today," said Jake.

"Thanks for the translation," Alyson saluted in Jake's direction, "but to answer your question, Oh Indecipherable One, I need you both to watch him because the two of you together are fairly close to one very nearly competent human being."

"She called us competent, Moz!"

"She said *very nearly* and that was *together*, not on our own."

"Still," said Aaron happily, "the word was in the same sentence as us so that works for me!"

"I need you there," Alyson said to Aaron, "to play with Milo and entertain him and make sure Jake doesn't tie him to a chair and forget about him because he finds him small and troublesome, and I need Jake there to make sure the two of you don't fall out of a window while you're playing or drink whatever blue shit you find under the kitchen sink."

"I do like to drink blue shit," agreed Aaron.

"And I do like to tie your tiny and problematic child to

stable and immovable objects," said Jake.

"Fantastic," said Alyson in false cheer, "I'll come back to find Aaron dead on the floor clutching a bottle of Windex and Jake tied to the bathroom sink and Milo sticking forks in electrical outlets."

"Probably not, Aly," said Aaron. "I'm sure Milo will be calmly reading or playing with his toys and all perfectly fine, but I'm sure you're right about me and Jacob."

"Yes, sadly, I probably am."

CHAPTER FOUR

ALYSON let herself into Jake's apartment later that night and got Milo settled down with some crayons and paper before going in search of Jake. Naturally, she found him in his studio. He was sitting cross-legged on the floor in front of a little stool where Aaron had put his most recent nighttime blue, as Alyson liked to call them. He was doing nothing but looking at it with an intent, almost piercing, stare.

"That blue is particularly close to your eyes."

Jake jumped a bit before turning to Alyson and muttering, "Huh?"

"The blue. Of the pot. It's close to the blue of your eyes. He keeps trying ... I think he's getting closer."

"Closer to what?"

"The blue of your eyes, asshole."

"Bitch."

"Cunt."

Jake laughed, "Why is it you can call me a cunt, but if I call you one, you kick me in the fucking nads?"

"Because the word cunt is degrading, you fucking cunt."

"That's what I thought."

"Stop trying to distract me from my blue conversation."

"I'm not sure I was a willing partner in this blue

conversation of yours."

"Maybe not, but I'm going to make you one."

"Make me willing?"

"Yes."

"Go for it, then."

"You sound all put out, like you have anything better to do, when you were basically just sitting here in the near dark spanking it to one of Aaron's pots."

"I wish I had that on tape because you know he'd put you saying *'spanking it'* on a loop and play it repeatedly."

"Whatever, the point of my conversation is not what would entertain Aaron's feeble mind, but what you're going to do about the fact that you sit by yourself and stare at things that remind you of him."

"I do not sit by myself and stare!"

"Then what are you doing right now?"

"Doing my breathing exercises so I don't go out there and kill your child."

"Yeah, okay."

"Okay."

"God, between you and Aaron, I'm in a stupid sandwich."

"If you were between me and Aaron, you'd be in porn."

"Well, that could be fun, too, but I have a mission here, and it's not breaking into porn … although, don't you think Aaron would be perfect in a porn? He could make a LOT of money."

Jake scowled at her.

Alyson raised an eyebrow and starting walking around nonchalantly picking up things and setting them down as she began talking again. "Seriously, he's gorgeous … and the gays love the pretty boys. I bet he's pretty bendy, too … that long lean body. Yep, I bet he's bendy. And the mouth on him, I bet he can talk dirty with the best of them. I mean, he talks dirty in everyday conversation … could you imagine him in the bedroom? Fuck me. Oh, and those legs, those are perfect and long and could wrap around you and pull you down and ... mmm, yeah, perfect for porn. I'll have to ask Matt his opinions, you know ... since he's sampled the goods. And repeatedly, from what Flip has told me."

Jake's eyes took on a dark look at the mention of Matt. He got up from where he was sitting on the floor and tried walking away from Alyson as he threw over his shoulder sarcastically, "Well, if Flip says ... what else does Flip say? I'd really love to fucking hear every minute little detail. I can't get enough of how Flip moons about Matt to you. I'm at the fucking edge of my fucking seat."

"I think he's in love with him."

Jake turned on her instantly and practically yelled, "He's not!"

"How do you know he's not?"

"He's not," he growled.

"Yes, but *how* do you know Matt's not in love with Aaron?"

"Matt? Matt ... I thought you meant Aaron."

"Yeah, I know that's who you thought I meant," said Alyson, "and do you want to know *how* I know you thought that?" Jake turned away from her again to fiddle with a camera. "Because whenever anyone gets within a ten foot radius of him, you go insane. Any time someone even *dares* to suggest there's anyone in his life other than you, you go insane. Any time he's not within touching distance, you go insane. And any time you think he's falling away from you, that he's not there, you go insane. You've put your whole life into him, what do you think that means, Jacob? How can you possibly explain that and not make it sound like he's the axis your world spins on? Because if you can explain him away, and everything you feel for him away, then I'd like you to tell me how you function without a heart."

"I don't function without a heart," he said angrily and then added under his breath as he grabbed at the front of his t-shirt, "he's right here."

"What was that?" asked Alyson as she crept closer.

"I don't function without a heart."

"I heard that part."

"That's it, that's all I said."

"Fine. That's all you said," said Alyson in frustration, "I'll let you believe that's all you said."

Jake watched Alyson as she stomped out of his studio and he began to absently rub at the spot in the center of his chest that suddenly felt as if it were on fire and was slowly caving in on him.

"MOMMA! Unc Dake!" yelled Milo from the kitchen.

Alyson was already on her way to the kitchen when she heard Milo call. "What is it, honey?"

"Unc Fip's wants Unc Dake to come get him in the eletator," said Milo as he pushed himself off his chair and walked the phone over to Alyson. She was about to take the phone out of Milo's hand when she heard Aaron yelling through the receiver.

"MOZ! Come and get me!"

Milo giggled, "Unc Fip said to hold the phone at Unc Dake and he yell real loud."

"Your Uncle Flip is a moron, Milo, remember that."

Before Alyson could grab the phone from her son, he put it back to his ear and said, "Momma says you a moron." Alyson watched as a smile broke out on Milo's face then he turned to her and said, "Unc Fip says you a vewy bootafull lady and he gonna hug and kiss you when Unc Dake brings him the eletator."

"Yeah, I bet he said that," grinned Alyson as she took the phone from Milo's hand, "Quit telling my son to lie to his mother."

Jake chose this time to shuffle into the kitchen, still rubbing at the center of his chest. Milo came over and hugged his leg and he reached down to pat him on the head. "Is that your Uncle Flip on the phone?"

"Yep, you gotta get him in the eletator."

Jake smiled at the "eletator".

"Tell him I'm coming," he mouthed to Alyson as he walked out the door.

"Your hero is coming to get you, ya wuss ... no, the elevator cable will not snap halfway up ... that was a movie, Aaron ... no, you won't go crashing to the bottom of the elevator shaft with Keanu Reeves and Dennis Hopper with an ugly hand ... trolls do not live in elevator shafts, there's no such thing as trolls ... because I know ... no there aren't ... I will not ask Milo if he believes in elevator trolls."

"Are there eletator tolls, Momma?"

Alyson sighed, "Great, now you've scared my son." Alyson listened to Aaron for a second, then turned to Milo and said, "They make cookies, honey, they're like the Keebler Elves on TV."

"Oh. Okay," Milo said agreeably and went back to his chair to color.

Alyson walked out of Milo's hearing range. "Where the fuck do you come up with this shit? Elevator trolls that make cookies? Honestly Aaron, I worry about you ... yeah, I do, you're seriously insane ... I said *insane,* not *in pain,* you dumbass ... I could make you seriously in pain ... no, kicking me first will not help ... isn't your bitch down there yet to get you? I'm tired of having this conversation, your mind is draining mine of all its smart cells ... yes, I do have them ... no, you don't ... he's there? Fucking finally ... no ... no ... no ... hang up now, Aaron ... hang up ... yes ... I'll see you in two minutes ... yes ... hang up ... okay, fine ... bye ... hang up!"

Alyson laughed as the phone finally clicked off, courtesy of Jake and his impatience. She could only imagine how Aaron would chew him out for that on the way up. She walked back over to Milo to sit down at the table and color with him until the whirling dervish and his sidekick got back up.

"... I was talking to Aly, how many times do I have to say this before you understand?" Aaron's voice drifted through the door he was pushing open, obviously still chewing Jake a new one. "It's just not right, hanging up the phone when someone else is on it, it's bad manners, you Neanderthal."

"Well, seeing as how you'd still be down there talking to her right now if I hadn't hung up the phone instead of standing up here in the same room as her face to face, I see only positive results to my actions."

"You would, you goombah."

"Hello, Tony Soprano."

"I *know*," said Aaron excitedly, totally forgetting his beef with Jake, "I heard it *on* The Sopranos! I love that word!"

"Does it bother you that you're only now watching The Sopranos, about six years after everyone else?"

"I don't like to be rushed into things, you know, the whole tortoise and the hare bit?"

"That doesn't make any sense."

"That very well may be, but it doesn't make it any less true."

Jake rolled his eyes and walked over to the kitchen table and sat down. "What're you drawing, Milo?"

"Unc Fip and the eletator tolls."

"Ooooh!" exclaimed Aaron as he smooshed in next to Jake on his chair, "are there cookies, too?"

"Yep."

"What kind?"

"All kinds."

"Like chocolate chip and peanut butter and gingerbread?"

"Yep."

"How about worm ones and booger ones?"

Milo giggled, "No one makes booger cookies."

"Yes they do, they're my favorites!" grinned Aaron, "They're green and filled with big slimey boogies."

"Jesus," muttered Alyson as she got up and turned to Jake, "remember to keep them out of the cupboard under the sink."

Jake looked back over his shoulder and grinned at her as Aaron and Milo went into great detail about the grossest things one could make into a cookie. She walked over to Milo and placed a kiss on his head and said, "Be good and make sure your uncles behave themselves."

"I will, Momma."

"Excellent, see you boys later."

She walked out the door as a chorus of "good-byes" followed her.

Aaron slapped his hands together and started rubbing them. "All right, she's gone, what kind of mischief can we get into now?"

Jake got up from his chair to start making them some popcorn and smacked the back of Aaron's head as he walked behind him. Aaron squeaked and started rubbing his head as Milo's giggles floated through the kitchen.

JAKE looked around him at the mess spread throughout his studio. Aaron had decided it would be the perfect place for him and Milo to make an obstacle course that ended in complete and utter chaos. Chairs, blankets, sofa cushions, a skateboard and ski poles, which Jake claimed were too dangerous because of the sharp tips, so Aaron found marshmallows to stick on the ends, which *then* prompted him to want to make s'mores and start a fire in Jake's metal trash bin, were strewn across the floor. Thankfully he had held Aaron back from tossing a match into the trash bin and setting off the sprinkler system. He had *not*, however, managed to rein him in anywhere else.

They had started the night by making popcorn to watch a movie. Aaron had insisted on adding gummy worms to the popcorn, telling Milo they were the worms he was saving to make worm cookies but that he'd sacrifice them to the popcorn. Milo thought popcorn and worms was the best thing he'd ever had to eat in his whole entire four years of life.

Jake thought he might vomit.

They ended up watching about half of a movie with talking fish before Aaron's ADD kicked in and the idea of the obstacle course popped into his head.

Milo was all about the obstacle course.

Jake took about six aspirin for his headache.

Once the obstacle course had run its course, so to speak, Aaron had moved Milo on to his clay and wheel. He had marched himself into Jake's closet and pulled out a vintage t-shirt Jake was pretty sure cost him about a hundred dollars to put on Milo so he wouldn't get his clothes dirty and Aaron wouldn't get his ass handed to him by Alyson. They spent the better part of an hour making an unholy mess on and around Aaron's wheel.

Jake thought he'd get mad when Milo clapped his hands suddenly, sending splatters of watery muck all over the window and floor, but he didn't, the ache in his chest simply flared up again as Aaron threw his head back and laughed at Milo's delight. It pulled and constricted as he looked at Milo sitting on Aaron's lap and Aaron holding him and guiding him so patiently yet with such joy.

Jake took several pictures of that part of the evening.

Jake thought that might be his favorite part of the night until he walked in on Aaron brushing his teeth with Milo standing on a chair next to him so he could see into the mirror. Both turned to him at the same time with foamy grins. His finger crooked involuntarily as if he were taking a picture.

Jake was positive *that* was his favorite part of the night, until story time.

Milo, decked out in his Bob the Builder pajamas, hopped into Jake's bed and Aaron tucked him in, then beckoned to Jake, who was standing in the doorway, to come and join them. Jake got into bed on the other side of Milo who had curled himself up into Aaron. Jake moved over as close as he could as he, too, lay on his side and curled himself into Aaron.

Jake almost fell asleep to the sound of Aaron's voice.

"*In the great green room there was a telephone and a red balloon and a picture of the cow jumping over the moon....*"

"I wuv this book, Unc Fip," yawned Milo.

Jake smiled as he watched Milo's eyes began to droop because of the soothing tone of Aaron's voice.

"*... goodnight room, goodnight moon, goodnight cow jumping over the moon....*"

Jake could hear and feel Milo's breathing even out against the hand he had laid on his back as he slipped into sleep.

"*… goodnight nobody, goodnight mush, and goodnight to the old lady whispering 'hush', goodnight stars, goodnight air, goodnight noises everywhere.*" Aaron's voice trailed off as he gently closed the book and looked up at Jake.

"I like this part best," whispered Jake.

A faint smile spread across Aaron's face, "Yeah, because we're both quiet and far away from your closet and ski poles."

"Well, yes … obviously," Jake rolled his eyes in mock exasperation.

They lay in silence for a while, Jake's hand running gently up and down Milo's back, purposely brushing against Aaron's fingers which were resting against one small shoulder blade.

"Do you want kids?" Jake asked suddenly, raising his eyes to look at Aaron.

"Yes, very much so."

"You do?"

"Yeah, I do. Although, what I'd like first is someone to raise them with, someone who will look at me and say, *'That one. I want that one.'* You know what I mean? I want someone who will know right away that he wants to be with me and raise kids with me and just … love me."

"That isn't hard."

"What isn't hard?"

"Loving you…" said Jake without thought, "uh, I mean finding someone to love you … it shouldn't … it shouldn't be too hard to do," he amended quickly.

"Oh yes, not hard *at all*, because it's been soooo easy so far and I've been soooo very successful at it," smirked Aaron.

"You'd make a great dad, you know," added Jake, hoping to draw the focus away from the topic of Aaron and anyone else.

"You think so?"

"I know you would."

"You're just saying that because I have the mental capacity and the attention span of a small child," Aaron grinned.

"That too, but you would be amazing. Absolutely amazing. I have no doubt about it."

"But, I'd need someone to balance me out, someone to make sure me and the kid don't drink the blue stuff ... or make sure I put the marshmallows on the ski poles. You know, the usual."

"Nah," smiled Jake, "I think you could handle it, you only pretend to be as stupid as you are."

"Yeah," sighed Aaron, "I'm not nearly as naturally stupid as I would hope to be."

"But, you're still very ridiculous if that helps at all."

"Aww, thanks, Moz."

"Welcome."

Quiet descended on them for a few minutes until Aaron asked, "Do you want kids?"

Jake sort of shrugged and said, "I don't know. They don't really thrill me all that much. They just seem to annoy me is all, and they're always loud ... and hungry ... or crying about something ... and sticky, they're always sticky."

Aaron laughed quietly, "You just described me, Jacob."

Jake grinned, "This is true."

"But you keep me around so I think you'd do just fine."

"Possibly."

"Definitely. You'd be a great dad."

"I'm not sure I'd know how. I didn't really have a dad around much ... and when he was, he pretty much wasn't all that great at showing what a good dad should be."

"So, you'll just do the opposite."

"But what if I don't do it right? What if I fail?"

"You've never failed at anything in your life. Besides, don't you think every other person who's ever become a parent feels the same way as you? You just never know what's gonna happen, you just have to believe."

"You know how hard it is for me to do stuff like that. I'm not you, Aaron. You do whatever you want without fear or hesitation. You live. Me, I'm just the guy that never leaves his apartment and has to think everything through a thousand times before he does anything. I'm the stick in the mud."

"Yeah, well, you don't want to take life lessons from me either. If you do, you'll end up in intensive care or on medication of some kind. I think it's better to find a middle ground."

"Maybe Alyson is right, I think someone should mix us up in a blender and then maybe we'd have one whole normal person."

"Or a very successful serial killer."

Jake laughed, "You still haven't let that go yet, have you?"

"No, I still maintain that there's a touch of the serial killer in you."

"And yet, you're still here bugging me day after day, egging me on closer and closer towards murdering you."

"Yep," Aaron grinned.

"As long as you know it. I think I'm going to have you sign a waiver of some sort that will get me off the hook in case I actually do decide to murder you."

"If you do murder me, please promise to make it kinky or horribly strange - don't be boring, Moz, because then nobody will watch the special on CourtTV."

"I promise."

"See, you're always doing things to make me happy and to please me, you'd make an excellent dad."

"I worry about you, Flip, you endorse my parenthood in almost the same breath as you declare me a serial killer."

"A *kinky* serial killer."

"You do realize that Milo is probably soaking this all in subliminally in his sleep and will start asking Aly what kinky means and what a serial killer does, and when he does, you're the one that'll have to answer to her. I was never here."

Aaron started looking around in confusion, "Huh? What's that? Is someone talking to me? Who's there?"

"Retard."

"Did someone just say something?"

Jake grabbed one of Aaron's fingers and pulled on it.

Aaron looked at him in surprise, "Oh, Jacob! You're here! When did you come?"

"About the same time you lost your mind."

"Why didn't you grab it as you passed by it then? Would've saved me a crapload of trouble."

"It was going too fast, and it looked scared."

"Yeah," said Aaron sadly as he shook his head, "I often have that affect on it."

"Shut up, Aaron."

"Shutting up."

Jake watched as Aaron played with Milo's hair.

"You really think I'd make a good dad?"

"Absolutely."

"Moz?"

"Hmm?"

"There's something I wanted to tell you all night."

"You're pregnant, aren't you?" Jake grinned.

The corner of Aaron's mouth curled up, "Be serious."

"But you're not pregnant, right?"

"No, I'm not, you tosser."

"Then what's up with the serious?"

"Dunno … just couldn't think of a good way to tell you."

Aaron's tone of voice made Jake's stomach start to churn. "Just tell me it then, don't piss around about it."

"Matt asked me to move in. I said yes."

CHAPTER FIVE

JAKE suspected he had heard wrong. Aaron couldn't have said he was going to move in with Matt. That was impossible. It simply couldn't happen.

It couldn't.

As all the blood slowly froze in his veins, as he felt them hardening beneath his skin, Jake was sure he could see frost beginning to form and cover his hands, his arms, and surely it must be climbing up his neck because he was so fucking cold he could hardly draw in breath.

He was so suddenly, so overpoweringly, cold to the bone that it physically hurt.

He ached.

And felt brittle.

He saw Aaron's fingers inch over Milo's back towards his own and he quickly snatched them away for fear that if he touched them they would shatter into shards of broken ice.

And then where would he be?

He looked up and saw Aaron's lips were moving but for some reason no sound was coming out and his eyes looked sad. Jake hated it when Aaron's eyes looked that way. So many of the things Aaron got away with were because of those eyes. Now, however, he wasn't so sure the eyes alone would be enough to let Aaron get away with what he just said.

There were only so many times Jake could indulge Aaron.

There was only so much he could take.

Before something twisted.

Before it broke.

Jake jumped when the phone next to the bed rang. There appeared to still be sound in the world, and Jake couldn't figure out how or why none of it was coming from Aaron's mouth.

Aaron made an annoyed face and reached over and picked it up before the ringing could wake up Milo. Even when he answered it, his mouth continued to move, but Jake heard nothing at all. He saw Aaron's hand come up to the mouthpiece to cover it as he mouthed, *"It's Alyson"*. Jake hadn't a clue why he even bothered trying to mouth the words, since even if he had screamed them at the top of his lungs, he wouldn't have been able to hear him anyway.

Aaron rolled off the side of the bed and walked out of the room so he could talk without disturbing Milo's sleep. Once Aaron was gone, a strange whoosh of sound entered the room in his wake. He could hear Milo breathing deeply beside him. He could hear his joints creaking and cracking as he curled his fingers into tight fists.

He could hear his heartbeat.

He could also hear his stomach roiling and churning.

He rolled off the bed as well and rushed out the door and down the hall in a panic. He had to get to his studio bathroom, far away from where Aaron was at the moment.

With shaky hands, he managed to get the doorknob to turn and he stumbled inside the small bathroom nestled within the safety of his studio. He turned on the water in the sink to try to mask the sounds, then fell to his knees in front of the toilet and puked his guts up.

Hacking.

Coughing.

Gagging.

Choking.

He threw up absolutely everything that was foul and sad

and lonely inside him. He felt the sweat break out in a sickly film on his forehead.

His sides ached.

His throat burned.

He shook from head to toe.

And still, he couldn't stop. There was so much in him he wanted to flush away, so much that blackened his insides, that he just couldn't stop.

He was afraid if he didn't stop soon, his heart would come up with everything else and he'd lose what little there was of it left. So much of it was gone already, he just couldn't spare any more and still stay alive.

When he finally stopped choking and gagging on his knees, he pushed away from the toilet and leaned forward until his face was pressed into the cool tile of the floor. The hands that had fallen away from their grip on the toilet now lay flat on the floor, slowly sliding up until they were resting on either side of his face.

And then, there was this noise. This strange broken noise. Like something cracking or shattering. It wasn't until he felt the burning tears fall down his cheeks and drop to the floor beneath him that Jake realized the noises were coming from him. His mouth was open as if he were wailing but no sound other than choked and splintered noises and crackles were coming out.

Nothing.

He wanted to wail and sob and howl but nothing would come but the scorching tears.

Everything was still stuck in his throat, in his guts. He had been so sure he had thrown everything up he could possibly have inside him, but there was still enough bitterness and hurt in there to tangle up and block his cries from falling from his mouth.

All that was left were the hot tears and silent broken wails.

"MOZ?" Aaron whispered when Jake's face turned white as the sheets.

"Moz?"

"Jake?"

Aaron's voice kept getting smaller and smaller and more unsure the longer Jake stared at him without seeming to see him. He was looking at him with those eyes Aaron hated. The eyes that were far away and lonely and lost.

Aaron hated those eyes.

Why had he even said it? Why had he told him? He had no idea why the words spilled from his mouth and he burned to take them back.

Anything at all to get rid of those eyes.

Those eyes ripped him to shreds.

He realized Jake was shrinking in on himself, was curling away from him, so Aaron reached out his fingers towards Jake's. Aaron almost jumped out of his skin when Jake quickly snatched his hand away. That little involuntary reflex, that split second when his mind told his body to pull away from him shattered Aaron. Jake had never pulled away from him before.

Never.

Aaron didn't know what to do.

But before he could do anything at all, the phone rang and he had to quickly answer it before the ringing woke up Milo. He broke eye contact with Jake to answer it. When he heard Alyson's voice on the other end and turned back to Jake to let him know who it was, he saw the same far off look in his eyes. It was as if he were frozen in place.

"It's Alyson," he mouthed.

Jake didn't make any indication that he had heard him at all. He was still frozen.

Aaron decided to leave the room while he talked to Alyson so as to not disturb Milo. And, if he were to be completely truthful, to get away from those eyes just long enough to gather his thoughts.

To come up with a plan.

A way to make the eyes go away.

Or at least construct a crude time machine that could take

him back about five minutes to the time when he still had his foot out of his mouth.

And this ache out of his gut.

He wandered into the kitchen, not really listening to Alyson at all, merely remembering Jake's pale skin and lost eyes.

"Aaron! Hello! Are you listening to me, you little cocksucker?" yelled Alyson on the other end of the phone.

"He didn't say a thing," mumbled Aaron as he walked over to a corner, turned his back to the wall and slid down to the floor.

"Who? What are you talking about?"

"I thought he'd fight for me. I thought maybe … after what you said … he didn't. He didn't say anything at all. Why didn't he?"

"Why didn't who say what? What the hell are you talking about?"

"Jake. He didn't say a thing. He didn't argue. He didn't tell me *'no, you can't.'* He didn't say anything at all."

"What did you tell him, Aaron?" asked Alyson in a low voice.

"I told him I said yes."

"Yes to what?"

"He didn't fight for me, Aly, I thought maybe he would."

"Goddammit, Aaron, tell me what the hell you're talking about. What did you say yes to and why isn't Jake talking to you?"

"Matt asked me to move in with him. Three nights ago. He told me he loved me and wanted me with him all the time because he missed me when I wasn't. No one has ever told me that, no one has ever wanted to be with me all the time."

"No one? You honestly believe that? What then do you call Jake calling you in the middle of the night because he needs to know you're there? What do you call him coming to your place when he barely goes anywhere at all because he knows you'll be there? What the hell is that if not missing you and wanting to be with you all the time?"

"I *know,* but he's never *told* me. He's never said the words like Matt did. I never know with him. One minute I think maybe, just maybe but then he'll turn it off and I'm left standing there like an arsey little girl waiting for her crush to bring her chocolates and flowers and sonnets."

"But you know Jake isn't like that. He's not going to tell you outright because he's a fuckwit. A scared little boy, but mostly a fuckwit. And he's only going to give you chocolate because he knows you'll let him eat half. And the only kind of flower he'd ever give you would be the 'ou' kind because he wants you to bake him a fucking cake or something because he has no idea how to use the oven, or measure anything. And if you don't think he gives you sonnets then you're not paying close enough attention. Every photograph he takes of you is a sonnet. And every day he writes you one, whether you know it or not. Five years worth, Aaron. Thousands of sonnets just for you."

"But he didn't say a thing. I told him and he never opened his mouth. He never fought. He *always* argues and fights with me when it matters. He *never* lets anything go," Aaron stumbled and choked on his words as his throat closed up on him. "He let me go, Aly."

"He didn't say a thing because you probably didn't give him time. If I know you, you probably just blurted it out because you're the stupidest person I know and he couldn't possibly take it all in. How do you expect him to process the fact that his world is falling down around him so he can open his mouth and argue with you quick enough for your liking?"

"I just wanted him to tell me no. He's forever telling me no whenever he thinks he has a say in the matter, which he never does, but he still says it. He could have just said no."

"Oh, honey," sighed Alyson, "I give up. I'm done. I don't know what else I could possibly say or do to make either one of you understand. I just don't know."

"Would it be all right if I just went home, Aly? Milo's asleep, Jake can take care of him. I want to go home."

"Just go. I'll be there soon anyway. I'll be there to pick up your mess."

"I'll come back and pick it all up in the morning. I promised Moz I would."

"That's not the mess I'm talking about, sweetie, and I think you know it," said Alyson as she hung up the phone.

ALYSON let herself in with her key and walked into Jake's bedroom to check on Milo. He was sound asleep, oblivious to the world.

Jake was nowhere in sight, but she knew exactly where to look.

She opened the door to the studio slowly, fully expecting it to be disaster area. It was, but not in the way she suspected; instead of broken pottery and torn pictures there was the usual detritus that followed in Aaron and Milo's wake.

There was no evidence that Jake had been through here.

Carrying a shattered and partial heart.

She did notice that the bathroom door was closed and there was light peeking out from under the door.

"Jake?" she whispered, knocking quietly on the door.

There was no answer so she tried his name again, "Jake?"

Nothing.

"Open up, it's Aly."

She reached out tentatively to try the doorknob and it turned in her hand. She opened that door slowly as well and looked down to see Jake curled up and asleep on the floor.

"Oh, sweetie," she sighed as she knelt down beside him and shook his arm, "wake up. I'm back."

Jake muttered something she couldn't hear then asked in a small voice, "Flip?"

Alyson wanted to cry and beat Aaron at the same time and she briefly wondered if she could do both. "No sweetie, it's Alyson."

Jake opened his eyes, "Did he go?"

"Yes, he did."

"Good," he said as he turned away from her.

"No, it's not good. It's terrible. Horrible. No good."

"A very bad day," finished Jake with a sad laugh.

"Don't joke, Jacob, this isn't a children's book and it isn't going to be all right in the end if you don't do something about it. I've tried with Aaron and I'm done with the stupidity, I'm counting on you to let go of the dumb."

"He said yes, just like that, he said yes."

"And you don't find that strange? He's never been anywhere close to moving in with one of his phases before, why now? Why Matt?"

"Because Matt's good to him and loves him."

"There have been a lot of others that were good to him and loved him. He always came back to you, though. Always."

"Maybe he just got tired of coming back."

"I think he got tired of having to come back unasked."

"It's not my place to ask him to come back, he needs to do that on his own."

"Oh, but it *is* your place to tell him over and over again, with every single one, that they weren't good enough for him and that he was better off without them."

"Well, they weren't and he was."

"Better off with you," said Alyson quietly as she curled up behind him, wrapped her arms around him and put her chin over his shoulder.

"Then why would he leave me?"

"Because he wants you to tell him he can't. He wants you to bring him back home. This home, right here, where he belongs."

"But what if his home really is with Matt? What if, in the long run, that's where he belongs, where he'd be happiest? I want him to be happy more than I want him with me."

Alyson tightened her hold, "Honey, hearing you say that is exactly what would make him happy. He's happiest with you even though you drive him mad and he drives you, fuck, I don't know where he drives you, most likely off the road and through some poor unsuspecting old couple's front porch like those drunk or senile old people you see on the news."

Alyson could feel Jake's mouth turn up in a smile against her cheek where their faces were pressed together.

"You make him happiest. You. Make. Him. Happy. And the most astounding thing of all is that he makes you happy in return. I've never seen anyone make you truly happy but he does, crazy porch driving and all."

"Could you imagine if we ever let him behind the wheel of an actual car?"

"I'd rather Milo drive."

"So would I," Jake agreed readily, "the only thing Flip has going in his favor is that his feet reach the pedals."

Alyson gave Jake another squeeze, "I love you, you know."

"I know, and I love you, too."

Alyson lay her forehead against the side of Jake's head and whispered in his ear, "You have to tell Aaron the same thing. Tell him you love him."

Jake's only response was the sound of his breathing.

"You do love him, don't you?"

Again, there was silence and just as Alyson was about to give up hope on Jake ever figuring things out either, she heard the word she had been dying to hear for such a long time.

"Yes."

"Say it," she whispered as she tugged him toward her chest and held him fast, "out loud."

And finally, in a louder, clearer voice than before Jake said, "I love him."

CHAPTER SIX

JAKE awoke the next morning in a funk to end all funks.

He had said it.

Out loud.

To Alyson of all people, the only person other than Aaron with a mouth bigger than the Grand fucking Canyon. He was sure she would just love to run off and tell Aaron everything he said but he also knew without a doubt that she would never betray his trust that way. She would keep it to herself even if it killed her, just as he would for her. It didn't make it any less painful and shocking, however.

He couldn't believe he had said it, said he loved him.

He knew he did. He *knew* it, like how he knew the sky was blue and grass was green, he knew he loved Aaron. But to say it and mean it with every piece of his heart was something so frightening that he was surprised he still wasn't curled up on the bathroom floor too paralyzed with fear to even move.

It had always just been him. For the longest time, he'd had to depend on himself. For a while Alyson had been there every day to hold him up and keep him functioning, but then came Aaron and within five minutes of meeting him he became all Jake ever needed. End of story. He was gone from the word "go" and he had tried to deny it, for five fucking years he had tried to deny it, but he was no longer able to play dumb. The words had fallen from his mouth and even though the fear sizzled through him like a lightning strike, there was no way he was going to take the words back.

He was done pretending Aaron wasn't his entire world. That he wasn't the reason he got out of bed every morning or was able to fall asleep each night. He was no longer going to deny that Aaron had pushed his walls further away from him than they had ever been. Before him, the walls were so close around Jake that he only had to spread his arms out and he could touch all four of the solid walls that formed his cage. Now that Aaron had tunneled in, created an escape route, he found there was a sun and stars and fresh air all around him. Some days he couldn't even see the walls for how far away Aaron had pushed them from him. Because of Aaron, he could stretch his arms out and spin and spin and spin like a top and never once touch anything other than life and warmth. Gone was the cold. Gone were the ever present walls. And in their place was Aaron.

But now Aaron would be gone, too, and Jake knew without him there to protect him the walls would sneak back and close in around him like a coffin.

Oh-so-slowly suffocating him.

Burying him alive.

But hadn't he known all along that would happen? Hadn't he known he couldn't keep a bright someone like Aaron trapped in his tiny world forever?

He had.

He had known.

Known it was too good, too real, too much life for him to ever keep.

How he had managed to keep Aaron contained within the confines of his world for so long would forever remain a mystery to Jake. He would always wonder what spell he had managed to cast that had kept him there to stand guard for so long. Something so beautiful was not meant to stay hidden away in a box. Jake had tried, he had kept every single picture he ever took of Aaron in photo box after photo box in an effort to somehow restrain the real one from wandering away from him. For some reason, he thought he could keep him tethered to him if he kept all those pictures of his face, his body, his brilliant soul close to him. Like some form of voodoo … trap the soul, the image, and you trap the man. But Aaron could never fit in such a small place, could never be confined to a box of flat two dimensional false images, so that was why he wasn't going to say a thing to him.

Not a single word.

He'd let him leave, let him out of the box, to go where he would.

Jake owed him that much. For how long he had trapped him, he now owed him his freedom.

He knew Alyson would all but kill him and throw him in the East River.

He knew it.

He also knew he'd probably never be able to breathe again but it would be worth it just to see Aaron outside of Jake's stunted existence.

Worth it to see him never grow dim, never fade away.

AS Jake wandered out of his bedroom and down the hall he realized he could hear noises coming from the studio. He walked over to the open doorway and looked inside. He stood still for a moment as he watched Aaron pick up the mess he had made with Milo the night before. He watched as Aaron suddenly stopped and sat down cross-legged in the middle of the floor and looked around him like he was completely bewildered as to where he was exactly.

Jake had never seen him look so small.

And lost.

To him Aaron had always been larger than his physical presence and seeing him sitting by himself amidst the mess of the studio, unknowingly clutching a blanket to his chest, was a shock to his system. He couldn't quite handle the lost look either. Aaron *always* knew exactly where he was and what he was doing.

Always.

Jake had always been sure Aaron had all the answers to all the fucked up questions he had floating around in his own mind. Almost daily he'd let one of those asinine questions slip from his lips and Aaron would laugh or smile and give him what Jake believed to be a completely plausible answer, never mind that it was more than likely bullshit, it was coming from Aaron after all. But, he believed him, and that was what mattered. It was foreign to him to see Aaron looking lost.

Adrift on a wooden sea of blankets, toys and skateboards.

It didn't fit, didn't feel right, and it made what he had to do all the harder because what he really wanted to do at that moment was let go of his life preserver and float out to Aaron and drift away.

"Hey, Flip," he whispered from the doorway.

Aaron actually jumped at such a small sound. He turned to look at him sheepishly, "Hey, I didn't hear you come in."

"I'm not technically *in* though, am I? I'm still in the doorway."

Aaron smiled at him faintly, "Hmmm, *An Arse in a Doorway*, could be the name of your next series."

"Maybe, or perhaps I could do one called *The Whore on the Floor*? That might make more of an impression."

Aaron snorted, "Yeah, how much are you gonna charge for admission to that one? I don't come cheap, you know."

"No, you don't," said Jake quietly as he leaned his head against the doorjamb.

Aaron picked up the ski pole that was next to him and started pushing the skateboard around with it. Jake listened to the sound of the wheels rolling across the wood of the floor.

Back and forth.

Back and forth.

Jake suspected Aaron didn't know what to do or say so he was dinking around in an effort to give himself something to do.

"When are you going to move?" Jake finally asked.

"Huh?" Aaron turned a confused face to him, "I don't want

... I ... what do you...." When Jake didn't say anything he sighed and added, "Friday, I guess."

"Is that your last day here too, or are you doing the actual moving on Friday during the day and will be done here Thursday? I need to know so I can ask Aly to take over until I find a replacement."

Aaron sprang up from the floor, "A replacement? I'm not ... why do you need Aly? I'll be here. I'm right here."

"But not for long."

"Yes for long. Where would I go?"

"To Matt's."

"I'm just moving in with him. Across the fucking park for fucksake, it's not like we're moving to Timbuk-fucking-tu!"

"But don't you want a fresh start? Moving in with someone is a big step."

"Yeah it is, which is why I need everything else in my life to stay the same. How am I supposed to adjust if you're not there?"

"I'm not going to be *there* there so why do you need me to be here there?"

"Because I do! And that sentence didn't make any sense."

"You understood it though, didn't you?"

"That's not the point. Quit speaking in circles."

"You don't need me anymore, Flip."

"Yes I do!"

"To do what? Make your life miserable? I don't think Matt will welcome the three a.m. phone calls or the two a.m. visits. I think it's best if we just cut the cord now, so to speak."

"You're such a fucking asshole, Jake. Why won't you fight with me?"

"I thought that's what we were doing, a mild fight, but a fight nevertheless."

"We are NOT fighting! You're standing there like a fucking lump and telling me to go away and never come back, you arse!"

"I just think it would be easier if we didn't work together."

"When am I supposed to see you, then?"

"I don't think you're supposed to, I think you should focus on your new life with Matt."

"And never see you again?"

"Yes," Jake's fingers curled into the doorjamb so hard when he said that one word that he could feel his nails breaking as they dug into the wood.

"Never? Never?! Well fuck you, then!" Aaron yelled at him as he threw the ski pole he was still holding across the room, "Fuck you, Moz! Fuck you and all your stupid boring insecurities and your stupid boring life! Fuck you and the five fucking years I spent putting up with you!"

Jake watched as Aaron stomped around the room, kicking everything in his path.

"You fucking fight with me every damn day and try to run my life for me and just like that you're going to fucking stop? You're done with me now? Am I too fucking much work for you?"

Jake remained silent as Aaron answered his own rant.

"Apparently. Apparently I'm not worth the effort. Have I ever been?" he asked as his arms flailed and his feet continued to kick things, "Have I ever been worth it?"

Yes. Yes. Yes.

God, yes.

Jake closed his eyes to Aaron's angry face and sad eyes.

"I give up! I give up. I'm done. No more of this. If you don't want me here then fuck it. I don't care any more. I'll fucking move in with Matt and live happily ever fucking after and you'll be the fucking footnote I left back on page five, way the fuck at the beginning that everyone has forgotten about by the end."

Leave. Leave. Leave.

While I'm still able to stand.

Leave before I tell you to stay.

Leave before I ruin you more than I already have.

Leave.

Jake's eyes shot open when he heard a loud crash. Aaron had picked up Milo's baseball and thrown it at the last nighttime blue on the shelf. The last one. The one Alyson said was the closest to the color of his eyes. So shocked was he at the shattered blue pieces on the floor that he didn't even register Aaron running out of the room until he shoved him out of the doorway to get past him.

Jake jumped when the front door slammed shut and then he stood still, trying to remain on his feet. Breathing in and out as he swayed.

Just when he thought he was going to lose the battle the front door slammed back open and Aaron was running toward him again. The force of Aaron's punch sent him slamming into the wall. He wobbled a bit, thrown off by the strength and suddenness of it, and then Aaron's arms were around him.

Pulling him back upright.

Holding him in a near stranglehold.

Like he was never going to let him go.

His nails digging into the skin of Jake's back.

"I hate you! I fucking hate you!" Aaron yelled and wept at the same time into the crook of Jake's neck where he had buried his face, "I hate you!"

I know. I know.

Jake winced as Aaron's hands tore at his shirt and scratched him as if he were trying to rip him open.

"I hate you!" he sobbed one last time before violently pushing Jake away from him and running back out the door.

The door slammed one last time. Jake waited for it to open again but it didn't so instead he said to it what he had wanted to say to Aaron all along.

"I love you."

FOR days on end Jake put up with Alyson's haranguing.

She yelled at him over and over. Asking him what the hell did he think he was accomplishing by pushing Aaron away. And over and over again he insisted he was doing what he thought would make Aaron happiest in the long run.

"But what about *you*? What would make *you* happy?" she had asked.

"Him being happy," he had answered.

After the first week he had asked her kindly, but firmly, to just stop. Stop asking him why. Stop telling him he was a fool. Stop saying how much he had hurt Aaron and himself.

Stop.

There must have been something in his eyes or the tone of his voice that reached out to her, that told her he had had enough because she stopped. She never brought the situation up again. Not once. She simply and quietly resumed her job as his assistant, telling him now that Milo was older and in preschool most of the day and since Aaron had managed to temper and mellow Jake in the years they were together, that she could come back to work for him. He needn't find a replacement for Aaron. Jake was thankful she didn't say it outright but the truth was there, floating between them.

There was no replacement for Aaron.

There never would be.

There would merely be an inferior substitute.

So, instead of inflicting that trauma on an unsuspecting victim, Alyson very quietly moved all of Aaron's things to a box and put hers in their place and tried as unobtrusively as possible to take over his duties but never his place.

The box full of Aaron's things that he had left behind sat sullenly in a corner like an elephant in the room. Alyson never commented when she saw Jake looking over at it more frequently than he looked at anything else. She also didn't comment when she'd see him walking over to the box and picking up something just to hold it in his hands. She let it go when the thing sometimes didn't make its way back into the box but instead went into Jake's pocket or was put back in its "place." She suspected Jake didn't even realize he was slowly putting all of Aaron's things right back where they belonged because the room was somehow wrong without them there.

This little dance with the box went on for almost three weeks before Matt showed up out of the blue to collect it. Alyson felt sorry for him because he looked so horribly uncomfortable. He seemed so apologetic. Over and over he said he didn't mean to interrupt but that Aaron just couldn't find the time to make it over to pick his things up so he was there instead.

Everyone in the room knew that was a lie.

Once he had the box in his hands he didn't leave immediately, but suddenly flushed red and tried to say something. "I was wondering if I could..." he stuttered as he pointed at the nighttime blues all lined up in a row, "he wanted ... can I take two?"

"Of course you can, they're his anyway. You can take them all," Jake feigned disinterest. Alyson knew he could do so only because Aaron had just asked for two and not all of them. If he had asked Matt to take them all Jake would have choked.

Matt nodded and smiled a bit as he muttered, "Thanks."

Both Alyson and Jake watched as he looked up at the shelf and started counting them to himself, his finger following the path of his counting. About a third of the way down the line he reached out to pick up a pot. He placed it gently in the box then continued with his counting.

Jake looked at Alyson questioningly. Never one to hold herself back, Alyson asked, "What are you doing?"

Matt looked back at her and flushed red again, "He only wanted certain ones. He said he wanted the eleventh one and the thirty-sixth one," he shrugged, "I don't know why but that's what he asked for."

Alyson somehow suspected Matt did a lot of things just because Aaron asked for them. She wouldn't be surprised to see him do an Irish jig as he counted them if that was how Aaron told him they would be best collected.

After Matt left with more embarrassed smiles and muttered

apologies, Jake said, "Well, that's done, then."

Alyson didn't comment, only noticed how Jake's attention was now drawn to the empty spaces on the shelf rather than the box in the corner. A couple of days later, when Jake was in the darkroom, she had rearranged the nighttime blues so there were no longer any gaping spaces for him to focus on.

When she came back the next morning they were put back exactly where they had been.

Gaping holes and all.

Alyson left them alone after that.

And she continued to help him set up all the photographs he had chosen for his next showing even though they tore out her heart and she ached to know what they were doing to Jake's.

JAKE had taken to going on walks in the evenings, about the time the sun set and the lights in the homes went on. He'd walk through the park until he came to the row of Brownstones that Aaron now called home. He'd walk back and forth along the street until either Matt or Aaron would turn on a light so he could see inside. He didn't know if he hated or loved the fact that they tended to leave their curtains open and blinds pulled up.

He hated it on the days when he'd see Matt pulling a laughing Aaron across the room.

He loved it when Aaron was home alone, reading in the chair by the window, Harold sleeping on the ottoman at his feet.

He hated it when he knew Matt had said something from the other room because Aaron would smile and say something in return.

He loved it when it rained and Aaron would sleep in the window seat, his face pressed to the window, just like he used to do in Jake's studio.

He hated it when it rained and Aaron would sleep in the window seat, his face pressed to the window, because the raindrops looked like tears streaming down his face and those moments made it all too easy for Jake to get up from the bench he was sitting on to walk over to the door of the Brownstone and almost press the buzzer before he could stop himself.

One day he wondered if Aaron had a new Wilbur and Charlotte. He longed to know if Matt loved him enough to know he needed to create, that he needed to draw pots and bowls and vases out of the lumps of clay that looked liked nothing at all to those that didn't know any better.

He couldn't tell since the only room he could ever see into was their living room, so he decided to pack up Wilbur and Charlotte and send them over to him. He was disappointed and relieved both when not more than a couple hours after they left the men who had picked them up returned with them still in tow and shrugging their bewilderment.

"When we told him what they were he just said he didn't want them and closed the door," said the burly and somewhat smelly man in Jake's doorway.

"That's fine," said Jake quietly, "could you just put them back in the studio where you picked them up?"

So they did.

And Jake went back to wondering whether Aaron had a new Wilbur and Charlotte and whether Matt loved him enough.

He also went back to walking the sidewalk across from their Brownstone just waiting for a glimpse of anything that would make him even remotely happy.

One evening, as it was drizzling just enough to make a person damp and bring out the smell of the earth, Jake was sitting on the bench across the street when the door of the Brownstone opened and Matt walked out with an umbrella. Jake didn't know whether to get up and walk away or sit there and hope he wouldn't be seen. As he sat there in indecision, Matt headed purposefully across the street and sat down next to him.

"Hey."

Jake was confused and disoriented by Matt's sudden appearance and such an ordinary greeting, as if they had planned to meet all along. Like it was just an ordinary day.

"Hey," Jake said in return.

"I have a few things I want to say to you," Matt began.

"Look," interrupted Jake, "I'm sorry, I didn't mean to bother you. Let's just forget about it. I'll go home and I promise not to hang around anymore."

"I know why you do. Hang around. I understand it. I don't particularly like it, but I understand it."

"I'll stop. You won't see me again after today."

Matt ignored him for a few moments before saying, "I think I know I'm not his first choice but he did choose me and I'm working on that being okay because I want him here more than I don't. It's fucked up but it's what works for me."

Jake knew about being fucked up. He had mastered the fucking up a long time gone.

"I don't know whether to tell you to never come back here because I'm waiting for the other shoe to drop and if you're out here waiting it'll make it easier for him to walk out the door and never come back, or if I want you to stay because I couldn't stop you anyway. Regardless of what you promise."

Jake was going to protest but decided against it because he figured Matt was probably right, even if he did promise not to come back the temptation of that lit window was too vast to ignore.

"I'm taking good care of him," Matt added awkwardly, "In case you were wondering."

"I was and I wasn't," answered Jake.

There was an uncomfortable silence before Matt got up and turned to him, with the umbrella held in his outstretched hand, "Here, take it."

Jake looked at him questioningly but took hold of it anyway.

"He said since you were too stupid to bring your own you might as well have this one or else you'll catch pneumonia or malaria, and he doesn't want it to look like an old hobo has died on the bench in front of his house. Might bring the property value down," Matt said with a slight grin and a shrug of his shoulders.

For the first time since Aaron left, Jake smiled. A genuine

smile as he looked up and saw Aaron looking down at him from the illuminated window, shaking his head and scowling at him but then turning away before Jake could catch the corner of his mouth turn up in one of his crooked off-balanced grins.

"Tell him thanks," Jake said quietly as he tightened his grip on the umbrella, the metal beneath his hands turning from clammy cold to softly warm.

Matt stepped off the curb, ready to walk back across the street. "Maybe you should keep coming by," he said over his shoulder, "He's calmer, happier, on the days you come by."

"He knows I'm out here?"

Matt looked at him like he was a simpleton.

"He always knows where you are."

Jake watched as Matt jogged across the street and loped up the steps leading into the Brownstone and disappeared.

And even though the rain had stopped by the time Jake got up from the bench, he kept the umbrella up as he walked home.

CHAPTER SEVEN

AARON stood at the window and watched Matt talk to Jake. He watched as he handed him the umbrella he had insisted Matt take. He couldn't believe how often Jake would sit out in the rain with no coat or umbrella to keep him dry. It was like he was completely unaware of what was going on around him.

Aaron understood that feeling.

Without Jake, he sometimes wondered what it was he was supposed to be doing. He'd start one thing and halfway through think of something he used to do for Jake. At those times, he would often find himself halfway out the door on a film run or grocery trip before he realized, yes, it was Tuesday but no, Jake wasn't in the other room waiting for his chicken salad on wheat.

He didn't know how to spend his days without Jake there to fill them.

When he had moved in with Matt, he had been able to sell a few of his pieces to a local gallery, so there wasn't a pressing need for him to go out and find another job. The money he earned from the sale was enough to get him through a couple of months. Matt never pressured him to find actual employment, only suggested he try focusing solely on his work and making his living off of that.

Aaron loved and hated Matt in equal measure in moments like those. He loved him for loving him and knowing exactly what he wanted. Aaron had always wanted to create, nothing more complicated than that. He had been lucky in finding Jake, the one person who would pay him to "work" while really letting him piss away hours on end at his wheel. Jake never interrupted him, and there were days when he'd get up to leave and realize he hadn't said a thing to him all day nor had he done a single minute of actual work for him. He also hated Matt for being so good, so loving. He hated him because he knew he was using him, knew Matt knew he was using him, and he let him keep doing it. He let him live in his home. He let him bitch about everything while knowing all the while it was actually Jake he was bitching about. Aaron hated him for being nice to him, for letting him walk all over him.

He hated him.

He loved him.

But not like he loved Jake.

He loved Matt like you would your favorite t-shirt or movie or book, you just did because they made you feel like you were home and safe.

He loved Jake because he *was* his home, and no matter how much Matt *felt* like home, he simply was not.

Jake was Aaron's home.

His stupid, fucked up home.

And he was achingly homesick.

Painfully.

Achingly.

Homesick.

But now he didn't know what to do. When he first told Jake he was going to move in with Matt, he thought he'd throw a fit and tell him he couldn't. He readily admitted he used the statement as bait to try to trap Jake into saying *something*, anything really, just something to show he cared ... maybe even loved Aaron. But instead, he had all but fired him and told him to have a nice fucking life, and Aaron was left no other choice but to actually move in with Matt, which he had never had any intention of doing in the first place. Now he hadn't only ruined his own life, but he'd ruined Matt's as well.

He had no idea why Matt even accepted his yes in the first place. It was an angry impetuous yes, nothing even close to the lovingly excited yes it should have been. Yet Matt had smiled his Matt smile at him and said, "Okay then," and that was that.

Three days later, he was out of his flat and in Matt's.

Three days and he was severed from Jake, although admittedly that had happened the day after he told him, when Jake had been all sad quiet resignation and Aaron had been the screeching angry harpy.

For the first week, he sat all day long in the apartment, only venturing outside to take poor Harold for a walk in the park and even then he sometimes finagled Matt into doing it for him. He just didn't want to be out *there*. He was afraid of it. He was afraid of stepping outside his doors and getting lost. The city he had come to know, the New York that he'd grown to love, had disappeared for him. The city was now strangely empty despite its millions of people. It was too quiet and too noisy both. It was too fast and too slow. It made him want to scream. Not even that first day he had stepped foot in Manhattan had he felt so lost. Then he had had a silly little map to tell him where to go, which bus to take, which subway line would take him where he needed to go.

After that he'd had Jake.

Jake told him where to go to buy film.

Jake told him where to go to buy food.

Jake told him where to go to find the book he had mentioned he wanted in passing but that Jake remembered for weeks after.

Jake mapped out the city for him in a way no real map could. The map Aaron had held in his hands that first day was only a two-dimensional outline, you couldn't breathe it in, you couldn't live in it. The city Jake mapped out for Aaron he could live in, he *did* live in. For five years, he lived in it, breathed it in, and now it was gone.

The shock kept him holed up like a hermit for an entire week until he spotted Jake for the first time out on the sidewalk across the street. He watched with elation as Jake walked back and forth, seemingly lost in thought and only occasionally glancing up to his window. He thought for sure he was trying to figure out what to say to him before ringing his buzzer. He was absolutely positive he was thinking over the best way to say he was sorry and to ask him to come home.

Home.

Aaron nearly wept, he wanted to go home so badly. If Jake would just come up the fucking front steps, he'd even make some ridiculous Dorothy joke about it, would call him the Wizard of Moz and tap his heels three times once he asked him to come back.

And he'd definitely bring up the flying monkeys.

Jake fucking *hated* the flying monkeys.

There's no place like home.

There's no place like home.

No place.

Aaron waited patiently for half an hour as Jake paced. He waited with a smile on his face and his heart pounding. He practiced saying yes over and over again.

Yes, I'll come back.

Yes, I forgive you.

Yes, I love you.

Didn't you know?

Didn't you?

He was so busy reciting his yeses that when he next looked out the window, Jake was gone. He had cried out in panic and run down the flights of stairs to the front door, looking up and down the street for Jake's retreating back. He ran blindly out onto the street and then into the park. Running down the path he knew would lead him across the park the quickest, the one that ended a block down from Jake's building.

He ran and ran and ran until he realized he was no closer to finding Jake than he had been standing still way up in his ivory tower.

So he stopped.

And looked around him in a daze.

Truly lost.

He had to ask a police officer patrolling the park on horseback where to go to get back home. The officer looked at him funny but had pointed out the way. It was only after he had made it back to the Brownstone and walked up through the still open door he had left flapping in the breeze on his mad rush out that he realize he looked slightly crazed, his hair uncombed and his eyes wide and shocked, pupils dilated. No wonder the officer had looked at him the way he did, how else would one respond to a grown man asking, *"How do I get home?"*

So stupid.

So very stupid to leave home without your breadcrumbs.

All he wanted was a sign, any slight indication that Jake wanted him back. Anything at all. If only once Jake would look up at his window and then come to the door, Aaron would rush down the stairs and be there in an instant. Right there in front of him, reaching out to him, grabbing onto him.

Never letting go.

He would watch from his window, euphoric with hope, dizzy and out of control, breath and heartbeat far too frighteningly fast.

Until Jake turned and walked away again.

Then it was the crash, the inevitable crash back to earth, where his legs gave out under him and he'd drop to the floor because he no longer had the rush that the sight of Jake shot through his system to keep him upright. He would shake like an addict bereft of his drug.

That lasted for two weeks.

It lasted until Matt came home one day and found him crouched down by the window. He had asked what was wrong and Aaron couldn't say a thing, couldn't form a word that wasn't crazy. He couldn't say anything other than "Jake walked away again," so he stayed silent.

After that, he vowed to no longer let Jake affect him that

way. He didn't want to run the risk of Matt finding him like that again and asking more questions he couldn't, and wouldn't, answer. So instead of the burning mania that had consumed him before, he tried seeing Jake's visits for what they were ... glimpses of the world he used to know. He tried replacing the hope with calm resignation, with that sad yet fond remembrance one bears for days long gone, days that won't ever return no matter how many stars you wish upon.

He tried turning Jake into a fond memory, like Sunday dinner at Gran's or jumping in puddles on your way home from school. Something that made you ache inside to remember but also smile and be happy from the sheer fact that it had happened at all.

He tried being happy he had splashed through the puddles at one time in the not too distant past.

He tried because he didn't want Matt wondering any more about why he found him crying at the window when he came home from work. One time was enough. It had to stop.

He had to make it stop.

So each time he'd see Jake across the street in the park, pacing the sidewalk or sitting patiently on the bench, he'd try to remember something good about him, something that would make him smile instead of cry. There was so much that could make him smile, so much he had loved, that it wasn't nearly as hard to hide the tears behind a grin and a happy façade as he had thought it would be.

There were still days when he'd forget his resolution and would lose it watching Jake do nothing to come closer to his door. Those were usually the days it rained and Matt was gone and there was no one home to fool. Those days, Aaron would lay in the window seat and press his face against the window and let himself cry, all the while telling himself it was only the rain sliding down his cheeks in the reflection of his face in the window and not the tears he tried so hard to hide.

The rain made it so much easier to be melancholy.

So much easier to forget what it was he was supposed to be pretending to do.

The rain made it so much easier to care for Jake as he sat without his coat or umbrella, soaked to the skin and alone.

So much easier to want to run out the door and sit beside him on that bench, soaked to the skin and together.

So it would stand to reason that on one of those rainy days he had let it all slip again and had asked Matt to take an umbrella out to him. Of course Matt had done it, yet another reason to hate him and love him all at once. He watched as they talked and his gut churned just thinking about what they could ever be saying to each other. When Matt handed him the umbrella and he had looked up at Aaron with one of his confused and beautiful 'Jake' looks, Aaron scowled at his stupidity like he would have done at any other time, but then had to turn away when the familiarity of it and the happiness of looking into Jake's eyes rather than simply at him made the corners of his lips turn up in a grin. He was waiting in the entry when Matt came back upstairs and through the door.

"What were you saying to him?"

"I told him you said he'd get malaria and die like a hobo."

"Funny."

"It's what I said."

"You said a lot more than that. That would have taken two seconds. I know it only used to take me two seconds to tell him he was a dumbfuck. You were out there more than two seconds."

"I told him to keep coming around."

"Why?! Why would you ever do that?" Aaron asked in alarm.

"Because it makes you happy when he does."

"And you see nothing wrong with that statement."

"Nope."

"Are you retarded?"

"Not that I know...."

"Why would you tell someone to keep stalking your boyfriend?"

"Because my boyfriend is stalking him too ... albeit from a

window, a kind of stationary stalking, but stalking all the same."

"What is *wrong* with you?"

"Nothing. I'm just wondering when I'm going to get my place back to myself."

"What?" Aaron all but shouted.

"Well, I figure if he keeps coming around long enough, one of you two idiots should finally crack and do something about the fact that you're both crazy and in love with each other and crazy and lost without each other and crazy. Did I mention crazy? Because you are. Crazy. Very, very, very crazy. Like 'all work and no play makes Aaron a dull boy' crazy."

"Me, crazy? I think you just bought yourself a straight jacket with that little speech, Matty."

"What? You think I don't know you're in love with him? I'd be crazy if I *didn't* know that. How dumb do you think I am, Aaron? I've got two eyes and a relatively perceptive brain. It didn't take me too long to figure it all out."

Aaron stared at him flustered and confused, "Well, how long, then?" he demanded. "How long have you known, oh wise one?"

"A while."

"A while? A fucking while? Since before we moved in together?"

"Yeah."

"Then why the hell did you ask me to move in with you, you tosspot?"

"I thought asking you to move in would be a big enough shock to light a fire under your ass. but apparently I vastly overestimated your intelligence."

"Duh! I'm stupid! Hello, arsehole! Where have you been?"

"Being stupid, too ... and completely infatuated with you. Must have been our stupids calling out to each other."

"Oh my god! Where the hell is this conversation going?"

"Certainly nowhere intelligent."

"Obviously."

"Listen," said Matt, reaching out to grab Aaron's arm and drag him over to the couch to sit down, "I know you love him. It's been obvious to me for a long time, but I wasn't sure if he felt the same way, so I talked to Alyson about it and she told me that Jake did. Love you, I mean. That's when I gave up. Before that, I thought maybe, if it was only one-sided, I could charm you away from him, which was a stupid idea all around, but since we just recently established our own stupidity, that was to be expected, yeah?"

Aaron nodded but continued looking at him blankly, not quite knowing what to do with the information overload.

"So I figured the quickest and easiest way to scare you away would be to ask you to move in with me, because that way you'd run and it would be *your* fault and not mine. You'd be the one that ran away from me, and I could try to believe I wasn't the one that ended it, that I wasn't the fool who loved someone more than he loved me."

"Matty...." Aaron quietly pleaded as he reached out to take his hand.

Matt curled his fingers around Aaron's outstretched hand and bent down to give it a quick kiss, "But you threw me for a loop by saying yes. Although I guess you didn't really *say* it, more like angry-yelled it, but it was still a yes."

"You fucker," Aaron whispered as he half-heartedly shoved at Matt's shoulder, "why in the hell didn't you tell me to fuck off?"

Matt shrugged, "Can I claim stupidity again?"

"No," Aaron said stubbornly.

"Fine, I didn't tell you to fuck off because you were so angry and sad and you looked like you really needed a place to go."

"Yeah, like my own home. You could have sent me on my merry fucking way."

Matt set his arm on the back of the couch and bent it so he could rest his head in his hand as he smiled at Aaron.

"Quit giving me the Matt look."

Matt kept looking at him.

"Stop it."

Matt raised an eyebrow.

"Quit being a penis!"

Matt's smile widened.

"I hate you. You always think you know exactly what's going on, but that's just stupid to think you know everything. No one knows everything. Not even Stephen Hawking. Or the Pope. Well, that's not a very good example because on the whole, popes are rather oblivious to what's going on in the actual world. Like in the year 2006, you know, because the way they talk, it's 1206 and we're all serfs harvesting wheat for the Lord or whatever. And now that I think about it, you're the Pope. Pope Matt the First. Wearing your big pope hat and waving to the crowd and telling people what to do even though you're stupid and way behind the times. You're the Pope."

"I love you, Aaron."

Aaron scowled then leaned forward until his forehead came to rest in the center of Matt's chest. "I love you, too, Matty."

"I know you do."

"Which makes me an even bigger fucker who should be kicked out and forced to catch malaria and die like a hobo on Jake's bench."

"Probably, yeah," Matt agreed, reaching up to run his hand through Aaron's hair.

"Uhhhhhhh," moaned Aaron dramatically, "I'm a hobo."

"But a hot one. Take some consolation in that."

"I'm only hot on account of the malaria."

Matt laughed, then yanked Aaron's head up by his hair so he was looking at him. "Okay, you malaria soaked hobo, I let you move in because I wanted to and it's what I thought you needed at the time."

Aaron's lips turned down as he muttered 'ouch' and rubbed

his head where Matt had tugged on his hair.

"Baby," muttered Matt before continuing, "Now, however, I'm beginning to wonder at my decision. I thought you two would be quicker about it. I didn't take into account your stubborn streaks."

"And our stupidity, don't forget that streak … it's Aly's favorite."

"Yeah, speaking of Alyson, seeing as how you've appointed me Pope, I think I'm going to grant her sainthood."

"She deserves it," agreed Aaron.

"That she does. But we'll talk about her shrine and crying statue later. Right now we need to focus on what you're going to do to get the hell out of my apartment and back into Jake's where you belong."

"I was never *in* Jake's apartment," said Aaron mulishly.

"Quit being literal. I'm done with the pouting and the denial and the stubbornness. I'm done being nice when all I want to do is kick Jake's ass and take you away so I can keep you for myself, but since that ain't gonna happen, I'll have to settle for getting your mess straightened out."

"Why are you doing this, Matty?"

"First of all, because I love you and don't get all sad looking about it because I know the way we work and I think we work better as friends, don't you?"

"You deserve a better friend than me."

"But I want you as one anyway, so let's just leave it at that," said Matt. "Secondly, you and Jake belong together no matter how fucked up the two of you are. You're absolutely volatile together, like a damn match and a can of gasoline, but I know you belong together. Nobody else could, or should have to, put up with your toxicity. You're each other's poison and there's no way around it."

"Yeah," sighed Aaron, "we're kinda like Pamela and Tommy Lee."

Matt laughed outright, "Jesus fuck, trust you to say

something like that."

"Well, we are!"

"Does that make me Kid Rock in this scenario?"

"Fuck, no, you're way cuter than Kid Rock. Besides, you don't even own a cowboy hat and you don't like beer, it just doesn't work."

"But Kid Rock and Pamela just got married, didn't they?"

"Pfft! Like that'll last. Pam and Tommy belong together."

"Now I'm picturing you in a halter top and blond wig."

"Why am I Pamela?"

"Because you've got the best tits I've ever seen?"

Aaron squeaked as Matt reached out and pinched a nipple. "You fucker!" he laughed.

"See, best tits in town."

"That was my nipple, thank you very much, you barmy sonofabitch."

Matt just grinned at him again as he rubbed his chest with a pained expression on his face. When Aaron stopped, he looked up to see him smiling at him.

"I love you, Matty, even if you give me titty twisters."

"I'll keep that in mind," said Matt thoughtfully, "I need to digress, though, and ask you what you're doing Friday night?"

"I don't know, you tell me."

"Well, there's this photography exhibition that Alyson told me you might like...."

AARON took Matt's hand and walked into the gallery. He had no idea what to expect. He only knew that he was nervous to see Jake again. He knew Jake wouldn't be mingling with the crowd, he hated crowds, he would probably be hidden somewhere trying to stay away from his admirers. That knowledge was the only thing that allowed Aaron to have enough courage to step inside.

He knew Jake had called his exhibition *The One I Want* but

nothing else. He didn't get much further than the doorway, however, because the moment he entered the gallery, all he saw was himself. Dozens and dozens of photographs of him staring back at him. They lined every wall, every pillar; every possible spot contained his face or his mouth, his eyes or his neck, his hands on a pot or a curl tucked behind an ear. Every photo was some part of him.

"He kept them," Aaron whispered. "I thought they were all gone. I didn't think they were good enough."

"Of course, he kept them, you shithead," said Alyson casually as she handed Matt a drink and started to pull him away. "Jake's outside, through those doors. You know him and crowds...."

Aaron looked at Matt in a panic as Alyson dragged him away. "See you on the Flip side," he grinned, saluting Aaron with his drink and disappearing with Alyson into the crowd.

"Stupid Matt and his stupid puns," mumbled Aaron as he stomped over to the door leading out to a courtyard lit with Japanese lanterns. He was so caught up in his petulant scowling that he almost missed Jake sitting by himself on a bench, his back to Aaron. He stood stock still for a minute before putting his head down and purposefully heading over to the bench where he sat down next to Jake, but in the opposite direction, looking back in at the party instead of out at the courtyard. His fingers curled over the edge of the bench and held on for dear life.

Jake didn't move, didn't turn to him, didn't give any indication he even knew Aaron was sitting beside him. Aaron wanted to say something but the words clogged his throat and he sat silently.

"Just so you know," said Jake suddenly but quietly, "I love you, Flip."

And just like that Aaron could suddenly breathe again.

CHAPTER EIGHT

JUST so you know, I love you, Flip.

The words echoed in Aaron's head and filled his body with a wave of calm. It covered and washed over him slowly like a warm, clean summer rain. Nothing had ever compared to this moment.

Right now.

Here.

With Jake.

Jake who was in love with him.

He exhaled the breath he had been holding for longer than it should have been possible and turned to wrap both his arms around Jake's upper arm, holding it to his chest and his peaceful and contented heart as he pressed his face into Jake's shoulder. Breathing him in. Holding him still.

Jake's body jerked at the contact, as if it wasn't prepared to feel Aaron's touch again but, as soon as Aaron's arms wrapped around his own and he felt his nose press against his shoulder and his warm breath weave its way through his shirt to his skin, he relaxed. The rigidity with which he had been holding himself, the strength he had been exuding just to stay upright finally was able to give up and let go as he slumped against Aaron and was warm again.

Although his body relaxed and slid into Aaron's, Jake kept

his gaze on the courtyard as he gathered more of his words.

"I wanted you to know that," he continued in the same quiet voice with which he had said those miraculous words. "I wanted you to know I loved you all along. You told me once you wanted someone who would love you from the start, someone who would look at you and say, *'that's the one I want.'* That was me, Flip. I'm the man that wanted you from the start. You're the one I want and if you never come back to me, never see me again, I wanted you to know that."

Aaron let the words flow over him, tears dropping from his eyes onto Jake's shoulder.

"Even if you stay away from me, even if you give up on me, just know there's someone across the park who loves you and wants to have kids with you and sleep beside you and argue with you and see you smile and all those things you said you wanted. I want them, too, but only with you. Only with my Flip."

Jake finally turned his head toward Aaron, leaning over and pressing a kiss to the top of his head. "I'll always be right across the park waiting for you, loving you, whenever you need me."

A happy sob broke past Aaron's lips as he let go of Jake's arm with one of his to reach up and wrap his fingers around Jake's neck, pulling his head forward to meet his own. Their lips almost crashed together, Aaron surged toward Jake so suddenly, but Jake reached out for Aaron's face at the same time he pushed forward and his hand on his cheek held him in check. Jake's lips parted and were soon covered by Aaron's. Both marveled at the taste of the other and wondered in the back of their minds what had taken them so long, why had they bothered to wait when this, *this*, kind of taste, feel, touch awaited them.

Jake's thumb ran along the top of Aaron's cheekbone, his fingers slipping into the curls surrounding his face. Aaron's thumb was resting in the hollow of Jake's neck, feeling every beat of his heart which, instead of being erratic and fast, was steady and strong, as his fingers and palm curved around his neck. The kiss was an odd mix of tender and fierce with both wanting more while still savoring that first taste, that first kiss. Lips were gentle until one pushed forward and teeth clashed, noses collided. Tongues, warm and determined, tangled. Both were losing every ounce of breath in their bodies but were unwilling to part.

Not when they had finally found the path to each other's lips.

Aaron was the first to pull away, but Jake kept his bottom lip firmly between his teeth in an effort to pull him back into the kiss. Aaron gave in immediately and reclaimed Jake's lips with a long deep kiss. Aaron's hand slipped from Jake's neck to grab at the collar of his shirt, he pulled the shirt into his fist as he used it to drag himself closer to Jake, pressing them together until their foreheads bumped and their teeth once again clashed.

Aaron tried pushing Jake away from him with the hand that was tangled up in his shirt as both struggled to take in air. Jake reluctantly pulled away and looked at Aaron with glassy eyes. Aaron smattered kisses all over Jake's face and then wrapped the arm that was still holding Jake's arm around his neck instead, tugging him close in a frantic hug and pleading in an almost desperate whisper,

"Take me home, Moz, please take me home."

"I will. I promise," said Jake, turning to the side to wrap his arms around Aaron's waist and lift him onto his lap. Once Aaron felt Jake lift him, he pushed up and all but scrambled into his lap.

"I love you, too, Jake. Please," he sobbed, "I just want to go home."

Jake's heart started to pound madly as he cradled Aaron in his arms. Aaron had always been the one to take care of him. Always. And now he clung to him like a lifeline and Jake was determined to never let go.

Never.

He was going to do right by Aaron. Give back to him all the love and shelter he had shown him for the past few years. He was going to give back to him every late night phone call, every reassuring smile, every single word of his belief in him, every time Aaron had held on to him in the night when he needed someone to keep him from drowning, he was going to do the same for Aaron. No matter how long it took.

Jake hoped it took forever.

Aaron's breath hitched as Jake tightened his hold and nearly crushed all the air out of him, but instead of trying to push him away, Aaron only clung tighter, drawing in air in long stuttering breaths as he repeated over and over, "*I love you. I want to go home. Please.*"

Love.

Home.

Please.

Please.

And over and over as he held him and almost rocked with him, Jake repeated, "We're going home. I could never leave without you. I love you."

I love you.

As Aaron's breath slowed down and returned to normal, he pressed his face one more time against Jake's neck before pulling away and looking at him with tear soaked eyes. "I'm sorry," he whispered as he brought his hands up to Jake's temples before stroking them slowly down the sides of his face and touching their foreheads together, "I'm sorry for … it's … too much, you know. Too much."

"But not enough," said Jake as he captured Aaron's hands in his and brought them to his lips. "Never enough."

"I know," Aaron said after kissing Jake's temple.

Even though they were curled around each other, it was as if they couldn't touch each other enough, couldn't possibly be close enough. Fingers roamed and warm breath left lingering trails across overly heated skin that were soon followed by slow careful kisses.

Suddenly Aaron burst into one of his heart stopping laughs.

Delighting in the sound but wanting to know why he was laughing, Jake smiled. "What?"

Aaron smiled back brightly and pointed behind Jake's head to the crowd inside, "We're putting on quite the show if anyone is interested in looking."

"You mean Aly's not standing in the doorway waving her pompoms and chanting, *'GO! GO! GO!'*? Because I thought she might be."

"Oh, she was," grinned Aaron, "but now I think she's around front getting a car ready for us so we can hop in and speed away to save the world and have sex."

Jake laughed, for the first time in a long while he laughed, and it lit him up from the inside out. "I'm all for the sex part of your scenario but I gotta tell ya, saving the world can fucking wait."

"Fuck, yeah, it can wait!"

Jake stood up with Aaron. Once he was upright, Aaron let his legs slide from Jake's hips until he was standing on his own.

"I love you, Aaron," said Jake gruffly, pulling him towards his lips for a quick kiss.

"I know," beamed Aaron, "isn't it great?"

"Pretty much the best thing ever."

Aaron laughed as he grabbed both of Jake's hands in his and started dragging him back into the party. Jake scowled at him when he saw where they were heading.

"It's the only way out!" Aaron sighed dramatically, "It's either the front door or we jump the fence."

Aaron's laughter crackled through the night air again as Jake broke away from him and made a beeline for the fence. He watched as Jake took a running leap over the sad excuse for a barrier.

"I can't," whined Aaron, holding his sides, "I'm laughing too hard!"

"Get your ass over here right now, Flip," Jake whispered loudly as he waved his hand, "I'll lift your laughing ass over the goddamn fence if I have to!"

"Oh, fine!" said Aaron, jumping over the fence easily.

"Hey, I thought you said you couldn't do it," said Jake indignantly once Aaron was with him on the other side, smiling.

"For godsake, Jacob, the fence is like four feet high.

Besides, I was being contrary. Have you ever known me *not* to be uncooperative?"

"No, not really. But I still hold out hope," said Jake brightly.

Aaron smirked, then grabbed Jake's hand again, pulling him along behind him. Jake was surprised a cab even stopped for them since Aaron was all but running down the street, dragging him behind him and waving his arm like a bedlamite to try to hail it down. Once it came to a complete stop, Aaron opened the door and shoved Jake inside, practically shouting the address to the cabbie. Jake was laughing as he sprawled across the backseat and Aaron dove in after him, halfway sitting on him in the process.

"Jesus, Moz, get up, don't you know how to get in a cab?" Aaron asked with exasperation as he pulled Jake by his arm into a sitting position. "Do you need a child seat or something? I could buckle you in and give you a juice box."

"And animal crackers."

"Yes, those, too."

Jake laughed and grabbed Aaron's face in his hands to plant a big sloppy kiss on his lips. After the kiss, Aaron dropped his head back to rest it against the seat, smiling at Jake.

"Pinch me," he said, raising his arm up in front of Jake's face.

"Is this some kind of kinky sex game?"

"Yes, Jacob, it's my kinky pinching game ... nothing says sex like pinching, I always say!"

Aaron suddenly yowled when Jake pinched him ... hard.

"You fucker!"

"You just told me to pinch you!"

"Not so hard, asshat! I only wanted to make sure I wasn't dreaming."

"Awww, that's sweet, Flip!" said Jake with a goofy grin. "Here," he said as he stuck out his arm, "do me."

Aaron rolled his eyes at Jake's "*do me*" comment but let it slide so he could concentrate on pinching him as hard as he could.

"Motherfucker!" howled Jake.

"Hurts, don't it?"

"Did you take some skin with you too, you little shit?" asked Jake mulishly, rubbing his arm.

"Possibly ... now, do you still think you're dreaming, sweetheart?"

"No, I'm very much awake ... *pookie*."

"Snookums."

"Darling."

"Honey-bun."

"Boo-bear."

"Oh my god, I so thought you were going to go for the *'boo-boo-kitty-fuck'* from *Jay and Silent Bob*!"

"Shit," laughed Jake, "I forgot about that one! I could call you that though, you're so a boo-boo-kitty-fuck."

"If you call me that, I'm going to call you dumb-ass-Jakey-fuck."

"That's fine by me, boo-boo-kitty-fuck."

"Don't call me that!"

"Come on, you like it," cajoled Jake as he nuzzled at Aaron's neck.

"How could I *not* like it when you're doing that to my neck?" asked Aaron, scrunching up his shoulder to try to catch Jake's face between it and his chin.

"Dunno," mumbled Jake as he continued nipping at his neck.

Aaron's mouth fell open slightly, a sigh escaping his lips. His hand moved from his lap and into Jake's, starting at his knee and working its way north, slowly up the inside of his thigh as Jake scooted closer and spread his legs, allowing Aaron's hand to slip higher. Jake's hand rested against Aaron's stomach for a moment before it wormed its way under his shirt to touch the heat of his skin underneath. As Jake's hand slid across his stomach and around his side, Aaron nudged at Jake with his forehead for him to lift his head so he could get at his mouth again. Jake raised his head and leaned in to kiss Aaron as his free hand slipped around the back of his neck. Aaron opened up to the kiss, letting his tongue snake between Jake's lips while his hand moved high enough to cup the bulge in his pants. Jake grunted into Aaron's mouth at the slight squeeze.

He lifted his mouth from Aaron's and breathlessly asked, "Where are we? How close are we to home?"

Aaron looked out the windows in a daze, trying to figure out exactly where they were and how much longer they'd be trapped in the smelly cab. "I don't know, I think we're close."

"Not close enough."

Aaron turned in the seat so he could drape his left leg over Jake's lap, his hand continuing to stroke his hardening cock while his lips returned to Jake's mouth. The hand Jake had at Aaron's side dropped to his ass when he hooked his leg over him. He ran it down the crease until he could hold one cheek firmly in his hand and pull Aaron toward him. Jake's insistent tugging caused Aaron's own aching cock to brush up against the outside of Jake's thigh. Aaron started rubbing up against him in an effort to alleviate the strain that was sending all his senses on high alert.

Their kisses were sloppy and wet as they pushed against each other and tried to relieve all the pent up ache in their bodies.

"I love you, Jake," Aaron whispered against the corner of his mouth.

"Love you too," answered Jake as the hand that was at Aaron's neck came up to brush away the errant curls from his flushed face.

They stared at each other in between slow kisses, just biding their time until the cab finally got them home.

Once the cab finally stopped at Jake's building, he threw a wad of money at the cabbie as Aaron all but fell out of the back seat in his rush to get out. Jake came tumbling out behind him and had to do some quick steps to right himself while Aaron laughed at him delightedly. Once he had gained his footing, he wrapped an arm around Aaron's waist to pick him up and swing him to the side, kissing him right there on the sidewalk in front of all the people passing by. Aaron wrapped his arms around Jake's neck and kissed him back as they stumbled towards the door of the building. They laughed as Barry, the night doorman, looked at them strangely before rolling his eyes at their antics.

"Hey, Barry," grinned Aaron as Jake dragged him through the open door.

"Mr. Bennet," Barry nodded formally to Aaron while trying to keep a straight face before turning to Jake and adding, "Mr. Wyzchek, good evening, gentlemen."

"Good evening indeed, Master Barry!" Jake yelled over his shoulder, preparing to run across the lobby with Aaron to the waiting elevator.

They crashed into the elevator and Jake almost missed the button as Aaron's wandering hands snuck around his waist and down over his ass. "Stop that, I almost pushed the wrong floor."

"Eh, small price to pay," grinned Aaron as he gave Jake's ass another squeeze and kissed the curve of his jaw.

Aaron yelped when Jake suddenly grabbed him behind his knees to lift him up and slam him against the elevator wall. Jake set his ass down against the railing running along the back wall, his mouth colliding with Aaron's and his legs wrapping themselves tightly around Jake's waist. Aaron's arms slipped under Jake's armpits to slide along his back. When they heard the bell ping for Jake's floor, he leaned away from Aaron just long enough to press a random button on a higher floor so the doors once again slid shut.

Trapped within the heat of Aaron's thighs, Jake rubbed against him, forcing their cocks into contact. The rough heavy denim stretched painfully across both their cocks. Aaron hissed as Jake pushed against him and his head dropped back against the slick shiny surface of the elevator wall. He hitched himself up higher in Jake's arms and arched his neck to offer it up to his searching lips. Jake's tongue trailed down his neck to suck at the hollow at the base of his throat. Aaron moaned and the vibrations passed through Jake's lips making them hum and shiver.

The ping of the elevator opening interrupted them yet again

and both groaned in frustration. Jake leaned back to push the button for his floor and the doors closed with a whoosh.

"Gotta get you somewhere," said Jake between kisses, "with no interruptions."

"Gotta get me *home*," emphasized Aaron.

Jake ran his thumb over Aaron's lips and looked into his eyes as he whispered, "Where I'll keep you forever and ever and ever...."

"And ever and ever and ever...." finished Aaron.

"And ever," added Jake with a grin, kissing right above the arch of his eyebrow.

They held each other until the ping of the elevator sounded again. Jake kept his hands on Aaron's hips as he backed away from him and his feet slipped back to the floor. Aaron curled his fingers around Jake's wrists, following him as he walked backwards out of the elevator, seemingly incapable of letting Aaron out of his sight, even to turn around and walk to his door.

Jake's back bumped into his door but still he didn't turn around. Aaron smiled at him and reached down into his front pocket to pull out his keys and unlock the door. Aaron broke eye contact with Jake to look inside the apartment as the door swung open. His eyes filled with tears, and he whispered, "*I missed ... so much, Moz ... so much.*" Jake shushed him as he held his head in his hands and ran his thumbs over his cheeks. Once the tears cleared from his eyes and he looked back at Jake, he let go of his wrists to wrap his arms around his neck. Jake let his own hands move from Aaron's hips to encircle his waist in a tight hold that he used to pick him up, just enough to lift his feet off the ground as he walked backward through the doorway and into the apartment.

"You're home now, Flip."

CHAPTER NINE

AARON'S hold on Jake tightened. "I am," he whispered into his neck, "finally."

Jake set him down and pulled away from him, only to take one of his hands in his own and start walking with him toward the bedroom. Aaron gripped Jake's hand and followed. Jake's smell permeated the apartment and Aaron closed his eyes in relief as he let Jake lead him down the hall. Jake looked back at him as they walked through the bedroom door. Once Jake's eyes connected with his, Aaron started to shake uncontrollably, so much so that his teeth started to chatter. Jake stopped to look down at Aaron's trembling hand.

"What's wrong?" he asked in quiet confusion.

He looked so much like a little boy asking that question that Aaron wanted to smile, but the only thing he could say in response was, "It just started, I don't know why. Maybe I want this too much."

Jake did the only thing he could think of doing. He walked up to Aaron and wrapped his arms around him, trapping his arms firmly at his sides. Jake tried to surround him completely, tried holding him still through the tremors. "Does this help?" he asked.

Aaron nodded. "Don't let go just yet."

"I won't."

Aaron stood there breathing in Jake's scent and

remembering all the reasons why this place, why *Jake*, was his home. All the reasons why he belonged exactly where he was.

He drew in a deep breath and stepped away from Jake.

"Better?" Jake asked quietly as his fingers stroked his face.

Aaron nodded and smiled as he reached out and curled his fingers over Jake's belt buckle, "I have a feeling it'll get even better really soon."

"You think?" Jake's eyebrow arched, "I was actually just bringing you back here to watch a movie or something ... then maybe take care of some stuff in the studio, you'd think Alyson had never worked for me before, she's messed so many things up. She just does *not* know how to do them properly."

"Tosser!" laughed Aaron, tugging on Jake's buckle to yank him forward, "and you know Alyson does everything perfectly."

"Nuh-uh. She does things in her Aly way. I prefer the Flip way of doing things."

"You mean letting everything pile up until the desk collapses under the strain? Because I think the Aly way may be more efficient."

"But it doesn't have that Flip flair."

"I'd think you'd enjoy an assistant that actually assists."

"You would think that, wouldn't you? But you see, I've grown accustomed to the Flip way. I'm kinda in love with it, in fact. I found I can't live without it."

"It can't live without you either."

"That's good to hear."

"Hmmm-mmm," hummed Aaron as Jake's lips took control of the situation.

Jake's hands slid down Aaron's sides until they came to his waist and his fingers could curl around the hem of his shirt to pull it up and over Aaron's head. Aaron stopped kissing Jake for a minute so he could raise his arms and let the shirt come over his head. He let Jake slowly and carefully unbuckle and unzip his pants. He waited patiently as he dropped to his knees in front of him, pulling the pants down with him. He let Jake lift one foot,

then the other, to ease off his socks and shoes. He closed his eyes
when Jake's hand came around the back of his leg to gently
squeeze his calf before it continued downward to wrap around his
ankle and lift his foot up at the same time he freed it from his pant
leg. He had to open his eyes again when he felt Jake's lips, hot and
wet, against the inside of his leg. He had to be able to look down
and see Jake on his knees in front of him, pressing kisses again and
again down his leg until he got to his ankle and the process was
repeated, the warm caress of his fingers circling his ankle to pull
the other pant leg off. He sighed as Jake laid his palms flat against
the front of his calves and ran them up his legs until they were
fanned out on his hips, so close to his cock as to be almost painful.
He sucked air into his lungs when Jake rose up on his knees so his
face brushed across the thin fabric of his boxer shorts, his nose
gently bumping the head of his cock and then again, the hot wet of
his mouth ghosting across it. His fingers knotted themselves into
Jake's hair when his tongue licked its way across his stomach,
along the skin at the edge of his waistband. And he moaned when
Jake's hands finally pulled his boxers off as well.

Jake sat back on his heels and simply looked at Aaron.
From head to toe. With that intense and unbreakable stare he used
when focusing in on a subject, an idea, an inspiration.

Aaron stood there, knowing he should be embarrassed to be
completely naked, cock bobbing and hard as a rock, in front of a
still fully clothed Jake whose eyes were capable of burning holes
through him, but he wasn't. Not even a little bit. He felt beautiful
and strong. Like a wild thing Jake would never want to let from his
sight for fear it would run away into the night. He felt powerful
and in control. He knew he was like liquor running through Jake's
veins and slowly bringing a flush to his skin. He knew he was
Jake's addiction. Knew it and it coursed through him. He looked at
Jake as he ran his hands over his chest and stomach, down to his
hips.

Teasing.

"You're taking my picture, aren't you?" he asked quietly,
the fingers of his right hand sliding through the trail of curls paving
the way to his cock.

"Yes," breathed Jake, his eyes following the path of those fingers.

"How many have you taken?"

"Hundreds," Jake answered, sweeping his tongue across his lips, "a day. Every day I take hundreds of you."

"Take one now," ordered Aaron as he took hold of his cock and started stroking it.

"No."

"No? Don't you want one?" Aaron asked, momentarily uncertain.

"I always want one, but now," Jake answered, looking away from Aaron's hand and up into his eyes, "I want the real thing. I took pictures because I couldn't have you. Thousands filled with my want, my need for you. I want to stop for a while so I can touch what only my film has been able to touch up until now."

Aaron took his hand away from his cock. "Touch it then."

Jake tentatively reached out and pressed his palm flat against Aaron's stomach, his fingers fanning out then staying still, letting the heat soak into them, deathly afraid to move any further. Aaron stayed still as well, unnaturally still for him, letting Jake simply touch him. The only thing moving either of them was Aaron's steady breaths as his stomach rose and fell slightly under Jake's hand.

"Beautiful," whispered Jake. "The pictures could never hold you. This is mine, this is what I was trying to find."

"Now that it's found," replied Aaron as his fingers combed through Jake's hair, "don't lose it again."

Jake shook his head, moving his hand along Aaron's stomach to his hip and then around to the small of his back where it met his other hand to hold him around his waist. He laid his head against Aaron, his cheek brushing the smooth skin at his hip. Aaron shivered as Jake's stubble prickled his skin. Jake immediately pressed his lips to the delicate skin covering his hipbones, trying to capture the shudder in his mouth and let it slide down his throat so it could live inside him.

Jake turned his head so his cheek scraped against Aaron's cock, and he smiled softly when he heard Aaron's sharp intake of breath at the contact. He moved his fingers from Aaron's hips to hold his cock, his other arm still around his waist, hand resting at the top of his ass. He did nothing but hold Aaron's cock in his hand as he felt it pulse with heat.

"Jake, please...."

Unable to ignore such a plea falling from Aaron's lips, Jake ran his tongue across the slit, teasing the tip of his cock before taking it in his mouth. As he let his tongue roll around his cock, he slid his fingers down the crease of Aaron's ass, just brushing across his hole. Aaron's hips jerked forward at the touch and forced more of his cock into Jake's mouth. Jake simply relaxed his jaw and let Aaron slowly fuck his mouth. Aaron's taste filled him and his scent wrapped around him.

Aaron pulled Jake's mouth away from his cock and groaned, "I can't stay in your mouth and not come."

"So come," said Jake as he tugged Aaron's hips forward and tried to take him back in his mouth.

"No," said Aaron, dropping to his knees in front of Jake. He wrapped his arms around his neck and whispered hotly in his ear, "I want to come all over you when you're inside me."

Jake moaned when he heard those words and abruptly dragged Aaron up from the floor and kissed him, shoving his tongue in his mouth as he stumbled backwards with him to the bed. Aaron shoved at him and he fell on his back across the bed, bringing Aaron down on top of him since he refused to relinquish his hold on him.

Aaron straddled him and cried out loudly when his cock pushed against the rough denim of Jake's jeans. As Aaron kissed him, Jake almost wanted to stop him just so he could push him up into a sitting position and look up at him, take him all in. It was driving him insane to have Aaron laid out naked on top of him while he had yet to remove a single item of clothing. He knew he wanted his skin against Aaron's, but the way his bare skin looked pressed against his clothing was gorgeous and dizzying all at once.

Jake could barely breathe from the sight of it and he wanted it to go on forever. He wanted to keep holding, keep running his hands over every inch of Aaron's skin he could reach and when Aaron cried out, he moved his hands to his hips and held on so tightly as he thrust up against him that it must have been painful for Aaron. But instead of pushing his hands away or telling him to let go, Aaron dug his fingers into the fabric of Jake's shirt and pushed himself up off his chest to writhe against him. He moved his hips as if he were riding Jake's cock, as if there were nothing between them. Jake wanted to sob, he ached so much.

It was almost violent the way they held and moved and pushed against each other. Aaron's head was hanging down and he was shaking it as if he couldn't let himself go further. A couple of times, he raised his right hand, Jake's shirt still bunched up and held in his fingers, and brought it down hard, beating Jake's chest with his fist. Jake gritted his teeth and closed his eyes and knew that even though his nails were short and blunt, they were scratching burning red lines down Aaron's hips and the outsides of his thighs as they flexed and moved against him.

It was harsh and desperate.

It was if they were trying to fuck through Jake's clothing, fuck through all those years they had been without this kind of contact. This kind of heat.

Finally, Jake could stand it no longer and literally threw Aaron from him, but since Aaron's hold on his shirt was firm, it pulled at his neck, nearly strangling him as it dragged him toward Aaron. He ruthlessly shoved Aaron's hands from his shirt so he could pull it off. He flopped onto his back and fought with his belt and zipper, thrashing against the bed as he tried to squirm out of his jeans at the same time he was kicking off his shoes. He could barely get his jeans and boxers past his cock, it was so rigid. As he struggled with his clothes, he noticed that Aaron had crawled on his hands and knees to the side of the bed where he threw open his nightstand drawer so forcefully he almost pulled it all the way out. The lamp wobbled on the stand and came precariously close to falling off it. Aaron was frantically digging through the drawer and throwing things across the room.

A book.

The remote.

Jake's glasses.

All thrown out until he finally found what Jake knew was in the very back. Shoved there so long ago after one of his *Fuck Du Jours*, when he had at last given up all hope of ever finding anyone that could come close to being his Aaron. Shoved there when he had come to the realization that he would rather die than fuck one more guy who wasn't Aaron.

Who didn't smell like him.

Or feel like him.

Or taste the way Jake knew he would taste if ever he would get the chance to drink from him.

Jake had managed to pull off everything down to his socks when Aaron crawled back to him. With eerie concentration and focus, he coated Jake's cock with lube, then swung his leg over him. Before Jake could even mention a condom or argue that he wasn't ready, Aaron reached back, took Jake's cock in his hand and shoved himself down on it, taking him in as sweat and tears rolled down his face. Jake cried out in alarm, was nearly sick at the thought of how painful the act of taking him without preparation must have been. He shook with the tremors going through his body at the sight of Aaron's tears. He reached out clumsily to wipe them away.

He could take anything, *anything*, but sad aching tears falling from those brown eyes.

Aaron slapped his hands away and started moving up and down on his cock. Jake hissed *"stop"* and tried to lift him off of him, tried to stop him. Aaron shook his head and grunted *'no'* and fought him, hitting at his arms, scratching at his chest as he tightened his thighs against Jake's sides and continued to ride him. Jake didn't realize tears were falling from the corners of his eyes as well until Aaron finally trapped his arms against his chest and leaned down to lick them away, even as his own left the bridge of Jake's nose wet when his cheek slid across it. Jake was unaware he had started pushing up into Aaron, rocking his hips with him, until

Aaron's hands slipped up into his hair as he held his head still and sighed against the side of his face, "Yes, like that … more … give me more."

Jake tugged his arms out from between his and Aaron's chests and reached down to grab his ass, to hold him still while he fucked up into him. As he bucked and rocked against him, Aaron was kissing Jake, wet and fierce, biting and tearing at his lips.

They couldn't get enough.

Fast enough.

Hard enough.

Close enough.

Deep enough.

Just not *enough*.

Jake broke away from Aaron's biting lips to bite his own way down the side of his neck, leaving angry red marks behind. Aaron was moaning and gasping above him, his hands moving everywhere he could reach in a frantic search for more skin to touch, his cock trapped between their stomachs, rubbing against the hairs of the trail down Jake's stomach. He could tell Aaron wanted more, and it wasn't long before he pushed Jake's face away from his neck and sat up, burying Jake even deeper inside him. He worked himself on Jake's cock faster and faster until all his moaning cries blended into one long, broken, stuttering wail. Jake kept reaching out for him, fighting with him to pull him back down onto his chest. He needed him closer. He was too far away. Finally, he got a grip on Aaron's biceps and was able to anchor his feet firmly enough against the bed to throw Aaron to the side as he rolled with him. Aaron started to kick out with his feet, trying to roll them back over, trying to take back control but Jake hooked one arm under the knee of a thrashing leg and pushed it back until Aaron was flat on his back and spread beneath him.

Once Jake started fucking him again, started pumping his hips at an almost obscene pace, Aaron stopped fighting for control and instead clung to him like he was the only light in the dark. The only safe place he would ever find. His free leg wrapped around Jake's lower back while the one he was holding curled around his upper arm and back. His arms went around his neck and back until their bodies were nothing more than a tangle of limbs that were too entwined to claim a single owner but were rather an extension of this new sweating, grunting, fucking creature they had created.

Aaron screaming for more.

Jake claiming him in a growling scratchy voice.

More.

Mine.

More.

Mine.

Both were breathless and gasping for air as Jake continued to fuck Aaron hard and fast. All his muscles burned from the strain, but he kept pumping his hips, kept pushing in and pulling out of that divine heat, that tightness that was consuming him and swallowing him whole. Only the feel of Aaron around him, the sound of his moaning breaths and the taste of him that still lingered in his mouth kept Jake moving long after he should have collapsed. He was overwhelmed by desire and need. Possessed by Aaron. By his ass, his hot breath, his strong arms and hungry thighs clutching him close, his heels digging into his back to the point of pain.

Possessed.

Crazed.

Never once wishing for an exorcism, for he'd rather be filled by Aaron, controlled by him, bound and tied to him, than be without him or to be free of such burning, all-consuming love.

He wanted to burn.

Suddenly Aaron's arms unwound themselves from around Jake's neck and his hands moved up the back of his neck and forward to the sides of his face where they held on firmly and forced him to look down into his eyes. Jake knew Aaron was about to come, he could feel him tightening, constricting around him. He could feel it in the way Aaron held him, in the way his breath hitched and it relieved him to know that they were already in tune to each other's bodies, they were already living inside each other.

"Look at me," whispered Aaron as his fingers dug into

Jake's scalp, holding his head in place.

Jake unhooked his own arm from under Aaron's leg to join his other so he too held Aaron's head firmly in both his hands and answered in a ringing chant that matched the movements of his hips, "Yesyesyesyesyesyes."

And before either one could breathe another breath or utter another *"yes"*, Jake finally found out how Aaron looked as he came, finally saw the glazed look that slid over those brown eyes, finally saw the beauty that he had always known existed in this world but had never been able to find.

Finally knew *his* Aaron. Bare, flushed, breathless and slick beneath him.

It was enough to send him bursting inside Aaron. Spilling and spilling and spilling as if he'd never stop, the pleasure so intense, so profound that it brought forth exhausted and painful sobs. Sobs that were the build up of five years of wanting and waiting to have what he finally possessed.

Aaron.

He fell to Aaron's chest and cried. Cried into the hollow at the base of his neck where the smell of the two of them combined was so concentrated that it brought forth even more sobs. Aaron brought the leg Jake had dropped in order to hold his face up and around his waist, pulling him in further, making him sink deeper. One of his arms slipped back around his shoulders as his other hand combed through Jake's hair.

"Shhhhh, I've got you. I've got you," hushed Aaron.

Jake continued to cry as he whispered into Aaron's skin, "You can't leave me now, not after … you can't … you can't leave again."

"No, I can't," agreed Aaron.

"I love you, Flip," Jake stuttered.

"I love you, too."

Jake raised his head and started to wipe away his tears as he gently rolled away from Aaron, who winced as they separated. "I'm sorry."

"For what?" asked Aaron as his fingers gently joined Jake's to wipe at his cheeks.

"For everything. For not appreciating you enough, not telling you I loved you every day I was with you, for keeping you out, for crying like a baby just now and for hurting you," he added, reaching out his hand to slide it down Aaron's side and back over the curve of his ass.

"You don't need to apologize for those things. I did all of them, too," said Aaron, touching his forehead to Jake's, "and you didn't hurt me."

"But, you didn't even let me prepare you ... you just ... I had to have hurt you."

Aaron shook his head, "You didn't hurt me. Besides *I* was the one that did it, now wasn't I?"

"Yeah, but why? Why did you do that?"

"Because," said Aaron as he pressed his chest against Jake's, settling himself in his arms, "I couldn't wait one more moment. I couldn't. I would have split into a thousand pieces if I had to wait one more second."

"You have to be sore now, though."

"I guess that means next time it's your turn then," smiled Aaron.

"Guess so," shrugged Jake in feigned boredom.

Aaron scowled at him and bit his chest.

Jake yelped, "Ouch! Fucker!"

"What? I slipped."

"I love how you can pretend that you *accidentally* bit someone," Jake laughed, pushing at Aaron's shoulder. Aaron pushed back and soon they were tussling and rolling around the bed in a pile of naked limbs, laughing and swearing at each other until Jake stopped Aaron's curses with a strategically placed kiss. "Stop fighting and start kissing me, you little bastard."

"Well, since you put it like that, let's make out all night long, Mr. Dreamypants," grinned Aaron.

"Sounds like a plan, Mrs. Dreamypants," smirked Jake, and

before Aaron could start bitching about being called 'Mrs.', Jake started kissing him again and all protests were forgotten.

For a good long while.

BY the end of the second day, Alyson had called a total of eleven times. Each time she called, Jake swore and growled that he'd throw the motherfucking phone out the goddamn motherfucking window. On the twelfth time, he did throw it, but at the wall instead of out the window because he was too particularly busy getting fucked by Aaron at the time to do anything other than reach out and grab it off its receiver and smash it against the bedroom wall. Aaron had only laughed at him and said she'd start calling their cell phones sooner or later, which prompted Jake to throw those out the window instead, once he was able to get up off his hands and knees. Aaron sat cross-legged on the bed laughing hysterically as Jake dug the phones out of their pants pockets and tossed them out the window while yelling *"Watch out below!"* then swearing up and down as he pulled his head back in from the window that Aaron's phone had started ringing on the way down.

"I heard it, Flip!" insisted Jake, "tiny little strains of *'It's Raining Men'* as it fell to the ground."

"That's *not* my ringtone, you asshole!"

"Okay fine then, tiny little strains of *'I Will Survive'*."

"Douchebag!" shouted Aaron, reaching out to grab a pillow to throw at Jake's head before realizing there were none there.

A few hours before, when they had awakened from one of their brief naps between fuckings, Jake had suddenly pushed all the pillows, blankets and sheets to the floor, insisting that they hurt, claiming he could only stand the feel of Aaron's skin against his own and nothing else. Aaron knew exactly what he meant because he felt the same way. It was like all of his nerve endings were exposed, all lying just below the very uppermost layer of skin and any time he brushed against anything, his skin would spark and burn and the only time he could stand the burn was when his skin touched Jake's. Hour after hour, they had fucked and kissed and fucked and kissed until there was almost nothing left to them but the little blue electrical shocks that crackled across their raw and brittle skin as they slid along each other's bodies.

Sometimes it was gentle and slow, other times it was frenzied and harsh and brutal. They just couldn't stop. Even though every muscle ached and their arms and legs could barely hold them up, they kept fucking. Even though they were dizzy and lightheaded, wasted and weak, they kept fucking.

Over and over and over again.

They became ravenous and would have to stop and stumble to the kitchen where they'd simply open up the refrigerator door and sit in front of it, pulling out whatever was edible and eating it with their fingers. They devoured everything in sight. It was like their stomachs were bottomless and they couldn't consume enough food to keep them going. They soon emptied the fridge and had to move on to the cupboards, eating everything they could get their hands on.

And the thirst. They were always thirsty, their throats dry and screaming for water. It wasn't long before they had gone through every bottle of water Jake had and simply had to stand at the sink and gulp down water straight from the faucet. So hot and thirsty and dry that they couldn't even be bothered to fill a glass because it took too long. They both felt like they were drinking gallons and gallons and gallons of water, but they also both felt as though they were burning alive and no amount of water seemed able to douse the flames.

It got so bad that at the end of the third day, Aaron had to actually stumble into the studio and use the phone in there to call Alyson and ask her to drop off more food, since they had eaten every last crumb of food in Jake's fridge and cupboards both. She had tried to ask questions and be nosy, but Aaron had abruptly mumbled "*bring food,*" and hung up. When she brought it over, she pounded on the door until Jake stopped yelling to "*leave it at the fucking door and go home, dammit!*" and Aaron came to the door to ask her more kindly to "*leave it at the fucking door ... please.*" She said she wouldn't leave it until he opened the door and she could see with her own eyes that he was still alive and that his voice wasn't a cleverly procured recording used to distract and divert her. He had scowled and cursed but went back to the bedroom to grab the sheet off the floor, wrapping it around himself so he could answer her without the fear of frightening Jake's old neighbor into a heart attack if she happened to be walking down the hall when he opened the door.

When Aaron flung the door open, Alyson stepped back in shock, her mouth hanging open as she clutched the bag of groceries to her chest and stared at him, took in his crazy matted curls, his chapped bruised lip, the faint purplish marks in the shape of fingers wrapping around his biceps, the scratches up and down his chest, the bite marks at his neck and the utterly glazed look in his eyes. She wrinkled her nose as the overpowering smell of sweat and sex wafted out the door and over her. She shoved the bag of groceries at Aaron, then threw her hands up in the air and hollered in relief, *"Fucking FINALLY!"* before simply turning away from Aaron without another word and walking back down the hall toward the elevators.

FOR five days, they never once left the apartment, and it wasn't until Alyson came back over on the fifth day and let herself in to throw open windows and push them out of bed that they finally took showers and got dressed. Alyson told them she feared for their lives, that they might fuck themselves to death if she didn't intervene. Jake had rolled his eyes and shot her the finger but got up nonetheless. Aaron just smiled at her lazily until she shook her head and walked away to see what she could do about the damage throughout the apartment.

But after Alyson's intervention, they settled down into the life they'd have together. Both had voiced their concerns to each other about how they were going to adjust to living together, but they soon found that there really wasn't any adjusting to do at all, because whether either one knew it, Aaron had been living there all along. The only change this time was that he had all his things physically there as opposed to across the city, but the apartment itself had always been his true home.

They soon became the old married couple they had always been but never acknowledged.

Aaron found that he didn't really mind all that much anymore when he'd snuggle up next to Jake in bed and breathe in the scent at the curve of his neck and find that it didn't smell like him.

Because now it smelled like Aaron.

Jake found that he was a happy person at heart. He had never known it before. But now that the weight and stress of losing Aaron, of not admitting he loved him, had lifted from his shoulders, he found he was actually happy instead of cantankerous and crabby. And he found he actually *enjoyed* being so, much to Alyson and Aaron's amusement.

One night when he awoke to an empty bed, he wandered into the studio and found Aaron busy at his wheel. The brightness of the moon was the only illumination in the room. He sleepily shuffled over to where Aaron was sitting. Without a conscious thought, or even stopping what he was doing, Aaron automatically scooted forward in his seat so Jake could slip in behind him. Jake swung his leg over the stool and sat down behind Aaron, wrapping his arms around his waist and resting his head against the silky skin of his back between his shoulder blades. Aaron kept working and Jake could feel the muscles of his back moving under the skin beneath his cheek. The steady hum of the wheel, as well as Aaron's own humming, was quickly lulling him back into sleep. He blinked a few times and looked at the moon through the window. As his eyelids became too heavy and his eyes dropped shut again, he thought about the book he had read to Milo and Aaron that day. He remembered how Aaron had been so excited when Milo requested it because it was his favorite of all Milo's books. He smiled faintly to himself as he also remembered how he had made him repeat his favorite lines over and over again until Milo told him, "*Unc Fip, let Unc Dake read the story. Stop 'rupting him.*" Aaron had smiled at Jake over Milo's head and let him continue with the story, but Jake knew why he so loved the book. It was all about acceptance and the overwhelming power of love and about how you can give and give and give even after you think you have nothing left because there's still love and that's really what you were giving all along. The thing you were always left with.

So, as Aaron hummed and Jake fell back asleep wrapped around him by the moonlit window in the middle of the night, he repeated over and over what he had repeated for Aaron that afternoon.

And the boy loved the tree....

very much.

And the tree was happy.

Giselle Ellis grew up on a farm thoroughly convinced she was Laura Ingalls; she was quite displeased to find out she was not. Giselle now lives just outside of Minneapolis, Minnesota. She spends a great deal of time roaming around the Twin Cities looking in bookstores, museums and any odd spot she can find. She also teaches, reads voraciously and obsessively watches movies which in turn has created an enormous font of useless knowledge of which she is quite proud. If it were up to her, she would spend all of her time traveling the world, writing fiction and trying to convince Major League Baseball that baseball should be played 365 days a year.

START FROM THE
BEGINNING

Chrissy Munder

CHAPTER ONE

"CHRIST, Kurt. When you said peace and quiet, you meant it." Miles looked around suspiciously. The one room cabin, while small, was fully modernized with all the conveniences one could hope for. Except for one....

"Where's the bloody phone?"

Kurt set Miles's suitcase down at the foot of the queen size bed covered in an attractive Indian patterned quilt.

"The whole concept of you getting peace and quiet entails keeping you away from telephones, fax machines, Internet and anything else that's going to keep you from the rest and recuperation you need."

Miles made a face at his friend. "I'll rest when I'm dead."

"And that, my friend, is the reason why you are here." Kurt shook his head at Miles. "You have to take this seriously, Miles. You had a heart attack. You could have another one if you don't make some changes."

Kurt watched Miles as he crossed over to look out the front window. Looking at his lean and fit friend, it was hard to believe that just a few short months ago he had his hands on Miles's heart, massaging the life-giving blood through it and demanding his friend come back to him.

"Well, if things are so serious, dumping me off in the back of the beyond with no auto and no phone to contact my doctor is asking for trouble now, isn't it?" Miles's green eyes sparked at his long-time friend, sometime lover and currently, full-time doctor.

Kurt sighed. "It's not like you're just post-op, Miles. Besides, I told you. An old colleague of mine lives in the cabin up the hill. I'm leaving him your file and asking him to look in on you. Brenda will come by once a week with your groceries and to do any errands you need."

"I'm a fuckin' prisoner, then?" As always when Miles became upset his accent thickened, emphasizing his British roots that the last several years in the States had never managed to erase.

Kurt ignored the sensual jolt Miles's rough voice always gave him. That was a step in Miles's recovery they hadn't addressed yet. "You're not a prisoner," he repeated for what seemed like the tenth time. "You can go anywhere up here you want. There's a lot to see here, there's the lighthouses and miles of beach to walk on. The sunsets are terrific and the town has some great little art shops."

"You've got to be kidding me." Miles crossed his arms over his chest, feeling the scar under his shirt as he did so.

"Come on, Miles." Kurt's frustration was evident. "It's the best I can think of. I tried to let you do it your way but you were headed right back into trouble. At least, just try it … for me?"

"Even though I can't believe you stole my cell, it's not like I could ever deny you anything," Miles grumped as he looked out the large picture window. Kurt was right about one thing. The view here was terrific. The cottage was situated behind and atop a small series of sand dunes and looked down onto the big lake.

"Feel like I'm going to turn into a bleedin' turnip just sittin' around."

Kurt reached out and caught Miles close in a tight hug. "You're going to be the tannest and sexiest turnip I know."

Miles returned the firm grasp of Kurt's arms, knowing it was one of the few ways his friend could show his relief while still trying to maintain some professional focus.

"I did say thank you, didn't I?" he mumbled against Kurt's neck, his breath ruffling the sandy hair on the nape.

"For what?" Kurt joked, not wanting the moment to get too emotional. "My amazing ability to ignore you when you're being a foul bastard? Or for carting you up here to the "back ass of beyond" as you so delicately put it?"

"It's certainly not the last part, I can tell you that!"

"I'm going to take your file up to Drew and fill him in." Miles watched as Kurt shifted his feet uneasily.

"Uh ... Miles, go easy on him, will you?"

"What do you mean?" Miles asked.

"Drew's a quiet kind of guy. He's had some ... personal troubles. Just don't push, ok?"

"What aren't you telling me here, Kurt?" Miles's suspicions drifted back to the fore.

"Nothing," Kurt muttered as Miles picked up the remote control to the television. "I gotta go, Miles. I'll see you in a few weeks."

Miles watched Kurt rush out of the cabin and sniffed as he turned on the television. No telling with Kurt sometimes. There was a large assortment of DVDs in the lower half of the entertainment unit but Miles thought he'd check out some international news instead, maybe he could catch a market report.

There seemed to be one small problem with that plan.

Even half way up the hill to Drew's cabin, Kurt could hear Miles's yell though the open window of his truck.

"No fuckin' cable either? Kurt, you wanker!"

CHAPTER TWO

KURT stood at the front door of Drew's cabin and stared down at the manila envelope that had just flown over his head to land on the path behind him. It really had seemed like a good idea at the time, he told himself once again. Miles wasn't getting the rest and lack of stress he needed to complete his recovery. The cabin just sat empty the majority of the time, and Drew ... well, there wasn't another world-renowned ex-cardiologist Kurt would rather trust Miles's life to.

He just had to get Drew to agree.

Bending down to pick up the envelope that held Miles's file, Kurt could only shake his head. Why was it that both of the men he loved the most were such royal pains in the rear? He stepped into the cool interior of the cabin and headed towards the back room where he knew Drew kept his studio. When Drew had moved up here permanently, Kurt had transferred his belongings into the smaller, one room cabin, opening up this one for his friend.

A quick glance showed him that as usual the interior was spotless. Drew might live here full time, but it didn't look any more lived in than Kurt's cabin did before Miles arrived. It would make Kurt feel a little bit ashamed of his own rather careless housekeeping, if it didn't make him so sad to think how hard Drew worked at leaving so little impact on the world around him.

"Can we talk about this?" Kurt quietly asked the figure already sitting down at the potters' wheel in the back room.

A shrug from the large back covered in blue denim that faced him was his only reply. Drew's bare foot found its way to the pedal on the floor and he began the rhythmic pumping that set the wheel spinning.

Kurt stepped into the room, walking carefully over the various clumps of clay that were strewn about the floor on his way over to the storage shelves beside the large kiln. Drew hadn't shipped his latest work down to the shop in town yet and the shelves were still full. Kurt wandered around, the bright light streaming in the open windows highlighting the different colors.

"That new glaze you're experimenting with looks to be working well."

Another shrug from the silent back that faced him, this time accompanied by a head toss that sent the long dark hair swirling before it settled back down in the middle of Drew's back, as his hands rested lightly on the wet mass of clay on the wheel before him. It was longer than Kurt remembered and his hands ached to reach out and feel the softness of that dark mass, but he knew what the reaction would be if he tried.

"It won't take up any more of your time. It's not like he needs care, he's almost fully recovered from the surgery. He just needed to get away from the stresses of his daily routine and make some decisions about his future." Kurt could hear the pleading note in his voice. "It would make me feel better about leaving him alone if I knew you were keeping an eye on him."

The foot stopped its motions on the pedal and both men watched as the wheel began to slow, water and rich red clay sluicing off as it spun down.

"Do it in lieu of rent while he's up here?"

How could a back be so expressive? Kurt wondered as he tried one last time to get a response.

"Do it for me?"

With perfect timing, the wheel stopped moving at Kurt's last words and Drew stood up, shaking his head as he turned to face his former colleague. Without a word, just a meaningful glance from his dark hazel eyes, he took the envelope from Kurt's hand before making shooing motions at the man.

"I know, I know." Kurt laughed. "You hate it when I'm in your studio." He let Drew walk him out to the living room and shook his head when Drew gestured towards the coffeepot.

"I wish I could, but I have to get back. It's a long drive and I've got too many appointments booked tomorrow to push it."

Drew smiled and ran a hand through his thick fall of hair. Kurt tried not to stare at the crooked fingers exposed by the gesture but couldn't help himself, anymore than he could avoid looking at the scar just showing under the dark beard line. Drew's smile faded and he shoved his hand down into his front pants pocket and dropped his chin towards his chest.

"Oh, Drew," Kurt breathed. "You don't have to hide, not from me."

As always when he saw Drew, tears pricked at Kurt's eyes. Tears he didn't dare let fall in front of his friend. It was just so unfair, he thought to himself. Even now, Drew smoldered with an intensity that pulled others toward him, but Kurt could remember a time when being in Drew's presence was like being caught in the hot burning sun of a summer's day. A time before, when the man laughed easily and loved life with a warrior's joy.

Kurt stood there, wanting to reach out and hug Drew close like he'd done with Miles, needing to reassure himself his friend was more than this silent ghost, wanting to feel the muscles of that long body pressed up against his, wanting to breathe in his familiar scent, but he did none of that. He just nodded at Drew before walking outside the cabin.

"I'll see you later then." Kurt kept his voice steady with an effort. "Thanks for looking in on Miles, I appreciate it."

"Kurt...."

The voice was low and rough from scar tissue and disuse, but it was strong enough to stop Kurt in his tracks. When was the last time he'd heard Drew say anything, much less his name? he wondered dazedly.

Drew walked out into the sun beside him and they stood there silently for moment, before Drew leaned forward and let only his lips touch the side of Kurt's cheek. The kiss was as soft as a butterfly wing, barely there, barely felt, but a small miracle none the less to Kurt.

Kurt's arms came up instinctively – only to clutch empty air as Drew shuddered and stepped back away from the touch.

"Drive safe," the dark man uttered gutturally. And then the door shut behind him and Kurt was left standing there with nothing but the silly smile on his face.

CHAPTER THREE

MILES lay on his back in the hot grass and watched the two seagulls coasting overhead on the breeze blown in off the lake. The winds here were pretty phenomenal. He'd almost think he was in South Dakota the way they didn't seem to ever stop blowing. Idly he wondered if these winds had names – like something out of an old myth.

He'd given up wearing his watch after the first three days, as watching the second hand refuse to move had almost driven him insane. But he didn't need it anymore; he'd gotten pretty good at reading the sun. Judging from the shadow on the grass cast by the cabin, it was almost time to check on that surly bastard next door.

The first week in the small cabin had gone by slowly for Miles. Actually in the journal Kurt had left him and encouraged him to write in, Miles had described it in far more graphic and forthright terms. Miles grinned; he couldn't wait to read bits of this journal to Kurt. Serve the bugger right.

By the second week, with none of his usual distractions, Miles's world had been reduced to little things. Things like naming the seagulls he watched for hours and walking down to the lake's edge and dipping his toes in the freezing water. He'd discovered a bit of a garden behind the cabin, abandoned ages ago and gone to seed in a wild and disreputable fashion. In desperation for something to do, Miles had begun clearing it out, finding an unexpected pleasure in the simple task of nurturing the neglected greenery.

Miles knew he needed to make some decisions. That was after all why he was here. It was time for him to face a few truths about his life and the way he lived it. He rubbed his hand down his bare chest, feeling the sweat beneath his fingers as well as the raised line from his surgical scar. Damn thing had itched like hell when the hair was growing back.

The heart attack had scared the absolute shit out of him – if he was going to be honest, he had to admit that. What made it worse was that there wasn't a physical reason for it to have happened. No blocked arteries, no defects. There was nothing that Kurt could tweak with his scalpels. It was all the result of high blood pressure brought on by the "s" word – stress.

Miles snorted to himself and watched a lazy bumblebee meander through the patch of clover beside him. Stress that had left him with his chest cracked open and the knowledge that Kurt could now claim to have put his hands on just about every part of Miles there was. So, if he'd been so scared, why did he fall back into his old, careless habits when he'd been released from his post-op care?

Truth was, Miles didn't need the money. He'd made a small fortune – enough to last him for this lifetime and beyond. He'd only kept going for the thrill; the adrenaline rush as he teetered on the edge of disaster and pulled himself back using only his wits, nerves and bollocks. Kurt said those days were done and God knows he did trust Kurt, no matter how much he ragged on the man. So what did a bloke newly retired from the global commodities market and perfectly happy residing in a foreign country do? Miles wondered. He wasn't interested in moving back to England, his parents had died several years back and there was nothing and no one there to lay claim on him.

Miles's thoughts were interrupted by a creaking noise. He was always amazed at how easily the sound traveled the distance between the two cabins in the afternoon quiet. But he was grateful as well. With a groan, he rolled himself over to his stomach and oh so casually laid his head down onto his folded arms. His eyes didn't close, however; instead they were drawn to the lounger outside the other cabin and the lounger's current occupant. Yep, there he was, right on time.

In addition to all his newfound pursuits, Miles had also discovered something even more fun. Watching Drew. That and seeing how long the man could ignore him. Miles wasn't sure how it had come about, not really. He supposed it began that first night when he had been restless and unable to sleep. He had prowled around the small cabin before finally being driven outside by his irritation, like a wolf leaving his den to howl at the moon.

With no street lighting, the world outside his cabin at night was a revelation. He sat on a bench and stared up at the night sky, unable to remember the last time he'd seen so many stars. There had been a light on in the rear part of the cabin up the hill and Miles could hear music, light and faint as it drifted through the dark night, soothing and calming his frustrations and leaving him able to wonder at the sounds of the night creatures as they accepted his presence and went about their business.

Miles had actually started to drift off, warm and comfortable in the cool night air, when he heard the now familiar creaking noise from the other cabin. His eyes had adjusted enough to the darkness to make out a large shape on the lounger, but no other details. Silently Miles sat and watched the other figure, hypnotized by the man's utter stillness, and amazed to discover later that he'd sat there and watched the man do nothing for three whole hours.

And so it had somehow begun. Miles's new obsession, he called it in his journal. Nothing else up here to bloody obsess about, he joked to himself. Of course, the fact that even from a distance, Drew was one of the most attractive men Miles'd seen in ages didn't hurt. Not that Miles could do anything about that right now.

After a few days, Miles knew more about the man's daily routine than he'd known about most of the partners he'd had in his life. What he didn't know, Miles had ended up pumping Brenda for when she came up with his groceries.

In between Brenda's visits, Miles had tried being civil to his neighbor; hell, he'd even tried being social. All that his greetings and conversational gambits had gotten him were dark glances and endless silence – always from a distance.

He'd even tried knocking on Drew's door, certain his neighbor was inside and thinking he'd at least like to meet the man before he'd needed his medical help, but Miles never received any response. "Better hope I don't try to drop dead tomorrow, with all the attention I'm getting from that one."

Thanks to Brenda, Miles now knew that Drew spent his time as a potter, selling his pieces in some of the shops below. She'd had a load of his work in her truck and Miles had peered at it in curiosity. Apparently Drew had kept his license to practice medicine and held a free clinic on Saturdays for any who cared to show. Well, that explained the line of people Miles had seen the prior weekend. They'd stood there for hours it seemed.

Mainly migrant workers, Brenda told Miles, afraid or unable to afford the doctor in town, but strangely comfortable with the silent man. "Not a big talker at all, is Dr. Drew." She'd laughed before her expression changed, quickly becoming somber. "'Cause of what they did to him."

That statement had made Miles question her further, and with a little pressing Brenda gave him the basics. Apparently, Miles's neighbor had led quite a different life than he did now. A much-lauded surgeon and cardiologist, he'd been working for a volunteer group in South America. Apparently civil unrest had led to violence and Drew's group had been captured and, well … "bad things were done to him". That's all Brenda would say.

So, okay, given that information, perhaps there wasn't anything personal about the man's ignoring Miles. But Miles was bored and that was a dangerous thing, plus he never could resist a challenge. So every time Miles was out and saw his new neighbor, he'd give him a wave and a smile.

Sometimes he'd beckon the man over, just to watch him stiffen and turn away. Other times, Miles would start to walk up towards him, only to see the man silently turn and enter his cabin, shutting the door firmly behind him. Miles had to give the man credit – he didn't even make a pretense at being polite.

The subject of Miles's solitary musings decided it was time to roll over and Miles caught his breath. *Damn, but he was a big, fine bloke,* Miles thought once again. Every day, like clockwork, the man would venture outside and strip down before lying out on the lounger, looking for all the world like a big lazy cat, basking in the heat of the day. The dark hair spilled off the back of the lounger, drifting down to the grass and shining like a mallard's wing in the hot sun.

Miles could still remember the first time he'd realized the man was naked. Granted, he wasn't prudish by any stretch of imagination. It was just the surprise. Either the man didn't see him, or he just bloody well didn't care that he had a new neighbor.

After the first day, it became obvious he just didn't care. The distance was such that Miles couldn't really see more than the large expanse of honey dark skin, set off by the dark beard and that waterfall of dark hair. But that was more than enough to add to Miles's sleepless nights.

He didn't know what to do about the situation either. He'd discussed these things – briefly – with Kurt, but his friend had just told him to worry about that later in his recovery. Well, here he was, wondering just how much later. Miles'd seen the commercials, used to laugh at them too. But now the words "…must be healthy enough for sexual activity…" took on a whole new meaning, one tinged with fear.

He'd lay there at night, feeling the tingle of lust, his hands itching to reach down and touch familiar ground, wanting to relieve himself of the images that came to his mind every time he thought of Drew. But fear stayed his hand.

Miles's sense of the ridiculous painted graphic pictures of Brenda finding him dead, cock in one hand, fingers of the other buried deep in his ass. Victim of a simple wank. It had been so damn long! He laughed about it to himself, but still couldn't take that first step.

Deciding he'd spent enough time being lazy and thinking silly thoughts, Miles stood and stretched, slowly enjoying the crack and pop of his joints. With a jaunty wave in Drew's direction, he smiled and headed off to his garden.

"Catch you later, you rude, soddin' bastard," he muttered affectionately.

It was definitely time to come up with something new to add to the game.

CHAPTER FOUR

DREW crushed the misshapen mass of clay between his hands and sighed. He was going to kill Kurt. He really was. Kurt knew that the reason Drew had moved up to the cabin was to get some much-appreciated distance from the rest of the world, that he needed the space and the quiet and isolation to be able to breathe after all that had happened. Drew also knew that Kurt disagreed; he knew Kurt thought what Drew needed was more contact with humanity – not less.

But Kurt didn't understand how just being in the same room as another person, much less being touched, could make Drew's skin crawl and burn as if a thousand ants were trapped underneath if he wasn't prepared. Kurt didn't realize just how bad the nightmares were or how many nights Drew was unable to sleep.

It was as if the walls were closing in on him, the claustrophobia building, memories filling his mind until he had to go outside into the darkness and gulp in the cool night air to still his pounding heart and the silent screams that were all his damaged throat would allow him.

Kurt didn't know how bloody tired Drew was of people looking at his hands or his neck or any of the other scars that bore brutal testament to the inhumanity of man. Up here, alone, Drew could relax and strip off his shirt without having to hear the gasps of horror or the questions. Up here, Drew could almost forget.

He had his work, enough to satisfy. His physical therapist had introduced him to working with clay as a way to strengthen the shattered bones of his hands and fingers. Drew would never wield a scalpel again, but this was creation of another kind. And he could still heal, offering his services free of charge to those that had no one else to trust their care to.

He didn't live in total isolation. It was more a chosen solitude. If there was some unacknowledged need for human companionship during the long nights, some atavistic desire to touch another, he just ignored it – his prior painful attempts to reconnect with humanity had taught him he wasn't ready for that.

Brenda brought him his groceries and supplies and took his finished wares down to the shops to sell to the tourists. He had his patients. He had a stray tom that had adopted him and visited when mood struck or the local pickings were slim. Again, it was enough.

But now he had Miles. Bloody, obnoxious, absolutely fucking gorgeous, Miles and the unwelcome surge of desire that accompanied him. What the hell had Kurt been thinking? Drew had become accustomed to his isolation. Kurt spent more time working than not and with the cabin unoccupied, Drew had forgotten how close the two units actually were, but not anymore.

He couldn't seem to get away from the man. Every time, day or night, Drew would step outside, there he would be, rooting about in the overgrown garden with his torso bare to the touch of the sun, walking along the beach with his hair tousled by the wind or just sitting and staring up at Drew's cabin like it was the center of his universe.

He insisted on totally ignoring Drew's efforts to ignore him – he would wave and flash an infectious smile in Drew's direction, gesturing to him like they were old mates no matter how cold a shoulder Drew turned to him. Was the man completely mental?

Even from the distance between them, Drew couldn't help but notice how much lighter the tawny hair became, how much darker the pale skin turned as the days passed. That was all right, he could allow himself to admire Miles from afar. The problem was that Miles refused to respect the distance between them. He kept pressing into Drew's space.

Drew knew he should get it over with. Just go and confront the man, let him look his fill, ask his questions and then shy away like they all did. But still he held back – not sure why until the day he hid behind the door of his cabin, hand pressed up against it to feel the vibrations from Miles's knock. It was then that Drew acknowledged the fear and desire hiding within him.

He didn't want to see the same pity or the disgust in Miles's eyes he'd seen so many times before. He wanted something more. It had been a long time since Drew had felt the eyes of another on him. But he could feel Miles's. Without thinking, Drew had gone out to sunbathe the first few days as was his habit, only to remember too late that Kurt's cabin had an occupant. Miles's attention turned his way and he'd almost felt … normal again.

He knew he should stop. It was a silly, childish game he was playing. He knew what the reality would be like if Miles were ever close enough to see the marks on his body the distance between them softened and hid. But he didn't, he couldn't, and he found he wouldn't.

If this was all Drew could have, if this was all he could bear, then what harm did it do? And if in the night his swelling flesh would tell him it wasn't enough, he would bury that still voice beneath the throbbing strains of the music he played to express the emotions he could no longer voice with ease.

CHAPTER FIVE

THERE was something different about today, Miles thought. He couldn't put his finger on it. It was something in the air, something almost tangible, something just out of his reach. He snorted at his fanciful thoughts. *Been up here too damn long.* But making fun of it still didn't make the feeling go away.

There was a hush, a stillness that surrounded him. Miles supposed he could call it a sense of waiting. But he didn't know for what. Even the winds seemed to have died down and the seagulls were reduced to walking along the edge of the shoreline, rather than lazily floating on their warm air currents.

Miles looked out at the lake though the clear glass of the window and thought that the color of the water and sky appeared different this morning from all the others. The clouds were tinged with a faint green haze that seemed to spark with an almost electric current. *Strange*, he thought. *And beautiful.*

Whatever seemed to be impacting the world outside the cabin seemed to be taking a toll on him as well. He couldn't seem to manage to sit still today. It was as if his skin was too tight. Miles felt agitated and angry and nothing seemed to be helping. He didn't want to rest, he didn't want to garden, he didn't know what he wanted to do!

Miles sighed and turned to survey the interior of the cabin in restless disgust. He was bloody well sick and tired of being cooped up in this bloody cabin, all because he'd had a bloody heart attack and Kurt was being a bloody mother hen. *Ha!* He ought to put that in Kurt's bloody journal, except he couldn't still his agitation enough to pull the bloody thing out and write in it.

Of course, if he was going to be honest with himself, he might have to admit that this disquiet he was experiencing had been building ever since he realized that Drew wasn't up at the cabin. As a matter of fact, he'd seen neither hide nor hair of his tall, dark and silent neighbor for three entire days.

Well, to be bloody accurate it was more like three bloody days, three long bloody nights and six bloody hours, not that he didn't have anything else to pay attention to, mind you.

It was the silence that first unsettling night that had clued Miles into Drew's absence. After weeks of thinking the music that Drew usually played hours into the night was responsible for keeping him awake, Miles couldn't understand why he now couldn't sleep and missed it so much. The darkness from the cabin was his next sign. Drew always seemed to have a light burning through 'til morning.

When Brenda had swung by with his load of groceries he'd (*very casually, of course*) questioned her about Drew's whereabouts. Miles had long passed whatever litmus test she held newcomers to before considering them locals and her prior hesitations about sharing gossip had vanished, leaving her more than happy to sit down to a soft drink or two and some conversation.

So, here he was, three days, three long nights and six hours later, stuck worrying about a man he'd yet to even speak to. Miles kicked at one of his trainers he'd left lying in the middle of the floor, smiling with grim satisfaction as it bounced off the couch and hit the wall with a satisfying thud.

He'd tried to tell himself he was just bored – after all, wasn't Drew-watching one of his main pastimes? He was just deprived of his daily amusement, that's all. But when even a night out at the local watering hole with Brenda and her friends hadn't cured Miles's restlessness, he knew he was in trouble. Deprived wasn't the word for how he felt; addicted and in withdrawal was more like it.

He just needed to *see* the man.

And that, given that he'd not yet spoken to Drew, didn't know a thing about the man's romantic preferences (he could hope, knowing Kurt – but still), and didn't even know what his own current limits were sexually, well, that was just pretty damn pathetic.

Miles sighed. Then he gave himself a mental slap upside the head. Miles Taylor was not a man given to sighing, or talking about himself in the third person for that matter. It must be this place. Maybe it was the air in this place. Or maybe it was just Drew.

When he gave it some thought, Miles could understand how, given the bloke's history, he needed to go see a specialist every once in a while, even a fancy-pants one in Chicago as Brenda had called him. But how long did that take? And what was he doing the rest of the time? Visiting old friends? Painting the town red? Getting shagged?

Fucking hell!

Miles's teeth ground together as he contemplated the last possibility. This was definite proof that life wasn't fair! Here he was, stuck in the back arse of nowhere, too damn scared of dying to even given himself a good wank, and Dr. Drew bloody-fucking-gorgeous Cole was wining and dining his way around Chicago. Miles had no doubt that even now the man was letting someone else enjoy stroking that golden skin and shining hair while leaving Miles here, alone, worrying about him.

And wait just a minute; wasn't Dr. Drew bloody-fucking-gorgeous Cole supposed to be looking out for Miles? Keeping an eye on him and making sure that he didn't need any kind of medical attention? Just wait until he could get a hold of Kurt and give him an earful about this! God knows what could have happened to Miles in the last three days!

Having managed to work himself into a foul mood, Miles decided it was time for action. He wasn't going to moon about here all day like some stupid git, just waiting for the man to come home! Ignoring the total and absolute irrationality of his thoughts,

Miles grabbed a sweatshirt and headed out into the strange afternoon air, cursing as he stubbed his bare toe on the door frame and somehow managing to successfully place the blame for that on Drew as well.

CHAPTER SIX

MEANWHILE, the object of Miles's frustrations threw himself heavily upon the patchwork quilt that covered his bed with a sigh of his own. He was finally home! And luckily, he'd managed to beat the monster of a storm that was brewing as well. *God, how he hated hospitals!* The irony wasn't lost on Drew given his prior occupation, but he could ignore it.

It wasn't really hospitals themselves that bothered him; it was everything else that went along with them. Drew hated leaving the life he had made for himself up at the cabin. He hated having to face the crowds of people that went along with the city, hated having to force himself to speak to strangers, hated being poked and prodded, forced to remember things better forgotten and this time, he had hated leaving Miles and the strange connection that had developed between them.

Drew knew he should have let Miles know that he was going away, or at the very least told him that he had made arrangements with the GP in town in case something happened. But to do any of those things, Drew would have had to talk to Miles, and he wasn't ready. Not yet.

Besides, he told himself, there hadn't been any time once he had decided to have the procedure. The sudden opening in the surgical schedule had left him scrabbling as it was. Add in to that the stress of knowing what was ahead of him, and it was a wonder he hadn't backed out. Drew'd thought about changing his mind and called himself all kinds of fool for going ahead with it. But in the end, he found he really didn't have any choice.

The look on Kurt's face when Drew had spoken his name was what had finally decided him. Drew just hadn't realized the power and meaning behind such a simple act. Not being able to talk easily hadn't bothered him at first, not really. After everything that had happened, it wasn't like he had much to say anyway.

Everything just seemed to jam up inside his head and that was where he thought it should stay. He didn't want to share what had happened, didn't want to remember most of it. It was easier to let others think that he wasn't able to talk. The expectations were lower and most people left him alone.

But now there was Miles – beautiful, golden Miles who filled Drew's days and nights with thoughts of what could be. Kurt had always said Drew had more pride than sense, and after enduring the esophageal stretching and removal of scar tissue he'd just undergone, Drew knew Kurt was right. It had definitely been pride that had driven him to Chicago and the hated hospital.

Pride that insisted Drew become more than just a silent spectator to life. A man ought to be able to speak his lover's name, plain and simple. And so, for Miles, for the unexpressed hopes and desires that had blossomed so unexpectedly in Drew, he'd put himself under the hands of those he'd rejected years ago.

And wasn't that a sad comment on his life? he asked himself. Here he was, unable to gracefully handle the mere presence of another human, much less their touch without preparation, having schoolboy fantasies about a man he'd not even spoken to.

Of course, never satisfied, the medical staff had pushed a little more, bringing up the additional procedures they had talked about before. But Drew wasn't ready for any of that. Hell, he didn't know what he was ready for now. He just knew that if he wanted to find out, he needed to find a place to start.

Drew did a few of the breathing exercises they had taught him, breathing in and out deeply while attempting to relax his throat. Feeling ready, he pursed his lips and exhaled gently as he gave voice to a husky whisper, pushing the words past the pain in his throat.

"Miles."

The name seemed to echo in the small room, hanging in the air with a life of its own. Drew shivered, amazed as he felt himself harden. The power of the spoken word. It was amazing, a simple but vital component of life that he had chosen to forget.

Suddenly Drew rolled over and buried his face in the pillow. Miles wasn't the one who was mental, it was Drew, and it didn't matter that he was a man grown – right now all he wanted to do was pull the covers over his head and hide.

CHAPTER SEVEN

DREW was awoken from his brief bout of self-pity by the sound of a car door loudly slamming shut. He groaned and pushed up off the bed, stretching as he did so and amazed at all the kinks he could feel. Hospitals just didn't agree with any part of him nowadays, it seemed. He recognized the sound of Brenda's flip-flops on the cement walkway and grabbed a shirt to meet her at the door.

"Hey there, Dr. Drew." As usual, Brenda was in a cheery mood. "Glad you made it back in one piece." She gave his large frame a quick, appreciative glance as he finished buttoning up his shirt. "They didn't keep anything useful there, did they, big guy?"

Drew just stared at her for a minute. What? He was gone for a few days and the world changed? While always cheerful, Brenda was never this familiar, almost flirtatious with him.

"Hi, Brenda," he uttered cautiously.

"Dr. Drew!" Suddenly he was enveloped in a quick hug. Before he had time to react and push her away, she stepped back, wrapping her arms around her waist as she smiled up at him.

"That's so cool! Your voice sounds a lot better!"

Without waiting for a reply, she went back to her truck and pulled out a couple of grocery bags. Handing one to Drew, she walked past him and headed towards his kitchen as she continued to chat.

"Bill over at the Gas and Gone left me a message. He saw your truck drive by, so I thought I'd bring you some groceries up 'til you had a chance to get a list together. So everything went okay with the doctors, huh?"

Drew nodded, still feeling groggy from his earlier retreat from reality.

"Miles will be real happy to hear that. I didn't know you guys had become such good friends. Poor guy, he missed you something terrible." Giving Drew a quick wink, Brenda reached into the grocery bag she'd placed on the counter. "Let's put these away and have something cool to drink. I can catch you up on all the local gossip and...." Brenda realized Drew had stopped and was staring at her again.

"Miles?" Drew whispered in shock, his brain having caught up to her flow of words.

"Yeah. He was really lost without you." Brenda giggled. "You should have seen him; he was trying to be so cool, you know, asking me where you were, how long you'd be gone. You really should have told him."

"He asked about me?" Drew parroted again, ignoring her scolding.

"Real cute about, it he was." Brenda winked at him again. "It's about time you had a little fun. He's definitely a fine looking fella."

"Cute?"

Brenda walked over and gave Drew a push into one of the chairs by the kitchen table. "You must be tired from being poked at so much. Sit down and I'll tell you about us taking Miles out to the bar the other night. You were the only thing he could talk about."

AN hour later, a very confused Drew was again at his front door, this time waving goodbye to a giggling Brenda. Maybe it was his dazed state, but he had found he really hadn't minded Brenda's longer than usual visit. He wouldn't have called it relaxing, but at least he hadn't felt the need to bolt like usual. Perhaps it had something to do with the subject matter of their conversation?

"Oh, Dr. Drew?" Brenda poked her head out her car window. "When you see Miles, be sure you tell him about the big one we've got heading in off the lake. I meant to be sure to warn him about it, him being new and all up here, but he was out when I drove by. Wouldn't want him blowing away now, would we?"

Brenda's parting words worried Drew more than he immediately wanted to admit. The storms that blew in off the Great Lake were astounding in their intensity and always managed to surprise those that hadn't experienced them. Usually not in a pleasant way.

Drew looked down at Miles's cabin but was unable to see any sign he'd returned. He debated whether or not to try to look for the other man, but without knowing where Miles had gone or how long ago he'd left, it would be pretty futile; there was just too much territory to cover. He'd have to keep his eyes open and catch him when he came back.

Drew set about his usual storm preparations, checking that his supplies of water and the oil for his lamps and candles were all stocked and readily available. He usually preferred not to use the generator unless power was out for several days, but that needed to be checked and cycled as well. He had a root cellar he used for cold storage in emergencies, but having been away, his fresh supplies were limited to what Brenda had dropped off, and he would go through those before they went bad if the power did cut out.

Confident that the interior of his cabin was ready for anything the weather could throw at him, Drew began checking on his exterior storm shutters. The wind had picked up and he could smell the difference in the air. He didn't know if it was the scent of ozone or just some innate animal sense, but he could tell this was going to be a hard one.

He decided not to wait until later but began closing the outer wooden shutters over the glass windows. Some closed easily with a hook and eye setup, but others on the side that faced the lake needed the reinforcement against the wind that only a hammer and nail could provide.

Drew welcomed the labor; his thoughts were still in chaos over Brenda and her coy hints and comments. Should he believe her? Was it possible that Miles felt the same fragile connection between the two of them that he did?

He glanced down at the other cabin yet again, but there was still no sign of the other man. Drew shrugged and went inside. He had a consignment due by the next week that he needed to get started on. As he sat down at his wheel, he reminded himself to be sure to check on Miles before too much time passed.

SATISFIED with the work he'd produced so far, Drew stretched and rubbed his long fingers along the base of his spine. Either he was getting old or the hospital had taken more out of him than he'd thought. He thought of the grey he'd noticed in Kurt's hair a few weeks ago and winced. But that was Kurt, he assured himself.

Drew grabbed a bottle of water and walked outside the cabin. The storm clouds were gathering in force, and the sun had disappeared in their wake. Even though it was only late afternoon, it appeared to be twilight. Normally he loved the greenish yellow color the sky turned before all hell broke loose, but today he could only think of Miles.

He picked up his phone and called into town, checking with a few of the locals to see if they'd seen the tall blond during the day. Everyone he spoke with was pleasantly surprised to hear from him, complimented him on his voice, and all answered his questions about Miles in the negative. This wasn't good.

Knowing what was ahead, Drew pulled on a heavy sweatshirt and slicker along with his boots. He grabbed his emergency bag along with some extra blankets and with a muttered curse threw it all into his truck. *Damn the fool man,* Drew thought worriedly as he drove off with a squeal of his tires. *Didn't he know enough to come in out of a storm?*

CHAPTER EIGHT

THE winds had changed, growing stronger and cooler, and the sky had darkened before he knew it. Miles had tried to get back to the cabin before the obviously rising storm with no luck. The thunder had started first, low and rumbling in the distance, before quickly building to a constant roar overhead that rivaled the sound of the winds that whipped leaves and debris around him and churned up whitecaps on the lake surface.

He'd paced himself, careful of his bruised feet and slightly fearful of his increased heart rate. Nothing he hadn't experienced in cardio rehab, but knowing he'd already excited himself enough for the day, the last thing he needed was to have something stupid happen.

Well, he amended, not anything stupider than what he'd already done. As if in answer to his thoughts, lightning had appeared, streaking through the dark clouds over the lake, and finally the rain had begun to fall in drenching buckets.

Miles limped gratefully back into the small cabin, struggling against the winds to close the door behind him. Rushing out in a blaze of righteous indignation, while satisfying for the moment, had left him a few miles out with sore, bare feet, feeling terribly foolish once the blaze had burnt itself out. Not to mention that he was now wet, freezing and creating his own interior downpour as he stood in the entranceway, dripping puddles onto the floor.

He was more than a little ashamed of his earlier behavior. The long walk and the unexpected onslaught of the storm had calmed him down, and looking at things with a fresh perspective, Miles didn't even really have a good reason why he'd gotten so agitated.   Could be simple frustration, could be the isolation. Cabin fever, he thought the Americans called it.

Or, *damn it*. It could just be Drew. Miles didn't know what it was, but something about the big man up the hill just kept getting to him on all levels. In the long run, he guessed it just didn't matter. One thing to come out of his association with Kurt had been an understanding and acceptance of his feelings. He felt it, and no matter how strange, it was what it was. Trying to deny it would only lead to trouble.

Right now, though, he needed to get warm and dry. Deciding his wet clothes couldn't damage the floor any more than the water running off him already had, Miles wiggled his way out of his drenched clothing and dropped it into a soggy pile where he stood, shivering as goose pimples formed on his clammy skin.

Towels, he thought as he padded into the kitchen, leaving dark and soggy prints in his wake. *Towels would be good.* A hot bath would be better and best of all would be.... "Aha!" Miles exclaimed triumphantly as he pulled a dusty bottle of whiskey from a cupboard under the kitchen sink where he'd been rummaging.

He poured himself a small glass, smiling at the amber liquid he could barely see in the darkened interior of the cabin with appreciation.   Outside, the intensity of the winds increased; he could hear the trees thrashing about, limbs creaking and mixing with the loud accompaniment of thunder. Ignoring his physical discomfort, Miles walked naked towards the front window, fascinated by the lightning show before him.

Most of the time in the city you could see only bits of a storm. Here, with only the fragile pane of glass between him and the outside, it was like being part of the elements. The lake was an open expanse that the light from the bolts sparked and cracked their way across in jagged arcs. Only once before had he ever seen four of the differing types of lightning at once, and never had he seen so many strikes in such a short period of time.

They spread out before him, lighting up the lake and for a few moments letting him see the rain that the wind was blowing almost sideways. It had been frightening when he had been at the storm's mercy; exhilarating and somehow cathartic now with the benefit of shelter. He sipped the whiskey, letting it warm him from the inside out, and wondered if Drew was watching the same display wherever he was.

Shrugging the thought away as soon as it crossed his mind, Miles walked to the bathroom and fumbled for the light switch so he could run his bath.

Nothing happened.

Even though he knew it was foolish he tried it again, flicking the switch up and down a few times as if he'd gotten it wrong the first time.

"*Bollocks.*"

So much for the hot bath idea; he'd been gone a lot longer than he'd thought and depending on when the power went out, the water in the heater tank could already have cooled. Miles was surprised at how little this bothered him; the storm raging overhead left him feeling strangely calm and serene. Without even bothering to try the hot tap, he grabbed a couple of towels and rubbed himself down briskly, enjoying the texture of the material against his skin and the tingle of circulation that followed.

Miles stumbled a bit as he left the bathroom, wincing as the awkward movement jarred his feet. He groped his way to the bedroom, finding and pulling on a pair of sweats and a t-shirt worn soft by time and too many cycles through the wash he'd left on the bed that morning.

He should have tossed the shirt long ago, but he had stolen it from Kurt and hated to part with it. The calm bubble hadn't left him, and he wondered idly at the cause behind it without feeling any pressure to investigate further.

He stood at one of the back windows, looking up the hill to the where he knew Drew's cabin sat, even though he was unable to see it through the deluge. *May as well change my name to Noah,* he thought wryly. Miles was thinking about the whiskey in the other room and how good another drink would be, but he was strangely reluctant to move. The wind seemed louder in the back part of the cabin and yet, over the crash of the thunder and the roar of the wind, he heard a loud snap, almost like a gunshot.

His strange bubble of calm seemed to burst at the same moment and Miles turned away from the window, his heart pounding and sweat breaking out on his forehead. Even as he turned he threw his hands up over his head as the ceiling of the small cabin exploded, collapsing down on top of him.

CHAPTER NINE

WHERE could he be?

Drew pounded the truck's steering wheel with his fist, frustrated as he peered out the windshield. Even with the wipers on full, they couldn't keep up with the driving rain, and he could hardly see the hood in front of him, much less hear anything over the water drumming on the roof.

He had pulled off the road on his way back to Kurt's cabin, hoping that if he waited a few minutes the intensity of the storm would lessen, but there was no sign of relief in sight and no sign of Miles. Drew didn't know if he really expected to see anything out in a storm like this, but he felt he had to try.

Drew didn't know how to feel right now. One minute he was blaming himself for not making more of an effort with Miles, maybe then he would have an idea of where to look; the next he was cursing Miles's stupidity for going out in what was shaping up to be the worst storm this year. The last weather report he'd managed to pick up through the static noted that a waterspout had been spotted out on the big lake.

Another bright burst of lightning convinced Drew that he'd better do something other than sit there, and he cautiously pulled the truck back on to the road. Not that he was worried about traffic, but parts of this road had a tendency to wash out during a downpour and he didn't want to end up with the truck stuck or worse yet, flood the engine.

His headlights didn't make a dent in the darkness of the storm, only the brilliant and blinding flashes of lightning illuminating his way to the cabin and helping him maneuver the truck past downed branches and other debris. He was hoping that Miles had made it back before the storm started, there weren't too many places to take shelter otherwise and Drew had checked them all.

Drew parked the truck before the darkened cabin, knowing the lack of light didn't necessarily equate empty. A storm this bad was going to knock out the power. He was already drenched from his searching, but pulled the useless hood of the slicker up over his head anyway as he ran for the front door.

Without the lightning, he couldn't see clearly and he grunted as his momentum pushed him up against the door, which swung open eerily from his weight.

"Miles?" he called as loudly as he could in an effort to be heard over the wind and rain. "Are you here?"

Drew stepped in, stumbling over something in the entryway. He knelt and felt for what tripped him, his heart beating swiftly. Nothing human, just a bunch of wet and soggy material.

"Miles?" he called again and coughed; his voice rough and throat sore from the abuse he'd already put it through.

Another bolt of light illuminated the interior of the cabin, and Drew felt his blood freeze at the scene before him. No wonder it was so loud in here, a portion of the roof had collapsed and the rain and winds were just pouring in the opening.

Drew pushed his way through the debris, knowing the bedroom was to the back, behind the downed timbers. He ignored the pain as jagged splinters of wood and sharp metal fought back, tearing and pulling at his clothes and skin, his focus on maneuvering through the twisted doorframe, fearful of what he would find.

"Miles?"

Miles raised his head groggily. *What had happened?* He coughed and felt a sharp pain in his side. Groaning, he attempted to sit up, shaking his head and regretting it instantly. What was he doing on the floor? What was that noise? *What the bloody hell?*

"Miles!"

He heard his name, and instinctively he knew who it was. He didn't know how, but he *knew* that low and rough voice.

"Drew?"

Miles coughed again and pressed one hand to his forehead. *Shite.* He strained to focus in the darkness as Drew pushed his way through the damage, frantic but still careful not to disturb as much as could.

"Are you all right?"

Drew was there now, kneeling beside him, his large form barely visible in the dark, his hands moving down Miles's torso, carefully feeling his limbs and where the debris had him pinned. All the while talking, words Miles heard but couldn't process.

"Yeah." Miles coughed again. He was fascinated by the brief glimpses of Drew's face the lightning flashes revealed to him. Nothing but dark eyes and stark, shadowed angles of face and jaw. Drew was still speaking, asking him questions, but all Miles could do was stare at the curve of his lips as they moved. *Christ.* Must have banged his head harder than he thought.

"I'm okay." Miles could feel the heat of Drew's hands through his t-shirt and shivered. "I don't think anything's broken, m'leg's pinned though."

"You're soaked." Drew looked around. "Hold still, I'll get you out of there."

Miles watched as Drew struggled to find something to lift the mess on top of him, the flashes of lightning adding a surreal, strobe effect to the unreality of the situation. Finally, Drew was back with a long piece of metal he carefully placed under the pile before putting his weight on the other end.

Drew's muscles flexed as he worked to shift the material. Miles could see the strain in his face and then there was pain again, sharp and insistent. He couldn't keep back the groan of pain from his lips and Drew hesitated for a moment before he tried again. Miles could feel the movement above him.

"Can you pull your leg out?" Drew gasped as he struggled with the weight, cursing his hands and their limited abilities.

Miles grunted and tried to use his hands to propel himself backwards. "Almost there, a little more," he panted.

Despite the gravity of the situation, his mind was working to fit their heavy breathing and exclamations into a different scenario. *Idiot!* he chastised himself, even as he used the images to distract himself from the pain. With a final burst of effort, he dragged his leg out from under the pile.

"Got it!"

Drew gratefully let go. Immediately he was at Miles's side, checking to make sure that Miles was right and that the leg wasn't broken.

"Can you put your weight on it?"

"Not much choice, eh?" Miles snorted even as he tightly grasped at the arm Drew gently placed around his shoulders. It hurt. It hurt a lot, to be bloody honest.

"Let's get you out of here." Drew lifted Miles up, the ease impressive to the injured man.

"I was right," Miles gasped. "You're a damn fine big bloke."

Drew didn't hear the words, just the rough drag and timbre of Miles's voice as he decided it would be easier to check out the extent of Miles's injuries at his cabin. He balanced Miles against his hip and removed his slicker, wrapping it around Miles before easing him out of the destroyed cabin and into the truck, ignoring the rain that drenched him even more in the process.

Miles leaned against the side of the door, watching as Drew climbed in the driver's seat. His head swam with the effects of adrenaline and the whiskey he'd drunk and he leaned his forehead against the cool glass of the window.

Drew's lips were moving again, but Miles couldn't hear what he was saying over the noise of the rain on the roof. Miles just nodded and closed his eyes; he was safe now, he was with Drew.

CHAPTER TEN

MILES'S peace was short lived. Instead of concentrating on the barely visible road ahead of them, Drew was staring over at Miles.

"Is something wrong?" Miles asked groggily, wiping the water off his face with one hand.

"What were you thinking?" Drew's voice was low and intense but somehow audible now over the rain and Miles blinked in surprise as his rescuer glared at him, the peace he'd felt being surrounded by Drew's presence in the confined space disappearing in seconds.

"What?" Miles was sure he'd misheard Drew's words in the din of the storm.

"Worst storm of the year and you go gallivanting off sightseeing!" The force of Drew's feelings had him leaning closer to Miles as he made his point.

"Gallivan…" Miles felt his own temper rising, even though he was bewildered by the sudden argument.

"I can't believe a grown man doesn't have the sense God gave a goat!" Drew continued. His hands were trembling now that he knew Miles was safe and he had to work to keep them steady on the steering wheel.

"Now that's bloody unfair!" Miles protested. His aches and throbbing pains were forgotten as he glared back at Drew in the small cab of the truck. His chin jutted forward in a sign of defiance his friends would have easily recognized.

"Do you have any idea how long I've been looking for you? Do you know what could have happened to you out there?" Drew snarled, the stress his throat had been put through making the words sound harsher than he intended.

"Well, at least a bloody roof wouldn't have fallen on me! As far as gallivanting, I'm not the one who was living it up in Chicago!" Miles's voice was peevish as some of his earlier agitation returned.

Drew gritted his teeth and gripped the steering wheel even tighter, as he swallowed back his angry response and looked away from Miles's piercing green eyes. This wasn't how he wanted his first conversation with Miles to go, not even close. But after the tension and uncertainty of the afternoon, he had been so scared when he'd seen Miles lying under that debris.

Miles sat there, waiting for Drew to respond, and when the man just ignored him threw himself back into the seat. An act he instantly regretted as the pain in his side and leg stabbed at him again.

"Are you okay?" Drew stopped the truck instantly when he heard Miles's involuntary gasp of pain and reached for the other man.

"I'm fine." Miles angrily swatted at Drew before he paused in shock, his anger forgotten as he took hold of Drew's hands. "Did you do this getting me out? Why didn't you say anything?" It was dark but Miles could just see the awkward angles of Drew's bent fingers.

Drew froze at Miles's touch. Confusion, fear and desire swirled inside of him. He didn't know what to do or what to say, so he pulled his hands back from Miles's warmth and steered the truck towards his cabin once again. The silence grew between them at his retreat, the only sound the rain as it continued to beat down on the roof.

"No," Drew finally said; his voice thick. "I didn't do that getting you out."

And then he didn't say anything more.

THE silence stayed between them even when they arrived at the cabin. Each man was lost in his own thoughts, each berating himself for his side of the silly argument. Each wondering what to do or say next. Once inside, Drew's face had been closed and shuttered against Miles's questioning gaze as he poked and prodded at the blond man's injuries, and Miles felt invisible and almost intimidated by the silent, dark and bearded man.

Drew was relieved that Miles appeared to just have some bruising and small cuts. He was pretty sure one of his ribs was cracked as well. It would be painful, yes, but nothing as serious as it could have been. He could have broken a limb or worse. Drew made sure to check Miles's heart rate and listen to the sound of it beating, finding the experience oddly intimate instead of clinical. It was a bit fast but that was easily explainable. Harder to explain was the increase in Drew's own heart rate as he touched and examined Miles so closely.

Drew only had to clean up and plaster the various cuts and put a wrap on Miles's ankle. He knew Miles was watching him with those intense green eyes, but he avoided his gaze and focused on the man's injuries. He was embarrassed by his outburst and nervous now that Miles was within closer contact with him.

Drew'd lit the oil lamps when they'd first arrived, but the soft glow didn't help soften their somber moods. After heating some water on the gas stove, one of the advantages of using propane that Drew had never been able to convince Kurt of, Drew found some dry clothes for Miles and silently showed him the small bathroom so he could clean up a bit better.

Drew busied himself in the kitchen, prepping the water for tea and trying not to think about Miles stripping off his wet things in the warm glow of a lamp or the softness of Miles's skin under his fingers. His broken fingers that Miles had commented on. Drew winced. He could have handled that better. Hell, he could have handled everything better. But at least Miles was here and safe and maybe Drew could get over his nervousness.

When Miles finally shuffled stiffly out of the bathroom, Drew had poured the tea and had the mugs sitting on the table in the living room. He gestured for Miles to sit on the couch and picked up his own mug. The two men sat quietly, Miles on the couch and Drew sitting in a rocking chair, watching as the lightning show continued outside.

Warm and comfortable now despite his injuries, Miles was able to appreciate the severity of the storm and he remembered Drew saying he'd been looking for him.

"I … uh, wanted to thank you." Miles's voice was almost as rough sounding as Drew's as he broke the silence between them. "I don't know what I would have done if you hadn't gotten me out from under that mess."

Drew coughed and looked down at his tea, not seeing the hot liquid that was helping to soothe the irritation of his throat, only his fingers, some of them splayed out and unable to fully bend as he held the mug gingerly in his palms.

"Want to apologize too," Miles continued doggedly when the other man didn't respond. "I didn't mean to make you uncomfortable there in the truck, you know … about your hands."

"No, it's fine," Drew said, meeting Miles's eyes for the first since the argument in the truck. "I'm sorry as well, for … yelling. I was worried, Kurt would've killed me if anything happened to you."

"Yeah, well," Miles shrugged. "He's a worrier, he is."

Drew smiled quietly at Miles's words and then looked back down at his hands.

"Do they hurt?" Miles asked tentatively, not wanting to upset or offend the other man.

"What?" Drew looked up again and for the first time Miles caught a glimpse of the scar on his neck, just visible under the beard line. "Not really. Not so much anymore."

"Can they … fix 'em?"

Drew sighed, better to get this all out in the open. "The doctors in Chicago, they want to try re-breaking them again. Want to see if they can clean up some of the damage to the ligaments and the like."

"Again?" Miles questioned, looking at the scarred hands and imagining the pain Drew must have endured.

"Twice already." Drew spoke to the storm outside rather than to Miles. It was easier. "There's been some improvement each time, but I've adapted. I have a career of sorts, there's only a few things I can't seem to do." He looked up at Miles, his eyes dark and liquid as he confessed. "I'm afraid.... What happens if I go through all of that again and I'm worse off than I am now?"

Miles held his breath for moment. "That's right, you're a potter, Brenda told me. Did you make these?" He gestured to the mugs in their hands, more to cover his emotional reaction to Drew's words than to change the subject.

"Yeah."

"They're nice. Man-sized too, I'm not afraid I'm gonna break one."

Drew laughed, even though the action hurt his already strained throat. "Don't worry, I've broken several."

"Your thumbs still work then?"

"What?" Drew asked again, baffled by the question.

'You know, opposable thumbs? It's what separates us from the lower orders and all that. Where would a bloke be without opposable thumbs?"

Unable to think of anything but one use for opposable thumbs, Drew laughed a deep belly laugh that hadn't escaped him in ages. "Get some rest, Miles."

"Easier said than done, with that racket still going on out there."

They sat there in silence again, lost in their thoughts. But this time the silence was restful and Miles felt his eyes closing. Drew stood up and reached over, taking the empty mug off Miles's lap.

"Let's get you to bed, then."

I wish! "Just throw me a blanket," Miles murmured. "I'm fine here."

"You'll be more comfortable on the bed. I'll take the couch." Drew leaned down and put his arm around Miles's shoulders, effortlessly helping him raise up.

"I can't kick you out of your bed." Miles relaxed back against Drew's supporting arm and kept his eyes closed, trying not to think about how good it felt.

"I'll just wake you up if you stay out here." Drew smiled at the boneless way Miles lay against him. "I'm up and down a lot in the night."

"That's right." Miles sleepily let Drew stand him up and lead him into the other room. "I always see your light shining into the night when I'm looking for you."

Drew put Miles in his bed, trying not to appreciate how right the man looked there, and pulled the covers up around his shoulders as Miles settled down into his pillow. *Miles watched for him?*

CHAPTER ELEVEN

AFTER making sure Miles was resting, Drew moved tiredly through the cabin, putting out most of the oil lamps he'd lit and straightening up the clutter they'd left behind. He put their mugs in the sink and picked up his medical bag, carrying it into the bathroom where he stopped for a moment, stunned.

Drew could only laugh at the state of the bathroom. Apparently neatness wasn't high on Miles's list when the man was knackered. He would have thought Kurt'd been there the way clothes and towels were strewn over the small area.

From the look of the floor Miles had managed to spill more of his wash water there than down the sink, and Drew wiped it up before he hung Miles's wet clothes over the tub and then picked up the damp towels. He took one of the towels, shrugged and used it to roughly dry his own hair.

He wasn't sure what condition the cushion on the rocker where he'd sat would be in, probably unsalvageable, but it didn't matter. He'd known Miles had been in shock, the fact the other man had never even noticed or commented on Drew's bedraggled and dripping condition spoke volumes. Recognizing it, Drew hadn't wanted to leave Miles alone, even for the short time it would have taken him to get dry.

Drew felt as stiff as Miles had looked earlier, and he knew it was the cold and exertion settling in. He heated more water and then stood shivering in the small bathroom as he attempted to peel off his wet clothing. It took him some time; his fingers were cramped and didn't want to function.

But finally he was able to hang the soaked and dripping garments over the rod of the shower curtain where he'd hung Miles's. It gave him a strange feeling to see his pants next to Miles's; he hadn't realized how alone he'd been until he saw that small bit of hominess.

The water felt soothing to his various aches and he held the washcloth over his face for a moment, letting the heat seep in and relax him even further. Finally, he felt ready to take a look at the physical damage he'd incurred.

Both of them had been lucky. So very lucky, Drew thought as, ignoring the ones he couldn't reach, he covered the worst of his cuts with antibiotic cream before pulling on some sweatpants. He didn't bother with a shirt; he knew he wasn't going to get any sleep anyway and might as well do some more work on his latest consignment. He peeked in on Miles again, pleased to see him deeply asleep, and then carried the oil lamp back into his studio.

Drew's thoughts were still whirling with the events of the day, and he let his mind wander where it would as his fingers sought solace and relief from their painful cramping by digging into the stiff clay. The material warmed and softened as he worked. It never failed to soothe him, both mentally and physically, as the clay gradually became more pliable and malleable to his touch.

He was surprised at how peaceful he felt. The storm was still raging outside, but Drew didn't feel his usual anxiety at having someone in his space and that was a welcome relief. Miles had been rather matter of fact about his damaged hands and that made it easier for Drew to relax around him.

Drew's idle musings were interrupted; it was a feeling more than an actual noise that caught his attention. He looked at the clay in front of him, amazed at how much time must have passed. Wiping his hands, he walked back into the living room searching for what had disturbed him, but everything looked fine.

He pushed the bedroom door slightly open and found the cause for his sudden unease. Miles was tossing and turning on the bed, undoubtedly reliving the tumultuous events of the night.

Not wanting to wake Miles but fearful the restless man could easily hurt himself, Drew sat on the edge of the bed and hesitantly pushed the tousled hair off Miles's face. His skin was warm to the touch, but not enough to worry. Drew gently stroked one finger down the chiseled line of cheek and jaw, savoring the contrasting textures of smooth skin and rough bristle.

Miles seemed to settle a bit under the caress of his hand and Drew continued to delicately map the surface beneath his fingers. He traced the curve of Miles's lips and then down under one ear, smiling as Miles exhaled and turned his head in his sleep, exposing more of his soft skin to Drew's exploring fingers.

The world around Drew seemed to shrink, closing in until there were only the two of them, warm and cocooned in this small circle of dark sensation. He learned the curve of Miles's neck, felt the blood pulsing under the skin, the heartbeat strong and decisive.

Desire.

Drew could taste it, and his mouth grew dry. It had been so long since he'd enjoyed the simple and sensual feel of another's skin.

Suddenly Drew wanted more, he wanted to let his hands drift down to Miles's chest, tease at the small buds he knew he would find there and then explore even lower still.... With a curse, Drew stood, embarrassed to find himself pawing Miles as the man slept.

Drew left the bedroom, full of agitation and unrest, and paced around the living room until he felt like he was choking. With a growl, he threw open the front door and stood there sucking in great gulps of air. The storm had settled down to a constant rain and there was only a far off rumble of thunder and the downed limbs around Drew's cabin as a reminder of its prior fury.

It wasn't his usual need to escape his memories that pushed Drew outside into the night. It was fear, fear and desire for the man even now sleeping in his bed. He had worked hard to make his life placid and uneventful after everything that had happened, and now Miles was forcing Drew to remember what it was like to feel.

Drew stood under the falling rain, his face upturned to the darkness of the night sky. He was confused about what to do next. He had let his fantasies about Miles continue because he had thought they were a diversion, an outlet with no chance of actual fulfillment. Now he seemed to have traded the security of unrequited want with the desperate uncertainty of reality.

MILES limped slowly back into the bedroom and lay down gingerly. He wanted nothing more than to go to the man standing outside like some primal warrior challenging the elements, but there was so much holding him back, including his own doubts.

He had awoken to feel callused fingers lightly stroking across his skin and it had taken everything he had not to reach out and touch Drew in return. Miles had continued to feign sleep, not wanting the man to stop, just wanting the moment to go on.

He'd just been playing around to pass the time, he'd told himself, nothing serious. But the imposing reality of Drew in the flesh was more intriguing than he ever would have thought. Miles shivered even though he was under the covers.

Miles could still feel the lines Drew had traced on his flesh, burning him with a fire he hadn't felt in years. Why had Drew done that? There had been such yearning in his touch. Such sadness. How was it the man could communicate so much with a simple touch?

In the end, it was only Miles's utter exhaustion that finally brought his mind to a halt and let sleep claim him once again.

CHAPTER TWELVE

THE next weeks seemed to fly by as Miles continued to stay with Drew. Arrangements had been made for the repairs to start on Kurt's cabin, but it would be a slow process as the rest of the county had been hit just as hard, and the local workman had jobs scheduled for weeks. Unlike many other families whose homes were destroyed by the high winds and collateral damage, Miles had a place to stay and he found he was in no hurry to go back to living on his own.

Kurt was overseas on a lecture circuit and Drew had been unable to do more than leave a few messages, letting him know Miles was staying with him and everything was fine. There was a chance the messages would catch up to him at some point. Until then, there wasn't anything else they could do.

Miles was surprised at the relief he felt at not having to deal with Kurt right now. He knew the other man would swoop in and attempt to arrange things and things were, in Miles's considered opinion, just fine.

He was now a part of Drew's daily routine rather than an observer, able to look up at any moment and see the dark haired man whenever he pleased. After a few awkward moments initially, things were going nicely and he didn't want any disruptions, especially a Kurt-sized one.

Miles used his prior observations of Drew's routine to fit himself seamlessly into the quiet man's life, taking on small and varied tasks around the cabin as his ribs and ankle healed, and they had settled into a surprisingly companionable co-existence that extended benefits to both of them.

There was now a telephone available to Miles, cable and Internet as well, but he found his interest in the world outside the cabin had disappeared. Gone was the restless agitation that had plagued him and he relished the opportunities their new closeness afforded. He greedily tucked each quiet moment between them into his memories as he learned more and more about the man he had watched for so long.

Drew wasn't much of a conversationalist, that was definitely true; he and Miles had developed a form of abusive verbal shorthand that Brenda and the other locals found amusing to listen to. But Drew made up for it by expressing his silent concern for Miles in a variety of small ways, including leaving a steaming cup of coffee on the nightstand each morning and making sure Miles followed his diet and exercise program closer than he had been doing on his own.

In return, Miles would notice when Drew's voice grew rough, his throat raw and painful; then Miles would set a cup of tea with honey beside his elbow as he worked. Or Miles would leave dinner warming in the oven if Drew returned home late. It was easier for both of the men to make and accept these gestures without acknowledging them.

All in all, Miles only had two complaints. The first was that Drew hadn't sunbathed since Miles had moved into his cabin. Much to Miles's chagrin, he hadn't even managed to see Drew up close with his shirt off period, and he missed the large expanse of honey-colored flesh he'd admired for so long. The second complaint Miles had was that the other man worked far too hard. He didn't know what he expected but it wasn't the constant activity that surrounded Drew.

Even though Drew no longer did field work, he was still very active in the charitable organization that had cost him so much, mainly on the administrative end. Miles was amazed at the correspondence and amount of paperwork involved in the fundraising process, and was fascinated when Drew let him take

over some of the computer work that the other man found
frustrating.

There was also an open door at the cabin for those who
sought Drew's medical skills, not just on the weekends as Miles
had thought. It was amazing the variety of human ailments that
found their way to be either looked at or referred off to the doctor
in town.

At first, curiosity and a desire to near Drew had kept him
watching, but as the weeks passed, Drew let Miles wrap limbs and
assist him with some of the patients that needed finer hand
coordination than Drew could achieve. Miles wondered how he'd
managed on his own before.

The man hardly slept, Miles fretted to himself as he
continued to add to what he was now calling his "Great Book of
Drew". He worked all hours of the night in his studio, the gentle
hum of the wheel a soothing background noise for Miles if he
awoke. If he wasn't working, he could be found outside, pacing in
the night.

Miles would get out of bed and sit by the window, hidden
in the shadows, watching as the darkness seemed to soothe Drew
and the pacing slowed and then finally stopped and Drew would
come back inside.

Miles would return to his bed then and feign sleep.
Because always, after Drew paced his fill in the dark night, he
would return to the cabin and silently enter Miles's room. Miles
would hold his breath with anticipation until the gentle touches
came, stroking gently down his face and neck, soothing Miles with
their softness even as they tortured him with the desire to
reciprocate.

With a soft sigh, Drew would leave and Miles would flop
over on to his back to stare up at the ceiling and wonder when he'd
become such a coward, fearful of disturbing the delicate balance
they had achieved.

Wanting, always the wanting.

But now it was different, stronger and gentler all at the
same time. Drew was no longer a beautiful object to admire from

afar; he was a man of depth and feeling who left Miles feeling better just for having spent this time with him.

THE morning sun streamed through the window, illuminating the tendrils of steam that rose from the cup of coffee on the nightstand beside Miles's head. Miles groaned and wiped his hand down his face. It had been a long night, full of thoughts and wonderings and wishes; he hadn't even noticed when Drew had brought in the coffee.

His mouth felt like something had died in it, and Miles swallowed some coffee before throwing back the covers and wandering out to the kitchen in his shorts, surprised to find Drew dressed in jeans and a long sleeve shirt on such a hot and humid day.

"What's this then?" he asked. Drew hadn't slept last night and Miles had hoped to get him to rest in the garden as he'd done before, letting the other man doze while Miles puttered around with deliberate, lulling slowness.

Drew continued to put items in the backpacks he used to hold his medical supplies. He'd planned to be gone before Miles was up and was dreading the grilling he knew would follow, even as he smiled with the simple pleasure of seeing Miles with his morning hair askew, slouching and half-naked in his kitchen.

"I'll probably be back late. Did you say you were going to work in the garden today?" Drew tried evasion, even though that never seemed to work with Miles. His voice was still low, but it didn't hurt so much to talk now. Having Miles around had forced him to speak more than he might have and it had helped.

"Where will you be?" Miles prodded with a scowl. He knew what Drew was up to and they both knew it wouldn't work.

Resistance was a waste of his time, Drew thought as he gave in and offered up the truth. Much to his amazement, he'd learned Miles was even more stubborn than he was. "I'm heading off to the back fields at the Winding Creek Farms. I heard some of the migrants there are sick."

Miles didn't bother to ask how Drew knew this. There was an information web among the locals that put the MI-6 to shame.

"I'll come help." Miles put down his coffee and headed back to his room. "Let me get dressed."

"No," Drew said sharply. "I'd rather you stay here."

Miles turned back to face Drew, folding his arms across his chest and narrowing his eyes as he waited to hear more.

Drew sighed in exasperation. Having Miles living with him had turned into a constant battle of wills. At least it did as soon as Miles wasn't getting his way.

"These could be illegals."

Miles just continued to stare at Drew.

"There could be trouble. I'd rather you not be involved."

"But you'll be," Miles pointed out without pity for the slightly flustered man. Someone had to look after him. Besides, Miles grinned wolfishly; it was fun. He knew Drew wasn't used to explaining himself and Miles always enjoyed their small skirmishes.

"That's different." Drew looked down at his backpack and started counting to ten in his head as he tried to ignore the piercing green eyes and the desire to kiss the grin off the handsome face before him.

"I'll be dressed in five minutes." Miles unfolded his arms and walked off with a parting shot. "If you're gone, I'll just get directions from Brenda and follow you."

CHAPTER THIRTEEN

THE two men were silent the first part of the drive as the scenery changed from rolling coastline and heavy woods to open, flat fields. Miles finished his coffee, smirking slightly at his victory in the small skirmish. Drew was amused as well, enjoying Miles's not so hidden delight. It was a silly game, this battling between them over the littlest things, but a fun one.

Drew didn't know which he enjoyed more, coming out the victor and watching Miles sulk (an act he denied vehemently when Drew called him on it) or giving in and basking in the glow of satisfaction that Miles would radiate for hours afterward.

As he looked over at the handsome blond beside him, Drew couldn't believe how easily the other man fit into his life. It was almost scary. Drew was sure a personality as obstinate and abrasive as Miles could be would have left him crawling the walls and looking for a way out, but that wasn't the case at all. For the first time in ages, Drew felt … comfortable. There was someone there for him to look after, and someone there looking out for him.

Harder to deal with were the nights. So many times Drew told himself he wasn't going to enter Miles's room; he wasn't going to risk touching the other man as he slept or sit and watch him just breathe. But he couldn't seem to help himself. Miles was a drug. The more Drew interacted with him, the more he wanted.

"What's that in the fields?" Miles interrupted Drew's thoughts.

"Asparagus."

"Really?" Miles craned his neck to better look out the truck window at the waist high, feathery growth in the field beside them. "Looks rather bare and spindly."

"Hard to see it from the road," Drew smiled. "We'll let you pick some fresh from the field and you can make it for dinner tonight."

Miles shuddered. "Not a chance, mate. Triffids."

Drew waited a moment, slanting his hazel eyes in Miles's direction. He was getting used to Miles's conversational tangents. Sometimes he thought Miles did this just to keep him talking.

"Triffids." Drew kept his tone flat and matter-of-fact.

"Yeah, asparagus looks just like Triffids. Not a chance I'll ever eat one." Miles tried not to smile as he looked back out the window and waited for Drew to grab the dangling bait.

"So are you going to tell me just what a Triffid is?" Drew put more exasperation than he was feeling into his voice.

"You've never seen '*Day of the Triffids*'?" Miles asked in dismay. "Classic horror movie. There's a meteor shower, see? Great special effects, shots of the meteors falling over Big Ben and the like. And there's this military fella in a London hospital, he's been wounded and his eyes are bandaged. Well, everyone who watches the meteor shower ends up blind, and when he takes the bandages off he's the only one that can see."

"And this equals asparagus how?"

"The meteors are actually a way for these spores to travel to Earth."

"Spores?" Drew played along a little more.

"Yeah, you know, spores. So they grow into these plant-like creatures. Only they can walk and they make this strange noise, kinda of a constant chatter. Scared the bejeezus out of me as a lad."

"And?"

"They eat people. End of story. Man-eating Triffids terrorize the countryside. So, asparagus looks like Triffids and I've never been able to eat 'em."

Drew tried not to smile as he nodded his understanding. "Wouldn't you be scoring a victory for us Earthlings if you would just eat the Triffid-resembling asparagus instead of waiting for them to kill us?"

It was Miles's turn to slant green eyes in Drew's direction and he sniffed. "See if I protect you when they rise up."

Drew pulled the truck off the road, laughing as Miles's coffee cup went flying out of his hands when the vehicle jounced its way through the deep ruts before stopping beside a large field and ignoring Miles's offended glare.

Drew got out of the truck, stretched and then pulled out the packs and a long sleeved cotton shirt which he tossed at Miles, who looked at it in confusion as he was already hot enough without it.

"What's this for?"

"Protection," Drew replied.

"Doesn't look like a rubber to me." Miles couldn't help his playful retort. "You know, sentences of less than three words could be perceived as a lack of intelligence."

"Fine," Drew growled, distracted by the heat in his groin at Miles's teasing words. "It's for your protection, to keep the pesticides off your skin."

Miles beamed at him. "See, I knew you could do it." The sarcasm that laced his voice was evident and Drew shook his fist at him, while Miles just stuck out his tongue, undeterred by the implied threat.

The blond pulled the shirt over his tee and shielded his eyes with one hand as he looked around. It was a huge and flat area with nothing but green stalks as far as he could see and a few portable toilets.

There were three or four tractor-type vehicles with strange covered extensions to each side that almost looked like the wings of an old bi-plane. Seated on the extensions were two or three people on each side, legs out in front of them and a small knife in their hands.

Miles watched as they tractor trundled its way through the long rows and the workers sliced and tossed the freshly cut stalks into the bins beside them.

"Not a faster way to do that?"

Drew shook his head. "It takes a trained eye to know what to harvest and what to leave for next time. Did you know that under the right conditions an asparagus plant can grow ten inches in 24 hours?"

"Like I told you, Triffids."

Miles walked behind Drew through the field, watching as he greeted the Field Supervisor and they agreed upon an area for Drew to setup his impromptu clinic. There was a steady stream of workers, always careful to make sure there weren't too many off the field at one time. He found it amazing to watch Drew at work, the large hands moving with competence despite their damage.

Drew hardly spoke, just smiled and nodded and looked where dusty fingers pointed and pantomimed their ills. Miles had aided him enough by now to know what was needed and the two men worked as one efficient machine.

"Lots of rashes," Miles observed, swabbing as Drew lanced a painful looking boil from the back of a man's arm.

"That's why I gave you the shirt. It's mainly a reaction to the pesticides. Rashes and respiratory problems."

"You're kidding, right?"

"I wish I were," Drew shook his head. "The farms have come a long way in their attempts to improve pest management and reduce the fungicide applications, but the risks are still high. There's a local Uni that's working on using spore traps to reduce the need for the pesticide spray programs but it's going to take a while."

"Spores." Miles nodded as if he'd known it all along.

Drew laughed as the other man intended him to. "Well, if it will keep down the risk of birth defects and lung disease, I'm all for your Triffids."

"Where do these workers come from?" Miles asked.

"The majority are registered migrants. They travel all through the US, from Mexico to the Upper Peninsular and then back again in a season. Some of these families have worked these farms for decades picking apples, cherries, asparagus, squash and the other local produce. The County provides housing and schools for the children. It has one of the best migrant service programs around, including health care."

"So why are you here?" Miles looked up from where he was cleaning a scrape on a little girl's leg; she couldn't have been more than twelve and Miles passed his hand through her dark curls to soothe her.

"Some still don't trust the service organizations," Drew shrugged. "And some are illegals."

"Do the farmers know that?" Miles wondered as he looked at the line of people before them.

Drew looked up, his eyes dark with knowledge. "It's kind of a 'don't ask, don't tell' policy."

The two men worked until Drew's bags of medicine and supplies were empty. Miles peeled off his last pair of latex gloves and put his hands on his lower back, groaning as he stretched.

"I told you it would probably be late."

"You did at that." Miles looked around in gathering twilight with satisfaction. They had accomplished something today and it left him feeling better than making money ever had.

"You do good, here." He touched Drew's arm softly, proud of this complex man and the things Drew had shown him.

Drew looked up in surprise at the unexpected touch, feeling the heat where Miles's hand rested on his sleeve.

"I just wanted to thank you, for letting me be a part of it."

Before Drew could react, Miles cleared his throat and turned away, picking up the bags and walking towards the truck.

"C'mon then," he called over his shoulder. "Hurry up or I'll let the Triffids get ya."

CHAPTER FOURTEEN

HOT.

Miles was hot. Not only was he hot, but he was restless and couldn't manage to fall asleep to save his life. The air was heavy and sticky and….

Who was he trying to kid?

Rolling over to stare at the ceiling, fighting the sheet that was clinging to his sweaty skin, Miles wondered why he was so determined to lie to himself. Over the last several weeks, things had changed for him in a fundamental manner. And he hated change.

Hell, if he was going to be honest, things had been in flux since even before the heart attack.

And what a catalyst for change that had been, he thought with a hint of gallows humor.

The result of this long and unexpected period of touchy-feel self-exploration, as Miles liked to think of it, had been the realization that there was something *more* out there, and he was damn tired of being too afraid to reach out and grab it.

Granted, that was the purpose behind this whole "come stay at the cabin" thing, but Miles hadn't actually expected anything to really come of it. He'd just thought he spend a few months in the sun, relax and get Kurt off his back.

The events of today, the satisfaction that he'd felt working so closely with Drew, only seemed to reinforce the conclusions he'd come up with. Now what to do about it? Miles listened for the familiar hum of the wheel from the back studio, audible over the classical guitar softly playing, indication that Drew wasn't sleeping either.

Could he take the chance?

Miles pushed the sticky sheets away and grimaced as he slid off the bed. He was still a little stiff from the roof collapsing on him and working all day at the impromptu clinic hadn't helped matters, but he couldn't deny he'd been a lucky man. That was part of his realization. He'd survived a heart attack and a bloody cave-in, what was he so afraid of?

Rejection.

The word seemed to hang in the air heavier than the humidity. It conjured up past relationships, past heartache. Past failures. God knows he'd never exactly been involved in what he would call a sure thing, but when he thought about it, did such an animal really exist? Life was a gamble and at least in the last several throws he'd done all right. Maybe it was time to take another?

He didn't know where to start on any of it, there was still so much he didn't know. Miles just knew he had to try. Shuffling his feet on the cool wood, Miles walked towards the back studio, drawn by the soft light, hesitant but hopeful. Things had come a long way between him and Drew and he really would like to see things go even farther. He stood outside the door and looked into the studio.

Drew was sitting at the stand, one leg rhythmically pumping as the wheel spun. His hands were agile despite their limitations, finding and coaxing his vision inside the clay to show itself. Dark hair gleamed as it waved down his back and Miles could only imagine how it would feel under his hands.

But it was the rest of Drew that made Miles draw his breath in loudly with awe and sudden sheer physical hunger. Drew had his shirt off. There he was, close enough for Miles to reach out and touch. Honey-gold skin flowing over the flexing muscles of back and shoulder. Miles shifted uncomfortably, moving the seam of his shorts to the side as it pulled from the sudden force exerted upon it.

Bloody Fucking Hell.

He didn't know if his exclamation was a plea for help or a paean of thanks.

It didn't matter because Drew heard Miles's indrawn breath and misunderstanding the reason the behind it he flinched, freezing for a moment. Panic was evident in the haste as he reached for the plaid shirt he'd tossed aside in the heat and pulled it back over his shoulders, hiding his back from Miles.

Miles made a guttural noise of protest, the sound coming from deep in his throat, deep from his soul.

"Just don't say anything, Miles," Drew whispered. His worst fears were coming true. Miles had seen his back, and Drew had heard his reaction.

Miles just stood there, stunned. Rejected before he even had a chance to say anything? Before he even took the risk and reached out? *No fucking way!*

With a growl, Miles entered the room, sudden confidence fueled by endless nights of desire, striding forward as Drew stood. Miles stopped mere inches away from the taller man, his body vibrating with denied want as Drew just looked at him with pain-darkened eyes.

"What do you mean, don't say anything?" Miles burst out angrily to Drew's amazement. "There's a lot of bloody things I'd like to say to you."

"I'm sorry, Miles," Drew began in that low husky voice that always went straight to Miles's gut. "I never wanted you to see the…."

Drew's words were cut off as strong fingers grabbed his arms and jerked his body forward with sharp impact and Miles's tongue forced its way into his mouth. It was brutal and biting, a savage, frustrated invasion of lips and tongue and Drew couldn't get enough of it.

One of Miles's hands gripped the nape of Drew's neck, trapping the hair and refusing to allow Drew to pull away. The other moved upwards to caress Drew's neck as the intensity of the kiss softened and slowed and Miles released his grip, pulling Drew's forehead down to rest against his.

"*Christ,*" Miles groaned again as he tried to catch his breath. "You're going to be the death of me yet."

Drew was speechless, his hand coming up to touch his bruised lips in wonder. He thought he'd prepared himself for every reaction he could dream of from Miles. But not this, never this.

"I don't know which is going to blow up first," Miles growled possessively as he watched Drew's hand move over his lips. "My heart or my cock."

"What?" Drew gasped as Miles's eyes narrowed with lustful purpose.

"You're a cardiologist, right?" Miles murmured as he leaned in and began to nuzzle Drew under his right ear. Miles's teeth caught and worried at the warm skin, licking and tasting the line of scar tissue and causing pinpricks of gooseflesh to rise on Drew's arms.

"You'll know what to do when you give me another heart attack."

Miles shoved the shirt partially off Drew's shoulders, trapping the bigger man's arms and pinning them behind his back before bringing his teeth to clamp tightly down on the sharp jut of collarbone before him, causing the dark-haired man to gasp and shudder in response.

Drew was adrift in a world of sensation. It had been so long, and Miles felt so very good. Miles rubbed against Drew's thigh, grunting as he continued to lick his away across Drew's broad expanse of chest. Every nerve in Drew's body was tuned to Miles and he felt overwhelmed by Miles's physical presence.

He felt dazed as he let Miles push him back against the wall, grinding against him in obvious desire. Drew wanted to reach out to Miles and reciprocate, but could only close his eyes and let Miles's sudden fury spend itself on his willing body. He would take this; he would make it a memory to warm him on all the cold and lonely nights ahead.

Hands opened his jeans, reaching in and possessing the hard length within. It was Drew's turn to moan as his hips hitched helplessly against Miles's knowing grasp, legs instinctively splaying open as he sought deeper contact.

Hot. Miles was on fire where his skin melded against Drew's bare chest. His heart was pounding, pulse beating, vision blinded by the sweat that dripped from his forehead. *Good Christ, this **was** going to kill him.*

He tightened his grip on the molten steel in his hand and listened to Drew's breathy moans. It didn't matter that the lights were on or that the music had stopped. The two men were trapped in a world where nothing existed except the feel of the other.

"*God,*" Miles muttered as he shoved his shorts down and grabbed his own cock, thrusting it into his hand alongside Drew's, feeling the slick, the stroke and glide as he mindlessly drove them both to satisfaction.

He plundered Drew's mouth once again as they panted in unison and Miles teetered on the knife-edge of release. He was afraid to let go, it had been so long, but he was more afraid to stop. In the end, it was Drew's broken and helpless moans, the gushing heat in his hand that sent Miles plunging headlong into delirium.

Miles buried his face in Drew's shoulder, shaking with the intensity of his release, inhaling the scent of sweat and savoring the salty taste, unwilling to move, but knowing he had to. He finally pushed himself away, ashamed to realize the other man's arms were still trapped in his shirt.

"Are you all right?" Miles asked as he freed Drew, removing the shirt and using it to wipe them both off before he hoisted the other's man's jeans back up; concerned at Drew's unexpected docility. "Did I hurt you?"

"You expect me to be able to talk after that?" Drew continued to lean against the wall, his eyes closed, his brain still too short-circuited by Miles's flare of passion to make any sense of what just happened.

Miles was exhausted and exhilarated at the same time. His legs were trembling and he was lightheaded. *Christ,* he thought. *I lived. All that bloody time I could have spent wanking.* He was unwilling to lose his new connection with Drew and he pulled the unresisting man into the other room, pushing him down on the bed.

"Are you sure you're okay?" Miles asked again, running a gentle hand down Drew's back, unable to keep from placing a soft kiss on the scarred shoulder blade before him. Drew made an inarticulate sound, struggling to find his voice.

"They don't bother you?" he whispered, almost too afraid to hope.

Miles blinded in surprise. "What?" he responded blankly before he realized what Drew was asking. "Oh, your scars, you mean? We all have scars, Drew." Miles picked up Drew's hand and ran the fingers down the line that zippered his own chest.

"Some inside, some outside. Some of them are of our own making. Yours should be worn with pride."

Drew heard the words but it was the tone, the complete and utter surprise in Miles's voice that brought the prickle of tears to his eyes.

Miles pressed another kiss to Drew's back and snuggled closer, letting his fingers trace over the raised flesh of Drew's back as he whispered into Drew's ear.

"When I was a wee lad, my Mam despaired of me. All the other kids slept with a plushie. But I would only be able to settle if I held my footie. There was something about the pattern, the seams that soothed me. When I held it in my arms, everything would all make sense then."

Drew's emotions surged again, he was unsure if it was the gentle touches or the surprisingly poetic words. "You're saying I resemble a football, then?" Somehow he managed to keep his voice light and teasing.

Miles smiled with pleasure and pressed another kiss against Drew's back. There was so much for them to talk about ... later.

"I'm saying you bloody well near killed me and I need to sleep. So lie here with me and let me take comfort from you."

Drew exhaled, feeling truly at peace for the first time in years as he let himself settle back against Miles. As his breathing slowed, he wondered if Miles knew that instead of taking comfort, the other man was giving it.

CHAPTER FIFTEEN

DREW stirred, feeling the warmth of Miles's body where it was tucked up behind him. He felt both restless and at peace all at the same time, full but somehow empty. He moved Miles's arm carefully off his waist, not wanting to wake the sleeping man, and edged his way off the bed, smiling down at the sight of Miles's face buried in the pillow and the blond hair awry. Drew resisted the urge to touch and walked stiffly into the living room.

It was early yet, the morning light just starting to creep across the lake and into his windows, and he enjoyed the feel of the cool breeze on his skin after last night's stifling heat. Drew stretched and twisted, working the stiffness out of his body.

Last night.

More than Drew had imagined. More than he had dreamed of. Always before when someone had gotten too close to him physically, he would panic. Against his will, painful memories would flood his mind and body and he would react … badly. He'd stopped putting himself in that position after a while. It was part of why he'd withdrawn from the world.

There had been a few moments last night when, blinded by the intensity of Miles's overwhelming need, Drew'd been afraid the same thing would happen again. But the now familiar feel and smell of everything that was so utterly Miles had soothed him, and the unsated desire had its chance to push the memories away.

It wasn't going to be that easy, not by a long shot, Drew knew that. But it was a start. And it was more than he'd been able to hope for in a very long time.

Drew heard the pad of footsteps behind him and smiled as strong arms curved around his back to rest against his waist, the lean fingers pressing into his hips and pulling him back against the warm body behind him.

Stubble grazed the back of his neck, raising goosebumps, and Drew shivered once again as he realized that even in the brightening light of day he didn't want to hide his scars from this man any longer.

"Good morning." Miles's voice was rough and deep. "You okay?"

"Good morning," Drew replied as he turned to face Miles, raising one hand and, ignoring his stiff fingers, caressing the cheek that had moments before pressed against his shoulder.

"I'm fine. How are you?"

"Top of the world." Miles turned his head, pressing his lips to the palm that touched him so tenderly. "Will we ... can I...." He broke off nervously; he'd been afraid he'd hurt Drew or scared him off when he'd woken up alone and he wasn't sure how to proceed, even though Drew's response was giving him hope.

"Hmmm?" Drew's eyes closed and he swayed slightly in Miles's arms.

"Are we okay? Is this okay?"

The dark eyes opened and Miles held his breath as they stared into his searchingly.

"What do you want here, Miles?"

Green eyes dropped for a moment before raising again, letting himself be seen naked and honest for the first time in ages. "We've started something, yeah? I'd like a chance to see where it goes."

Drew nodded, smiling as the words echoed his thoughts. "It's a beginning." His smile faltered. "I don't know what I can...."

Miles tightened his arms around the large man, feeling both the strength and vulnerability that called to him in so many ways. "We'll figure it out, we'll figure it out together."

Drew let his head drop onto Miles's shoulder, feeling truly free for the first time in years before he groaned. "God, I'm never going to hear the end of this from Kurt."

The joke in Chrissy Munder's family is that she was born with a book in her hand. Even now, you'll never find her without a book or seven scattered about. Forced to become a practicing realist in an effort to combat her tendency to dream, her many years of travel and a diverse assortment of careers have taken her across most of the U.S. and shown her that there are two things you can never have enough of: love and laughter.

http://chrissymunder.livejournal.com/

EVAN'S
HEAVEN

Nicki Bennett

I was in paradise, and I would have given everything I had to be able to leave and just go home.

I hadn't even wanted to take this part, but Evan had convinced me it could be fun. "You've never done a comedy before, and after the sociopath you played in that last movie, this will be a good change of pace," he'd reasoned. "Besides, it'll let you work on your tan – you're too pale, Mac."

So I found myself on location in a tropical paradise, with a suitcase full of sun tan lotions and skin care products provided by my spa-owner lover. The movie, a light-hearted heist caper set in a Caribbean resort, <u>had</u> been fun at first, and I certainly couldn't complain about the accommodations – until the monsoon season started early. Russ – the director – only needed a few more clear days to wrap up filming, and insisted on waiting out the storms. He wouldn't let any of the leads fly back to the States, in case the sun came out while one of us was gone.

I normally wouldn't have minded staying past the projected wrap date, but today was the first anniversary of the day Evan and I had met. I'd planned something very special to celebrate, and here I was stuck over thirty-five hundred miles away from him.

Alone.

In the fucking rain.

I was sitting under the covered patio of my cabana, nursing a Corona and watching more storm clouds gather over the ocean, when a knock sounded at the door. A rather soggy-looking bellman stood outside, holding an umbrella precariously over a large package. I tipped him and took it from him gingerly, carrying it back to the patio and setting it on the table next to my beer. It had to be from Evan, and knowing my lover, there was no telling what might be inside.

Tearing open the paper eagerly, I was a little disappointed to see what looked like a standard spa gift basket. Did our anniversary mean so little to him that he'd just picked something up off the shelf to send me? There was a note taped to the top, and I sank back into the wicker chair to decipher Evan's handwriting.

Dear Mac,

I'm so very sorry we can't be together for our first anniversary. So I've sent you a few of our favorite things to bring you happy memories until you're back where you belong – with me.

I love you,

Evan

Looking at the basket more closely, I saw that instead of tissue, the contents were wrapped in a dark blue silk robe. Ashamed of my earlier doubts, I blinked away the sudden moisture that blurred my eyes. I could blame it on the rain, and frustration, and bad temper, but the truth was I just plain missed Evan. Untying the bow fashioned from the robe's belt, I let the material fall away and laughed out loud when I saw the first item nestled inside.

A bottle of blue nail polish.

FOOTWORK

I expected to feel out of place the minute I stepped into the salon, and I wasn't disappointed. The obviously high-maintenance female behind the counter looked at me like I was something particularly nasty that had just crawled out from under her refrigerator.

"Can I help you?" she drawled, obviously wanting nothing more than to help me right out the door. I'd be there before it could hit me in the ass, too, if I didn't have to be here.

"I have an appointment," I told her, probably not sounding any more pleased about it than she did. "Name's MacAlester Kerr."

I still thought it was a stupid idea, but Mark had insisted. He wanted some barefoot shots for the picnic scene, which was more than fine with me. But he wanted my feet to look more "polished" than their current natural state. I didn't see why the makeup people on set couldn't do whatever was needed. But when your director tells you he's booked you an appointment for a pedicure, there's not much you can do but go along. Even if it means spending the afternoon pissing off the help at a place called *"Evan's Heaven Salon and Day Spa"*.

The receptionist frowned (creating some wrinkles she'd probably be horrified by if she only knew) and began clicking away at her keyboard. I took the opportunity to look around in amusement. The salon obviously catered to a top-tier clientele.

Fine marble, expensive woods, and silky fabrics created an elegant atmosphere. Soft "lite" jazz (the kind that always set my teeth on edge) played quietly in the background. The customers waiting in the plushly upholstered lounge, sipping flutes of wine or imported sparkling water, were all highly made-up, expensively dressed women. I couldn't blame the receptionist too much for her attitude – my flannel shirt and jeans were glaringly out of place amid all this sybaritism. Hell, I was probably the only male in the place.

Or … not. The young man who stepped through the cut-glass doors from the salon's inner sanctum was definitely at home in the spa's refined aura. In his pink silk shirt and charcoal pinstriped slacks, he could have stepped straight from a photo shoot for GQ. He was tall and slender, with an angel's face and a barely-restrained mop of dark ebony curls that obviously benefited from plenty of the salon's "product". The receptionist was ridiculously happy to see him, leaning toward him to whisper urgently with just enough twitches of her head toward me to make it clear who she was talking about.

The young Adonis turned his attention to me with a dazzling smile. "Mr. Kerr? Would you follow me, please?" Since he was heading into the salon and not out to the street, I nodded and trailed behind him, silently enjoying the view of his trim hips swinging perkily in front of me.

He led me into a private room that was, if possible, even more luxurious than the reception area. Closing the door behind us, he offered me his hand. "Welcome, Mr. Kerr. I'm Evan York."

"As in 'Evan's Heaven'?" I asked. "I must have really scared your receptionist if she had to call the owner on me."

Evan chuckled. "I just bought the spa a few weeks ago, and we don't have much male clientele yet. She'll get used to it."

I realized Evan was still holding out his hand to me, and offered my own in return. Something quivered in my stomach at the feel of his soft fingers sliding over my callused palm.

"A pedicure, eh? Sure I can't talk you into a manicure too, Mr. Kerr?" he asked, turning my hand over and running his fingers lightly over my knuckles.

The quivering turned into full-fledged tremors. My cock decided to stand up for a closer look at what was going on. *Down, boy,* I told myself. *This is his job; just because he's the most stunning thing you've seen in a month of Sundays doesn't mean he's coming on to you. Hell, he works surrounded by beautiful women. Why on earth would you think he's attracted to men?*

"Just a pedicure, thanks," I growled, the tone coming out much harsher than I intended. "And please, call me Mac," I added in a softer tone of voice. He glanced at me curiously at first, then flashed his alluring smile again.

"Fine, let's get started then, Mac," he said, nodding toward something that looked suspiciously like a throne against the opposite wall. I must have looked totally lost, because his smile faded slightly.

"Have you had a pedicure before?" he asked.

"You're my first – I mean, no, this is my first one," I stammered. *Get a grip, Kerr,* I told myself sternly.

The smile was back. "A pedicure virgin? I promise not to do anything you don't like," he teased. Our eyes met and held for a moment. I recognized the look in those rich chocolate depths. Damn! Maybe he *was* coming on to me after all.

Taking pity on my ignorance, Evan gestured toward the chair. "This is the pedicure station," he explained. "We'll start with a foot soak to relax you and soften your skin, followed by moisturizing, trimming, exfoliation, and a massage." He leaned over the chair and turned on a faucet, testing the water temperature as it began filling the basin at the foot of the "throne". I took the opportunity to once again admire the trim ass bent before me.

Once he was satisfied with the water temperature, Evan selected a bottle from a shelf above the chair and poured a capful into the basin. A tangy scent wafted up in the steam rising from the bowl.

"Grapefruit, mint and eucalyptus," he told me. "It's my own blend. I prefer it to the floral scents we offer for the ladies.

"If you'll take off your shoes and have a seat…." Evan hesitated, glancing at my slim-legged jeans with concern. "You'll never be able to roll those up enough to keep them out of the water," he observed. His eyes glittered wickedly. "Perhaps you should just slip them off."

Fuck – he was *definitely* coming on to me. The way my cock was dancing against my zipper, it thought Evan had made an excellent suggestion.

If I'd known I was going to be dropping trou, maybe I would have worn some boxers underneath them.

I could feel my cheeks reddening involuntarily. The look Evan gave me said he knew exactly why I was blushing. Chuckling again, he turned to a closet nearby and, after rummaging inside for a moment, offered me a deep blue silk robe. "Here," he said, "why don't you slip into this? I'll get a few supplies together and be right back." He winked at me over his shoulder as he left the room.

I stripped off my jeans and, after a moment's hesitation, my shirt as well. Hanging them on a hook behind the door, I slipped into the robe, belted it firmly around my waist, and climbed up gingerly onto the pedicure chair.

Evan returned carrying a basket filled with bottles, tins and mysterious utensils. "That's a great color on you," he commented admiringly. "Really brings out your eyes."

I leaned back in the cushioned seat, discreetly making sure the robe hid my growing erection. A good thing, since when Evan straddled a stool in front of the chair, his eyes were directly level with my groin.

Reaching beside me, Evan flipped a series of switches on the side of the throne. The seat cushions began to vibrate gently as a series of jets in the basin churned to life. Evan slid my feet into the water, his hands lingering on my calves just a moment longer than necessary.

"Just relax," he said quietly, beginning to arrange the items from the basket on a low table next to the pedicure chair. I closed my eyes for a few moments, letting the warmth of the water and the soothing vibrations of the chair lull my senses.

They snapped back to full awareness the minute Evan reached down to lift my feet out of the water, settling them on a thick towel draped over the lip of the basin. He pumped a handful of lotion into his palm and began slathering it over my right foot.

"This is a moisturizer," he explained, his strong hands smoothing the lotion up my calf. I could imagine those hands smoothing over another part of my anatomy, which quickly signaled its enthusiasm for the idea. I tried unsuccessfully to will it down as Evan repeated the treatment to my left foot.

"Do you go barefoot a lot?" he asked, wiping the excess lotion from his hands on another towel.

I snorted, which had the unfortunate effect of causing the sides of the robe to slither down my thighs. Catching them just before I flashed the spa owner, I settled them back over my legs, tucking the ends under one thigh to hold them tight. Evan's lips twitched, but he refrained from commenting on my reaction.

"Yeah," I admitted, "as often as I can … how can you tell?"

He slid his fingers gently over my toes. "You have fewer calluses than most people," he said, trailing along the outside of my feet to my heels. "But it tends to dry your feet out more than normal." His touch was sending tingles pulsing up my legs. "You really should moisturize them every day."

I really hoped he hadn't noticed the way my cock twitched against the robe when his fingers caressed my insteps.

"You have beautifully shaped feet," Evan told me, rubbing them lightly. "Have you ever considered modeling?"

"I'm an actor," I admitted, surprising myself. That wasn't something I normally told people, especially when we'd just met. Something about this gorgeous young man was definitely getting to me. "That's why I'm here – my director wanted my feet to look a bit neater."

"You mean my work is going to be displayed on the silver screen?" Evan grinned. "Then I'll have to give you my extra special treatment."

I knew what kind of treatment I'd like to give *him*.... Swallowing hard, I gritted my teeth and told my cock firmly to behave itself. It was unimpressed.

"I'm going to clean up your cuticles first," Evan continued, picking up an implement that looked like something someone would threaten you with in a dark alley. He concentrated for the next few minutes on pushing back and trimming away the skin around my nails, giving me a chance to talk my arousal into uneasy submission.

"You keep your nails nice and trim," he said, sounding a bit surprised. "I'm just going to smooth off the edges."

"I do own a nail clipper," I protested. "I even know how to use it."

Evan just smiled as he ran a file over the tip of each toe. Then he picked up what looked like a small white block and buffed the surface of each nail vigorously.

"Let's see what we can do with these heels," he said next, selecting something shaped like a shoehorn. Dipping it into the water, he lifted my foot and rubbed it firmly over each heel in turn, pausing occasionally to pass his hand over the skin before rubbing some more. After a few moments of this, he nodded in satisfaction and returned the tool to the table.

"This is an exfoliant," he said, dipping his fingers into a jar of deep green goop. He massaged some of the gel over each foot in turn, paying special attention to the heels. My cock, which had taken a break while Evan was holding sharp implements, began to respond again to the feel of his hands touching me.

Evan dipped my feet back into the water to rinse off the gel, then dried them tenderly. Flipping a switch to let the water drain, he pumped out more moisturizer and began to massage my right foot in earnest. I realized his slim hands were much stronger than they looked, as they firmly pressed every sensitive spot on the underside of my foot. I shifted my hips, trying to hide my growing erection without freeing the robe from where I held it closed beneath my legs.

Evan turned his attention to my left foot. It became increasingly hard – literally – to hide my arousal, since my cock was throbbing with each stroke of his hands over my skin. When he slid those strong hands up my calves, I couldn't hold back a soft moan of pleasure.

Evan's melting brown eyes met mine and searched them before dropping to my lap. Following his gaze, I was mortified to see a glaring wet spot staining the silky fabric of the robe. The sound Evan made could only be described as a purr, as he lifted his eyes to meet mine once again.

"I'm so glad I'm not the only one feeling this way," he murmured. "I've been hard since the minute I saw you in the lobby."

"Evan," I groaned helplessly. My spa angel stood up from his stool and climbed up the side of the chair, swinging his leg across to straddle my hips.

"Is this what you want, Mac?" he whispered, leaning forward to tease my lips with his own. "Because it's sure as hell what I want."

I pried my hands from their death grip on the arms of the chair and pulled him against my chest. My tongue surged past his open lips, searching out the contours of his warm mouth as he slid his hips against my crotch. He tasted as rich and heady as his spa was elegant.

"Mac," he moaned, reaching between us to pull open the tie of my robe. This time I let the silky material slip down my sides. Evan began kissing his way down the base of my throat, his hips maintaining a steady rhythm against mine. I managed to unbutton my Adonis's shirt to reveal his smooth chest. His pert brown nipples called to me, so I slid his body upward until I could reach them with my mouth. He arched back hedonistically, whimpering softly as my tongue traced their outline. Taking one gently between my teeth, I reached under the waistband of his loose slacks to find he was telling the truth about his arousal. I also discovered why he understood my earlier embarrassment. Evan had gone commando himself.

When my hand closed around his impressive length, Evan cried out wordlessly. He let me stroke him for a moment, his eyes closed in bliss, before leaning forward to kiss me again, deeply, and still my hand.

"Not yet," he whispered, pushing himself up against the arms of the chair and swinging off me. My cock protested the loss of contact immediately. Evan quickly stripped off his clothes and stood proudly naked before me. He was glorious, and I started to rise myself, needing to hold him again. He placed a palm against my chest to stop me and smiled into my eyes.

"Will you let me...." He hesitated, his eyes flickering briefly away. *Anything*, I thought to myself. *I'll let you do anything you want.*

"Will you let me paint your toenails?" he asked quickly. Whatever I had expected him to ask, it sure as hell wasn't that. He must have seen the confusion on my face, because he leaned forward to brush my lips again.

"I find it very erotic," he said, his eyes promising that I'd enjoy the benefits of indulging him.

"I'm not sure Mark had polished nails in mind," I protested feebly.

"I promise to remove it when we're done," Evan countered.

"Okay, then," I agreed, immediately rewarded by the pleasure that lit his face.

He turned away for a moment to select a bottle of quick-dry polish from a crowded rack. I smiled when he waved the bottle happily in front of me.

"Blue?" I asked, unable to resist grinning myself at Evan's obvious glee.

"It matches your beautiful eyes," he answered. "Now just lie back and let me have my way with you."

Evan pulled the stool back in front of the chair and lifted my feet back onto the ledge. With quick, practiced strokes, he covered my nails in the deep blue polish. Each touch of his hands on my feet sent tremors through my over-sensitized cock. When he was finished, he crawled up my legs to once more straddle my hips.

"Now we have to let them dry," he crooned, claiming my mouth forcefully and fucking me with his tongue. If this is what a little polish did to him, he could paint me every night. I reached between us to where our eager cocks strained against each other. Circling them both in my fist, I matched the rhythm of my strokes with Evan's ravenous tongue. A deep groan rumbled in his throat.

I tore my lips away to suck in a much-needed breath. "Fuck, baby," I groaned, "feels so good. You're so fucking hot."

"I want you inside me," Evan moaned, pulling my hand away reluctantly. He slid back down my legs until he could reach the small table at the foot of the chair. Lifting a towel, he revealed a foil-covered condom.

"I don't do this," he confessed. "Especially since the clients are all women. But when I left you to get undressed, I couldn't help but hope."

"I'm glad," I told him truthfully. Our eyes met again, and then Evan was rolling the condom down my hard length. I stopped his hand from stroking me with a rueful grin.

"I won't last if you do that," I admitted. Evan pressed the bottle of moisturizer into my palm. "Make me ready for you," he pleaded, turning around so that his tight ass was facing me, his stiff cock bumping against my groin.

I pumped a stream of lotion over my fingers, gasping when Evan's tongue slid over my toes. I had never considered my feet erogenous before, but Evan might as well have been licking my cock directly. I moaned as he sucked my big toe into his mouth, sliding a finger into his tight channel at the same moment.

We both groaned as my fingers worked their way inside him, finding the bundle of nerves deep within. The suction on my toes increased as Evan writhed above me. With my other hand, I grasped his cock, the lotion still on my palm letting it glide over him slickly. Evan shuddered and threw his head back with a sob.

"So good," he gasped.   "Oh god, Mac, stop, gonna come...."

"Let it go, baby," I urged, needing to see my beauty find his release. I twisted my wrist, my fingers brushing his prostate as I flicked my thumb over his slit. With a cry, Evan came, spurting his creamy fluid over my abdomen. He lay gasping against my legs for a moment before catching his breath and crawling around to face me once again.

"You are incredible," he told me, after kissing me all but senseless. "What can I do to make you feel that good?"

"Ride me," I pleaded, pulling up at his hips. "I need to feel that tight ass I've been admiring all day wrapped around my cock."

Evan ran his palm down my chest to the pool of come still warm against my belly. Gathering the creamy fluid in his hand, he coated the condom and positioned himself over me. His eyes locked with mine as he lowered himself over my hard length in one smooth stroke.

"Fuck, Evan," I gasped as he squeezed his muscles around me. "Fuck me, baby. Fuck me hard."

Evan grasped the arms of the chair, lifted himself up and then slammed back down, impaling himself on me again and again. I thrust my hips up against him, fighting to bury myself as deeply as I could in his welcoming heat.

"Tight," I growled, reaching for his reawakening cock. "Knew you'd be tight ... feels so goddamn good...." I pumped him fiercely as he rode my throbbing cock.

"Close," Evan moaned, reaching down to flip the switch that started the chair vibrating beneath me. "Gonna come again ... come with me, lover...." He tightened around me one more time, and we both cried out as we found our release together.

Evan collapsed against my chest as we each fought to recapture our breath. I ran my fingers through his sweat-dampened curls, loving the feel of his weight pressing against me.

"Congratulations," Evan whispered after a moment. "You're the lucky winner of our grand opening contest."

"And what do I win?" I asked, nuzzling his cheek.

"Free pedicures every week for life," he replied dreamily.

"Only pedicures?" I pouted. "I had my heart set on that manicure you offered me."

Evan smiled at me, his heart shining out from his dark chocolate eyes. "We're a full-service salon," he stated proudly. "And it will be my pleasure to service you any time."

"It'll be a pleasure for us both," I promised.

I shook the bottle in my hand, setting the silver glitter mixed into the polish sparkling. Maybe later I'd paint my toes and give Darryl, my ex-NFL-linebacker co-star, a good laugh. Except he'd probably want to borrow it himself, and I wasn't about to share any of Evan's presents.

Setting the polish on the table, I dug into the basket again, a warm glow igniting inside me when I removed the next item – a mesh bag of smooth river stones. Glancing at the directions for warming them in the microwave to create a "do it yourself hot stone massage", I knew they'd never be as satisfying as Evan's version of that treatment.

HAND JOB

"MR. KERR! Welcome back!" the receptionist gushed as I entered the salon. Even my rattier-than-normal jeans and t-shirt didn't dim her unctuous smile. I'd definitely risen in her esteem over the past several months since she realized I was a VIP – at least in the eyes of her boss. I think I preferred her original disdain – at least it was honest.

She peered at her computer screen in confusion. "Er … did you have an appointment?"

"Not today," I admitted, anticipating her unconscious frown. I had a standing 'appointment' with Evan every Friday afternoon, but I'd been filming on location for over two months. I'd just gotten back into town for a brief break, and there was no way I could wait until Friday to see him. Now, however, I felt a twinge of uncertainty. As much as I'd been tempted, I'd never even called Evan while I was away. He'd given me no indication that he wanted anything more than the casual relationship we currently enjoyed. Was I being presumptuous to expect him to disrupt his schedule just to see me?

"I just wondered if Evan had a free moment?" I faltered.

Her manicured fingers flew over the keyboard. "You're in luck … he's between clients," she determined. "Make yourself comfortable – I'll let him know you're here."

I wandered over to the luxurious waiting area, noticing with interest that I was no longer the salon's only male customer. A young man of perhaps thirty nodded to me in greeting. His frosted, spiked blond hair and rakish grin looked vaguely familiar – I wondered idly if he was another actor, or perhaps a musician. Before I could puzzle through where I might have seen him before, the doors to the inner spa flew open and my dark-haired Adonis flew across the lobby to catch my hands in his. A dazzling smile bloomed across his face and danced in his bottomless eyes. I couldn't help but smile back at him, squeezing his hands in return. He was dressed all in black today, the silky fabric of his shirt and slacks clinging to his willowy frame. I'm not sure how long we stood there, just grinning at each other, until the sycophantic tones of the receptionist greeting another client broke us out of our spell.

"Come on back," the spa's owner beckoned, leading me through the cut-glass doors of the salon into a large private treatment room. As soon as the door closed behind us he was in my arms, attacking my mouth with his lips and tongue, molding his body against mine. "God, I missed you," he moaned, nipping at my lips with his teeth. "How long can you stay?"

I did my share of reacquainting myself with Evan's mouth before I pulled away enough to answer him. "A few days," I murmured, giving into the temptation to thread my fingers through his silky curls as I kissed my way down his graceful neck. "Sorry I couldn't wait until Friday – I just had to see you," I admitted, forcing myself to pause and wait for his reaction.

"I'm glad you didn't wait," he purred, running his palm caressingly down my face. He frowned as he noticed the cuts on my cheek and the side of my chin. "What have you been doing to yourself?" he demanded, pressing a gentle kiss over each scratch. "This face is too handsome to abuse this way, love," he rebuked me teasingly. "How about a facial to make them all better?"

I shook my head at him repressively. There were many things I'd dreamed of Evan doing to me over the past months, but smearing my face with herbal goop wasn't one of them. "I might take you up on that manicure, though," I offered in exchange, holding out my scratched and scabbed hands. "Those fight scenes were hell on my knuckles."

Evan ran his fingers tenderly over my hands, tracing the bruised nail beds, the broken, abraded knuckles, the chunk of nail missing from my thumb. I wasn't usually so accident prone, but these months of filming had been especially draining, and my concentration had slipped at times. As it always did from the first time I met him, the touch of Evan's fingers on my hands brought my cock to rigid attention. Raising my hands to his face, my dark-haired angel soothed each injury with his lips and tongue. The feel of his mouth on my battered skin stirred my insides to Jello and my cock to rock hardness. When a salty drop stung the torn flesh, my heart lurched. The thought of Evan crying over my clumsiness was unbearable.

"Don't, baby," I pleaded, lifting his head and wiping the moisture from his impossibly long lashes with my thumbs. "A few nicks and dings aren't going to kill me."

"If you won't take care of yourself, I'll have to do it for you," he scolded thickly, pressing a final kiss into my palms. "I have some very special treatments in mind for you."

He picked up the telephone hanging next to the door, his sparkling eyes never leaving mine. "Margaret, clear my schedule for the rest of the afternoon," he instructed, smiling at me beguilingly. "See who else is free to take my clients, or reschedule them. Offer them a free facial for the inconvenience."

"You don't have to do that," I protested. "I just wanted to see you."

"I don't want to touch anyone else when I can be with you," he insisted, locking the door to ensure we wouldn't be disturbed. The seed of unacknowledged jealousy, which had sprouted on seeing another man in the lobby, withered immediately at the honesty of Evan's admission. "Besides, if just one of them starts booking facials as a result, it will more than pay for itself."

I chuckled at my beautiful lover's business sense, until the feel of his palms slipping underneath my shirt drove all other thoughts from my mind. "Why don't you get out of these and get comfortable?" he suggested, handing me one of the spa's signature silk robes, in the deep blue I'd learned he offered only to me.

"Do you keep one of these in every room?" I asked, amused that he had one immediately at hand.

"Only the ones I think I might want to fuck you in – so, yeah, that would be all of them," he laughed in reply. "Give me just a minute to get a few things ready."

I quickly shed my clothes as Evan stepped through a connecting door, returning a few moments later. Holding the robe open for me to step into, he wrapped his arms around me with the silky fabric, nuzzling the spot he'd discovered beneath my ear that always made me shiver. "Missed this so much," he murmured, tying the belt and smoothing his hands lower across my stomach.

"Me too," I admitted, turning to pull him against me. He was already as hard as I was, and our mouths fed from each other hungrily as I pressed my hands against his tight ass, rubbing us together. "Evan," I groaned, wanting nothing more than to sheathe myself inside him immediately.

"Manicure," my angel insisted, pulling back with a final nip of his teeth. "I promise, you'll enjoy it."

My cock was throbbing in protest as I sank into the seat Evan indicated. It stubbornly ignored my attempts to convince it of the benefits of anticipation.

Evan filled the shallow basin with warm water and his favorite citrusy aromatic oil. Tracing my scarred knuckles gently with his fingers, he slid my hands into the water. "We'll let them soak for a few minutes first to soften the skin," he explained, "then I'll clean up your cuticles, shape the nails, and give you an exfoliating massage." He arranged his implements beside him on the table between us. "And then I have a little surprise for you."

You'd think after this many months I'd have gotten used to his touch. But every brush of his palms against mine, every stroke of his fingers sent a thrill of excitement through my nerves, just as strong as the first time he touched me. I watched him in growing stimulation as he concentrated on caring for my scarred and callused hands. Each time he unconsciously gnawed at his lower lip, or wet it quickly with his tongue, my cock stirred in response. At least now I no longer had to make any attempt to hide my arousal. By the time Evan had finished trimming and filing, and began to gently massage lotion into each hand, my erection had escaped the confines of the robe to stand proudly, if damply, before me.

Evan leered appreciatively across the tabletop at the obvious impact of his caressing touch. "Is Little Mac feeling jealous?" he teased.

I'd never had a pet name for my genitals before, but Evan could wrap a pink ribbon around it and call it Mary Sue if it made him happy. "I think it objects to being called 'little'," I replied, as it stood up even straighter under his gaze.

"Well, we'll take care of that in just a minute," my lover promised. "But I have a special treat for you first." Rising, he circled the table and spun my chair to face a small, square appliance that looked like a deep fryer. "Dip your hands in here," he instructed, lifting the lid to reveal a steaming, clear liquid.

"What is it?" I asked, eying it suspiciously.

"Hot paraffin wax," he replied coaxingly. "It's great for healing and moisturizing."

"Won't it hurt?" I hesitated.

"It's not a fucking bikini wax, Mac! It'll feel wonderful," he promised. "Have I ever disappointed you yet?" I had to admit that going along with Evan's sometimes exotic suggestions had always proved most rewarding for us both. I eased my hands tentatively into the steaming liquid, feeling as Evan promised a warm glow as the slippery substance coated my skin.

"Dip them a few more times," Evan directed, watching until I had coated them both to his satisfaction. He knelt between my legs to slip a cloth mitten over each hand in turn.

"How long do these have to stay on?" I asked, resenting anything that prevented me from touching my lover.

"Long enough to let me do this," he replied, pushing open the robe and sinking his mouth over the length of my erection. "Oh, fuck, Evan," I moaned, arching with pleasure as his tongue swept around my shaft. Nine weeks of dreams could never compare to the reality of Evan's hot mouth engulfing me. He slid slowly up and down my throbbing cock, teasing the ridge of skin around the head with each stroke. The sight of his dusky curls bouncing between my legs and the insistent suction of his lips quickly stole what little control I had. With a guttural groan, I shot my load into his hungry mouth. As soon as I stopped shuddering, he crawled up onto my lap, capturing my mouth to share the saltiness of my release.

"Damn, I needed that," I groaned, resting my forehead against his. "Now take this stuff off me so I can touch you, baby."

Evan stripped the mitts from my hands and peeled away the now-cooled layers of wax. He smoothed a final coating of moisturizer into each arm, but stood up when I reached to encircle him.

As I rose to follow him, my cocoa-eyed beauty caught my hands in his and led me forward into the adjoining room, where a wide, sheet-draped table beckoned. "That's more like it," I growled eagerly, trying to maneuver him against the side of the bed. Evan sidestepped my grasp and pushed me to sit on the padded surface instead.

"You're still too tense," he murmured. "I want to give you a massage first."

"What about you?" I pouted, reaching forward to cup the bulge that strained against his slacks.

"Trust me, this will be worth waiting for," he promised, sliding the robe off my shoulders and pressing me to lie with my back against the cool sheets. Stepping away for a moment, he dimmed the lights and flicked on some soothing, Celtic-sounding background music. He unbuttoned his shirtsleeves and began to roll up the cuffs, but I eyed him pleadingly. "Take it off," I urged, and after a moment Evan complied, revealing his smooth chest to my appreciative gaze.

"Now lie there and behave yourself," he commanded, pouring a handful of aromatically scented oil into his palm. Rubbing his hands together, he brought them down on my shoulders and began to massage the muscles firmly but soothingly. After a few moments, I let my eyes drift shut and gave myself over to the bliss of his hands. Suddenly, I felt something firm and warm settle into the hollow of my collarbone. Opening my eyes, I saw Evan draw a smooth, flat stone over my skin before settling it into the matching spot on my other side.

"These are warm river stones," he explained. "I'll place them in all your chakra spots – the focal points of your body's energies – to soothe and strengthen you."

Evan's talented hands stroked and soothed me from head to toe. He drew each warm stone slowly over the planes of my muscles before placing them – down my chest, in the center of my belly, between each finger and toe. The stones held me as immobile as any bonds might, preventing me from reaching for my lover, as I was increasingly tempted to do when he worked his tantalizing way up my legs. By the time he had settled stones in the hollows of my hipbones, my cock was once again hard and leaking against my abdomen. I moaned as Evan skirted it with his oil-slick palms, straining in frustration when he lifted his hands at last.

"Evan," I pleaded, but my dark angel shook his head inexorably. "Not yet, love," he admonished me with a smile.

Removing the larger stones from my torso but leaving the smaller ones between my fingers and toes, he urged me to roll over onto my stomach.   The finely-spun cotton of the sheets rubbed stimulatingly against my stiffened cock as I settled uneasily against the cushions. I turned my head at the sound of rustling behind me, to see Evan stripping off his slacks before kneeling to straddle my hips. I pushed up against him, only to have him swat me down reprovingly. "I said behave yourself," he scolded, reaching for another handful of oil.

If anything, Evan paid even more attention to my back and shoulders, massaging them firmly before placing stones against each shoulder-blade, inside my elbows and knees, down my spine and across the small of my back. Each languid stroke, rather than relaxing me, was beginning to arouse me unbearably. I hitched my hips against the bed sheets, moaning softly at the friction against my aching cock. When Evan's strokes reached the top of my thighs and began kneading my buttocks, I could no longer restrain the groan his touch wrenched from my lips.

"Please, baby," I begged him, thrusting up into his touch. "Need you now, please...."

Evan moved to kneel between my legs and lowered his head to kiss me hungrily. "Do you trust me?" he broke off to whisper sensuously into my ear.

"Yes," I hissed in response, knowing it was the truth. Following Evan's lead in our lovemaking had resulted in some mind-blowing experiences for us both. Until now, my dark-haired beauty had always preferred to be taken, but I had high hopes that this might be the day he was ready to change that. I arched against him, pressing myself against his own rigid arousal. "Anything you want, baby, always...."

Claiming one more passionate kiss, Evan knelt up again and began to stroke his hands tantalizingly over my backside. Spreading the cheeks gently, he trailed alluring fingers up and down the cleft between them until I was undulating beneath him. An oiled fingertip circled my entrance enticingly, pressing teasingly against it as I clenched and released involuntarily. I gasped with pleasure as the tip entered me at last, only to slide away immediately, then repeat the motion again and again, until I was wild with the need for more. Suddenly, something warm and hard and wider than Evan's fingertip slipped within me. It felt like he had slid one of his hot stones inside me. It felt fucking incredible.

"What the fuck?" I gasped, straining to lift my head and see what Evan was doing. He raised his hands to show me a strand of smooth, marble beads, each about an inch around, threaded and knotted onto a silky cord. "These are love beads," he told me, his dark eyes smoldering with desire. He slowly slipped another stone into my channel until it clicked against the first. "Can you take all of them for me, lover?" he crooned seductively.

I moaned inarticulately as Evan slid another oiled bead past my trembling entrance. The motion pressed the first stone deep enough to brush against the bundle of nerves within me. I cried out in pleasure at the exquisite sensation. Evan continued to slide the stones slowly inside me, the rhythmic stretch and release of my opening, the growing feeling of fullness, the erratic press of the beads against my prostate building my arousal to levels I'd never felt before. Each time I was sure I couldn't take any more, Evan pressed another stone inside me. He held my hips firmly to keep me from thrusting my cock against the slick-smooth sheets. "Not yet, love, you're doing so well," he praised me, "just a few more, you can take them all...."

As he slipped the last bead past my straining muscle, Evan bent forward to lap soothingly over my overstretched entrance with his wet tongue. I bucked back insistently against his mouth, crying out deliriously as he thrust his tongue inside me, stirring the beads into motion against my pleasure center. I rocked my hips wantonly, seeking relief. The sheets beneath me were so wet I'd have sworn I'd already come, but that my balls were still rock-hard and aching. "Fuck, baby, please, no more, oh god, please...." I babbled, writhing wildly.

Evan clenched his teeth around the end of the silken cord and slowly pulled the last bead back out. I groaned as he thrust his tongue inside me again, alternating between removing the stones and stirring the remaining beads within me until I was trembling uncontrollably. The sense of emptiness as he slid out the final bead was so strong that I physically ached. As I gasped to find the breath to speak, I recognized at last the feeling that had haunted my last few months. Emptiness. I was empty without Evan in my life.

Dropping the cord of beads to the floor, Evan slid up my body to kiss me passionately. "Can I make love to you, Mac?" he whispered against my lips.

"Love ... me...." I gasped, panting with need. Stones flew heedlessly as Evan flipped me onto my back. I pulled my knees up to my chest, reaching out to clutch for him. Evan pulled me forward onto his thighs and slid deep inside me with one smooth stroke. I pushed my heels into his back, urging him deeper as I rocked against him wildly. Leaning forward to thrust his tongue down my throat, Evan grasped my hips and pumped fiercely. I was so sensitized that I came almost immediately, painting both our chests with the force of my release. Evan threw his head back and shouted my name as he convulsed against me in ecstasy.

We both collapsed back against the massage table in exhaustion, totally spent. Our breathing slowly quieted as our hearts settled back into stable rhythms. Evan nuzzled his cheek against my chest like a kitten begging to be petted. "I wish you didn't have to leave again so soon," he whispered sadly.

"Come back with me," I offered impulsively, before I could censor myself. "Let that hot-shot assistant you hired take over here for a while."

"Jordan *is* ready for more responsibility," he mused. "It would give him a chance to show what he can do...." He lifted his head and eyed me consideringly. "So I'd be there as what – your personal masseur?"

"If that's what makes you comfortable," I said. "But as soon as they see us together, it'll be obvious to everyone that I'm in love with you."

I may spend the rest of my life trying to rekindle the light that shone from Evan's eyes at that moment. He cradled my head in his hands and kissed me deeply, lingeringly. "I've loved you since our first time together," he admitted shyly. "I didn't know what a famous actor like you would see in me."

"I'm not a famous actor, Evan," I protested. "I'm just a guy doing a job, like anybody else. A guy who happens to love you very much. If you come with me, you'll get to see how un-glamorous acting really is. But it will be a lot easier for me to take if I have you by my side."

"At least I can make sure you take better care of yourself," he sighed. "And who knows? Maybe some casting agent will discover me, and I can be the next Brad Pitt! We can make blockbuster movies together!"

We both laughed at our innocent daydreams. When you're in love, anything seems possible.

NEEDING to cool off from the heat of my memories, I padded into the kitchen for another Corona. My cock was hard against the zipper of my shorts as I walked back to the patio, complaining that none of the presents so far had been for him. I couldn't help but smile when I lifted out the next item, one that I definitely wasn't going to be using on my cock – or at all, until I was back with Evan again – a jar of ginger-scented sugar wax.

WAX OFF

I was so intent on sharing the awful news with my lover that I barely paused as I barreled through the door of the salon, storming right past the elegant waiting lounge. Fortunately, *Evan's Heaven's* receptionist was used to me by now, and barely raised an artistically-shaped eyebrow at my attitude or my attire.

"Evan's just finishing up with a client.... I'll let him know you're here. Treatment room six is open if you want to wait in there," she suggested calmly. Probably a good idea, since in my current mood I might have barged in on some socialite's manicure – or bikini waxing – without thinking. Taking a deep breath, I flashed her a rueful grin and nodded my thanks, careful not to slam the cut-glass doors behind me as I entered the inner sanctum of the salon.

Like every room in the day spa, treatment room six was opulently outfitted with plush furnishings, watered-silk walls, and marble flooring, but it could have been as ratty as my first apartment for all I noticed. I paced in bad-tempered impatience for several minutes, oblivious to the restful music and soft lighting. Even the delicate hint of patchouli and lemongrass in the air – the spa's signature aromatherapy fragrance – was powerless to relieve my irritation. Only one thing had the power to do that, and I was wallowing so deep in my self-pity that it caught me by surprise when strong, graceful arms enfolded me from behind in a soothing embrace.

"What's wrong, love?" Evan's charmingly musical voice murmured against my ear. "Margaret was concerned – she said she's never seen you look so upset."

"Margaret said that?" I challenged, leaning back into his encompassing warmth as he dropped a slow trail of kisses down my neck. I could feel him smile against my throat.

"Actually, she said I'd better intercept you before you scared away the rest of the clientele," he admitted, pulling aside the collar of my t-shirt to leave a gentle bite-mark on my collarbone. I could feel the tension draining from me already, just from his presence. It may seem odd for someone with so much energy and enthusiasm, but Evan can always calm me out of my darkest and most disgruntled moods. Of course, the fact that we inevitably get off every time we're together might help to explain it.

Apparently, I wasn't relaxing fast enough for my lover. He turned me around and pinned me gently but firmly against the nearest wall, leaning forward to nip at my other collarbone in turn. The weight of his body pressing against mine was easing my mental frustration, replacing it with another, more physical variety.

"You going to tell me what's bothering you, or am I going to have to bite it out of you?"

My cock, never quiet for long when I was with Evan, signaled its opinion of that option by pressing eagerly against my zipper. "That's not much of an incentive to tell you," I countered, trying to pull him closer.

Shaking his head of artfully tumbled curls, he held me at arm's length. "Then I won't touch you again until you tell me," he replied in mock-anger. "Out with it. What happened to make you this testy? You didn't lose the part, did you?"

Suddenly the reason for my anger seemed petty – but damn it, I still remembered how much it hurt the last time. "No, I didn't lose the part, but I'm beginning to wonder if I still want it," I grumbled. "Remember the shower scene I told you about? Jerry decided he wants my character to have a smooth chest."

Evan's hands slid from my shoulders down my sides until they reached the hem of my t-shirt. I shivered as they slipped underneath to tease at the short curls of hair he found there. "But your chest is perfect the way it is," he argued, his thumbs unerringly finding and fondling my nipples to aching hardness.

I swallowed hard to choke back a moan of pleasure. "I'm glad you think so, baby, but Jerry doesn't agree. He wants me to lose the hair."

Pulling the t-shirt up to my armpits, Evan bent to nuzzle at the tightened nubs he'd raised, seeming not to understand what this meant. "I had to do it once before, a few years back," I complained. "That wax hurt like a sonofabitch. I don't think I want to go through that again … oh God, do that again," I moaned in response to a particularly firm nip of my lover's teeth.

Evan obligingly complied, then raised his head to kiss me passionately. I could see excitement kindling in his chocolate-dark eyes as he pulled away. "Do you trust me, love?" he asked playfully, pulling my t-shirt back into place.

'Fuck yeah!' my cock agreed enthusiastically. It knew what that sparkle in my lover's eyes meant. Every time Evan asked that question, it led to a new and mind-blowing sexual experience. But it was more than just the slightly kinky games he introduced me to … somehow, the trust and love we felt for each other shone clearer in those moments than any other.

"Always," I assured him, sealing my vow with a kiss. "Always, and in everything."

"No one but me is laying a hand on this gorgeous chest," he proclaimed possessively. I couldn't hold back the shudder of pleasure that ran through me as his hand slid down the planes of my abdomen to flirt beneath the waistband of my jeans. "But I can't have you jumping like that while I'm trying to work." His voice took on a stern tone I had never heard him use before. I was surprised at how fucking erotic it sounded. Evan suggested and coaxed, he never demanded – but I realized with surprise that the thought of him taking control made me incredibly hard.

"What do you have in mind, baby?" I asked huskily.

"Do you remember that leather store I found when Molly was misbehaving?" The last time Evan had accompanied me on a location shoot, he'd brought along the large golden lab he'd rescued from the local shelter. The two of them shared the same exuberant personality, and like her master, Molly had charmed everyone on the set – that is, until the day she devoured the prop food for the pivotal family dinner scene.

"I bought more than a leash for Molly," Evan admitted, his voice dropping to a sultry whisper. He glanced at me from beneath his long lashes, his eyes smoldering. "I bought some … restraints…. I wasn't sure if you were ready for them yet."

Evan had introduced me to pleasures I'd never dreamed of, but our play had never extended to bondage – until now. He raised my hand to his lips and kissed the inside of my wrist tenderly. "I can't make it not hurt at all," he murmured regretfully, "but I can promise you'll feel so good, the pain won't matter…."

I pictured myself held down with leather straps, subject to anything Evan chose to do to me – and found the image shockingly arousing. He wasn't touching anything other than my wrist, and I was already so hard I was almost shaking. "Fuck, yes," I whispered, cupping his chin and raising his head to kiss him fiercely. "God, I want that so bad…." My hands slid to his ass, pulling him to me and grinding against him wantonly.

He allowed the contact for a heady minute, but when our breathing grew ragged he pushed away with reluctance. "We can't do it here," he groaned, drawing a calming breath. "The …

equipment ... is at my apartment. And besides," he promised, "I'm going to make you scream ... and not in pain."

"Let's go, then," I urged, trying futilely to adjust myself to a more comfortable position. My cock knew what it wanted, and it wanted it *now*. "But you're gonna have to drive. I'm so hard I don't think I can fit under the steering wheel."

EVAN fastened the buckle with a hungry glitter in his bottomless brown eyes, running a finger beneath the butter-soft leather. I was so high already with anticipation, even that simple touch made me tremble. "Not too tight, love?" he asked solicitously, tugging gently to test the strength of the straps that held my arms to the headboard.

I growled with pleasure and shook my head wordlessly, trying to catch his hand with my lips. Evan smiled and let me kiss his palm before sliding it caressingly up the side of my face. "Good," he responded, rising from the bed and letting his gaze rake over me. I could tell he liked what he saw – me, naked, shackled to the headboard of his large bed, already hard despite the pain I knew was to come.

"You're so beautiful like this," he marveled, bending forward to kiss me gently, his tongue barely penetrating the seam of my lips before he rose, all too quickly. "Give me just a minute to get everything ready." He left the room, leaving me to savor the anticipation of what he had in store for me.

A moment later he returned, carrying a bowl and a handful of long muslin strips. Setting both on the bedside table, he unbuttoned the cuffs of his yellow silk shirt and began rolling up the sleeves. I wasn't sure if it was proper protocol for me to speak without permission, but I wanted to enjoy the feel of him against me as he worked. "Please," I asked quietly, "take it off for me?"

He looked at me thoughtfully for a moment, then smiled. "You aren't going to make this easy for me, are you?" he asked, unbuttoning his shirt and letting it pool on the floor. Feeling bolder, I shook my head again. "It's better for both of us when it's hard," I teased, watching with growing excitement as he stepped out of his slacks and stood proudly before me. You can keep David and Alexander – to me, Evan nude is the most sublime work of art I've ever experienced.

Straddling my hips, Evan kissed me, his tongue dancing sensuously against mine until I was undulating beneath him, hungry for more. With a final nip at my lips, he sat up and reached for the bowl, stirring its contents with a small wooden paddle. "This is sugar wax," he told me, letting something that looked like melted caramel drizzle back into the bowl. "It's less irritating than regular wax. I'm going to spread some on your chest, then cover it with a strip of muslin. When I pull off the cloth, the hair will come with it." I nodded my understanding, but my face must have revealed some of the trepidation I was feeling.

"Trust me," he reminded me, painting a broad swathe of the sticky substance down the right side of my chest. It certainly felt more soothing than the hot melted wax I remembered. Evan's hands caressed me as they smoothed the first muslin strip over the syrupy goo. He leaned forward to nip at my lips again, tantalizing touches that refused to linger, until all I was thinking about was how to capture his mouth for a deeper kiss. Without warning, he straightened and yanked the strip from my chest.

It felt – well, it felt like you'd expect it would to have hundreds of short hairs suddenly torn out by the roots. I bit my lip to keep from crying out at the pain. Instantly, Evan dropped the cloth to the floor and slid downward, swirling his tongue around the head of my flagging erection. All thoughts of pain were quickly forgotten as every nerve ending in my body focused on the deliciously depraved things his tongue was doing to my happy cock.

When he'd reduced me to whimpering incoherence, he slid forward again and smoothed a second strip onto my chest. This time after yanking it away he turned his attention to my balls, sucking them into his mouth and using his tongue and teeth to entice them to indurate hardness. After the third strip, he spread my cheeks with his thumbs and rimmed me until I was moaning uncontrollably, pressing them inside me alongside his plundering tongue.

He continued to work his way across my chest and stomach, alternating between the short, sharp pain of the waxing and the increasingly intense pleasures he lavished on my cock, balls, and ass. By the time he removed the last strip, my torso burned and I was harder than I could ever remember being.

Bestowing a last loving lick between my cheeks, Evan knelt over me and ran appraising hands across my now-hairless chest. The feel of his palms gliding over me without the usual resistance was arousing as hell. He caressed the irritated skin soothingly, brushing away the last dried crumbs of the sugar wax, circling my reddened, distended nipples. When his fingertips traced across them at last, my entire body jumped. He repeated the motion sadistically, his eyes twinkling. "Like that?" he inquired, brushing with agonizing lightness over the sensitized nubs.

"Please, baby," I groaned, needing more than that fluttering contact. "Put your mouth on them … please…."

Evan dragged his tongue in a broad sweep across my chest, humming at the lingering sweetness of the sugary treatment. "Tastes good," he acknowledged, licking and nibbling each tight peak in turn until I was arching up wildly underneath him, close to coming just from the wet slide of his mouth on my nipples. "Oh fuck, Evan," I pleaded shamelessly, "need more … need you…."

My lover raised his head from my chest and ran a hand down its length, over my stomach to the thatch of curls, wet with his saliva and my pre-come, that was the only hair left on my torso.

"You did so well, Mac. Will you let me do something else?" he asked seductively, threading his fingers through the damp thicket. My cock wilted noticeably at the thought of wax – even sugar wax – coming anywhere near its home turf.

Evan noticed my tremor of discomfort and laughed merrily. "Don't worry love, I'm not planning a bikini wax," he chortled, enjoying himself more than was called for in my opinion. "I want to shave you. Do you remember how good it felt when I shaved your mustache?" It *had* felt incredibly sexy when he'd used a straight-edge to remove the thick mustache I'd grown for an earlier role, though the fact that we were both naked and I was buried balls-deep inside him at the time might have had something to do with it. My cock wasn't sure it liked the idea of six inches of razor-sharp steel so close to its base, but I could never say no to Evan, especially when he used that pleading puppy-dog look on me.

"Okay," I grumbled in agreement, hiding my own smile when his expression transformed with glee. It was little enough to make him this happy.

The feel of Evan smoothing the warm shaving cream over my pubes and the slow, careful strokes of the razor were still surprisingly arousing, even if he wasn't clenching his sinfully tight ass around me this time. When he removed the last of the foam with a warm cloth and ran his palm appreciatively over the denuded flesh, the pleasure was indescribable. And when Evan lowered his head and engulfed me in his mouth, his fingers tracing patterns over the newly-bared skin, I nearly bucked myself off the bed. His talented mouth tantalized and teased me, his fingers gliding from base to balls to butt and back again, until I was straining against the restraints and all but gibbering with need.

'Please, baby. Let me go," I pleaded, needing to hold him, to touch him. He lifted his mouth, leaving my cock screaming for him to come back and finish what he'd started, and shook his head.

"You're so fucking sexy like this," he crooned, teasing his fingers beneath the soft leather cuffs on each wrist. "I'll let you do whatever you want to me later, but I have to have you this way. I just can't decide if I want to ride you or fuck you…."

My cock is usually not shy about making its opinion known, but at this point it was so damn hard it didn't care how it got off. "Whatever you want, just make up your fucking mind," I growled unrepentantly, shifting to wrap my legs around his waist in an insistent embrace. I was going to be sore as hell tomorrow, but I wasn't letting him go until he fucking did *something*.

Evan dragged his fist over my leaking length, making me hiss. "Feels so good when you're inside me," he considered, raising his hips 'til the tip of my cock danced against his entrance. I pushed upward eagerly, but he pulled away to kneel again between my legs. "Evan," I growled dangerously, tightening my legs around his hips. "But I'd have to take time to prepare myself, and you're already open for me, aren't you, love?" He plunged his thumbs inside me, pushing against the sides of the tight channel and nudging the opening with the tip of his cock.

"Yesss...." I gasped, thrusting forward to force him deeper inside. "Fucking do it, Evan, fuck me already...."

He leaned forward and slammed his tongue into my mouth, thrusting to the hilt inside me at the same time. I rocked wildly beneath him, setting a desperate pace for his shuddering strokes. When he unlocked my shins from around his waist and raised them to his shoulders, changing angles to hit my prostate with every snap of his hips, I howled out my release, spraying creamy fluid over both our chests. Evan came inside me a moment later, crying out my name before collapsing on top of me in a boneless heap.

I must have spaced out for a minute, because the next thing I knew Evan was unbuckling the restraints, lovingly kissing the reddened marks around each wrist. "Are you okay, love?" he asked with concern, rolling off me to curl against my side. "It wasn't too much for you?"

"It was incredible," I reassured him, kissing him tenderly. His hand played in the puddle of pearly liquid that pooled around my belly button, the sensation of his fingers sliding without friction against my skin already beginning to reawaken my desire. "You're pretty incredible yourself," he murmured, spreading the moistness over my rapidly resurgent erection. "I did promise to let you do anything you want to me...." One kiss from his delectable lips quickly turned from languid to urgent. This time it was his turn to moan needily as I broke the kiss.

"Hold that thought," I told him, rising to pad noiselessly into the kitchen. I sometimes wondered if Evan found my sexual tastes too vanilla, but his reaction to the leather restraints had inspired an idea that I hoped would bring my love as much pleasure as he had just given me. Finding what I sought, I returned to the bedroom, grateful that Molly was a large dog and Evan had a slender throat.

"Hands and knees," I commanded, watching his eyes light up when he saw what I held. As I buckled the collar around his throat and positioned myself behind him, I thought it might be a good idea to check out that leather shop myself sometime soon. Anything that got Evan this excited was definitely worth exploring further. I patted his curly head with one hand and wrapped the lead around my other fist with a smile.

"Good boy," I praised him, my cock nudging his ass as he wriggled happily against me.

"Let's do it doggy-style."

SHAKING my head at the memory – that idea of mine had turned into more of a success than I'd ever imagined – my breath caught in my throat at the next item in the basket. It was a bottle of champagne – the same brand I'd bought the last time I'd shared champagne with Evan, on his birthday. There was a thin black ribbon around the neck of the bottle, with a tiny pink satin rose attached. I lifted the flower to my lips and closed my eyes, letting remembrance wash over me.

BIRTHDAY SUIT

MY gaze flicked to the clock for the fifth time in as many minutes, willing the moments to pass more quickly, smiling to myself at my impatience. Glancing around the room and checking over the supplies one more time, I confirmed again that everything was ready. I, personally, was more than ready.

Drawing a deep breath, I tried to tamp down the arousal that was already building in anticipation of what I was about to do. I had a full day to indulge in all the activities I had spent the last week or more fantasizing about, twenty-four hours to turn the tables on the man who had come to mean more to me than I had ever imagined possible, twenty-four hours beginning – *now*!

I could feel the smile spreading across my face as I entered the bedroom and sat on the edge of the bed. As eager as I was to begin, I took a moment to indulge myself in merely gazing my fill at my lover's face. In repose, the energy and enthusiasm that were so much a part of Evan's being were muted, making the pure beauty of his features – the wide, smooth forehead, the gracefully arched brows, the fringe of dark lashes hiding his bottomless brown eyes, the elegantly carved cheekbones, the hint of stubble that shadowed his chin, the delectably bowed lips – all the more striking. I would never understand what I had done to deserve this angel in my life, but I had stopped questioning my good fortune. Right now, my only goal was to show him exactly how much he meant to me.

Leaning forward, I gently drew back the sheet that covered him and pressed a soft kiss to his cheek. "Wake up, baby," I murmured against his ear as he stirred restively against the bed linens.

His long lashes fluttered and then swept open, his sleepy gaze focusing on my face. "Mac? I'm sorry I fell asleep. What time is it, love?"

"Don't apologize, you needed to rest," I told him lovingly. Since I was stuck on location for at least another month, Evan had flown in to spend his birthday with me, but the eleven hour flight from L.A. to Amsterdam had taken its toll on him, especially since he hadn't yet learned my trick of being able to sleep anywhere. When I'd met him at the airport yesterday afternoon after filming wrapped for the weekend, he was barely able to keep his eyes open. I'd taken him to the hotel, ordered him a light meal and then put him to bed. After indulging in some quick, sweet lovemaking – it had been three weeks since we'd seen each other, after all – no matter how tired he was, there was no way we'd been able to resist! – I held him in my arms until he fell asleep, and then slipped away to begin my preparations for today.

"It's – " I checked the clock – "three minutes after midnight on November 15th. Which means it's officially your birthday. Happy birthday, Evan!"

He wrapped his arms around my neck and pulled me into a deep, heart-stopping kiss. My cock awoke from its own nap to strongly recommend getting horizontal and giving him his birthday present right away. Evan seemed to agree, sliding a hand to my hips and urging me silently to join him in the bed.

I broke the kiss and lifted my head reluctantly, rising to my feet and extending a hand to my sleep-rumpled lover. "Get up, baby. I have a special birthday surprise for you."

"I'm up already," Evan admitted, stroking languidly over his lengthening erection. He smiled at me seductively, licking his lips as he played with the droplets of fluid already moistening the tip of his slender cock. "Why don't you come down here and wish me a happy birthday properly?"

I was sorely tempted, but today was about his pleasure, not my own. Shaking my head with a smile, I pulled his hand away from his cock and drew him to his feet, letting him wrap himself against me for a brief moment of delicious full-body contact before turning to lead him the short distance to the bathroom. "I think you'll enjoy what I have planned for you," I told him over my shoulder, opening the door to let him precede me into the adjoining room.

The hotel I'd been living in for the last six weeks was much more luxurious than my average location accommodations. Normally I was so exhausted by the end of each day's shoot that the only amenity I was interested in was the bed, but I was glad I could offer Evan something that approached the elegance of his salon. I'd left the lights dim but lit several candles around the marble-tiled room, and drawn a warm bath in the deep Jacuzzi tub. The air was fragrant with Evan's favorite citrusy scent, from the candles and the scented oil I'd added to the bathwater.

I led him to the tub and helped him settle into the water, shaking my head again when he raised his arms, inviting me to join him. The tub was big enough to hold us both, and I promised myself we'd take advantage of it before the weekend was over, but on this day I had other plans for my lover.

"You just relax for a little," I told him, turning on the radio to a soft jazz station. "I want to be sure your back isn't bothering you after that long flight." I slid my hand into the water to be sure the temperature was just right, turned the jets on low, and padded to the living room to pop open the bottle of champagne I'd left chilling. I carried a flute back to the bathroom and offered it to him with a smile.

"Mmmnnnn ... aren't you joining me?" he asked, a puzzled note in his voice when he noticed I had brought only one wineglass. I shook my head again before turning to gather some supplies from the dressing table.

You're all the intoxication I need, I thought to myself, but it sounded too much like a line from one of my movies to say out loud. Instead, I knelt beside the tub and took the flute from him, setting it on the side of the tub and gathering his hands in mine.

"You always take such good care of me," I told him, my voice thick with emotion. "Today it's my turn to take care of you. Let me do this for you, baby. Let me show you how much your love means to me."

Tears sparkled on his lashes as he nodded, a smile of pure joy lighting his face. My heart swelled to know that I had put that look there. Another part of my anatomy simply swelled, making me glad I was wearing only a loose pair of soft linen trousers. The way my cock was throbbing already, I was in for a long day. *Easy, buddy*, I told myself sternly. My cock, never very attentive at the best of times, merely twitched in disdain and told me to get a move on.

Deciding that wasn't bad advice, I reached into the steaming water and drew Evan's feet out to rest on the edge of the tub. Opening a small bottle of polish, I carefully painted his nails a deep burgundy, admiring the contrast of the rich tone against his olive skin. His breathing quickened as my fingers cradled each foot, enjoying the contact with his warm skin but not lingering. I painted his fingernails in turn, dropping a moist kiss into each palm before I arranged his hands on either side of the tub to dry. He looked up at me with heavy-lidded eyes, passion simmering just below the surface of his umber gaze.

"Very nice," he purred, examining the fingers of one hand more closely. "I like the color." He leaned back, a picture of relaxed languor as he reclined in the marble tub, his limbs outspread, his semi-rigid cock swaying gently amid the swirling bubbles.

I watched him in heart-filled silence for a moment, but when he sat up to reach for another sip of champagne, I held his shoulders to keep him from lying back down. "Lean back and let me wash your hair," I instructed him, sliding an arm around his back for support and running the other hand through his sable curls when they slipped beneath the water.

I couldn't resist kissing him when I helped him sit back up, slicking away the streaming water from his face and cradling it in my hands to drink the moisture from his lips. Before I could lose myself in that temptation, I broke away and poured a handful of shampoo into my palms, working it into a lather in his silky tresses. He moaned as my strong fingers massaged his scalp. I'd been the recipient of such caresses from Evan enough times to know how erotic the seemingly mundane act of washing a lover's hair could be. The feel of his fingers moving through my hair and rubbing circles onto my scalp always left me achingly hard, and I did my best now to bestow as much pleasure on Evan as his touch always gave me. The groans escaping his lips as I continued the massage seemed to indicate I was succeeding.

I could have gone on playing with Evan's hair for hours, but after a few more minutes he arched his back, dropping his head below the water and incidentally revealing a now fully-hard cock to my appreciative gaze. My hand reached out to ghost over its tip before I could stop myself, but I drew it back almost immediately. It was far too soon for that.

Returning the sharp glance Evan gave me when he erupted out of the water with my best innocent stare, I sluiced the excess moisture from his hair. Turning off the jets and opening the drain, I gave Evan my hand and helped him to stand. My pulse pounded as I watched the rivulets of water stream off his smooth, firm flesh. Venus rising out of the sea had nothing on Evan's beauty. Then his eyes met mine, filled with so much love that even his physical allure was dimmed by it. I fought back another urge to simply lead him into the bedroom and make love to him immediately. No matter how many times I had demonstrated the rewards of patience, my cock never managed to retain the lesson.

"Careful, it's slippery," I cautioned as he climbed out of the tub, holding open one of the luxuriously thick towels for him to step into. His hands reached for the terrycloth, but I brushed them aside. "This is my pleasure," I insisted, kneeling to blot up every drop of water from his body, from his toes up. "You don't have to do anything today but enjoy." A purr of contentment issued from Evan's throat, and his hands closed around my shoulders for stability.

When I had dried the last glittering droplets from the curves of his ears, I tucked the towel around him and sat him in the swiveling stool before the dressing table. With a dry towel, I blotted as much of the dampness as I could from the thick mane of his hair. Knowing how much I love his curls, Evan had begun to let them grow, and by now they nearly reached his shoulders. I pumped a handful of glossy conditioner into my palms, rubbing them together and working it into his curls until they bobbed and gleamed. A hum of pleasure rumbled in Evan's chest as I tweaked and patted the dark locks into a semblance of barely restrained order.

Wiping my hands and setting aside the towel, I considered my lover's face for a moment, rubbing the back of my hand over the light shade of stubble on his chin. Evan arched into my touch, for all the world like a cat nudging to be petted. The slight scratchiness didn't bother me, but knowing how much care Evan took in his appearance, I though he'd prefer to be clean-shaven. So I retrieved my razor and shaving cream, spreading the lather over his face and carefully working the blade against his skin. I could feel my cock thickening inside my slacks as I remembered the times Evan had shaved me, and the slight tremble as I held his chin told me Evan was remembering too. Careful not to knick his flawless skin, I stripped away the last light whiskers and toweled off any lingering foam, leaving his face smooth and clean – the perfect canvas for what I planned next.

I bent my knees until my face was level with Evan's, and cupping the back of his head in my palm, I brought him forward to touch my lips to his. The fire of passion that always lay banked between us flared to life, and his tongue met mine hungrily, surging into my mouth and dueling with mine until we were both gasping for breath. Disengaging myself gently, I rested my forehead against his and met his eyes, darkened with desire.

"Evan," I asked softly, "do you trust me?"

The thrill of excitement that flashed across his face eased any doubts I might have felt. Until now, it had always been Evan saying those words to me, words that had become a signal that he was about to introduce me to some new form of sensuous play. I had always been content to let Evan take the lead in our games, and the results were never less than mind-blowing, but today was the first time I had asked for control. To my surprised delight, I saw that Evan was not only willing but happy to cede that power to me.

"Always," he told me seriously, though an imp of mischief danced in his eyes. "Always, and in everything." I didn't really need to hear the echo of my own words; the trust in his voice was as obvious as his love and his need.

"I love you," I whispered against his lips as I claimed another kiss before drawing away. Opening a nearby drawer, I took out the small case I had placed there and paused to consider. It would be easiest for me to sit on the edge of the dressing table, but I didn't want Evan squirming to look in the mirror as I worked. Instead, I knelt before him, placing the case on his lap and opening it to reveal…

"Makeup?" Evan husked, the quaver in his voice betraying his excitement.

I shrugged a bit diffidently. "I wasn't sure I could carry off some of the treatments you've given me, but makeup, I know. And I thought it might be something you'd enjoy." Given his enthusiasm for painting my nails, I'd been fairly sure it wouldn't turn him off, but I was thrilled by how much it seemed to appeal to him.

"Oh, yeah," he rasped breathily. "Fuck, Mac, yeah."

His perfect skin didn't need any foundation, but I brushed a sweep of dusty rose blush over each high cheekbone to emphasize it. Selecting a dark pencil, I outlined each eye with a thin line of kohl, then covered the lids with a smoky brown shadow. Though his lashes were already long and thick, I combed a coat of mascara on to accentuate them, leaning over him as I worked. The towel covering his lap couldn't hide the growing swell of his arousal, not that I was in any better state myself.

"Does this turn you on, Evan?" I growled, running my hand lightly over the tented fabric. "Does it make you hard to imagine what you look like, how beautiful I'm making you for me?"

His moan was so wanton that I couldn't stop myself from kissing him again, tasting his lips so hungrily that they were swollen when I pulled away at last. The deep wine-red lipstick I stroked over them looked sinful against his honey-toned skin.

When I was satisfied with my artistry at last, I turned the stool to face the mirror, letting him see himself in the glass. The image that stared back at me was a sloe-eyed houri from some oriental fairy-tale, a seducer sent to lead men to paradise.

"Mac," he groaned, rising to pull me into his arms. I buried my face in the curve of his shoulder, not wanting to mar the results of my efforts. My cock surged as our bodies molded to each other, our groins rubbing together needily, but when he reached for the soft cloth tie of my trousers, I forced myself to step back. I ignored the howl of protest from below my waist, knowing that once he touched me I would be lost, and there was still so much more I wanted to do to him first.

Evan's own wail of protest when I pulled away turned to a coo of delight when I returned a moment later with a large, brightly wrapped package. "I bought you a present," I told him, my nerves dancing with anticipation. Evan all but snatched it from my hands and tore into the wrappings with the excitement of a six-year-old. I held my breath as he opened the box and pushed aside the layers of tissue. His gasp of surprised joy was exactly the reaction I'd been hoping for.

"Mac," he exclaimed, his eyes flickering back and forth between the contents of the box and my face. "Mac, I fucking love it! Where did you find it?"

"Just something I saw in a shop window," I murmured. That was true enough, though it had been a woman I'd seen wearing it as I browsed Amsterdam's red-light district in search of gift ideas. The image of Evan that flashed through my mind at that moment had made me so hard, it was all I could do to keep from stroking myself to completion right there on the street-corner.

"Help me put it on," he pleaded, lifting the confection of dusky pink silk and delicate black lace from its nest of tissue. I wrapped the corset around his torso, my fingers shaking as I fastened the dozens of tiny hook-and-eye closures. It would be hard as hell if I wanted to take it off quickly, but that didn't concern me – I hoped to enjoy him in it the rest of the day.

When the last closure was fastened, I straightened the ribs and smoothed my hands over the filmy lace top. I'd gotten the smallest cup size they had, and Evan's nipples were already so hard they peeked through the gauzy fabric. My fingers teased at them as I nuzzled the base of his neck, his moans of pleasure encouraging me to suck harder until I'd left a purpled mark.

Sliding to my knees, I reached into the box for the matching black lace stockings. Lifting one foot to rest on my thigh, I gathered the fragile material and carefully worked it over his toes, past his calf and up the length of his thigh. As I fastened the thin elastic garter strap to the stocking top, Evan rubbed his foot over the firm bulge in my crotch.

"I think you're enjoying my present as much as I am," he whispered seductively.

"We're both going to enjoy it even more," I promised, raising his other foot and sliding the second stocking into place. Evan repeated the teasing pressure as I did, and my cock was so wet it was leaking through the front of my slacks by the time I fastened the second garter into place. Ignoring its increasingly insistent demands for relief, I removed the next items from the box, buckling the black ankle-strap sandals onto Evan's slender feet.

Sitting back on my heels, I gazed up in awe at the vision my lover made, his lithe body encased in silk and lace, his eyes dark with passion beneath the sultry outlines of kohl. "You are so beautiful," I breathed, burning his image into my memory. "I wish I were an artist and could paint you, or a photographer so I could capture the way you look right now."

"You make me beautiful," he whispered, "what I feel for you is beautiful ... make love to me, Mac, please...."

He tugged at my shoulders until I rose and seized my mouth, kissing me passionately. He tasted of lipstick and champagne and every sweet thing I'd ever savored. Our hips rocked together, finding a rhythm that pressed us together constantly, fanning the conflagration that burned between us. Only when Evan reached again for the waist of my slacks did I regain enough awareness to stop him.

"Please," he whimpered, "want you, want you to fuck me...."

"Oh, I will, baby," I panted, fighting for control over my own spiraling desire. "I will, but there's so much I want to do to you first...."

I pushed him gently back onto the seat and knelt between his legs. Lifting one of his sandal-clad feet, I brought it to my mouth, lapping at the polished toes that peeped through the gossamer lace. Evan had shown me, our very first time together, how erogenous feet could be, and I re-taught him that lesson now, sucking each toe into my mouth, tracing the straps of the sandals with my tongue, thrusting into the hollow of his instep. I licked and nipped my way up his ankle, following the circumference of the leather band that encircled it, then kissed a slow path up his leg, laving his skin through the openings in the lace.

When I reached the top of the stocking, high up his thigh, I paused, spending long moments tracing and re-tracing the lacy border, delving beneath it to taste his skin directly, until Evan was trembling steadily beneath my mouth. Then I repeated the entire amorous journey up his other leg. Evan whimpered and gasped, his fists clenching and unclenching at his sides as my ministrations drove him higher and higher.

Once I had lavished equal attention on each limb, I straightened and pulled Evan forward, so my mouth could reach the top of corset where it hugged his smooth chest. He rocked his pelvis against my stomach as I echoed the trails I had traced on his thighs over the lacy corset-top, using my thumbs to tease his nipples to diamond-hard points. When he cried out my name, I lowered my mouth to engulf first one and then the other, soaking the diaphanous fabric with my saliva as I suckled him through it. His cock leaked a ring of pre-come onto my trousers, adding to my own wetness.

"God, Mac, please," he whispered brokenly as my hands slid up and down the line of the corset-ribs, moving lower on each stroke but never trespassing below the hem. "Please, oh god, please...."

"Please what, baby?" I asked him, slowly kissing my way down the center of his chest, nipping at each spot where a silken flower adorned the dampening lace. "Tell me what you want me to do to you...."

He canted his hips with abandon, rubbing himself against me shamelessly. "Your mouth ... want it ... on me ... Mac, please...."

Dropping back to my heels, my mouth returned to the tops of his stockings, but this time I traced a path upward, drawing the flat of my tongue on either side of the thin line of his garters, sliding beneath them when I reached the top to follow the crease where his leg and hip met. He was undulating constantly now, trying to force the contact he craved.

"Please, Mac ... aahhh ... lick me ... suck me, please...."

"Put your legs on my shoulders, baby," I coaxed him, helping position his sandals against my collarbones, his knees falling apart so he was opened to me completely. We both groaned as I slid my hands from his ankles up the length of each lace-clad leg to cup his buttocks beneath the hem of the corset.

Unable to deny what we both wanted any longer, I buried my face in his crotch, breathing in the fragrance of citrus mixed with musk. I'd debated whether to shave him earlier, remembering how erotic it had felt when he'd shaved me, but I loved the scent and the feel of Evan's curls too much to sacrifice them. I licked and nuzzled my way through his thatch, drinking in the taste of his sweat and pre-come, while my hands gently cradled his heavy sac.

"You taste so fucking good," I moaned, sliding one hand back into the folds of his crease as I sucked his balls into my mouth. He groaned beneath me until I let them slide from my lips and followed the path my fingers had traced with my tongue, lapping over his opening as I teased it with my fingertips. A steady stream of whimpers, interspersed with gasping breaths, fell from Evan's lips as I delved into the hot channel, spreading his cheeks with my hands to let me probe deeper with each thrust of my tongue. My own hips were rocking now, keeping time as I fucked him with my mouth, the friction of the soft cloth against my rock-hard erection nearly enough to bring me off myself.

That wasn't how I wanted to come, though, so I slid two fingers into my mouth, wetting them thoroughly before slipping them inside him as I withdrew my tongue. Curling them until I felt the bump of his prostate, I let my mouth taste his cock at last, licking around the base and in long, wet swipes up its length. Evan was moaning with every breath, writhing against my fingers in an ever-increasing frenzy.

"Fuck, Mac, close … so fucking close … gonna come … please … gonna come…."

"Come for me," I pleaded, my fingers stroking deep inside as my mouth devoured him, licking and biting but never closing around him. "Come for me … come on me…."

With a wailing cry, he stiffened underneath me and then erupted, creamy spurts of come splashing onto my lips and cheeks. Only then did I let my tongue caress the tip of his spasming cock. Dropping his feet from my shoulders, Evan seized me and dragged me up the length of his body, his mouth plundering mine, the come on my face smearing the color from his lips as he lapped it up. I thrust my tongue into his mouth, the kiss hard and deep and wet as I humped against him, desperate now to find my own release.

This time it was his turn to draw back, framing my face in his hands and covering it with small, moist kisses. Panting raggedly, I fought for control over the screaming need to come that wracked me. I groaned harshly when Evan's hands trailed down my chest to reach once again for the waist of my trousers. One hand slid open the tie that held them closed, while the other stroked teasingly over the soaking fabric stretched over my cock.

"Poor Little Mac," he crooned, pushing the slacks over my hips to pool at my feet. "He hasn't been enjoying the party very much yet, has he? And he's the best present I could possibly get."

Evan's pet name for my cock always made me smile. "He's yours," I assured him, sliding back to my knees, "always, any way you want to use him...."

A sense of rightness filled me as I spoke the words. This was a gift I hadn't thought to give, but seeing the flare in Evan's eyes, I suddenly knew it was one I wanted to offer. I bowed my head and knelt quietly, ignoring the ache between my legs, holding my breath as I waited for Evan's response.

His hand lifted my chin gently, a look of wonder suffusing his face. "Just knowing you trust me enough to offer that to me means so much," he whispered, his thumb caressing my cheek. I could feel the love between us like a physical connection, a chain of gold that linked his heart and mine. "Some day, yeah?" he murmured, drawing me back up against him, "but not today ... I'm enjoying your pampering me too much to want you to stop."

My cock, free of all restraints at last, surged eagerly against Evan, indulging in the contrast of slick silk and raspy lace against its hyper-sensitive skin.

"Tell me what you want, then," I pleaded, my body rocking against his as our mouths melded together again, gasping the words between kisses. "Tell me ... how you ... want me...."

"Fuck me," he moaned against my lips, sucking on my tongue as if he were giving me head. "So deep ... want you ... so deep ... need to ... feel you...."

I let myself glide back down his body, kicking off my slacks after grabbing the lube from the pocket. Kneeling back on my heels, my cock jutted up stiffly, quivering with need. He'd been so patient, really, but as I smoothed a slick handful of gel over its length, that patience reached its end. Luckily, Evan was eyeing me with a predatory hunger that matched my own.

"C'mere, baby," I urged, opening my arms to him. He crawled onto my thighs and straddled me, his hand joining mine around the base of my cock. Shifting until my head nudged against his wet opening, he lowered himself onto me, taking all of me in a single slow stroke that left both of us gasping for breath.

"Oh God, Mac, so good, you feel so fucking good...."

We were both too desperate now for slow and gentle. My fingers dug into Evan's hips as he rode up and down fiercely, clutching my shoulders and biting at my neck. I freed a hand to push his head upward, crushing his swollen, stained mouth against mine. I slammed up into each pump of his hips, the ribs of the corset scraping against my belly, his cock leaking between us where it jutted out from beneath the dampened black lace.

"Never like this ... never ... with anyone else...." he moaned, throwing his head back as his body bowed with the strength of his thrusts.

"Always," I insisted, "...always ... this perfect ... every time ... with you...."

I grabbed Evan's ass and embedded myself in him, rocking in short stabbing jolts as my orgasm roared through me, shaking me with wave after wave of ecstasy. Evan cried out my name and collapsed against my chest, his cock coating my stomach with come, the thick droplets catching in the corset's lacy trim.

I cradled him to my chest as we panted in repletion, stroking his back until our careening heartbeats slowed to a normal rhythm. He turned his head to nuzzle at my chin, working his way toward my mouth. We traded lazy, languorous kisses, still kneeling on the cool marble tiles, until the hard-worked muscles in our legs finally demanded relief.

"This is the best birthday ever," Evan purred as he slid off me slowly and helped me to stand.

"And it isn't over yet," I told him, turning him back toward the box that still held the last part of his present. His eyes lit again as he held the long, side-slit skirt against his legs.

"Try it on, babe," I cajoled. "I hope it fits, 'cause I want to take you dancing...."

My cock did its own happy dance as Evan launched himself back into my arms.

UNDERNEATH *the bottle of champagne, padding the bottom of the basket, was a thick, soft terry-cloth mitt. "Use this for washing ONLY!" said the note pinned to the wristband. I guess Evan didn't trust me with the rest of that particular treatment....*

CLING WRAP

"FRENCH Body Gommage."

Evan's words caught me completely by surprise. I looked up from my current obsession with the hollow between his neck and collarbone with a startled frown. "Say what?"

"French Body Gommage," Evan repeated. "That's what I'm going to do to you. It's an exfoliating body rub." He leered at me most intently. "Just think about it, Mac. My hands rubbing over every inch of your skin for over an hour. I know you'd like that." He prodded me to sit on the edge of the table and settled on my lap. "It would feel so good."

Evan's hands on me in any way whatsoever sounded pretty damn fantastic. If I had to put up with some herbal-smelling goop as part of the package, well, that was fine with me. I'd been away on location shooting for weeks, and while we spent every night on the phone with each other, my own hands never gave me a tenth of the pleasure Evan's did. Besides, the sun and wind at the desert camp had been pretty brutal – my skin probably *could* use some exfoliating. I snorted as I realized how much my lover's fascination with personal care had begun to infect me.

Evan took my silence for consent and stood, pulling me to my feet as well. "Strip," he ordered, going to the cabinet where he kept all his supplies. My eyes followed him hungrily. We'd been apart too long and not back together long enough for me to let him out of my sight any time soon. I did as he said, though, beginning to unbutton my flannel shirt and jeans. Getting naked sounded pretty damn good, too.

I watched him stretch and bend to gather the things he needed, his every move elegant and graceful, and gave thanks once again to whatever god watched over B-movie actors for blessing me with my priceless lover. A particularly deep bend stretched the softly clinging material of his charcoal grey slacks over the delectable curves of his ass, and my cock was quick to signal its appreciation of the view. "Does getting naked apply to you, too?" I asked hopefully.

Evan turned back around and grinned at me. "Now, Mr. Kerr," he teased, "it is not the policy of this salon for the employees to have relations with the customers. It's unprofessional." I knew he was joking – we'd had 'relations,' as he put it, the first time I came in – but then his hands moved to the hem of his sweater, pulling it up slowly, and I decided to simply enjoy the pleasure of watching his olive skin come into view.

"I'd hate for you to be unprofessional," I agreed, licking my lips as I caught a glimpse of the rising sun tattoo that was such an uncanny counterpart to my own moon and star tat. Evan had insisted, the first time he'd noticed them, that they meant we were fated to come together. I wasn't sure at the time how we'd make it work – we seemed to be such opposites in every way – but he'd more than convinced me there was no one else I'd rather share my life with. He completed me, soothed me when I was irritated, healed me when I ached. And if he didn't finish taking off his clothes and do something about the ache he was causing right now, I was going to take matters into my own hands.

Fortunately, Evan seemed to feel the same way, because his pants hit the floor only a second behind his sweater, leaving him wearing nothing but a tiny g-string. I raised my eyebrow at that, but he just smirked at me. "Lie down on the table," he said firmly. I almost obeyed, but decided I needed a kiss first. Walking over to where he was standing, I cupped his cheeks between my hands, angling his head so I could close my lips over his, mating our mouths the way we had already mated our hearts.

Evan let me control the kiss for a heady moment before a slap on my ass reminded me firmly who was in charge here. "I said lie down," he ordered me again, pulling away from my arms and pushing me toward the linen-covered treatment table. I lowered myself onto the decadently soft sheets, adjusting my position on the headrest, while my cock grumbled about being flattened beneath my body. A mental image of a spa table with a strategic hollow to accommodate a raging hard-on flashed through my lust-addled brain, and I couldn't help but chuckle at the idea.

I could hear Evan moving around in the room, bottles clinking as he finished his preparations. Then his hands were on my shoulders, spreading a thick, gritty cream onto my body. It felt incredible on my dry skin, like a sip of water after a long day of filming. I could swear I felt my skin absorbing the moisture immediately. Little by little, he worked his way down my back, the thick layer of lotion heavy on my flesh.

"This is gommage," he explained as he coated me in the aromatic paste. It smelled fresh, like some kind of herbs mixed with citrus. "It's made with natural plant extracts, kaolin, and macadamia oil. Gommage means 'erasure' in French – it erases the damage that exposure to sun and the elements does to your skin." He paused to drop a moist kiss on the tanned strip at the back of my neck. "The clay helps slough off the top layer of skin cells, and the oils rehydrate the new layer underneath. It's going to leave your skin incredibly smooth and supple." Yeah, whatever – as long as it involved his hands on my body, it was all good with me.

Once he had spread the cream over every exposed inch of my skin, he began to massage it in, using deep, circular rubbing motions. Starting with my arms, he stroked and circled until the cream was fully absorbed, working his way from my fingers and palms, up my forearms and biceps, and higher still to my shoulder-blades, lingering over the spots, like the insides of my elbows, that were especially sensitive. Then he repeated the same sweet torture on my legs, caressing toes, insteps, ankles, calves, knees, thighs, until I was quivering in the hope of where he would put his hands next.

I almost asked. I wanted to ask. I wanted his hands on my ass, kneading the skin there, giving it the same loving treatment he had given the rest of my body. Before I could voice the request, his hands were there, smoothing over my butt, rubbing the cream into skin that rarely saw the sun – certainly not in the desert – but that didn't seem to matter. He lingered there as he had lingered everywhere else. My cock was throbbing against the sheets again, especially when a gritty finger teased along my cleft and over my hole. My whole body clenched at that touch, and a moan escaped my lips.

I couldn't help but push up into that tantalizing caress, but I knew my lover too well by now to expect that he was ready to end my torment so soon. The finger slid away as his hands started to work their way up my back, leaving my cock to call him every rude name its aching little head could think of. "Tease," I hissed as he straddled me to reach my deltoids, his ass pressing down on mine as he let me feel his weight settling against me.

"Mercilessly," Evan agreed, rubbing his silk-covered erection into my crease. I pushed back against him, only to feel another firm smack dissuading me. "Not with this cream on you," he cautioned. "The grains that exfoliate your skin would really hurt if I made love to you now." He lifted up a little. "Turn over."

He raised his hips just enough to let me roll onto my back. I groaned as my cock, ecstatic at being freed from captivity, sprang up eagerly, rubbing itself against the front of the sinfully abbreviated sack that covered him. To both our dismay, he slid away from the contact to scoop up another handful of the thick exfoliant cream.

"Just relax," he told me. "Let me see to the rest of you." My eyes drifted shut as his hands started at my neck and worked lower, covering me in the thick lotion, not rubbing it in yet, just letting it rest on my skin. My abs tightened as his hands spread the gel over my stomach, coasting to the very edge of my curls before moving away to work down my legs. I groaned in protest, my cock twitching in its bid for attention.

"I can't use any of this on Little Mac," Evan told me in a sympathetic voice, though I could see the mischief dancing in his dark chocolate eyes. "The skin there is too sensitive, the abrasives in the gommage would tear him up." Despite my cock's insistence that it was tough enough to take it, I knew Evan was right, so I tried to will myself to patience while he continued massaging the rest of my skin. My success was sketchy at best – my cock was leaking a steady thread of fluid down its length before he finally worked in the last of the cream.

Reaching for a damp towel on the cart next to the table, Evan wiped his hands free of the exfoliant and squirted liquid from another bottle into his hand. "This, on the other hand," he said with a smirk, "is perfect for Little Mac." And with no other warning than that, he circled my cock in his hand and subjected it to the same thorough massage he'd given the rest of me. I couldn't help it. I bucked up into his hand frantically.

Threading my hands into the tangle of curls I loved so much, I pulled him down into a hard kiss, moaning into his mouth as the smooth friction of his hand brought me the fierce pleasure I craved. My own cream pulsed over my stomach as he continued to stroke me gently, as if he were rubbing that into my skin, too.

"Feel better?" Evan asked me, laughter tingeing his voice. I managed a weak nod. "Good, because that was just the first stage of this treatment." He reached over to the cart again and came back with a thick glove that he slid over his right hand. Coaxing me onto my stomach, he set his hand on my shoulder, letting me feel the heavy nap of the cloth. Then he started to rub, the thick cloth gently scrubbing the gommage against my skin.

It's a good thing he'd let me come already, or I would have done it even without his hand on my cock. The soft nub of the mitt felt so good smoothing over my skin, especially when he rolled me on my back again and focused his attention on my chest, rubbing the mitt over my nipples until they were as hard as the river stones he'd used on me once before. By the time he reached my abdomen, the slow circle of his hand had brought my erection back to demanding life. And this time, I promised it, I wouldn't be coming alone.

Except that his hand avoided my erection, yet again. I knew it was because the mitt was covered in the gritty lotion, but that didn't stop my desire to feel the cloth on my eager flesh. I was just about to ask if he had another one of those gloves when he stopped touching me entirely and got up off the table. "Evan?" I asked softly.

"Into the shower," he replied with a leer as he removed the mitt and offered me his hand.

I followed him into the sybaritic shower area that adjoined the treatment rooms, gathering up an armful of thick towels as Evan adjusted the water temperature in one of the stalls. Since it was after hours, there was no possibility we'd be disturbed, so I had no hesitancy in pulling him inside the spacious cubicle with me before closing the etched-glass door. "No more teasing," I growled, backing him against the tiled wall and holding him there with the weight of my body as I kissed him thoroughly, plundering his mouth with the insatiable need to taste him.

Evan returned the kiss, and I could feel his cock pressing against mine as I rubbed demandingly against him. Reaching down, I tore at the g-string he still wore, pulling it off and baring his erection. He indulged me for a moment, then pulled away and angled my back into the water. "After we get you clean," he declared firmly, his hands renewing their journey over every inch of my skin.

I relented long enough to let Evan rinse the last of the gommage cream from my body. Whatever was in that stuff, I had to admit it had done an incredible job. Evan's hands slid almost frictionlessly over me as he angled me this way and that under the water. It felt as if my skin had gained a million new nerve endings, every one of them tingling with electricity at my lover's touch.

When I didn't think I could stand it a minute longer, I pushed him back against the wall and dropped to my knees, reaching behind him to grasp his butt cheeks and pull him to my face.

Evan let out a most gratifying moan when I buried my nose in the dripping curls around his cock. I sucked him into my mouth, eager for the taste of him again. My hands closed around his hips, holding him in place as I licked up and down the hard flesh and then between his legs to tongue his sac. I couldn't get enough of his taste, and it seemed he couldn't get enough of my mouth, because his fingers clutched at my hair, urging me closer.

Needing to make him half as needy as he'd made me, I let my fingers play up and down his crack, following the trail of water that ran from his back. The increased tugs at my hair told me it was working, so I refined my touch to just tease around his puckered hole. When I felt him clenching under my fingers every time I slid over it, I worked in the tip of one finger, just enough to push through the tight ring of muscle.

He obviously liked that, if the muffled moan he let out was any indication. Encouraged, I pushed in a little farther, hoping the water running freely over us would provide sufficient lubrication. I certainly didn't want to return all the pleasure he'd given me with anything that even began to resemble pain.

Sucking as much of Evan's slender shaft as I could into my mouth, I probed with my finger for that little knob of nerves that would short all his circuits. I was so focused on these two extremely pleasant tasks that I was caught off guard when Evan suddenly pulled out of my mouth. I would have fallen on my ass if he hadn't grabbed me by the shoulders and pulled me back to my feet.

"As wonderful as your mouth feels," he told me, dropping playful kisses on the corners of my lips, "I don't want to come down your throat. I want to come buried in your tight, hot ass. If that's all right with you?"

All right with me? As wonderful as Evan feels filling my throat, he feels even better filling my ass. "You're the professional," I agreed, turning to lean against the shower wall in eager anticipation.

Those well-loved, pampered, deceptively strong hands ran down my back to part my cheeks. I couldn't see what he was using for lube, but his fingers were slick when they started to toy with me as I had been toying with him. I pushed back against his probing, hungry for his touch. He obliged me instantly, a sign that he was as desperate to come as I was. That was good. I didn't know how much longer I could wait, and I really, really wanted him to come with me this time.

I wasn't the only one who knew just what buttons to push on my lover – with just a few swipes of those talented fingers, Evan had me all but gibbering. My cock thumped against the slick tile wall as I squirmed against him, telling me firmly that fingers were no longer enough. "Please, baby," I moaned, too far gone to wait any longer. "Just fuck me, already."

Almost immediately, the fingers were gone and the head of his cock was bumping against my hole. "Yes," I hissed, pushing back against him, wanting him inside me. He steadied me with his hands on my hips and pushed inside. "Oh, God, angel, fuck, please," I babbled nonsensically. All that made sense to me in that moment was his cock inside me again after so long.

Bracing myself with one hand against the shower wall, I reached behind me with the other, grabbing his ass cheek and pushing him even deeper inside. I wanted to feel every long, hard inch of him inside me, filling up all the emptiness of our weeks apart. Evan must have felt the same way, because he wrapped an arm around my chest and pounded into me, so strongly that I rocked into the wall with each powerful thrust.

As much as I hated to let go, I needed to brace myself or I was going to get hurt. Putting both hands back on the tile, I spread my legs a little more to give Evan better access. His rhythm never faltered. If anything, it picked up speed, as if knowing how I felt. "Touch me," I begged, needing his hands on my cock to help me come.

His teeth fastened on the spot on my neck, just below my ear, that he'd long since discovered was extra sensitive to his mouth. I could tell by the erratic rasp of his breath and the unsteady rhythm of his fist around my cock that he was nearly as ready to blow as I was. I squeezed my internal muscles around him, even harder when the deep moan vibrating against my back told me it was working. "I'm so fucking close," I panted, trying to hold off just a little longer. "Come on, baby, come with me, come on...."

He did. He slammed into me twice more, hitting my prostate as he bit down on my neck and squeezed my cock. Then I could feel him flooding me, hot and wet inside my hole. With a shudder, I came in long, ropy spurts, coating the wall in front of me.

Feeling boneless and pretty damn wonderful, I leaned my weight against the cool tiles of the shower, Evan's body plastered against my back. "That treatment wasn't too bad," I mumbled contentedly. "Guess you can add it to the 'keeper' list." To be honest, there weren't many of Evan's 'treatments' that hadn't made the list – even the ill-fated attempt at an Egyptian mud facial had had its redeeming moments.

"We're not done yet," Evan replied, kissing my neck. "I still have to put the moisturizer on your skin." Before meeting Evan, I would have scoffed, but now, the thought of his hands smoothing more potions onto my skin bothered me not at all. I had long since learned to enjoy his pampering – and the lovemaking which seemed to be an inevitable after-effect.

"I'm not going to smell like a fruit salad again, am I?" I asked, turning to rest my back against the wall and take him into my arms. The moisturizer could wait for another few minutes, while I took advantage of the opportunity to hold and kiss my alluring lover for the first time in far too many weeks. "The last one you used attracted every bee in a twenty-mile radius."

Evan laughed and lounged against me. "I promise not to use anything fruity," he replied, nipping at my lower lip. "This one smells like sandalwood. I think you'll like it." He pulled back and tugged on my hand. "I'll even let you smell it first, and if you don't like it, I'll get another one."

With a show of reluctance that Evan knew was only an act – after all, my cock was already half-hard again just from our few minutes of languid kisses – I let him lead me out of the shower, wrap me in one of the spa's amazingly thick and soft towels, and guide me back to the treatment room. "How's this?" he asked, waving the cap from a bottle of lotion under my nose. "It's made with aloe, shea butter, jojoba and sandalwood oils."

I sniffed at the bottle, surprised at the masculine smell. This was no woman's brew. "Did you get this for me?" I asked. I grabbed the bottle and poured a little onto my hand. It was thick and creamy, but when I rubbed it into my palm, it absorbed right away. I started to pour some more when Evan snatched the bottle back. "That's my job," he told me imperiously.

"I love it when you get all demanding," I told him archly, fluttering my eyelashes at him. He laughed and pushed me back down onto the table, letting his towel drop to the floor as he began to smooth the lotion onto my legs. My laughter changed to a low rumble of pleasure as his touch became firmer. With each stroke of his warm palms, nerve endings that had calmed in the aftermath of our shower re-awoke to tingling life.

He worked his way up my legs and over my hips, deliberately ignoring my reawakening cock as he spread the lotion further up my chest and down my arms. By the time he had finished with my front, I was as hard as I'd been before my first climax. It never ceased to amaze me how easily he could rouse me. All it took was a look, a touch, and I had a raging hard-on that only he could ease. This time was no different.

My cock protested mightily when Evan motioned me to roll over so he could reach my back. There was no way it was going to put up with being flattened a second time, not as hard as that sensuous massage had made it. "You're going to have to do me like this, baby," I teased him, settling onto my knees and elbows but leaving my ass poking up in the air. "Either that or get some more comfortable tables."

To my delight, Evan leaned forward and ran his tongue up the cleft of my ass in a long, loving lick. "I'll do you like this anytime," he assured me. I pushed back, wanting more from his tongue, but he had pulled away and was rubbing lotion into the rest of my skin. I moaned in half-hearted protest, knowing he wouldn't leave me hurting for too long.

Sooner than I would have liked – as much as I pretend to protest, I never get enough of Evan's hands on my body – he was wiping them on a towel and putting away the lotion. But instead of handing me a robe – or, better yet, joining me on the table – Evan turned to a counter at the other side of the room. He opened a door, and a cloud of aromatic steam poured out, filling the room with a fresh, herbal scent. When he turned back to me, his arms were filled with warm, steaming sheets.

"The last step is an herbal linen wrap," he told me, setting the sheets on the bottom of the table. "The cloth is steeped in organic herbs to relieve tension and draw toxins from the body. The heat will make your pores open so you can absorb all the moisturizer." He patted the surface of the treatment table, encouraging me to lie back down. "I promise it will be the most relaxing half-hour you've spent all week."

"Oh no, you don't," I protested. "If you're swaddling me up like a baby, you're getting in there with me."

He quirked an eyebrow at me. "Now why would I do that?" he teased.

"Because I can't think of a way I'd rather spend half an hour than holding you in my arms," I answered, opening mine to him in invitation. He stepped into them and I closed them around him, marveling as I always did how perfectly he fit against me. I kissed my way up his throat to nuzzle at the shell of his ear. "Come on, baby. Wrap us up together."

Evan hesitated for a minute, considering the practicalities, before reaching for the sheets. "This won't work on the treatment table. It's too narrow," he protested, looking around the room. "Maybe on the couch?"

I eyed the couch suspiciously. "Doesn't look any wider than the table to me," I answered, though we could use the floor for all I cared, as long as I could hold my angel in my arms. Evan's face fell into one of his adorable pouts, making me grin. "Guess you'll just have to lie on top of me, baby."

That brought the impish smile back to my lover's face. He opened the sheets, one on top of another, and stood back. "Lie down then so I can climb on," he urged.   I didn't hesitate, stretching out on the smooth, scented sheets, the table supporting my body perfectly. I opened my arms again, waiting for Evan to join me. He did, moving to straddle me first, then settling atop me until we were perfectly aligned from head to toe. He reached down and pulled the sheets up over us, tucking them tightly around us to swaddle us in their herbal warmth.

For a minute or two, both of us were content to just lie there, soaking in the warmth of the fragrant linens. Before long, though, the inevitable result of Evan's body molding to mine made itself apparent. My cock nudged against his as I nuzzled his neck, working my way toward the nectar of his mouth. "Turn your head," I urged him, "so I can kiss you properly."

He did as I asked immediately, angling his head so our lips met in a tender kiss that quickly turned heated. As our lips moved in concert, I could feel his cock swelling against mine. At least I wasn't the only one affected. Then I felt his hands shift, moving over the skin of my thighs, tracing small, teasing circles.

Having my arms and legs immobilized by the tightly wrapped sheet had some definite disadvantages. Not being able to pull Evan against me as I tried to deepen our kiss was one of them. Squirming underneath him, I was able to move my legs an inch or so further apart, which had the happy side effect of bringing our cocks into even closer contact. We drank in each other's moans at the sweet friction as they pressed together. Managing to wiggle one hand free inside our cocoon, I slid it up my leg, picking up as much moisturizer on my fingers as I could along the way.

I worked my arm around Evan's body, one destination in mind. He had loved me thoroughly in the shower. It was time to return the favor. Fortunately, he seemed willing to abet in his seduction, moving his legs enough to part the sweet cheeks of his ass for me. It was a good thing, too. As tightly wrapped as we were, I wasn't sure I could have freed my other hand to help. Rubbing the lotion into his skin, I pushed at his hole, trying to work my way inside.

Evan's hips rocked against mine as I gently eased my finger into the puckered opening. He couldn't move much, and neither could I, making every touch more sensual, more arousing. A droplet of sweat trickled down his temple as I slowly worked my finger inside him. Unable to resist, I released his lips to catch it on my tongue, tracing its path to capture every hint of my lover's flavor.

"Now who's teasing?" he asked me hoarsely, leaning into my lips and trying to push his hips back against my finger. I just smiled at him. Turn-about's fair play, after all.

"You're the one who insisted on thirty minutes in this wrap," I reminded him. "Have you changed your mind?"

He hesitated, clearly considering his reply. "No," he said finally. "The treatment doesn't work nearly as well if you don't spend your time wrapped up in the sheets."

"Well then," I declared. "Don't complain."

It wasn't often I was able to render Evan speechless, so before he could think up a suitable retort, I kissed him again, circling and stretching my finger until the tip found the nub of his prostate. *Pay dirt!* His entire body stiffened against me, increasing the subtle pressure on our cocks. Flexing my knuckle minutely, I rubbed over the sensitive bundle of nerves, each pass making him tremble and whimper against my mouth.

Of course, every tremble pushed him harder against me, every whimper went straight to my cock until I felt like whimpering, too. I tore my lips away from Evan's long enough to look at the clock. "It's been thirty minutes, baby," I moaned. "Get us out of here. I want inside you."

I knew Evan was as desperate as I was when the sheets hit the floor almost before the words were out of my mouth. Kicking the last of the wrappings free from our legs, Evan reached down and grabbed my cock, pushing up onto his knees to put his ass within reach. Pulling my finger away impatiently, he aligned the head of my cock with his quivering hole. "Fuck me," he demanded, "right now. Fuck me hard."

What's a man supposed to do when his sexy-as-sin lover is demanding a good reaming? My answer was to give it to him. I flipped us over, just managing not to land us both on the ground,

and pulled my knees up under me, giving me the leverage I needed
to pound into him unrestrainedly. He met every thrust with a solid
one of his own, reassuring me that he was with me completely.
Despite my earlier orgasms, I wasn't going to last long at this pace.
I snaked a hand between us, searching for his cock so I could take
him with me when I came.

Evan's own hands weren't idle – he'd grabbed my sides
and raised his head so he could reach my chest. When my hand
closed around his shaft, his lips latched onto my nipple, sucking
firmly. I slammed into him so hard that his teeth bit down
instinctively, and that was all it took to make me lose it
completely. My hips jackhammered against his, my hand fisting
his cock until it erupted between our heaving bodies. With a
hoarse shout, I pumped into him as my orgasm shuddered through
me, filling him until we both collapsed into a sweaty, sated heap on
the crumpled sheets.

Somehow, I found the strength to roll onto my side to keep
from crushing Evan beneath me. He pillowed his head against my
chest and sighed in blissful satisfaction. "So, did you like your
treatment?" he purred.

Resting my chin against his damp curls, I nodded, content
to simply snuggle with my lover, passion spent for the moment.
Knowing I had this to come back to – Evan's care, Evan's love –
made leaving each time just a little bit easier to bear. "I loved it,
but I'm never going to be able to hear a director say 'That's a
wrap' again without getting hard."

THERE were only two items left in the basket. The first was a small black velvet bag. I opened it and spilled the contents onto my palm – two small pieces of jewelry, slender barbells surrounded by the stylized images of a golden sun and a silver moon. 'We're going to share these, baby,' I promised my lover as I curled my hand around them, imagining the sun shining against his honeyed flesh.

CHAIN REACTION

"YOU ever consider getting pierced, Mac?"

Since Evan had pulled my cock out of his mouth to ask, I think I can be forgiven the shudder that ran through me at the question.

"I didn't mean Little Mac," Evan laughed (what can I do? he insists on calling it that), stroking soothingly over its saliva-coated length. It signaled its appreciation of the sensual massage by adding a dribble of pre-come to further lubricate his talented hand.

The ostensible reason that had brought me to the salon that morning was to let Evan color my hair. Over the years I've had to change colors so often for various roles that I can hardly remember what the natural shade looks like any more. Since I'd be playing a killer-for-hire in my next film, the collar-length locks and heavy moustache I'd grown for the Western I'd just finished shooting needed to go too. I'd worked with David – the director – before, and he'd left it up to me to decide how my character would wear his hair. "As long as you don't show up still looking like Snidely Whiplash," he'd added, twirling the end of my 'stache.

I'd honestly been leaning toward just getting a number three buzz to be done with it. I hate having to sit for hours in a styling chair – as far as hair is concerned, my favorite role ever had been when I'd played a Marine drill instructor, since I'd had practically none to bother with. When I brought up the idea to Evan, though, you'd have thought I'd suggested cutting off his own hair instead. (Which is something I'd never do – I love being able to bury my hands in his long dark curls while I bury my cock in his hot, tight ass.)

"Vic's a stone cold killer, right? Trust me, he'd rather be caught dead himself than wear his hair like that," Evan had protested. Before I knew it, he'd talked me into letting him come up with the perfect hairstyle for the modern urban hit-man.

The 'stache was the first to go. To my cock's considerable regret, my personal stylist was so eager to get his hands on my hair that he didn't even look for the straight razor, let alone suggest we get naked to shave me. As traumatized as my little head had been the first time Evan casually whipped out a six-inch length of sharpened steel, I thought it was pretty funny that it was pouting now at his taking off my 'stache with a few quick swipes of an electric shaver instead.

Next thing I knew, Evan had wrapped a cape around me and was running his hands through my hair, humming consideringly. Since meeting Evan, I'd discovered that my scalp is a definite erogenous zone. Of course, since meeting Evan I'd discovered that practically any part of my body is an erogenous zone if he's the one touching it. I leaned back into the chair, spreading my legs to give my balls some room to move inside my jeans.

"I'll leave you brown, I think, but take you a couple of shades lighter, maybe add a little bit of red to warm it up," he mused, his long fingers massaging my skull.   He could have suggested coloring it in rainbow stripes and I would have agreed, as long as he didn't stop rubbing my head. "And then frost the tips to give it some contrast. How does that sound?"

"Feels – sounds wonderful," I mumbled, slumping lower in the chair and wondering if it would be rude to unzip my jeans and have a quick whack off while Evan was mixing up the color. He must have been reading my mind again, though the bulge against my zipper was a pretty obvious give-away, because he gave my hard-on a quick squeeze and wagged a finger in my face. "None of that, now. Tell Little Mac to behave and I promise I'll make it up to him later."

"Like he ever listens to anything I tell him," I complained, but I tried to distract myself from imaging how Evan was planning to "make it up later" by working on creating a back story for Vic instead. Once Evan started painting the thick color onto my hair a strand at a time, it was a toss-up whether the sensuality of his rhythmic touch could offset the acrid chemical smell of the dye. I had high hopes once he'd finished applying the color – even daubing some carefully onto each eyebrow – that enough time had passed to be considered 'later', but he only wrapped a plastic baggie over my head and rolled over a contraption that looked like one of those 1950's helmet dryers but turned out to emit steam instead. "Ten minutes under this to set the color, then I'll wash it out and style you before I do the tips," he advised me.

I'd come up with an entire life history for my character by the time Evan declared himself satisfied and let me look at the new me in the mirror. I had to admit that the short, spiky style he'd come up was exactly the way I'd begun to imagine Vic – tough, hip, and definitely cutting-edge.   I let myself slip into the character's headspace a little bit, trying on the persona to see how it fit the image staring back at me.

"As often as I've seen you do that, I still can't get used to it," Evan murmured over my shoulder. "I swear your eyes have changed color."

Vic's hard, flat killer stare took in Evan's slender form, the willowy allure of his frame accented by his dark parachute pants and gauzy white shirt, sheer enough that his tawny nipples showed clearly on either side of the suspender straps. A surge of pure lust, raw and urgent, took control of me. I started to reach for him, to rip open that shirt and bite those taunting nipples 'til they bled, to slam him against the wall and fuck him until one of us passed out – and it sure as fuck wouldn't be me.

Evan took an instinctive step back and the moment was gone. I inhaled roughly and dragged my hand over my face, trying to wipe away Vic's taint. For once, I was glad this was a location shoot – I wasn't going to be a pleasant person to be around until filming was over.

"Sorry, babe," I shook my head ruefully, running a hand through my damp hair. "Afraid Vic's kind of an asshole."

"Under the right circumstances, he might be interesting," Evan retorted, though I noticed he was still clutching the styling scissors like a weapon. He chuckled when he noticed the direction of my gaze. "At least we know the look is right."

"It's perfect, baby," I told him, wrapping him in my arms as soon as he'd laid the scissors on the styling table. "David is going to love it."

Evan nuzzled a kiss against the newly bared side of my neck and drew back, his nose crinkled adorably. "You're covered with little bits of hair, and I reek of chemicals. I think a shower's in order for both of us."

"Sounds like a plan," I agreed immediately.

After the time Evan's assistant manager, Jordan, had walked in on us as I was doing my best to fuck his boss through the wall of one of the spa's showers, Evan had installed a private unit adjacent to his office. The glass-and-cedar enclosure was nearly as large as the entire bathroom in my first apartment, with dozens of shower heads lining the walls and ceiling that could be set to anything from steam to hydromassage to tropical rain forest. It had built in heaters, a chromatherapy lighting system, and a pair of wide cedar benches that could be folded down to form a king-size platform. Right now the benches were folded out of the way against the walls, leaving plenty of room for both of us (and for half a dozen of the salon's customers too, if either of us had been the type to share, which we weren't). We were so happy with the luxurious shower that Evan had installed a couple of smaller units in the spa itself, where they'd become so popular they'd quickly paid for themselves and our private retreat as well.

I had my clothes off before the office door closed behind us, but Evan was rooting around in the cabinets next to the shower enclosure with a look on his face reserved for only the most important of concerns, like...

"Stress relief scalp treatment," he purred, retrieving a bottle from the crowded shelves. I'd learned it didn't pay to argue with Evan when it came to treatments – it was easier just to give him his head, since he was usually more than willing to return the favor. I snuggled behind him, letting my cock nudge his ass by way of reminder as I bent over his shoulder to sniff at the product. "Smells okay ... what is it?"

"A blend of essential oils – lavender, chamomile, ylang ylang and sandalwood – to relax you and eliminate tension, with almond and jojoba oils to strengthen your hair and restore the moisture the coloring chemicals strip from your scalp." I tended to zone out while Evan rattled off the properties of whatever gunk he planned to use on me, but it was going to have to be some powerful shit to relax the hard-on I was developing just from the rise and fall of his body against mine as he spoke.

"Do you have to be naked to use it?" I prompted hopefully, working at the fastening of his trousers.

"I'll apply it out here, then let you sit in the steam for fifteen minutes or so to help it absorb," he countered, stepping out of my embrace and guiding me to a seat on the antique fainting couch he'd moved into a corner of his office. It was a deceptively sturdy piece of furniture, as we'd proven on more than one occasion, but it didn't seem like this was going to be one of them as Evan poured a handful of oil into his palm, working his hands together before starting to massage the concoction onto my head.

I may have said it before, but Evan has magic hands. His strong fingers drew tiny circles all over my scalp, turning my muscles into putty and my cock into an iron bar leaking against my thigh. I had to clench my fists to keep from reaching for it, or for him, but even biting my lip couldn't prevent the low moans of bliss from escaping as he worked his way down the back of my skull. This put his chest directly in front of my face, and I couldn't resist the temptation to nip at the dark nipple peeking at me saucily. Evan's fingers faltered and I suckled the tip into my mouth, leaving a wet ring against the sheer fabric of his shirt.

"I think it's time to get naked now," Evan agreed hurriedly, wiping his hands on a towel before slipping the suspender straps off his shoulders and kicking off his pants. As usual, he wasn't wearing any boxers underneath them. He started to unbutton the shirt, but I stopped him, entranced by how transparent the damp material had become. "Leave it on?" I asked, rising to my feet and leading him into the already steam-filled enclosure.

My imagination wasn't disappointed – it only took a few seconds in the thick steam to plaster the gauzy fabric to his torso. I can't tell you why I found the idea of that so erotic, but it brought me to my knees, feasting on his olive skin through the wet cloth until he was so hard his cock was poking me in the chest. Before I could turn my attentions lower, Evan pulled me to my feet and adjusted the controls to turn the water to a warm, gentle spray that caressed us from all directions. He rinsed the last of the oil out of my hair and then sank down gracefully himself, proving once again that his mouth was even more talented than his fingers by giving me the blow job of my life.

Until he asked that question about piercing.

"I didn't mean Little Mac," Evan repeated, using his nearly-as-talented hands on my suddenly softened cock until he'd restored it to stony hardness.

"I was thinking something a little higher up," he added, nipping his way across my wet abdomen (after a brief pause to leave a love-bite over my moon-and-star tattoo). "Maybe a nipple ring?" His mouth closed over the potential site, biting down to demonstrate what it would feel like.

We'd already experimented some using clamps, so I had an idea how much a little pain could sensitize me. And I knew David wouldn't mind – it was just the kind of accessory Vic would affect.

I could always take it out when I needed to – it wouldn't leave enough of a mark to be a problem with other roles.

"As long as you get one too," I agreed, a sudden image popping into my mind.

"Matching rings?" Evan purred. "I know that look, lover – what are you thinking?"

"A silver chain connecting us while we make love," I admitted, just the thought of the erotic tugs as we moved nearly enough to make me come in his hand.

"Hold that thought," Evan groaned, pausing to kiss me thoroughly before heading out the glass door of the enclosure. I was relieved to see him replace his sodden shirt with a robe before leaving the office – it was something he'd been known to forget, though I don't think any of his clientele, female or male, would complain about catching a glimpse of that delectable body.

The salon did piercings for both earrings and more intimate spots, but Evan didn't bring back the gun-like device I'd seen used for ear piercings. Instead, he carried a box of latex gloves, a set of clamps that looked more lethal than the ones we'd played with, and several packages of slender needles. After rummaging through the cabinet again to locate a bottle of antiseptic, he seated us side by side on the antique couch.

"If you're sure about this, I'll do you first so you can see how it works, and then you can do me," Evan offered.

I didn't think I'd ever turn down a chance to do Evan, but – "I've never pierced anyone before," I hesitated, unwilling to risk hurting my lover. "Maybe you should get Jordan to – "

"You're the only one I want touching my body, ever," Evan insisted, stilling my protests with a kiss. "Let me show you how easy it is – it'll be over before you know it."

Pulling on a pair of latex gloves (which started my cock hardening again, an idea I wasn't sure I wanted to think about), Evan smiled at me reassuringly. "Left or right?" he asked, pinching both nipples to hardness.

"Left," I answered without hesitation. *Over my heart.* I didn't say the words, but Evan seemed to understand anyway, bending forward to place a soft kiss on the site before cleaning the nipple thoroughly with antiseptic. He positioned the clamp so the pink nub stood erect and immobilized, then opened one of the individually packaged needles. "I'm going from side to side, right here, through the base," he told me, and before I could draw a full breath he had pushed the needle through the skin. I barely felt it – the pressure of the nipple clamp biting into my flesh was far more uncomfortable. Evan threaded a silver ring through a thin plastic tube I hadn't realized surrounded the needle, pulled the needle and tube through, and twisted the ball closure. "All done," he said brightly, disposing of the needle in a sharps container before easing off the clamp and carefully cleaning the area again. He snapped off his gloves, tossed them in the trash and turned back to me with a kiss.

"Doing okay?" he asked.

"Not bad at all," I answered in surprise. I'd expected it to be far more painful than it was.

"That's your endorphins kicking in," he explained. "It'll be sore enough later, I'm afraid. Ready to do mine now?"

With Evan talking me though it, I repeated the process on him, having to grit my teeth to push the needle through his skin. But it was worth it to see the matching silver ring adorning his dark, flat nipple. I was so tempted to lean down and kiss him there, but it probably wasn't the most hygienic idea, so I settled for kissing its rather forlorn looking mate instead. Somehow I had an idea that Evan, at least, wouldn't be wearing only one ring for long.

"I've got some decorative chain we use for belly button piercings," he continued, "though maybe we should wait until you've healed a little...."

"No way," I insisted. I was going to be leaving for filming too soon as it was – there was no chance I'd let an opportunity like this wait. Evan measured several lengths of the fine silver chain before clipping it off, making sure the ends were smooth, and slipping it onto first his ring, then mine.

The gentle tug sent a wave of pure fire burning from my chest straight to my groin. "Fuck, babe," I groaned, "that has to be the sexiest thing I've ever seen." The chain swayed between us in a graceful arc that connected his chest, his heart, to mine.

Moving carefully, Evan guided me to recline onto the couch, following me down to make sure the chain stayed loose. It didn't take much of the gentle friction of our chests rubbing against the new piercings while we kissed before we were both achingly hard. Evan reached to the nearby shelf to grab the lube – I said we'd tested the couch out more than once – and squeezed some of the gel onto his fingers, but I stopped him before he could start to prep himself.

"Make love to me," I asked him, spreading my legs wide and offering myself to him. Evan didn't top often enough to suit me as it was, and the memory of Vic's violent lust still haunted me. I needed to have this image of him kneeling over me, the feeling of him filling me, to carry me through the weeks we'd be apart.

Evan kissed me lingeringly before mouthing a path down my body. The chain was just long enough to let him kneel between my legs, lifting my butt to rim me until I was moaning and stretch me until I was fucking myself on his fingers before finally taking me in a long, slow slide. I draped my legs over his hips and pulled him closer, pushing up each time he drew back to try to keep him buried inside me as deeply as I could hold him. He braced his palms behind himself and leaned back, the chain measuring the space between us as our hips rocked together, the tug on my sensitized nipple and the love in Evan's eyes carrying me over the edge. The warmth of his release filled me and I splashed white streaks all over our bellies, finally pulling him down to lie on top of me with a purr of pure satiation.

"We should shower again before the sweat starts to sting," Evan said eventually. "And we can put an ice pack on it later if it hurts too much. It'll take a couple of weeks to heal completely."

I wasn't worried. If there was pain, it would just remind me of this moment, and by the time I returned from location, we should both be healed enough to do this again.

THE last thing in the basket was a small padded envelope. Inside was a metal dog tag in the shape of a heart. 'Mac' was engraved on it, and underneath, 'If lost, return to Evan York'.

"Just as soon as I can, babe," I promised. "I'm coming home as soon as I can."

DOGGY STYLE

A warm nose bumped my palm, disrupting my sleep and interrupting a dream in which Evan was doing something sinful involving shea butter and avocado-seed-oil body balm to my willing cock. A wet tongue lapped at my fingers, stirring more than just my mind to wakefulness.

"Evan, your damn dog's in the bedroom again," I muttered without opening my eyes. Molly had a bad habit of sneaking in when one of us forgot to close the door securely – we'd caught her more than once curled up at the foot of the bed, stealing an unfair share of the duvet cover. Hoping to slip back into my erotic reverie, I groped around behind me blindly for the interruption's owner, but instead of a warm body my free hand met only cool, rumpled bedsheets.

The raspy tongue moved to the still-sensitive contours of my recently pierced nipple, the surge of pleasure more than enough to seduce my attention from the sensuous dream to an even more vivid reality. Forcing my eyes to open, I saw Evan crouched on all fours next to the bed, his agile tongue teasing my nipple to aching hardness. He was naked except for a rim of kohl around his eyes and an embossed leather collar around his throat. The matching leather leash trailed enticingly over the crease of his delectable ass.

While he was usually the leader – though too rarely (to my taste) the top – in our sexual adventures, Evan had a surprising fondness for playing puppy. After the third time he 'borrowed' Molly's accessories, I'd bought him his own collar and lead from our favorite leather shop, complete with dog tags that proclaimed his name and had my name and phone number engraved under the "If lost, return to" heading.

Evan's mouth moved across my chest to my other nipple, the tags jingling on his collar as he bobbed his head. Rolling onto my back to offer him better access, I sank a hand into his dark curls and gave him a good scratching.

"What do you want, boy?" I asked, smiling at the glow in his warm brown eyes when he lifted his head. "Do you want me to take you for a walk?" Evan panted, wiggling his butt in eager anticipation. "Or better yet, maybe I'll just take you." He nosed my crotch impatiently, making my cock bounce, his meaning as plain as if he'd spoken when he grinned up at me.

"Yeah, Little Mac thinks it's a good idea, but then Little Mac never thinks anything else when you're around," I groaned, rising as his tongue worked its magic on my equally eager cock. When I felt my balls starting to tighten, I pulled him upward into a wet and messy kiss. When he's in puppy headspace, Evan doesn't kiss so much as lick and nip, which is fine with me – I can never get enough of his tongue, no matter how he uses it. His body squirmed against mine as I deepened the kiss, working my tongue into his mouth and holding him still as I tasted him. I'd take a long drink of Evan over my morning coffee any day, and for a caffeine addict like me, that's saying something.

Evan was humping my thigh by the time I'd finally gotten my MDR of his mouth. While my cock was more than ready to move things along, the rest of me was in the mood for some more leisurely lovemaking. "Easy, boy," I soothed them both, petting Evan in long, slow strokes down his back as I turned us onto our sides. Evan whined softly but arched into my touch. My cock wasn't nearly as obedient, but I'd had plenty of experience ignoring its complaints by now.

"Good doggie," I told Evan as I kissed my way down his neck, my palms gently rubbing his belly. I spent a long time tracing the line of the black collar against his elegant throat with my tongue, the scent of the leather and the tang of it against my tongue surprisingly arousing. I wondered if I would find it as arousing if I were in Evan's place. I had no interest in playing puppy myself, but I'd spent more than one lonely night on location wondering what it would be like to wear a collar. I'd never once regretted following Evan's lead as he introduced me to the world of kink, but as mind-blowing as our sexual exploits were, I wanted to offer him more.

Evan pawed at me restlessly, pressing against me until he'd rolled me onto my back again. Straddling my hips, the weight of his body held me down as he lapped long, wet stripes over my chest, his bottom half still wriggling. Watching his toned ass cheeks shimmy from side to side, I wondered if I could find him a butt plug that had a doggy tail attached. Who knows, they probably make them in all different breeds. Yeah right, *cocker cocks*, I thought with a silly grin, which quickly morphed into a moan as Evan rediscovered the nipple ring. His agile tongue swept over it, flipping it back and forth, each movement zinging along my nerve endings. He nuzzled at it with his nose and then nipped it, the not-so-gentle tug just this side of painful.

"No," I told him, swatting him lightly on the butt. "Bad dog, no biting."

Evan's eyes met mine for a moment, a spark of mischief glinting in them before he lowered his head and, very deliberately, bit me again. Harder.

I jerked reflexively, whacking his butt with the leash I still held in my hand. Evan whimpered, lowering himself on his forearms until his face was buried in the middle of my chest, his ass quivering. A pink line ran across one cheek where I'd caught him with the strap. His nose bumped my sternum, his ass poking up higher, sending a message loud and clear – 'more'.

"Are you a bad boy? Do I have to spank you?" I asked, going along with the game but also needing his assurance. This was a kind of play we'd never indulged in before, and I wasn't sure I was completely comfortable with it. But if it was what Evan wanted … I'd never gone wrong yet following his lead.

The sound that escaped was more human moan than puppy whimper, but the urgent bob of his head was unmistakable. Wrapping the slim leather around my fist to the optimal length, I laid a half-dozen stripes across his ass with the wider handle of the strap, not hard enough to break his perfect skin, but enough to raise a couple of fair-sized welts. The smack of the leather was surprisingly loud against his cheeks, and Evan yelped into my chest at each blow, but he didn't try to pull away. His cock had leaked a thick string of pre-come onto my stomach by the time I finished.

"That's enough," I said, dropping the leash and running a gentle hand down his back. His ass cheeks felt hot under my palm. "You'll be good now, won't you?"

Evan whined, lifting his head and lapping at my mouth as hungrily as if it were a bowl of Alpo. I buried a hand into his tousled hair, holding him still for a long, deep kiss. Then I slid from underneath him, pointing down at the pillow before slipping behind him on the bed.

"Stay … good boy, stay…." I crooned as I checked Evan's ass more closely, relieved to see I hadn't done any real damage. His cheeks were a warm pink, the welts where the leash had made contact already fading. Holding his hips, I leaned forward and traced each one gently with my lips, ending with a soft kiss in the dimple at the base of his spine. Evan whimpered loudly, pushing his hips up in a blatant request to be fucked. I might have woken up in the mood for some leisurely lovemaking, but that definitely wasn't what Evan had in mind. Still, I wasn't about to argue with that. My cock certainly wasn't complaining.

"Who's a good boy?" I praised, my probing fingers finding him already lubed and ready for me. I sank into him in one long glide, mating my chest to his back and nuzzling the arc of his ear. Evan hummed his pleasure and pressed back against me eagerly.

"C'mon, baby," I prompted, tightening my grip on the leash. "Let's romp."

If there's anything in the world that feels as good as Evan clenching around me, I haven't found it yet, unless it's being fucked by him in return. Since I'd forgotten to grab more lube from the bedside table, it was a good thing his cock was already leaking steadily as I fisted him. It didn't take more than a few deep thrusts and a few tight strokes before Evan was coming all over my hand. His groan of fulfillment and the way his channel rippled around me as he came wrung a pretty impressive orgasm from me in turn. I was panting as hard as he was by the time we finally collapsed back onto the bed in a tangle of sweaty limbs.

"That was fucking brilliant, love," Evan murmured, arching his neck as I carefully unbuckled the collar. Instead of setting it aside, I ran my fingers over the stylized design. The thought of placing myself completely under Evan's control, of offering him my full and willing permission to use me in whatever ways he wanted, was so arousing that despite just having come, I was already hardening again. "Maybe next time I should be the one wearing this," I suggested.

"I'd pegged you for a pony, not a puppy," Evan said teasingly.

"That's not what I mean," I answered, my voice softening as I bowed my head. "I want to give myself to you – to give you unconditional control."

I could feel Evan tensing in my arms even before I finished speaking. I'd offered something similar once before, on his birthday, but although Evan had brushed aside the gesture at the time, I'd been sure it was because the scene we already had going was enough for us. Now, his uncharacteristic hesitancy made me wonder. We'd said we loved each other, but maybe Evan wasn't willing to make the kind of commitment I was ready for.

"I'm not sure that's a good idea," Evan said quietly.

"Why?" I asked, unable to hide the hurt from my voice. I'd just spanked Evan when he wanted it, even though I wasn't sure about it before we started – couldn't he trust me the same way to know what I wanted? "Don't you think I'm ready? I've taken everything you've ask me to – I've *loved* everything you've shown me," I insisted, forcing him to look at me. "Don't you think I can handle this?"

"It isn't you I'm worried about," Evan protested. "It's me." My gut turned over at his words – every breakup I've ever gone through has started with some variation on the *'it's not you, it's me'* theme. "I mean it, Mac," Evan asserted. "You're the most amazing lover I've ever had. But you're asking for something I don't know how to give." His hand traced the scruffy line of my jaw, and I could feel his fingers trembling.

"I play at kink, but I've never been in a real Dom/sub relationship. I'm not sure how it would work for us. I don't know enough to be sure I wouldn't hurt you."

"You've never hurt me," I argued vehemently. "You never would."

"Not intentionally," Evan countered. "But collaring isn't a game, Mac. You don't understand what you're asking for."

"Then why don't you show me?"

"What if I do something wrong – something that does wind up hurting you?" Evan objected. I pulled him closer, stroking his curls away from where they hid his face. "You mean too much to me to fuck this up, Mac."

"I want this because I trust you," I insisted. "I want to be able to show you how much. We don't have to start with anything heavy – whatever you're comfortable with."

Evan does puppy-dog eyes way better than I can, but I gave it my best shot, staring at him soulfully until he realized what I was doing and broke into laughter. "All right," he agreed finally, "we'll try something. I suppose I owe it to you, after all the treatments you've let me experiment with on you," he teased, ruffling my still-frosted hair.

I sat up and handed him the collar, but he shook his head. "Not yet," he said, setting it on the bedside table. "Let's see how this works before we decide whether we're ready for that."

I was about to press the point when I realized that arguing with your dom wasn't a very submissive thing to do. I took a deep breath, trying to let go of all my tension as I exhaled. "What do you want me to do?" I asked quietly.

Evan thought for a minute, during which I tried to calm myself, breathing evenly and not letting myself speculate on what he might be considering. I trusted that whatever he decided would be good for both of us.

"Lie down on your back, hands over your head, and hold onto the headboard," Evan said finally. I positioned myself as he instructed immediately, my cock already hardening again without even knowing what it was getting itself into. "Whatever happens, don't move unless I tell you to, and don't speak unless I ask you a direct question. Do you understand?"

"Yes," I said huskily, a hot spiral of arousal spreading through my veins. My cock was already standing rigidly at attention – if it could figure out how, it would have saluted.

"Oh, and Mac, no matter what I do to you, don't come until I give you permission."

The sensual promise in Evan's voice alone was enough to make me shiver in anticipation. I knew exactly how seductive my lover could be, and Evan demonstrated it to me again, starting at my feet and pleasuring every centimeter of my body with his touch and his mouth. He had me quivering within minutes, biting my lip to keep any wayward sounds from escaping. Evan had made love to me while I was restrained before, but knowing I was free to touch him but couldn't was even harder to endure. My knuckles whitened around the bedposts as he nibbled his way across my chest, kissing me everywhere except my tightened nipples. I could feel them throbbing in anticipation, could imagine his mouth closing over them, but each time I thought he was going to give me what I ached for, he veered away to nip at another patch of skin, until all I could think of was his hot, wet mouth closing over them.

It was even worse when he started down my abdomen. My cock was already leaking a puddle of fluid in the hollow of my hipbone. As soon as Evan started kissing his way down the same path, it twitched with every movement of his mouth. When he spread my knees apart and began nuzzling at the crease where my thighs joined my torso, I was pleading with him silently to touch me, kiss me, take me into his mouth – anything to relieve the desperate need he'd incited. His tongue flicked over the wrinkled skin between the base of my shaft and my balls, and I nearly arched off the bed in shock. He pulled away immediately, leaving me panting as his attention turned to the inside of my knees, starting the cycle all over again.

By the time he'd made a second slow circuit of my body, again avoiding all the most sensitive spots, I was nearly ready to start begging. Only the determination not to disappoint him by disobeying his very first order kept me silent. Every muscle in my body was corded with the effort not to squirm beneath him. My cock was so hard it felt like solid granite. Evan was licking my thighs, each swipe coming millimeters closer, closer, to where it felt like every nerve in my body had redirected itself. *Please*, I chanted to myself, *please, sweet God, Evan, do it, please....*

"Don't come," Evan reminded me, before fluttering little kitten-licks over my balls. I tried to think of the most horrendous filming experience I'd ever had, that sci-fi flick where I'd played an alien, buried under so many prosthetic attachments I could barely breath – anything to keep myself from immediately shooting my load. When he'd moistened every inch of my sac, he teased lower, skittering over the sensitive skin of my perineum, tracing a wet circle around the quavering ring of muscle. *Fuck me*, I pleaded wordlessly, *dammit, Evan, ram your tongue up there and fucking fuck me!*

He didn't, of course. I was cursing steadily by now in my head, while he spread my cheeks apart and blew warm air over the superheated skin. Then he did the same to my cock, leaning in to lap at the pool of pre-come. The edge of his tongue brushed against the tip of my shaft and a bolt of pure electric current galvanized my body. I jolted and couldn't bite back the gasp of need fast enough to keep him from hearing it.

"You're doing so well, love," Evan praised me, rubbing his thumbs down my iliac crease and framing the patch of tawny pubic hair. "I need you to hold out just a little longer...." He dipped his head and began to lick at my cock, little swipes of his tongue that never lasted long enough, never traveled far enough, and they were driving me crazy. I needed to come more than I needed to breathe, gasping to fill my lungs only when they were burning; rocking, though I didn't realize it, to the litany that filled my brain, *please, please, please, please, please....*

"Come," Evan said finally, his lips closing over the head of my cock, and I lost it completely. I came with every cell in my body exploding in pleasure, overloading me with sensation until I think I must have blacked out. When I was alert to what was going on around me again, Evan had me cradled in his arms, his own cock sticky against my thigh, his head resting on my still-shuddering abdomen.

"Mmmmnnnn," I said intelligently, trying to pull him up so I could kiss him. "C'mere."

"How was it?" Evan asked when I'd let go of his lips. "It wasn't too much?"

"It was torture," I told him. "I never came harder in my life." I bent my head and pressed my forehead against his. "Not that I'm complaining, but it wasn't quite what I expected. It seemed to be all about me. I thought you'd want me to – I dunno – do something to – for – you...."

"Maybe I'm just a lousy dom," Evan chuckled, his dark eyes sparkling. "I got exactly what I wanted out of it, love, which was to make you come completely unglued." He pulled back and ruffled my hair so the spikes stood back up. "Don't worry, I still have plenty of things I want you to do for me. And no matter what anyone tells you, D/s is <u>always</u> about the sub."

As sated as it was, my cock did a little jig at the thought of the kind of things Evan might want me to do for him some day. I didn't need to push a commitment on him he wasn't ready for, not when we were already this good without it. "Thank you, baby," I told him. "Even if you're never ready to let me wear a collar, I need you to know that whatever you want me to do, ever, I'll do it."

"You say that now," Evan countered, his voice thick. "Wait 'til I want to try out a Moor Mud Body Wrap on you."

"Anything," I promised, "even mud. I trust you, angel. I love you."

"Love you too," Evan answered, kissing me again.

What more than that could I possibly ask?

I was reaching for my cell phone, hard and hot and missing my lover fiercely, when it rang before I could flip it open to dial. I didn't need the special ring-tone to tell me it was Evan – somehow, it made perfect sense that he'd know how much I needed to hear his voice at that exact minute.

"Did you get my present?" he asked eagerly, sounding close enough to reach out and touch. I swallowed around the tightness in my throat and answered, "Sure did, baby. I love it – thank you for sending me so many wonderful memories."

"There's one more bit that goes with it," he said. "I think they might have left it outside your front door."

"The bellman didn't say anything about more," I fretted, heading toward the entryway. "I hope it won't get ruined in this rain...."

I really should have known, but I guess loneliness and horniness had made me stupid. I was taken completely by surprise when I opened the door and Evan launched himself into my arms, sending us both skidding backward on the wet terrazzo floor. Evan took advantage of my shock to tackle me onto my ass and ravage my mouth, not that I was putting up anything like a fight.

"What are you doing here?" I asked when I could talk again. "And how long can you stay? I thought you were registered for that seminar on couples massage therapy this weekend."

"I'll reschedule it," Evan answered distractedly, busy pulling my shirt over my head. "I'd rather go when you can come with as my partner anyway." His lips closed around my nipple

ring and I gave up any hope of being able to carry on a rational conversation. Only when he pulled me to my feet, letting my cutoffs drop around my ankles, did I remember that I had a gift for him, too.

"Hang on, baby," I insisted as he tried to drag me in search of the bedroom. I dug into the pocket of my shorts and stayed on one knee, determined to do this right.

"This past year has been the best one of my life," I told Evan, for once letting my heart and not my cock do the talking. "I love you, and I want to spend the rest of my life loving you." Reaching for his hand, I showed him the rings I had carried around for the last month, waiting for this day. "When filming is over, if you want to, I'd like to fly back to Amsterdam and get married."

If only Russ could harness Evan's smile, he could dry every cloud from the sky and finish up filming tomorrow. "Yes!" Evan shouted, knocking me backward again and jumping on top of me to kiss me. My only complaint was that while I was happily naked, he still had far too many clothes on, and they were wet. I stripped him as fast as I could, considering he wouldn't take his tongue out of my mouth, and then rolled him onto his back to do some tongue-sucking of my own. Finally remembering that I had a big, cushy bed that would be a lot more agreeable for what I had in mind than a wet tile floor, I helped my lover up and started toward the bedroom.

"Don't forget your robe," Evan prompted. I had no intention of letting anything but his skin cover me for the next several days at least, but I grabbed it out of the basket anyway, revealing the final gift that had been lying hidden beneath it.

A soft, narrow, black leather collar.

"Guess we're both ready to make a commitment," Evan said as I ran it lovingly through my fingers. We'd each learned a lot about what we were comfortable with over the last few months, and while our take on kink might never fit anyone's definition but our own, who cared? We didn't have anything to prove and only ourselves to make happy. And at that moment, I was in paradise.

"C'mon, lover," Evan urged, pulling my body against his, cock to cock, heart to heart. *"I'm going to take you to heaven."*

Growing up in Chicago, Nicki Bennett spent every Saturday at the central library, losing herself in the world of books. A voracious reader, she eventually found it hard to find enough of the kind of stories she liked to read ... and decided she needed to start writing them herself.

Printed in the United Kingdom
by Lightning Source UK Ltd.
133909UK00001B/403/A